Treasure in Paradise

Written by Anna Tikvah

Cover Illustration by Hannah Young

THE BIG PEOPLE

PROFESSOR
LEMANS

EVAN

SETH

THE FIRST TINY

UNCLE LOUIS

The Forest Girls

AIMEE

GEORGIA

SANAA AND
MUFFY

LILY

DIYA

Rainbow Hill Boys

ZAHIR

MILAN AND
RUSTY

The Orchard Girls

Vinitha and
Mimi

Tina

Yu Yan and
Mia

The Farmer Boys

Charley and
Bojo

Kenzie

Vahid

The Storekeeper

NANCY AND
RIPPLE

The Beach Boys

DAMIEN AND
EMMA

LEMA

FRANZ

North Forest Boys

ODIN

PONCE

Other Books in this Series:

The Enormous Tiny Experiment

Inside the massive Biosphere, showcasing living plants and animals from all over the globe, Professor Lemans and his assistant, Evan, have secretly put together the most intriguing display. Having discovered the process to miniaturize life, they have created a beautiful paradise hoping to give twenty-one Tiny people and lots of animals and birds a life with minimal suffering. The Professor believes that his giant terrarium, complete with hills, forests, a surfing lake, and productive gardens, will be the best place to keep his little family safe and happy. He hopes that his fantastic experiment will eventually become an opportunity for novel research around the world.

However, the Professor didn't count on a foolish 'science experiment' which set off the emergency fire response...

Pain in Paradise

The Tinys are sent back to the nursery, as Professor Lemans and Evan clean up from the catastrophic accident. Baby animals, new activities, and a restored Paradise keep everything exciting for a time

Entering adolescence, the Tinys discover that even in a perfect world, human misunderstandings, greed, envy, and pride can undermine happiness and ruin friendships. As the Professor and Evan attempt to showcase Paradise to their colleagues, will the evidence of suffering turn the world against this project? And what happens when some Tinys continue to use their newfound knowledge in destructive ways?

Dedication

Dedicated to my dad,
Frank Abel,
who like Uncle Louis,
through kind words and a wonderful example
led me and many others to Jesus Christ.

Chapters

First Aid

Chapter 1

*I*n less than an hour, life in Paradise had been drastically altered. Five Tinys were now suffering painful burns in varying degrees and everyone had been traumatized by the fearful experience. Smouldering ruins stretched across one end of the large terrarium. The very first fire, recklessly lit by Odin, Ponce, and Franz, had incinerated many trees in the North Forest near the train tracks. Even with the rainmaker on full power, the fountains around the perimeter spewing water from behind, and the Tinys doing their best to douse the flames, it had taken over forty minutes to fully extinguish the blaze.

One courageous fighter who had laboured intensively to quench the inferno now lay writhing on the ground next to the Tiny he had saved. Both were seriously injured. Zahir was groaning and Ponce was crying loudly. Uncle Louis had fallen beside them, but he wasn't moving at all.

Aimee and Tina had found the First Aid kits in the store and came dashing out to assess the damage and help the wounded. The beach boys, who had been on the front lines, were examining their singed limbs. Tina ran in their direction with the Burn Remedy in her hand; she knew it could only be used for minor injuries. Everyone was wet from the constant rain. Two dogs were racing around trying to share their love, but for the first time, the Tiny who cared most for the animals begged someone to take them away. She was fearful they might inadvertently do more harm than good.

Milan took charge of the dogs.

With her eyes on the dark-haired young man who was lying on the ground in agony, Aimee headed straight for Zahir. He had saved Ponce's life, but after lifting the heavy, burning beam he had tripped and fallen into the flames. She yearned to know the extent of his injuries and to stay by his side. With dismay, she heard his girlfriend, Georgia, yell from close behind, "I'm looking after Zahir! You go help someone else!"

Opening her mouth to protest, the copper-haired girl suddenly noticed that Uncle Louis was in a worse state. Lying motionless, close to Zahir, his eyes were shut and his face was a strange grey colour.

Crying out with alarm, Aimee ran over to kneel by the older man's side. Quickly, she determined that he wasn't breathing and he had no pulse! "No! *No!*" she wailed. "Uncle Louis! Uncle Louis!" Suppressing panic, she tried to remember what he had taught her about CPR. She checked that his airway was clear. Placing her hands on his chest in the exact location he had shown her, she began pumping rhythmically.

Kenzie and Vahid were right behind her. One look at Uncle Louis' complexion filled them with alarm. "If you get tired," Kenzie implored, "I'll take a turn."

Aimee glanced briefly upwards and nodded her thanks. Her mind was fully on the task before her. Everything else seemed to blur into the background as she desperately tried to bring Uncle Louis back to life. Although they were only an arm's length away, she barely overheard Kenzie accessing Zahir and Ponce's needs.

Completely focused on her task, Kenzie's questions and Georgia's sobs faded in and out of her consciousness. As she breathed two breaths into Uncle Louis and watched his chest rise and fall, reproachful cries caught her attention. "Zahir, you look terrible! Your face is black, and your skin is peeling! Why did you go into that fire? Ponce started this. He deserved what he got. I begged you to stay out of it because *I love you!* I love you so much! Oh, *what* have you done to yourself?"

Deep dismay welled up inside as Aimee kept pumping... thirty compressions and two breaths of air... thirty compressions and two breaths of air... over and over. She longed to praise Zahir for his courage, but Uncle Louis was in critical condition! She didn't feel she could stop for even a moment. To her relief, she heard Kenzie speak up sharply in Zahir's defence.

In the office room, on the other side of the glass, the Professor and Evan were frantically trying to manage the situation. All the visiting scientists had been dismissed and the doors to the viewing hall locked. The tall blond assistant had responded immediately to the alarm on his phone, dashing through the university halls, through the gardens, and frantically into the Rainforest Biome. Thinking only of what was best for the Tinys, he had been the one to insist that all the scientists and the cameraman leave immediately. Now that the flames were finally out, he pressed the white button to restore the oxygen levels, and then he reached up and turned off the rainmaker.

A wild-eyed Professor was on the phone with Dr. Farouk Khalid, the best heart surgeon in Greenville. With his eyes desperately focused on Aimee's attempts to perform CPR, he anxiously explained the crisis that had enveloped Paradise. "I think Louis has had a major heart attack!" he agonized. "We're sending in the train to get him out right away. I have an emergency centre set up in the lab, and I'd appreciate any advice you can give me. It also looks like Zahir and Ponce sustained serious burns. They are lying on the ground barely moving! I'd say the beach boys were injured too... hopefully just minor burns."

Responding to Farouk's advice over the phone, Jacques called out to Evan. "Keep the rainmaker on in that same location. Farouk says we need twenty minutes of cooling rain on the burn patients."

Worried about hypothermia, his assistant replied, "They've already had fifteen."

"At least five more," the Professor insisted. Then responding to Farouk's inquiry, he said, "*Non, non*, I don't see any evidence of smoke inhalation. The ventilation system worked well. I'd say it was more like putting out a bonfire than trapped inside a burning building.

Turning the rainmaker back on, Evan made a call to Rachel Khalid, the head Biosphere Animal Doctor. Explaining the whole situation, he implored her to come immediately. With the phone up to his ear, he listened to her advice as he ran to the train supply room. Placing a small stretcher in the first car, he hastily scribbled instructions to the Tinys. *"Put Uncle Louis on the stretcher,"* he wrote. *"Place him on the train carefully but as fast as you can. Don't worry about the alarms that will go off. Then stay with the burn victims. Elevate Zahir and Ponce's heads and feet about a finger span. Keep them warm, but don't do anything else until further orders arrive. Don't put anything on their wounds just yet. However, the Burn Remedy will be effective for the injuries that the Beach boys have sustained. Apply it liberally on them."*

Hitting the button, he sent the train into Paradise with the stretcher and the note.

Receiving a text that Rachel had reached the private office door, Evan ran to let her in. Together, they peered through the windows, watching Aimee's rescue effort and hoping they could get Louis into the Emergency bed as soon as possible.

Rachel was impressed. "She's got the right method," she nodded. "Oh, I do hope Louis survives!" Glancing at Zahir and Ponce, she fretted, "They look like they are in *severe* pain! We'll need to assess those burns up close."

"You mean on *this* side?" Evan clarified anxiously. He knew the Professor would only agree to transport Tinys out of Paradise if it was an absolute necessity! They didn't want to arouse curiosity about the other side.

"Yes, I mean on this side!" she nodded fervently. "I'll just run and get some supplies."

When the train whirred through the charred landscape and stopped at the store, Vahid ran to it and opened the doors. Kenzie rushed over to help him. Together they pulled out the stretcher and read the note, then they rushed the stretcher over to Uncle Louis.

"We're to put him on the train," the young men relayed anxiously as Aimee continued CPR. "Right away!" Kenzie pleaded.

The girl with the copper-brown hair didn't stop immediately. She gave her unconscious uncle the next breath of air and watched his chest rise. She was oblivious to the impatience of her friends. Everything seemed to be in slow motion as Aimee watched Uncle Louis' chest fall, and then, it seemed as though it was rising again on its own! Astonished, she placed her hand close to his mouth and felt a slight breath of air!

There was no time to take a pulse as the guys were determined to follow their instructions. As they began to carefully lift the limp, heavy body onto the stretcher, Aimee stood up reluctantly. She was certain she saw Uncle Louis breathe again! Once they had his body secure on the stretcher, Kenzie and Vahid grabbed the poles and dashed as quickly as they could to the train.

As soon as the precious cargo was on board, the train reversed down the tracks and out through the secure tunnel, with all the alarms blaring. The noise added to the chaos.

Picking up Evan's note that Kenzie had left beside her, Aimee read it through quickly but carefully. Without Uncle Louis there to guide them through this emergency, Aimee felt a fearful loss of direction. Always, in any crisis, the older Tiny had been the steady one they could depend on.

She called out Evan's instructions as she read them.

"I'll get blankets and cushions," Tina yelled, running into the store to grab the supplies that sat on the shelves for trade.

"Help me! Help me!" Ponce wailed. "I'm in *so* much pain!"

Glancing over, Aimee was shocked to see that Georgia was no longer with Zahir. Instead, the young man who had courageously saved another was lying on the ground alone and shivering. Quickly glancing around, Aimee saw Georgia bent over near the store, vomiting.

"Zahir!" Aimee cried, dashing to his side. She dropped to the ground and gazed in horror at his wounds. A bloody, blackened patch ran up the visible side of his face from his beard to the dark hair on his head. Around his neck, the gold chain had heated up in the flames and left a black charred line. She saw large burns on his right arm and the lower part of his right leg.

Trembling, Aimee reached over and undid Zahir's Shining Moon necklace, fearful it would rub against the raw wounds and cause more pain. It dropped to the ground. "Are you okay? Are you okay?" she begged anxiously, knowing that he wasn't, but hoping with all her heart that he would say he was.

Shivering uncontrollably, Zahir chattered, "Stay with me. Please stay with me."

The cold rain stopped again suddenly to Aimee's relief. Tina threw her a blanket and two cushions and ran over to help Ponce. Kenzie came running back over as well. Picking up the cushions, he helped Aimee position them under Zahir's head and feet, as he encouraged his friend to stay strong. Reaching for the blanket, they both spread it carefully over their patient, avoiding his wounds and tucking it under his body where they could. Chilled, dripping wet from the rain, and shivering with shock, Zahir didn't open his eyes, but he did groan appreciatively.

Hearing Tina and Lily call out, Kenzie left to help move Ponce into a comfortable position. The bronze-faced troublemaker cried out in anguish with every jarring motion.

Sitting down, Aimee asked, "Are you in *terrible* pain, Zahir?" She was greatly distraught by the severe injuries she saw, remembering the small burn she'd once sustained from hot glue.

"So much!" Zahir murmured, barely moving his lips. "Will I... will I *die?*"

"No!" she exclaimed fervently, as her heart skipped a beat. She reached for his left hand and he gripped hers gratefully. "No! We are going to help you! The Professor is sending in supplies. You aren't going to die, Zahir!"

Seeing the extent of her friend's injuries was nauseating, but she battled against a reaction. "I'm staying with Zahir!" she determined fiercely. "If Georgia can't, I will! He needs a friend. He can't suffer alone!" She remembered how much she had longed for someone to stay with her after she had almost drowned. Resolutely, she decided that the two most severely injured young men would have her best care. Regardless of what anyone else might say or do, their needs would be her priority. Kenzie came back to rummage in the First Aid kit for another tube of Burn Remedy. Picking it up, he dashed over to the beach boys.

"You're going to be okay, Zahir!" she promised fervently, as tears fell from her eyes. She hoped with all her heart that he would. "You're going to be okay and I'll stay right beside you!"

She saw Kenzie, Yu Yan, and Tina spreading cooling gel on the three other young men and elevating their singed limbs. She wished she could do something for the others.

Lily felt the same. "What can we do to help?" she wailed, holding tightly to Ponce's hand. Ponce's face had been spared, but his arms and legs looked as badly burnt as Zahir's.

Aimee assured her friend that instructions would come soon. "Just stay with him," she said.

"Don't leave me!" Ponce begged.

A few of the girls were having the same reaction as Georgia. Unable to stomach the sight of the wounds, Vinitha, Sanaa, Nancy, and Diya, were a safe distance away. They looked anxious to help but reluctant to come any closer.

"Play some nice music, read some books," Aimee called out to the others. "We need something to distract the injured! They are suffering so badly!"

Happy to find a way to help, Georgia ran to the xylophone, still stationed on the deck of the store, and played music, all the best tunes that she and Zahir had created, and even some more. The xylophone was far enough away that the music was soft, not jarring, just a quiet, soothing voice in the distance.

Vinitha and Sanaa plucked up the courage to return to their friends. Diya and Charley had gone to the store to help Nancy make food for dinner, although doubts were voiced that anyone would have an appetite.

Holding Zahir's hand with both of hers, Aimee praised the injured fighter. "You were *so* brave," she said, her voice trembling. "You saved Ponce's life. You helped to save Paradise and all of us. I'm going to do my best to help you, as soon as I know what that is. We're just waiting to hear from the Professor."

The large burn on Zahir's right cheek made it painful for him to move his face in any way, but he opened his eyes briefly and whispered, "Thanks." Then he squeezed her hands.

"I'm so, so proud of you, Zahir!" she expressed earnestly. "You did the right thing! I wanted to help you, but I was too scared. You had so much courage! I'm so glad *you* were brave!"

Looking up, she did a quick check to ensure that everyone was being cared for. Lily was faithfully doing her best to comfort Ponce.

Every time he called out in pain, she assured him, "I won't leave you, Ponce. I love you." Tina was helping Damien sit up. Kenzie was applying Burn Remedy to the blond surfer's leg, and Vahid was bringing drinks of water to the injured. Franz was propped up against a tree and Yu Yan was beside him. Sanaa had returned to Lema. Milan had locked the dogs in the store and was ensuring the fire was completely out. He doused any stray wisps of smoke.

Humming softly to the xylophone music, Aimee stayed beside her patient and desperately hoped the train would return. Zahir's eyes were closed, but she could tell from his groans and the occasional, intense pressure in his grip that he was struggling to endure. Once again, he asked if his life was in danger, and she tried to reassure him that he would be okay. With all her heart she hoped she was telling the truth!

Finally, they heard the train whistle as it came back through the highly secure tunnel. It seemed like it had been gone for ages but, only ten minutes had passed. After Jacques and Rachel had stabilized their living, *breathing* patient in the Emergency Care bed and put Louis on oxygen, they had run back up to the Paradise Room to look closely at the burn victims' wounds through binoculars. The animal doctor had then phoned her husband, the heart surgeon, who initiated a conference call with the Greenville Burn Specialist. They had all agreed the severe burns needed proper visual assessment, so two stretchers had been put on the train with a second note.

It was with great dismay that Aimee helped Kenzie and Vahid gently place Zahir on the stretcher. She had promised to stay with him and do her best to help and now, only minutes later, he was being carted away to the other side – a side that no Tiny had ever returned from! Her heart was full of fear and concern. Lily wailed and begged to go with Ponce, but the instructions clearly stated that only the two most severely burnt victims were to be put on the train.

Most of the Tinys gathered around as the train departed again with all the alarms blaring. No one knew what to do or how long it would take before they saw their friends and uncle again. Aimee began to cry and Kenzie put his arm around her. Neither one of them knew what to say. Three Tinys had just been taken out of Paradise in serious condition. They had all fought a terrible fire and everyone was exhausted. Wet, weary, anxious, and overwhelmed, they huddled on the store steps, waiting for directions that could take hours to come and hoping they would see their loved ones again.

The Emergency Response

Chapter 2

While the sad little group of Tinys congregated miserably by the store, three fully masked, full-sized humans stood around the miniature stretchers. The oxygen levels had been raised in the supply room since Zahir's facial wounds prohibited anything touching his face. A bright spotlight shone on the two burn victims, so bright indeed, that they could barely open their eyes. Jacques had intentionally chosen an intense light not only to expose the wounds but so that Ponce and Zahir would see as little as possible of those on the other side. On a Zoom conference call, Jacques held his phone so that Dr. Mark Montgomery, the Greenville Burn Specialist, could view the full extent of the injuries. Rachel sedated both patients with a minute amount of painkiller, dropping it into their mouths with the smallest pipette she had.

Back at the Greenville Hospital, Dr. Montgomery was taking the Zoom call on a giant screen. Observing the wounds, he felt confident the burns were severe second-degree and that they would be healable with diligent care. He postulated that the fragile injuries were best treated with tiny hands in the more suitable and sterile environment of Paradise. Rachel weighed both patients and imparted the data to the doctor. She wrote down his precise instructions and cautionary concerns, while Jacques and Evan piled the train full of sterile bedding and mattresses, soap, buckets and towels, and the two bedpans they had in stock for potential emergencies. Caring for the burn victims would require setting up a make-shift hospital. Having keenly observed the various reactions to the latest crisis, Jacques was confident that a few of his Tinys were well-suited for nursing care. While Rachel's husband, Dr. Farouk Khalid, and the burn specialist tried to calibrate the correct dosages of antibiotics and medications, the train was sent back in with the first load of supplies and the third hand-written note.

Eagerly the Tinys rushed over, hoping to find their friends, but instead, there was only another message and cars full of bedding. Specific directions were listed. *"Milan, Vahid, and, Kenzie,"* Kenzie read out loud, *"Take the seven beds you will find on the train and carry them to the girls' mansion on Rainbow Hill. Choose two rooms for a Caring Centre. Zahir, Ponce and Uncle Louis will need to be in one and the beach boys in the other. Take out the girls' beds and set up the new beds. You are then to carry anyone who has been wounded up to the Caring Centre. For the next three weeks, Kenzie and Vahid are to remain dedicated to helping the injured, especially during the nights. Take turns doing the night shift. Sleep in the same room as Zahir and Ponce, so you will hear them if they need you. Read the instructions for how to use the two bedpans you will find on the train. During the day, you must ensure the beds stay clean and help the patients get up and stretch their limbs every few hours..."*

To Aimee, Tina, and Yu Yan, the Professor had requested that they also become full-time nurses until the firefighters recovered. *"Two patients will be coming back with the next train load,"* Kenzie read. "Uncle Louis is recovering but will need a little longer..."

Cheers from the others interrupted him momentarily. This was encouraging news. With a smile of relief, the young man wiped his eyes and continued, *"There will be sterile wipes, antibiotics, special 'Wonderdrink' and painkiller. Be very diligent to read labels and measure quantities exactly! More instructions will follow. Read them carefully!"*

Looking up, Kenzie directed his listeners. "All right, everyone. Let's get things set up before they return. This is an emergency! We need to act quickly!"

The tired crew flew back into action. At least, everyone that heard the message got moving. Odin was still nowhere to be seen.

The young men found the foam mattresses on the train. Piles of blankets, gauze cloths, bandages, and towels were neatly piled inside each car.

"Use my room," Aimee called out to Kenzie, as the guys set the first mattress on a large carry cart. "It's the biggest and has the best view. I'm happy to make it part of the Caring Centre."

"Mine too," Georgia piped up with a resentful tone, as she pulled a bundle of gauze out of the train. She wasn't happy that she had been overlooked as a potential caregiver.

Damien tried to get up and help, but nearly fainted on Tina.

Kenzie told him to rest and promised a stretcher ride. Franz and Lema looked over wearily and decided they were quite happy to wait for a lift as well.

With seven carts full of supplies, many of the Tinys carried the beds, bandages, and bedding up Rainbow Hill.

On the other side of the glass, Farouk arrived in the Biome with large containers of medication that had to be distributed into small bottles for the Caring Center. Evan and Jacques set to work filling those flasks and labelling them carefully. With her small pipette, Rachel administered the first doses of antibiotics and the specialized protein formula that Dr. Montgomery had formulated for burn victims. Taking some antibacterial ointment, she also carefully dropped it on their wounded limbs, but she avoided Zahir's face, worrying the liquid might seep into his mouth. Then she sterilized her small instrument and put it on the train.

Once the final list of instructions had been written, and the medications filled, Jacques gazed into Paradise. He was pleased to see that all the supplies had been taken off the train and the Tinys were now coming back down Rainbow Hill. With a nod of approval, he was glad that so many had sensed the urgency and worked together to prepare the Caring Center. Pressing the reverse button, he brought the train back to the supply room. Carefully, Zahir and Ponce were placed in the cars, still lying on stretchers and drugged into a deep sleep. In the last car, Jacques placed the medications and instructions that Rachel had meticulously listed out.

Sending the train back in, the four big humans gathered in the viewing hall to watch the transfer of care take place. How they hoped that everything would go well for the sake of their patients and those who had been entrusted to their new and very important roles.

"How will they cope with suffering?" Evan wondered to himself.

Aimee was the first to spot the train coming in. She called out to Kenzie and they sprinted across the meadow. Reaching the train shortly after it had stopped in front of the store, they yanked the first door open. The copper-haired nurse was elated to see that two patients had been returned. "You're back!" she cried out with relief. However, neither young man responded.

"Let's find the note first," Kenzie reminded her. "We need to know what to do."

Very concerned about the lack of response, Aimee reached out for Zahir's hand, but he was sound asleep. His hand was limp. "Are they okay?" she questioned fearfully. "What happened to them?"

Finding the handwritten message, Kenzie grabbed it quickly. He glanced over at Zahir with a worried expression and then began reading out loud. "Both patients have been sedated to help them deal with the pain," he read. "They will be asleep until the medication wears off..." He sighed with deep relief and so did Aimee.

The others had now reached the train and were crowding around.

"I want to be a caregiver too!" Georgia insisted, pushing forward to the front. "Zahir will be in my room and I will be his nurse!"

"And I'll look after Ponce!" Lily added.

Ignoring their demands, Kenzie continued reading the instructions. The burns were to be cleaned gently with sterile wipes and bandaged with clean gauze and antibacterial ointment. There were three bottles of liquid and specific amounts and timing for each dose. There were details concerning life-threatening infection and fever, dangerous symptoms to watch for, the importance of handwashing, and how to tell time on the new clock. Notebooks and paper had been provided so they could write daily journals for each patient. Those notes were to be put on the train every day.

And then the message clearly reiterated who would perform the various duties. There were to be five nurses, Aimee, Tina, Yu Yan, Kenzie, and Vahid. Kitchen and gardening duties would be shared by Georgia, Sanaa, Charley, Nancy, Vinitha and Lily, who were also to bring food to all the workers in the Caring Centre. Tina, Yu Yan and Diya were to help wash and repair the patient's clothing and blankets. Bold words stated, "Everyone must shower before entering the Caring Centre at any time. Extra towels are on the train."

As the young man with the brown curly hair continued to read, Georgia argued, "I don't care what it says! I'm staying with Zahir."

"And I can't leave Ponce!" Lily insisted. Neither of them were used to being told what they could and couldn't do.

Kenzie glared in their direction. "For the next week, at least, all of us will follow these instructions exactly." Pointing to the words near the end of the message, he stated firmly, "Look, right here. The Professor has said that both of you, and even Vinitha and Sanaa, can bring books to read to the patients every morning after breakfast. You can visit all you want when you've finished helping with the gardening and food preparation. Just remember to shower *first.*"

Georgia grumbled to herself and shrugged her shoulders. "I also don't know how to *cook!*" she complained. "So why would I be sent to the kitchen? That's Aimee's job! This is *so* dumb!"

Looking around, Kenzie ignored her complaints and asked, "Has anyone seen Odin?"

No one had.

"There are instructions for him as well," the tall, freckled young man muttered. "But for now, let's get these guys up to their beds. We have a lot to do!"

Just in case Odin was nearby, Aimee spoke loudly, "I sure wish Odin would show up! We could really use his help with these stretchers."

In a few minutes, a shame-faced Odin came hesitantly into view. His hair and beard were dishevelled, and he looked fairly wild. "Did you say you need help?" he asked awkwardly.

He was met with angry stares from everyone.

"You *Rollin' Tumbler!*" Damien shouted savagely, from where he sat with Tina. He punched the air with his fist. "When are you going to stop destroying things? Look what you've done. Look at the damage! Look at the people that nearly lost their lives! If you ever do anything like this again, I'll drown you myself! *I will!*" Exhausted, his voice trailed off and he slumped back against the tree.

Damien's angry outburst was frightening to everyone. Yet, most felt that some sort of a rebuke was necessary. This was the second time Odin had put everyone's lives in danger. The flood and the fire had both been terrifying calamities.

"We sure do need help!" Tina snapped. "You've caused so many problems!"

"It's time you started making up for all you've done!" Lema added harshly. "This was not just another dumb science experiment! Do it again, and *I'll help* Damien put you under! And you too, Franz!" he

16

said, turning bitterly toward his surfing buddy who had also suffered burns. "If you're going to follow Odin's crazy ideas, you'll get what he gets!"

For once, Odin wasn't defensive. "What do you want me to do?" he mumbled.

"All of these brave, injured firefighters need to be carried up Rainbow Hill," Aimee murmured, uncomfortable with the beach boys' terrible threats. She hoped Odin and Franz would try to make up for what they had done, and she knew that Ponce was already paying a heavy price. "Let's get started with the ones who have the worst injuries," she suggested. "Kenzie and I will take Zahir. You and Vahid take Ponce."

"I can help too," Georgia protested.

"We need water," Kenzie told her brusquely. "If there isn't anything for you to do in the kitchen right now, please bring a few buckets of boiled water to the Caring Center."

As Georgia reluctantly headed to the store, Aimee struggled with her end of the stretcher. Seeing their need, Milan ran over to help. With his assistance, Aimee and Kenzie began heading for Rainbow Hill. Charley and Sanaa brought the supplies over in the carrycarts.

Tears ran down Aimee's face as the limp bodies in the stretchers remained unresponsive to noise or jarring. She had never seen anyone sedated before and it worried her. They looked nearly dead. She hoped she would be able to follow the instructions carefully enough; there was a lot to remember.

Eventually, one by one, all the injured were brought into the Caring Centre and settled onto the brand-new beds. Under Kenzie's direction, the most severely injured were taken to Aimee's room and the others to Georgia's.

All the nurses showered, washed their hands with soap in the water that Georgia brought up, and then the work began.

Taking charge, Kenzie directed Tina, Yu Yan, and Vahid to start cleaning the beach boys' wounds, while he and Aimee took on the others.

Cleaning and dressing the wounds was not a pleasant task, but as the pain medication took effect, the hollers and complaints coming from Georgia's room subsided. Part way through the process, Zahir and Ponce began to flinch and groan. Thankfully, it was just in time for the caregivers to give their first round of medications.

As Kenzie and Aimee measured carefully to ensure that all five patients received their required dosages, Odin brought Zahir's gold chain up to the room.

"Thank you so much!" Aimee said, as her eyes flew wide open, realising she had left Zahir's precious treasure lying on the ground. She took it from Odin and hung it around the bedpost.

Having not yet had a chance to share the instructions with everyone, Kenzie told the strong young man that he was to oversee cleaning up the mess in the burnt forest, hauling boiled water every day to the Caring Centre, and carting new supplies and garbage back and forth to the train.

Both were amazed that Odin didn't argue.

Late that evening when all the patients were finally cleaned, bandaged, and sleeping fitfully, Kenzie lay down wearily in the extra bed, following the Professor's instructions for the male nurses. He had offered to do the first night of bedpan duty and be on call for help.

Knowing that the patients would be well cared for, Aimee was thankful to head to Lily's room. She would have preferred to be in with her best friend Sanaa, but Sanaa's room was only big enough for one. Deep breathing indicated her roommate was already asleep. Collapsing into bed, Aimee didn't take long to join her.

Emergency Planning

Chapter 3

*L*ouis was sleeping soundly with an oxygen mask on his face and a monitor hooked up to record his vitals when Rachel, Evan and the Professor came down to the underground lab to check on him. Three hectic hours had passed since he had been transported out of Paradise on the train.

Pleased with the stats on the monitor display, Rachel smiled. "I think he's going to make it," she said. "But his heart is damaged. He can't ever exert himself again."

With a huge sigh of relief, the Professor shook Dr. Khalid's small hand with both of his. "*Merci beaucoup.* I can't thank you enough, Rachel. The Tinys aren't ready to lose Louis, and neither am I! I'm so appreciative!"

Evan shook her hand as well, saying, "And we're both very grateful for all the advice and supplies that you and your husband have sent in."

"You're most welcome," Rachel acknowledged warmly as they headed toward the elevator. "But please do remember, we have only made our best estimates on the proper dosages." With a look of concern, she straightened her white lab coat and cautioned, "None of us have worked with tiny humans before. *Never!* I'll check back tomorrow and ensure things are going smoothly."

As the elevator brought them up to the next level, she reiterated the need for the nurses to take daily notes of the patient's activities and to record their temperatures. "If there are any spikes in temperature, loss of appetite or consciousness, please call me immediately," she said.

"I have a small thermometer that I will send in," the Professor assured her. The elevator doors opened, and they walked down the long corridor toward the train supply room. "We will pass everything we hear on to you. I can't thank you enough for helping us to organize this rescue mission."

Entering the train supply room, Rachel nodded. "If your Tinys are diligent and follow all the instructions carefully, the victims will do well in their care. Aimee saved Louis' life; you know."

Evan and the Professor exchanged astonished glances. Rachel had been the first to assess Louis when he came in unconscious on the train. "*She* saved his life?" Jacques stuttered.

"Yes, Louis was breathing on his own when he came in. Her hands are just the right size; her pressure was perfect. I might have broken his ribs with my thumb."

Pointing to a bottle of the highly nutritious protein formula procured by her husband, Dr. Farouk Khalid, Rachel continued, "I can't stress enough how important this special formula is for those who are severely burned. In our world, this would be delivered intravenously, but obviously, we have no miniature medical equipment. Ensure that your nurses encourage the patients to drink it every two hours during the day, whether they want it or not."

Nodding, Evan jotted a quick note for the next page of instructions.

They all walked into the viewing room and took one more look into the Paradise dome. "I am concerned about Zahir and Ponce," Rachel fretted, wringing her hands anxiously. "I'm so thankful we had them accessed properly. Dr. Montgomery is the best in his field." She looked up and pleaded, "However, the next seventy-two hours will be crucial. It may be best to remind your nurses to be extra cautious..."

"I will," Jacques promised. Considering the uniqueness of the Tinys, he added, "They may heal faster than normal. Their cellular systems are generally in a fast-forward state, since the full growth potential has been restricted."

"Very true. It's all so unpredictable, isn't it?" she nodded, watching three Tinys carry Damien across the meadow to the Caring Centre on the hill. "I feel for Zahir," she fretted. "His face will be quite physically scarred from this ordeal, if he survives. It's going to be hard on him! To think it was all because he wanted to save one of the arsonists."

"*If* he survives?" Evan clarified anxiously. "Is his life in doubt?"

"Your nurses are new to this," she replied. Turning to the Professor, she asked, "Are you certain you've chosen the most caring, dedicated individuals? Will they follow the instructions thoroughly?"

Jacques nodded. He had no doubts about his five nurses. "Absolutely," he said.

"Um, when can we send Louis back into the Caring Centre?" Evan begged uncertainly. "They need his guidance in a crisis like this!"

Dr. Khalid nodded. "Your Louis needs solid bed rest for the next few weeks, but it would do him good to be with the other patients as soon as his vitals are steady. I can explain to him all the particulars for healing burns, so he will be able to guide the others. Louis will never be strong again, but he will heal faster surrounded by the people he loves. They all will."

When the doctor left through the office door, Evan turned to the Professor. "I'm so thankful Rachel is willing to help us."

Nodding, the Professor agreed. "She adores this project. I believe she and her husband will be watching over everything carefully."

"That is quite fortunate for all the Tinys!" Evan exclaimed.

Watching the three young men labour to get Damien up the hill, the Professor remarked wistfully, "We won't be able to count on Louis anymore for cell phone communication."

21

"No," Evan agreed. "He certainly won't be able to make any trips to the cave if we send him to the Caring Centre. What is your plan? Should we just keep sending messages back and forth on the train to whoever opens the door first?"

With a serious expression, the Professor replied, "I plan to ask Aimee to take on the communications."

"Why Aimee?" Evan inquired curiously, folding his arms across his chest. He knew that she was special to the Professor, but he wasn't exactly sure why. "Zahir, Kenzie, Sanaa, or even Tina would be equally responsible," he suggested. Then he corrected himself, "I realize Zahir is injured, at the moment, but Kenzie..."

Observing the action inside the dome, Jacques quietly watched Charley, Milan, and Odin dash back to the charred forest for Lema. Finally, he replied, "I'd like to choose Aimee. I've given this a lot of thought, and I want to work with her."

"Okay... I'm sure she will do a fantastic job," Evan nodded. "Just like she is taking to nursing. Who would have thought?"

With a light laugh, the Professor acknowledged, "The reaction to the sight of blood is a great separator. When I saw those five Tinys take charge of the victims in such a brave, compassionate way, I had no doubt who the nurses were. It's not for everyone, but some do excel."

Evan smiled, "The others may miss Aimee's cooking."

"It takes talent to be a chef," the Professor agreed. "Not everyone can make food *'Magnifique'*, but most can make it edible. It's good for some of the others to learn how to cook."

Pondering the Professor's choice of Aimee, Evan wondered if there might be something else motivating his decision. Aimee certainly had some leadership qualities, but he didn't consider her to be the top choice. She was a sensitive, somewhat timid girl, and he wasn't sure she would always rise to the occasion when adversity set in, even though she had responded remarkably well to the medical crisis.

22

An intriguing idea had been forming in Evan's mind ever since the Professor had called out to Louis during the fire.

"May I ask you something?" he said to the Professor.

"Of course. Anything you like."

"You called out to Louis when he was hobbling over to help Zahir lift the catapult. You said, 'Not my son. Not my ageing *son.'*"

Jacques was watching Charley, Milan, and Odin position the stretcher so that Lema could get on it. Sanaa was trying to help. Lema was hopping on one leg and for a moment it looked like he might end up on the ground. After some tottering back and forth, the tall dark youth fell onto the stretcher. Thankfully, Odin was able to keep his end up, or the fall might have hurt. Sanaa praised the stocky, wild-eyed youth and began walking with them towards the hill.

With a furtive glance in Evan's direction, the Professor hesitated to reply.

"Is Louis actually... *your son?"* Evan prodded.

There was a very long pause and then a deep sigh. "Yes, he is," Jacques admitted slowly. "When Wendy and I were attempting to have a family, we used IVF. There were plenty of embryos available to me without requiring consent forms from anyone else."

For a moment, Evan was dazed. His suspicions were true. "Is... is Aimee also your daughter?"

Tears welled up in Jacques' eyes. *"Oui, "* he nodded.

The pieces of the puzzle were fitting together, but Evan was still curious. "Who else belongs to you?" he asked gently.

Folding his arms across his chest, Jacques confessed, "Franz... is also my son..."

"What? I would never have guessed Franz!" Evan remarked in astonishment. "The son of the famous scientist surfs all day and sleeps on the beach." Then Evan thought carefully. "Although Franz has shown some clever ingenuity when he applies himself," he conceded. "That ball slinger was exceptionally well made."

Jacques nodded. "He has some skills, but Franz is definitely not someone that I would ask to lead Paradise."

Trying to ensure that he had worked it all out, Evan clarified, "So Louis, Aimee, and Franz are yours... ah, *the Europeans,*" he smiled, remembering how the Professor had once labelled them. "No one else?"

"No one else," the Professor promised.

They watched as Lema was taken across the meadow. Sanaa held his hand all the way. She helped with the stretcher once they reached the hill.

Now that he fully understood the relationship dynamics, Evan clarified, "So you want to choose Aimee because she is your daughter?"

Jacques shook his head fervently. "*Non, non,* Evan, that's not all there is to it. Aimee has lovely qualities that I feel I can work with."

Nodding his head, Evan didn't push the matter further, but he was concerned that the Professor was becoming partial. How could he not? Of course, he would want to choose his own daughter!

"I really hope I'm not biased," the Professor lamented, knowing it would be against his own principles and suddenly second-guessing himself. "But I genuinely see in Aimee a kind heart and a willingness to put others first. She's a lot like her mother..."

Evan glanced over with a kind smile. He understood. He tried to determine how they would proceed with reinstating communication on the new phone in the cave, asking, "How will you tell Aimee about this?"

Looking into the dome, the Professor replied, "I'll write a private message to her and send it in tomorrow."

Nodding slowly, Evan wondered how it would all work. Between becoming a nurse and learning how to use a Smartphone, Aimee had a steep learning curve ahead.

A Conversation in the Lab

Chapter 4

*L*ying alone in the peaceful, dark chamber, Louis felt very comfortable. Oxygen was flowing freely through the mask on his face. He could see the monitor on the wall, beeping softly in a regular pattern as it kept track of his heartbeat. The blankets were satiny-smooth, and he felt like he could sleep forever. "How long have I been here?" he wondered wearily.

A new noise startled him. He opened his eyes and realised that the Professor was sitting on a makeshift bed beside him!

"You're awake!" the Professor rejoiced, happy to talk to his son before going to sleep for the night. "How are you feeling, Louis?"

Jacques was sitting close to the tiny, elevated emergency chamber that had been prepared for such a time as this. There had only been a few times in their lives that they had seen each other without a glass enclosure between them.

Unable to reply with the mask on his face, Louis motioned with a 'thumbs-up.' The Professor reached over and placed his hand beside the Tiny. With a smile, his ageing son clasped the finger closest to him. It felt like a hug.

"Thank you for saving Ponce and Zahir," Jacques smiled as tears welled up in his eyes. "I would never have asked you to risk your life like that! *Ça alors!* You were very brave to run in there, especially in your condition! I'm so thankful that you didn't lose *your* life!"

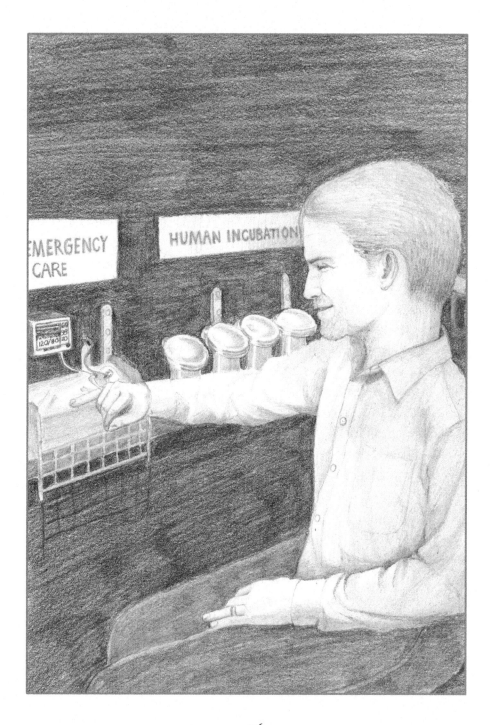

Louis looked at him thoughtfully. Even though he was unable to speak, the Professor could tell by his son's wrinkled forehead that he was thinking deeply.

While the elder Tiny appreciated the Professor's protective sentiments, he wondered how he would have felt if Zahir and Ponce had died in the fire. Weren't two lives worth the risk of one?

Moving one hand in a questioning fashion and shrugging his shoulders, Louis longed to ask about the fire. He remembered seeing the girls running towards him, but nothing after that.

"Do you want to know what happened?" Jacques inquired.

Louis nodded.

"You had a heart attack," the Professor explained, "but Aimee knew what to do. You taught her well. She brought you back to life with the CPR training you gave her. The boys put you on the train and we stabilized you once you came down here. Your heart is quite weak, but you're alive and I'm *so thankful!* I love you, Louis!"

Stroking the big finger, Louis tried to express his deep feelings without words. "Aimee saved me!" he thought with astonishment. He remembered back to the day he had taught First Aid, recalling how eager she was to learn. He was so pleased she had succeeded – for her sake and for his! Then he thought about the terrible burns two Tinys had incurred and wondered how they were doing. With great anxiety, he weakly raised one arm and drew a 'Z', then a 'P' in the air.

It took a moment or two for Jacques to understand. Finally, he smiled, "Ah, you're asking what happened to Zahir and Ponce?"

Louis nodded earnestly.

The Professor told him they had very serious burns, but he was hopeful that with the right care and medication, they would recover well. He explained they had set up a Caring Centre in the girls' mansion, and that the doctors had given him a lot of medical advice and assistance. "I've put Aimee, Tina and Yu Yan in charge of nursing them back to health during the day," he relayed. "Kenzie and Vahid are doing the nightshift and bedpan duties. We'd like to send you back into Paradise as soon as you are stable. However, you will need to be on complete bed rest for at least three weeks."

With a frown, Louis wondered how he would endure three weeks in bed with nothing to do? He wouldn't be able to continue his research on the Bible!

But the Professor was insistent that complete rest was necessary. "We'll recommend you go into the same room as Zahir and Ponce," he informed him. "The medical instructions we've sent in must be followed exactly and the medications given just as prescribed. Their temperatures and wounds must be carefully monitored. If not, infection could set in quickly. They aren't out of danger yet and the next three days will be crucial. We considered keeping them here on our side, but their wounds are too fragile. The doctors feel that tiny hands will give better care than we can."

Louis nodded. With all his heart he wanted to ensure the young men recovered. He longed to be with them, helping Aimee, Tina and Yu Yan make the best decisions concerning their care.

"Rest now," the Professor encouraged. "We'll send you back in tomorrow morning, if your heart remains stable."

With a thankful nod, Louis agreed. Tears welled up in his eyes as he considered that Zahir and Ponce were still in danger.

Jacques saw the tears. "Their situation is troubling," he assured him, "but we have the best doctors overseeing their care. If you are in there monitoring the situation, I feel very confident that full recovery is possible." With a smile, he added his hopeful thoughts that due to the Tiny's rapid cell reproduction, they might heal faster than normal.

For a moment, the two sat together in thoughtful silence. Louis gently rubbed the Professor's finger as he pondered what lay ahead. He desperately hoped that the nurses were taking good care of their patients.

"There's one more thing I want to say to you, Louis," Jacques relayed quietly. "Since you will be confined to bed, I'm going to ask Aimee to take on the communications with me. I will send a private letter in for her with written instructions, but she may need your guidance to work it all out."

Louis nodded slowly. He was pleased that Aimee had been chosen but wondered why she had been singled out. Feeling that there were at least three other Tinys that were quite capable of handling the position, he motioned 'Z?,' 'K?,' 'S?'

The Professor didn't immediately understand what Louis was trying to say. After three tries, he nodded. "Yes, those would all be good choices and Evan agrees with you. Eventually, Aimee will need someone else to support her... and balance her decisions, but right now she seems rather... *alone.* I think it will be best to have a male and a female with a strong friendship to interact with me." He paused and then asked, "Do you think that maybe Zahir would be a good choice to help her? Last week I overheard the beautiful song that they sang together. Have they reconciled?"

Looking up with consternation, Louis shook his head. He had been privy to Zahir's outpouring of grief the day after the song, and he knew that the sensitive, dark-haired young man was fully committed to Georgia. Louis felt that if he and Aimee were given a secret mission, this would be terribly upsetting to Georgia and emotionally disconcerting to Zahir. Having his own personal thoughts on the matter, Louis drew a 'K' in the air.

"Kenzie?" the Professor deliberated. He had his heart set on Aimee and Zahir for a number of reasons. Thinking it through, he pondered, "Perhaps I have it all wrong. I've certainly been wrong about many things with this experiment. Am I completely biased? Louis has a much better idea of the relationship dynamics; he witnesses the personal interactions. Why have I been so set on Zahir? Is it only because he reminds me of a good friend?" Reluctantly, he acknowledged to himself, "Kenzie is certainly capable of sincere, compassionate leadership. He would be a very good choice. And the Tinys must have freewill," he reminded himself with a sigh. "I can't force things to happen or I will be going against my own principles."

Louis patted his finger affectionately.

"Maybe you're right," Jacques acknowledged reluctantly. "You know the Tinys best. For now, I'm thankful that Aimee can turn to you for help."

In the peaceful, darkened room, with soft beeps and fluttering lights, there was one more thing that Jacques wanted to tell Louis face to face. While they had this private opportunity, there was something he wanted to say.

"You're probably wondering *why* I've chosen Aimee," he asked.

Louis nodded.

"First of all, she is a loving, thoughtful person, much like you," he smiled warmly. "She wants to do good and she cares about choosing right over wrong. She trusts me. Those are the most important reasons and without those qualities nothing else would matter. But... there is something else I want you to know. You and Aimee are both my *real* children," he said, happily sharing the secret which he had often alluded to but never fully revealed. "You have the same mother and the same father. Aimee is your sister even though you are many months apart. I loved your mother dearly. She was a very special person. If you lived here in my world, Louis, you and Aimee would have grown up together in my family."

The heart monitor beeped erratically, and warning lights flashed.

Worried, Jacques looked over, but within ten seconds the monitor signs settled back down. He didn't tell Louis about Franz. In his son's fragile state, he only wanted to share a little joy.

Tears welled up in Louis' eyes. He had always thought of the Professor as a father-figure, but it was heartwarming to know that he truly was his son. And while he loved all the Tinys that the Professor had placed in his care, there had always been a special connection between himself and Aimee. "She's *my* sister!" he considered radiantly. "I have a *real* sister in Paradise. I can't wait to tell her!"

He looked up at Jacques with a puzzled expression, wondering if he were free to share this news. He also wished that he could take off the oxygen mask, so they could have an actual conversation!

"You can tell her," Jacques smiled, anticipating Louis' thoughts. "Make sure she understands that I consider *all* the Tinys my children. I love you all. This relationship doesn't give her any special status," he cautioned, "except the privilege to communicate with me. Tell her that I am looking forward to speaking with her on the phone." With a happy smile, he added, "And please tell Aimee that I *love* her."

Louis nodded eagerly, longing to witness the new family interactions. "I'm so thankful that I lived to be a part of this," he thought with a grateful prayer upwards. Still exhausted, his eyes began to close.

"You're tired," the Professor acknowledged, nudging Louis gently with his finger. He showed him a small button by the bed. "This is for emergencies," he explained. "I'll be sleeping here beside you tonight. If you wake up in the morning and I'm not here, you can always press this button and I'll come immediately." Holding up the slim black device he now rarely forgot, he said, "The heart monitor is linked to my phone."

Lifting his hand from Louis' side, the grey-haired researcher was about to lie down on his cot, but then he felt there was *one more thing* he had to say.

"If I don't get another chance to speak to you privately," Jacques begged, "please do your best to guide Aimee to choose her partner carefully. He must be loving and caring and have servant leadership qualities. I trust you, Louis, to work this out. I don't want to force anyone together, but please provide encouragement if she asks you for advice."

Wearily, Louis nodded. As he and the Professor drifted off to sleep in the dark, peaceful room, he thought to himself, "I'll do my best to guide Aimee to find a good partner, but I will not force anything. They all need genuine relationships of their own choosing in order to be truly loved and appreciated for who they are. At least... that's what I would want if I had the choice."

"However," he reflected dreamily, as he thought about the Professor's failed attempt to give him a partner, "I'm sure I would have enjoyed Loretta, *whoever she was*. It would have been really nice to have had a wife."

Louis' Request

Chapter 5

*J*acques met Evan at eight the next morning in the Paradise Room. He was tired. Sleeping on the cot beside Louis hadn't been the most restful experience. With all the soft beeps on the monitor and his anxiety over what might be happening in the Caring Centre, Professor Lemans was feeling quite stressed. However, exams were over and he knew he might never run them again. His teaching career was likely to be terminated, based on the decisions made by the Ethics Committee, and the University was now shut down for the summer break. All the scientists that had come to tour Paradise had gone home with plenty to discuss. He and Evan were both thankful they had a break in duties while so much was at stake in the dome.

Walking over to look into the enormous terrarium with his assistant, the Professor noted that very few were outside. Charley, Lema and Sanaa were watering the gardens, and Odin was dragging burnt trees from the front of the forest to the back. Plenty of activity could be heard coming from the store as the Tinys came in and out for breakfast. Sadly, he could also hear moans and cries coming from the girls' mansion.

"They must be changing the dressings," Evan sighed sorrowfully. "I feel so sorry for the burn victims."

"Yes, there is a lot of pain and suffering right now in the Caring Centre," the Professor agreed sadly. "Zahir and Ponce must be in absolute agony. I hope the nurses read all of Dr. Khalid's instructions," he fretted. "As Rachel said, the next few days will be vital."

"Do you think Aimee will figure out how to communicate with us?" Evan asked.

Reaching into his lab coat, the Professor pulled out his phone. "I know how we can help her," he smiled. "How about we make a video? You can tell her what to do with a demonstration on your cellphone? Then we just have to explain in our note how to get into the cave, turn on the device and press the WhiteDove App."

Noticing the Professor was positioning his phone to take a video, Evan smiled, "Now?"

"This is as good a time as any," the Professor nodded.

It took two tries, but a video was made and sent off to the control cave phone. Jacques sat down and wrote a little note to... his daughter.

Rachel knocked at the door and delivered a small eye dropper bottle with a special concoction from Farouk, for Louis' recovery. It was well-labelled with clear instructions in a very small font. "I just had a good visit with Louis," she told them. As she and Evan loaded the bottle on to the train, along with another supply of downsized gauze strips, a few more mattress covers and the tiny thermometer that Jacques had found, she relayed, "I've explained everything he needs to know about burns."

Looking over at the Professor who had just finished his note, Rachel added, "Jacques, when you have a chance this morning, could you please come and have a look at the boa constrictor. I think it swallowed some litter. Maybe someone threw garbage into the pond. I need help to get it down from the tree."

Jacques raced off to have a look, while Evan finished packing the train. He put the Professor's note into a tiny brown envelope to send in with Louis. Once he was done, he decided to check again on the very important patient in the basement laboratory.

Louis was awake and looking around.

"Glad to see your eyes are open," Evan smiled kindly. "You're looking well."

Gazing up at the tall young man with the spiky blond hair, Louis' eyes brightened happily above his oxygen mask. He had been thinking hard about an urgent matter which he had found difficult to mention to his father the night before. With one arm in the air, Louis made a typing motion with his finger. Evan studied his actions with a frown and then finally understood. "You want to write a message!" he smiled. Taking out his phone and wiping it carefully with disinfectant, Evan opened the Notepad app and held it in front of Louis.

With a happy nod, Louis quickly typed a few sentences. "Evan, do you have any thoughts about God or Jesus? Are they real? Have you read God's Book?"

When Evan looked at the message, he was thoroughly astonished. Running his hand through his hair and causing it to stand straight up in a spiky fashion, he thought about how he and Seth had discussed sharing the Gospel message with the Tinys only a week ago! He remembered Seth's prayer. At the time, Evan had felt it was impossible to take a 'missionary' initiative without going behind the Professor's back. The whole idea seemed preposterous. He had never imagined that Louis would ask him these questions, especially not after the older Tiny had read the Professor's book – *'Faith or Fact – An End to Delusion'*!

With an uneasy glance in Louis' direction, Evan was struck by his earnest gaze. The elder Tiny's hands were tight together as though he were begging for an answer.

"I haven't always known about God," the young researcher replied hesitantly, keeping things sterile and positioning the phone in front of Louis again, "but I've been learning about Him. I've been finding

35

more reasons to believe He exists than to believe that He doesn't. I have read some of His book."

Louis' eyes filled with relief and joy. He typed on the screen, "I learned about God on the Internet. I started to read His book weeks before the fire, but I didn't get far. Evan, I prayed to Him to give me more time, and I'm still alive! I survived a heart attack and a fire! I believe God has extended my life. If I'm going to be confined to bed, I'll have so much time to read, but no opportunity to get to the cave. Please, please, is there some way you can help me continue my research?"

Reading the message, Evan felt his spine tingle with excitement and apprehension. This was an opportunity like no other to send the Gospel message into Paradise. Yet, he felt unsure whether he should go against the Professor. He knew Jacques would be furious if he sent in a Bible!

Glancing up from his phone, he was moved by Louis' pleading eyes. "You know how the Professor feels about the Bible and God, right?" Evan inquired nervously, "I know you have read the Professor's book."

Louis nodded and moved his fingers in a typing motion. When Evan repositioned the phone, he typed, "Life matters to me, Evan. I don't have much of it left... maybe a few weeks, but not likely months. I'm desperate to find out if there is anything more. I believe the Bible offers a hope that is beyond anything the Professor can give. I love Jesus and his extraordinary teachings which go far beyond servant leadership. I want to read more about him. I believe that God heard my prayers and gave me this extra time to investigate. Please Evan, is there some way you can help? Can you print out some of the pages of the Bible and send them in on the train every day?"

Evan pondered the matter thoughtfully. "I could send you in a complete copy," he murmured anxiously, remembering that Seth had one that he was willing to lend. "Only, I feel the Professor would never forgive me. And I don't know *for certain* that the Bible is true, or reliable, but it is very intriguing..."

Louis' eyes opened wide. "You have a *small* copy?" he wrote.

Evan nodded. "My friend has one that he is willing to share."

Typing on the phone, Louis said, "Evan, please, please send this book to me!"

"I'll tell you what," Evan replied decisively. "Send a message to the Professor and ask him if you can have a copy of the Bible. Beg him to allow you the opportunity to *investigate,"* Evan chuckled, "and use the word *'investigate,'"* he emphasized. "Any true scientist appreciates the necessity of a full and fair investigation."

Louis wasted no time in finding the Professor's name in the WhiteDove app on Evan's phone. Assuming that his relationship with the Professor was still unknown to Evan, he didn't begin his message with 'Father' as he would have liked. Instead, he typed in,

> *"Dear Professor, I would really like to do a thorough investigation on the Bible. I have read your book and I would also like to read God's. I don't have much time left to live and I want to be sure I have fully examined the evidence on both sides of this argument before coming to my own conclusion. Please allow me this vital opportunity to investigate while I am confined to bed.*
>
> *With much love, Louis"*

Looking up at Evan, the eldest Tiny pressed the send button. Together, they anxiously waited to see what the response would be. Minutes dragged by. To pass the time, Evan told Louis about various happenings in Paradise that day.

"You'll be pleased to know that Odin worked all day on the rock stairway for Rainbow Hill," Evan said. "It's more than halfway done."

Louis was astonished. "Odin is working without supervision?" he pondered.

"And on his own initiative!" Evan nodded. "He has also been carrying water back and forth without complaint, liked we asked him to," Evan said proudly. "He apologized outside at dinner last night for all the damage he caused and even helped to unload the train this morning."

Wide-eyed, Louis was hopeful for change.

"And there are a new group of kitchen helpers," Evan explained. "Georgia and Lily have been asked to collect the food from the garden every day and help Nancy and Milan to prepare it. Feeding everyone will be more complicated as there are so many deliveries that need to be made to the Caring Centre, but those who weren't injured are readily volunteering to help..."

The lab door creaked opened and footsteps sounded in the hall. The Professor came around the corner with a baffled expression. He had his phone in his hand.

"Louis," he said, addressing the Tiny in the small white bed, "I am astonished at your request. This isn't the time to fill your head with... well... *nonsense.* If you feel you only have a short time left, you should spend it talking to the other Tinys and encouraging them to carry on in the wonderful, loving manner that you have shown."

Evan could see the look of deep disappointment on Louis' face. He felt Louis was quite disadvantaged with the mask on his face, unable to speak. "Jacques," Evan spoke up in his defence, "Louis began this search before the fire, but his time was cut short. He longs to finish his research and determine for himself what is right and wrong, and where hope lies. I suggest we allow him to do this investigation in a full and fair way. Louis has rarely requested anything for himself."

Holding his own phone up for the Mastermind of Paradise to view, Evan said, "Read what Louis wrote to me."

Folding his arms across his chest, Jacques read Louis' pleas on Evan's phone. He tingled with alarm. Looking at the two earnest faces staring at him, he was distressed that they both thought this was a good idea.

"Evan," the Professor reasoned, "if Louis were to stay here on our side, I would readily allow him this opportunity to research whatever he wanted. But taking a Bible into Paradise will potentially cause confusion among the Tinys. They only have a short lifespan to sort anything out. It has taken me years of scientific study and careful analysis to come to the conclusion that God is a foolish fantasy created by humans to control other humans. I don't want to see this concept brought into Paradise. It will throw everything into chaos. I *can't* allow this!"

Pacing back and forth, Evan felt his mentor's reasoning was unfair. "In class you have always promoted the importance of investigating *both sides* of a matter," he reminded him. "You say we should consider *all* the evidence before drawing our own conclusions. You warn your students about the dangers of bias and demonstrate how many times bias has skewed the results of crucial experiments. On top of all that, you are against rules and restrictions in Paradise. So how can you *ban* the Bible?"

"Because it has been proven wrong! Because it is archaic. Because it promotes false hopes and ideas! I feel I must make an exception to my principles. The Bible cannot go into Paradise!"

"Proven wrong?" Evan frowned. "By whom?

"Evan, there is no God!" the Professor protested. "How can an intelligent person like you let Seth fill your head with all this foolish nonsense? It is very evident that there is no one looking after us when we see the lack of protection for those on our planet. The Bible itself is *riddled* with contradictions and error. There are *thousands* of discrepancies between the manuscripts that have been found. The promises that God has made have not occurred. Think of all the predictions that Christians have made over the last one hundred years that God will intervene and Jesus Christ will return. *None of them have happened!* With all the disease, pestilence, wars, potential for nuclear annihilation, natural catastrophes and climate change – we will either blow ourselves up, or pollution and disease will snuff out life...”

Lying back, observing the discussion, Louis was distressed to hear the bitterness in his father’s voice. He had read rather accusatory words in his book, *“Faith or Fact”,* but now he heard the tone. He wondered if such intense emotions might have hampered his father’s ability to be objective. “But why?” he thought. “Why is he bitter? And are there really *thousands* of contradictions?” he wondered anxiously. “That would certainly deal a serious blow to the reliability of the record. And if promises have not been kept, that would indicate the book may be a fraud...”

“But, Jacques, you’re overlooking many promises which God made, that *have occurred,*” Evan pleaded. “Seth is still confident that Jesus will return to save the world and restore God’s creation. It just hasn’t happened *yet.* ”

“What promises have been fulfilled?”

“Well, for instance, from the beginning of Creation, God promised to send the Messiah. He gave hundreds of details in the Old Testament about him, of which the majority were realised when Jesus Christ came to earth the first time. Some remain as promises for the future – the ‘last day.’”

“But that’s all part of the book itself,” Jacques pointed out, “of course the Bible is going to tell you that its prophecies came true. How do we know *Jesus* really existed, *apart* from the holy book?”

“I’ll need to ask Seth about that,” Evan replied, not being entirely sure himself. Undaunted, he chose an example that he had researched. “As Seth told us, God promised to bring the Jewish people back to the land of Israel from all over the earth and make them a nation again in their own land. That happened *against all odds* in the last one hundred years."

The Professor was shaking his head in disbelief.

Having spent hours looking at passages from Ezekiel and Zechariah[1] with the Bible study group that Seth attended, Evan gestured with his hands in a pleading way, "Think how small Israel is compared to the numerous hostile nations all around them who continuously rally for their destruction. God promised that the Jews' neglected land would once again be productive and that they would dwell on the *'mountains of Israel'*[2]– the disputed West Bank. We are seeing it happen before our eyes."

"*Ça alors!* Do you realise you are condoning the oppressive and illegal takeover of Palestinian land?"

"That may be how the media spins it," Evan acknowledged, "but not how the Bible portrays it... or even the *unbiased* historical records." Responding to the skeptical look on the Professor's face, Evan continued, "Professor Lemans, none of this has happened easily. Israel has had a daily struggle against the human forces that openly threaten its existence on many sides. Without God fulfilling His promise to the Jewish people, there would be no nation of Israel today. It is a real miracle, and more is still to come. Sadly, the Bible indicates that more destruction will come before the greatest miracle ever!"[3]

Lying comfortably in his bed, Louis found the open discussion helpful in determining his own viewpoint. He hoped he could research the miracle of Israel returning to their land, the 'thousands of discrepancies,' and some other things that he had come across in his previous investigation. Desperately curious, he made motions to type on the phone. He had rarely, if ever, argued against his father, but he

---

[1] Ezekiel 36 – 39; Zechariah 12 – 14.
[2] Ezekiel 34:13-14; 37:22; 38:8
[3] Ezekiel 38 – 39, Zechariah 14:1-4; Joel 3

felt he must insist on doing this research. If the Bible were true, he knew from what he'd already read that lives were at stake in a much greater way than the Professor acknowledged.

Both researchers heard Louis' heart rate go up on the monitor and turned to him. Evan noticed he was motioning to type and passed him his phone. While Louis was entering his message, Evan kindly asked, "If Louis believes the Bible is true and yet it isn't, what will happen?"

"Well," the Professor muttered. "He'll die believing *a lie...*"

"Like the 'hope' that you can restore life to the cells and bring Rosa back?" Evan prodded. Instantly, he grimaced as he saw the Professor flinch. "I'm sorry, Jacques," he apologized, placing his hand on the older man's shoulder. "That was uncalled for."

Walking away and pacing around the room, the senior scientist didn't meet Evan's eyes.

In a more conciliatory tone, Evan continued, "If God *is* real and Louis dies with a hope for the future, what has he gained?"

Shaking his head, the Professor didn't want to answer the question.

Quietly, Evan gave his own reply. "What he gains is the hope of resurrection from the dead. If the Bible *is* true, then Louis gains God's salvation and the hope of living forever. Why wouldn't we allow him the opportunity to make this choice for himself? Six years hardly compares to a promise of eternity."

With the heart monitor still beeping quite fast, Louis finished his message and pressed send.

Receiving the text instantly, the Professor read,

> *"I love Paradise. I love every Tiny that you've put in my care. I dearly long to be with them and help them through this crisis, but this research means much more to me than even my own life. If I'm only allowed to research on this side of Paradise, then I*

beg to stay here for another week and finish my investigation. Please may I have access to the Internet somehow? Perhaps you could put me in the nursery?

However, if you allow me to take a copy of the Bible into Paradise, I will only share it with those who are with me in crisis care – Zahir, Ponce and whichever nurses remain with them in the evenings. We will keep our investigation private while we try to determine what is right and what is wrong. I will also share the book that you wrote with them if you make it available to me in a small format.

You must remember that it is very easy to find God's Book online. Potential leaders in Paradise will certainly come across it. It will be better for the future of everyone that the leaders have opportunity to discuss the options thoroughly and make our own conclusions as a group."

With a heavy heart the Professor pondered the message. It wasn't like Louis to make insistent demands. He saw the desperation in his son's eyes. Fearfully, he wondered what would happen to Zahir and Ponce if Louis didn't return for a week. The next three days were critical, and he was counting on Louis to oversee the healthcare providers and coach the nurses through the dangerous infection that could soon set in. He knew Louis longed to take part in the recovery process and was not likely to cast this opportunity aside unless he felt something drastically more important was at stake. Was finding a hope for the future so crucial that Louis would give up everything else that mattered?

As Jacques quietly deliberated his decision, he realised that his son had raised a good point. "Aimee is likely to come across the Bible online someday," he acknowledged. "Without Louis to help her sort through what she reads, she may be turned against me. He's promised to read *both books* to the Tinys. Surely truth will prevail."

Turning to the eldest Tiny, he said evenly, "You may have a Bible in Paradise." He looked over at Evan, "I assume you have this copy?"

"I can get it," Evan nodded.

"And I will find a way to make a small copy of my book," Jacques relayed to Louis, "so you can lead the investigation fairly. However, I would like you to carefully minimise the number of Tinys who are involved with you in the room. Aimee and Zahir should both be there," he insisted. "And Ponce, of course," he added. Since Louis felt Kenzie was the best choice, he granted his attendance as well. Then he begged, "But please do not invite *anyone* else until the five of you have reached a consensus on the matter."

Louis nodded gratefully. "When do I go home?" he typed. "I'm ready to go."

Jacques' phone rang. Looking at the screen, he saw that it was Tom Freeman from Canadian Broadcasting, calling to request an interview. He had already left a voice message that morning and there were at least six unanswered emails.

"Today," Jacques assured his son, before dashing off to the elevator to take the call in private. Once inside the enclosure, he answered the phone.

Tom chided him for his lack of response. "You promised a full disclosure once Paradise was open to the public," he reminded him. "I assume that will be happening in the next few weeks *as planned,* even though I hear you had *another* catastrophe. I hope everything is okay. When should I schedule you for an interview?"

With a sigh, the Professor felt very weary. "Listen Tom," he pleaded, "Paradise has gone through enormous upheaval in the last two months. To be honest, it hasn't gone according to plan. I'm not really sure what to make of it all. I... I don't know what I'd say in an interview."

"You can say exactly what you just said," Tom laughed. "After all, everyone only wants to hear *the truth.* I should just mention," he remarked in a serious tone, "that the very graphic video of the fire will be airing tomorrow night, and it's going viral on social media. There will be a huge public outcry for information. Everyone will want to know how this disaster is being handled and how you intend to avoid such a dangerous situation occurring in the future. It is essential for you to keep the public informed."

"I'll send daily reports," Jacques promised, "but please give me another month before requesting an interview. I feel I'll have a better understanding by then. I'd like to have answers for you, but I'm just not prepared at this point to go public with any of my opinions."

"It's that bad, eh?" Tom goaded.

"It's just... not what I expected," the Professor replied.

"A disappointment?"

"In some ways, yes," the Professor admitted. "In other ways, no. I feel I'm gaining some important insights from this experiment, but I'm not ready to make any conclusions just yet."

"Ah, this bodes well for the future," Tom chuckled. "The Professor has learned something new! I'll call you again in a month and see what we can set up."

"In a month then," the Professor agreed with a sigh, wondering if he should have asked for a year.

A Most Important Delivery

Chapter 6

Carrying Louis in his hand, Jacques brought the eldest Tiny up to the main level and headed toward the supply room where Evan was getting the train ready. Louis still wore his oxygen mask, and was holding the small, attached cylinder.

"We're going to send you back in with oxygen," the Professor told him. "When the train enters Paradise, you will likely be able to remove your mask. But it's fine for you to keep it on until you reach the Caring Centre. I don't want you to have any physical distress."

Louis nodded.

Handing him a very small brown envelope, the Professor added gently, "This letter contains information about the cave and how to use the phone. Give it to Aimee when you have a private opportunity - the sooner the better - as we need daily reports on the patients. Ensure she understands that she is not to publicise this message. I'd like to keep our communication a secret for as long as we can."

There was another nod as Louis slid the little envelope into his pocket.

The Professor picked up the stretcher and gently placed Louis on it. Then Evan loaded him carefully on to the first car of the train, hoping he would be discovered as soon as possible. For good measure, they placed an extra oxygen bottle beside him.

"Goodbye, son," Jacques said sadly, reaching one finger into the train to pat Louis's folded hands. "I'm so thankful that you are still with us. Take it easy and don't be in a hurry to get out of bed. Your books will come soon. Remember how much I love you!"

Louis closed his eyes briefly and patted the giant finger. Evan's eyes welled up with tears as they shut the doors and sent the train in.

"We've got to watch this," the Professor said earnestly to Evan. "Are you okay for time?"

"Summer holidays," Evan smiled, although he wasn't sure what 'holidays' meant anymore. His classroom studies were over until September, but he had no plans to leave the Biosphere.

Walking through the long corridor into the Paradise Room, they witnessed Kenzie, Vahid and Milan rush down the half-finished stairway on Rainbow Hill to meet the incoming train. The young men grabbed carrycarts from the store and ran over.

"Hey, is that Odin joining them?" Evan asked quietly.

Sure enough, Odin came from the charred forest towards the train.

"He's already cleared quite a lot of the debris," the Professor whispered.

"And look at that," Evan pointed out. "He's collected a cart full of rocks!"

"That's incredible," the Professor observed. "He doesn't even have Louis to supervise his work or Ponce to help him. This *is* encouraging!"

Curiously, the scientists watched Odin approach the train. From the microphone near the store, they could hear him ask if the guys wanted any help.

"Sure," Kenzie replied. "There's likely a lot to carry." Opening the first car, he discovered *live* cargo!

"Guys!" Kenzie called out with great excitement. "Uncle Louis is in here and he's alive!"

Everyone peered in to see.

Uncle Louis's eyes were smiling, but he kept his oxygen mask on.

"Should we take you to the Caring Centre?" Kenzie asked, seeing that the older Tiny was lying on a stretcher.

Removing his mask briefly, Uncle Louis said, "Yes. Please take me there. I'm so glad to be back with you all!"

With a happy smile, Kenzie called out, "Grab an end, everyone."

Slowly they pulled the stretcher out of the car and everyone took one end of the poles.

Together the young men marched slowly, yet triumphantly, up the hill. Never had there been a more important delivery in Paradise. Odin didn't meet Uncle Louis's eyes, but he put all his muscle into bringing the stretcher up the hill as evenly as possible. The rock stairway made the climb easier. Once they reached the narrow path, Kenzie warned, "Careful you don't trip." Then he said to Odin, "See what a big difference you've made already! Your staircase will be appreciated by everyone who goes up and down this hill!"

Odin acknowledged the compliment with a grunt and he didn't complain about the work.

Just before they reached the clearing at the top of the hill, the stocky Tiny with the wild blond hair asked, "Uncle Louis, what do you have on your face?"

Taking the mask off, the elder Tiny answered, "To survive in the big world, I had to wear this constantly. The tank holds the right mixture of oxygen. It comes through the tube and into the mask and then I can breathe it in. I am likely all right now without it," he acknowledged, but with a shrug he put it back on anyway.

Frowning thoughtfully, Odin nodded. "What was it like on the other side?" he asked.

"Quite dark and boring," Uncle Louis replied, taking off the mask again and deciding he didn't need it. "If your life is in danger, it's a good place to recover, but it's not nearly so beautiful as Paradise!"

"Really?" Odin questioned dubiously.

"I'm very glad to be back home," Uncle Louis smiled.

When they reached the girl's mansion, Kenzie yelled out toward the upstairs' windows, "We've got Uncle Louis! The Professor brought him back to life!"

The nurses were first to run downstairs and open the door. Sanaa and Lily excused themselves from holding hands with their patients and raced after the others. It was a jubilant welcome for Uncle Louis as he entered the house in a prone position. Once inside, he was pleased to receive hugs from Aimee and Sanaa while still lying down. "I'm so thankful to be back with you all!" he rejoiced. "How are my injured boys?"

"We'll show you," Kenzie replied with a smile, encouraging his team to continue with the stretcher. Marching up the stairs they brought Uncle Louis to his new bed, right next to the big window and beside the two most severely injured young men.

Right away, Uncle Louis noticed that Zahir and Ponce were only semi-conscious. They barely acknowledged his presence. "The sedation is working," he thought.

There was a joyful reception from everyone else. The beach boys hobbled to the doorway of Georgia's old room to say hello while Sanaa danced and sang. Vinitha, Georgia and the kitchen crew stood with the others, panting a little from their long run from the store. They hadn't had time to shower so they weren't allowed in the room, but they waved happily and called out cheerful greetings.

On his own initiative, Odin carried up the pink sofa from the living room. "You will need this chair for visitors," he said flatly.

Kenzie and Aimee thanked him and positioned it against the wall. With great joy, everyone celebrated that Uncle Louis was home and still alive!

Hurting to Help

Chapter 7

*A*imee awoke the next morning to a loud crash outside the window. Bright light shone into the dark room. "Time to get breakfast ready," she told herself sleepily, and then she realised she was not in her own room. Lily was lying in the bed beside her.

Curious about the crash, she ran to the window and saw that the big pine tree that had once shaded Lily's window was lying flat on the ground. Its tiny roots were helplessly exposed.

Hearing Ponce cry out in pain, the copper-haired girl remembered that she was now a nurse and her patients needed her help.

Slipping quickly into her clothes with a smile, Aimee glanced out Lily's newly bright window. With their room at the far end of the house, she could see out over the forested hills, and to the left the lake was sparkling in the distance. She was sad the beautiful tree had fallen over, but happy to have morning sunshine and a better view.

Lily looked up wearily. "Are you getting up already?" she groaned. "Why is it so bright in here?"

"The patients need their medicine," Aimee replied. "And your tree fell over."

Heading into the hallway, the copper-haired nurse saw bags of clean bandages, equipment and medication piled neatly outside of her old room. With a smile she washed her hands carefully in the pot of

50

soapy water. It was the second day since the fire and she *loved* her new assignment!

Vahid came out of the critical care room. He had been on night duty. "I had to give everyone more pain medication last night," he told her quietly. "They were really suffering. Did you hear them?"

"I didn't hear anything last night," Aimee admitted. "I slept so soundly! I'm really thankful you guys are doing the night shift."

Rubbing his dark beard with both his hands, Vahid nodded wearily. "I think they are anxious for the next round of medications," he yawned. "Do you want some help?"

Aimee laughed kindly. "You look like you need a break," she smiled. "Tina and Yu Yan will be here soon. I'll be fine, but thanks for the offer."

"Okay, I *really* need more sleep," Vahid yawned, heading for the stairs. "I'll check back in later."

Looking at the tall bottles of painkiller, antibiotics, medication and formula, Aimee read over the instructions twice. They had pinned up the important messages in the hallway. She was anxious to get everything right. Glancing over at the clock in her old room, she saw that it was seven in the morning. As Vahid had said, many of the patients were awake and two were groaning in pain. Using the pipette, she carefully filled everyone's cups with the exact amount prescribed. By the time she had given all six the first dose of painkiller, Tina and Yu Yan had arrived with wet hair from their showers, ready to help change the bandages. Lema and Damien were standing in the doorway. "Let's get this day going, girls," Damien teased, holding out his bandaged arm. "We have important things to do."

Kenzie came running up the stairs as Aimee picked up a new wad of gauze. "Can I help?" he asked eagerly.

"Sure," Aimee agreed. "I've done the pain killer, but not the protein formula or the antibiotics."

"Great!" he said. "I'll do that."

Emma, Damien's golden retriever, waggled into the Crisis Room to say good morning to the patients. She had been sleeping in the room next door, unable to get through the night without her master.

"Dogs should not be in this room around open injuries," Uncle Louis objected sharply. "We can't afford infection right now."

Aimee coaxed Emma out of the crisis room and brought her back to her master. Damien was admiring Georgia's artwork that decorated her walls. "She's really good, isn't she?" he remarked, pointing to a painting of Freddo that hung by the window.

"Georgia and Vinitha have the creative touch," the young nurse agreed, with her hand on Emma's head. "Umm, Uncle Louis says dogs aren't allowed in the Crisis Room. I'm just going to take her outside."

Damien turned around and smiled. He had a bandage on one leg and his right arm, but he could walk fine. "I'll take her outside," he said. "She'd probably love a walk on the beach."

"Actually," Aimee smiled back, "you aren't supposed to go outside until you have scabs on those wounds."

"Says who?"

"Come and see," the girl with the deep blue eyes encouraged. Outside the room, she showed him the instructions pinned up on the wall. "If you get any dirt or unsafe water onto those wounds right now, you could wind up in the Crisis Room."

"This is terrible!" Damien protested. "I can't stay inside all day!"

The other beach boys had been listening in to the conversation and added their disapproval. "What are we going to do? It's so boring in here!"

Sanaa burst through the doorway one level below. Georgia, Milan and Nancy followed her in with boardgames and books. "Look what came in on the train!" they shouted.

"Check it out!" Damien exclaimed, clapping his hands together. "Now we have something to do!"

Aimee took Emma downstairs and let her outside.

Washing her arms and hands again carefully, Aimee returned to her old room. Tina and Yu Yan were across the hall, attending to the surfers' moderate injuries, which were already forming scabs. "When I'm finished here, I'll come help you with Ponce," Yu Yan told Aimee.

Georgia and Lily ducked in to say a quick good morning to Zahir, Ponce and Uncle Louis. Then they hurried off to get breakfast ready.

The Caring Centre reverberated with cries of distress as the nurses tended to the messy sores. Zahir and Ponce were finally awake and aware of everything that was happening. It took much longer to care for their burns than for the other three Tinys, as their injuries were larger and much more severe. Dead, peeling skin and oozing fluid had to be gently cleaned and removed if it came off easily. It was not a job for the faint-hearted or those with sensitive noses. While Kenzie carefully measured doses from the eyedropper bottles and brought them around to both rooms, Aimee and Yu Yan applied antibiotic cream with very clean hands onto the gauze and then wound it around their patient's injured legs.

Having Uncle Louis in the room was reassuring for them all. He couldn't do anything to help in a physical way, but he could offer advice and encouragement. As Aimee worked, he explained many principles behind germs, infection and compassionate caring. He passed on all that he could remember from Rachel's explanations.

Even though he had been given the pain medication that morning, Zahir cried out and flinched badly when Aimee tried to take the gauze bandages off his arm. Even the slightest movement against the injuries caused him to react.

"I'm so sorry I have to do this to you," she apologized sadly.

"Moisten the gauze first," Uncle Louis instructed both nurses, recalling a tip he hadn't passed on yet. "That will help."

Zahir nodded weakly, closing his eyes and clenching his jaw.

The tip worked well. When the copper-haired nurse had changed the dressings on her patient's right forearm and lower leg, she turned to his face and neck. With a sterile wipe, she dabbed at the oozing sores, trying to gently remove any loose dead tissue. Following the instructions on the wall, she soaked a new strip of gauze in a saline-solution and rubbed it with the antibacterial cream. Then she gently covered the wound and wrapped it around his head. It was such a large burn, stretching from his jaw right up into his hairline.

Once she was done, Zahir reached out his left hand for hers. "Please stay," he begged, closing his eyes.

Yu Yan arrived to begin caring for Ponce. Chairs had been positioned near the beds to make it easier to dress the wounds. With great compassion welling up inside, Aimee walked around and sat down between the two burn patients. She took Zahir's hand gladly.

"Hey, what about me?" Ponce pleaded. He held out his hand. With a kind smile, Aimee took his as well. Her second patient was mischievous and had made a lot of mistakes, including starting the fire, but there was something endearing about the comical troublemaker.

For a few minutes the young nurse told them both about the way the sun was sparkling on the lake and that the deer were walking around outside the mansion, wondering why she had forgotten to bring treats the night before.

Having followed Uncle Louis' helpful advice as well, Yu Yan was trying to unwrap the bandages around Ponce's legs. Never a one to suffer quietly, Ponce vocalized every stab of pain and squeezed Aimee's hand so hard that it ached.

"Just lie still," Yu Yan begged. "I can't wipe this sore if you are thrashing around like this."

"But it hurts so badly!" Ponce yelled.

Kenzie was still helping Tina with the beach boys.

"I need to help Yu Yan," Aimee apologized, letting go of both the hands she was holding. "I think Ponce needs more pain medication."

Zahir winced.

"Is your pain bearable?" she asked.

With his eyes closed, he nodded.

"Is there anything you need?"

"A drink, please."

Aimee got up to measure the dosages for both patients. Ponce was given more pain medication, and then she brought over their special protein formula.

Zahir had only been injured on his right side falling into the flames, and he was able to drink from a cup himself. Both Ponce's arms hurt to move, so Aimee helped him with his dose.

Hearing the kitchen crew coming up the path with breakfast, Aimee assisted Yu Yan with Ponce's wounds. While the vocal, bronze-skinned Tiny had severe injuries just like the patient beside him, his face was untouched. However, there were burn wounds on all of Ponce's limbs and a narrow section on his chest. Had Lema not doused the fire on their clothes quickly during the flareup, the damage would have been even worse.

Uncle Louis was able to sit up a little and watch as they worked. "Ponce," he said with concern, "you will need to move your arms every few hours. That one burn is over a joint, and you don't want the skin to grow back too tightly to move."

"But it hurts to move," Ponce complained.

"Just move it whenever your pain medication is working well," Uncle Louis suggested. "Girls you may need to help him exercise that arm," he encouraged, "just a little every few hours. Sometimes you have to hurt to help."

"Hurt to help?" Aimee echoed curiously, wondering to herself how that fit with the Professor's rule – 'No Hurting'. "Did you hear that, Ponce?" she teased kindly. "Sometimes you have to hurt to help."

"Ah no, no, no!" Ponce cried out dramatically. "No more pain!"

"Breakfast has arrived," Sanaa sang out merrily, standing in the doorway. She and Milan passed bowls of fruit salad and loaves of bread to Aimee, who placed them on the window seat.

"Fruit salad!" Uncle Louis rejoiced. "Thank you!"

Staying at the door, since they hadn't showered that morning and the stench from the patients had grown stronger, the kitchen crew briefly asked how everyone was doing and received varied replies. Kenzie walked in with a large jug of orange juice and cups that Nancy had given him.

"Thank you for breakfast," Aimee and Yu Yan called out gratefully, returning to finish loosely winding the medicated gauze around Ponce's leg.

"You're welcome," the kitchen workers replied and then they made a rather hasty exit, putting their hands over their noses as they dashed down the stairs.

Zahir and Ponce didn't want any food, but Uncle Louis wasn't concerned since they were drinking a potent formula every couple of hours.

Georgia appeared at the door with Lily, who had helped her carry a new book that had come in on the train. "Do you want me to read to you today?" she asked. "It's an adventure story."

"Please," Zahir said.

"Sounds great," Uncle Louis piped up.

"Me too," Ponce agreed.

However, Georgia never stepped inside the room. Her face screwed up slightly as the smell of dead skin and unwashed bodies overpowered her. "Oh, I'm so sorry," she said, covering her face with both her hands. "It smells really bad in here."

Uncle Louis chuckled. "You've got a sensitive nose," he remarked. "Try again in a few days. Things may improve as everyone heals."

"I love you, Zahir," Georgia called out in a muffled fashion, as she dashed away.

"I love you too," the dark-haired patient replied quietly, as he always did. Then he asked, "Do we stink?"

With a sudden lump in her throat, Aimee laid her hand on his good arm and smiled. "My nose isn't sensitive."

"Thanks for staying with us," he murmured.

Rachel's Inquiry

Chapter 8

*I*t was a cold, rainy April morning, when the Professor opened the blue-tinted doors of the Rainforest Biome to head inside. He had plenty on his mind. Paradise had made headlines on the Canadian news after the first scientists had arrived earlier that week. He had been told that the video of the Tinys fighting the fire would air that evening, and already the news was out. The cameraman had relayed what he'd filmed to the scientists and from there the news had spread. Now, Facebook, Instagram and Twitter were sharing the story far and wide. He could hardly keep up with incoming messages. Everyone wanted to know how the courageous Zahir was doing. Was he badly burned? Had Uncle Louis survived? Was Ponce okay?

To Jacques' surprise, generous donations were flooding in to handle the health care expenses. The media interest and the expressions of grief coming in from all sides were rather overwhelming. Even the University Governing Board had softened their stand on his 'reprehensible project' and were now asking if they could do anything to help. Bewildered, the Professor found it hard to accept that the disaster he would have expected to bring a shameful end to his experiment and the popularity of Paradise was actually promoting it worldwide.

Walking into the warm, humid greenhouse, Jacques savoured the soothing environment. A chorus of Howler monkeys greeted him. The macaws chimed in and even the leopard roared. With a slight smile, he looked around at the lovely oasis that brought him so much joy. He adored the Rainforest Biosphere.

"Good to see you this morning," Rachel called out. Kneeling by the fishpond, she was checking the PH levels.

Jacques waved. "Great to see you too," he replied.

"How are all the patients?" she asked.

"Why don't you come with me and see what is happening this morning," he encouraged. "We are still trying to establish communication. Hopefully, I'll hear from Aimee soon."

Nodding fervently, Rachel replied, "Thank you! I'd love to come."

Leaving her box of tubes and chemicals by the pond, the young doctor followed Jacques into the viewing hall. Walking through all the doors and hallways, they discussed the glum April weather, Uncle Louis' return to the dome and their hopes that all the patients were progressing well. Reaching the Paradise Room, they stood outside the dome near Rainbow Hill and looked through the tinted, one-way viewing glass. Only a few Tinys were outside, attending to their morning activities.

"I wish we could see how the burn victims are," the lovely dark-haired doctor fretted quietly.

"I know," Jacques whispered. "While I strongly believe they should have complete privacy in their own homes, it would be helpful to have a camera in the Caring Centre." He shook his head. "It's too late now. I have an emergency room prepared down in the lab, but I never anticipated the need for Paradise to have a proper hospital. I hope Aimee will send us an update soon. She just needs to figure out how to use the Smartphone..."

"How will she do that?"

"I sent in some instructions this morning. Louis will help her if there's anything she doesn't understand. We should hear from her tonight. I'll message you as soon as I hear any details."

"These are the crucial hours," Rachel murmured anxiously.

"I know," Jacques agreed quietly. "I hope it will all go well."

They watched as Georgia and Lily carried breakfast up the path to Rainbow Hill. Odin was working on the stone stairs.

Georgia's voice carried well over the microphone. "You're working *before* breakfast?" she said with surprise.

"Got to get these stairs done," Odin grunted as he lifted a heavy rock into place. "They are needed right now."

Impressed, the Professor watched the stocky young man as he wheeled his cart back down the hill for another rock. "Just three more rocks and he'll have the job done," he observed quietly.

"He's feeling badly about what he did," the young doctor whispered.

"Yes," Jacques nodded. "I'm really glad to see his response. He's demonstrating real remorse for his actions."

"Jacques, I've been wondering about something," Rachel murmured a little nervously.

"Yes," he encouraged.

"It may just be my imagination, or perhaps a foolish hope," she relayed, "but I do wonder sometimes... well, I wonder if any of the Tinys might be related to me?"

With a smile, Jacques looked over. "You did tell me once that you were an embryo donor," he whispered kindly. "So, I've wondered the same thing myself."

"You have?"

"Certainly," he replied, stroking his goatee. "In fact, I've been very hopeful that this might be the case."

Fidgeting with her stethoscope, Rachel asked, "Do you think anyone ... *in particular*... might be mine?"

Relieved to finally have the opportunity to share his precious thoughts now that his experiment was no longer secret, Jacques nodded. "Well, there is a certain young man – it's hard to tell if he is maybe an Arab Israeli... or of Jewish descent."

"Zahir," she said breathlessly. Trying to remember to speak quietly, she exclaimed, "I know! I thought the same. He looks so much like Farouk, but..."

"He has blue eyes," they both said together.

"Just like yours," Jacques smiled.

She nodded wistfully. "And I've listened to their songs," she relayed. "Maybe it's just my imagination, but Zahir sounds like *my father*. My father sings in the Jerusalem Symphony."

"Come," Jacques said eagerly, suddenly struck by an idea. "I have something for you. It's in the train supply room. Come with me."

Rachel followed him back through the elevator and down the hallways. In the loading room Jacques picked up a few messy, soiled gauze bandages. "These came in on the train this morning," he told her, sliding them into a plastic bag. "Some will be Ponce's. Some will be Zahir's. They are all mixed together. If you do a DNA test, then we'll know for sure if there's any connection."

Taking the bag gratefully, Rachel held it close to her heart. "Thank you!" she said.

With an anxious expression, Jacques pleaded, "I just don't want to get your hopes up."

She nodded. "I appreciate that. I'll try not to get too excited. But thank you, thank you for this opportunity. I've been thinking about it a lot! I'll let you know what I find out!"

The Basis of Morality

Chapter 9

A message came in from Evan, asking if he could bring Seth to view Paradise from the main room.

"If you want," the Professor replied, sitting down at his computer, now that Rachel had left. He had a lot of emails that he hoped to answer that morning. Seth was still not his favourite student, but Jacques knew the young man had become close friends with his research partner. Since the tall, blond assistant was integral to the future of Paradise and very dear to his heart, the Professor was willing to grant Evan almost anything, even if it meant allowing a questioning, probing creationist to come right into the actual Paradise Room.

Evan showed Seth around and cautioned him to speak very softly if he was close to the dome. They looked in at the charred forest and Seth was distraught to see the extent of the damage. For a while they whispered quietly to one another as they walked around the tall, glass terrarium.

Coming around to the lake, they watched Odin dig deep into Mining Hill. "What are the consequences for those who started the fire?" the redhaired student whispered.

Looking over in the direction of the Professor, Evan replied quietly, "Consequences? Well, Ponce certainly paid a heavy price for his involvement. He will be suffering for a while. Franz had some minor burns, but I suppose we hope that the whole situation was terrifying enough that he won't ever consider fooling around with fire again. And Odin... well, Odin is trying hard to make up for what he did. He's given himself consequences. I believe the experience has changed him, and if better behaviour continues, then we may leave it at that."

The Professor looked up from his desk and nodded. "I don't think any of them realized they were igniting such a destructive force."

Seth nodded. "So how do you determine the basis of morality in Paradise?" he whispered curiously. "Is it just based upon the 'no hurting' and 'no stealing' rules? What do you do if someone wilfully disobeys?"

"Louis talks to them and tries to reason it out," Evan explained.

"And when Louis is gone?"

"We'll come up with something else," the Professor retorted, his eyes fastened on the computer screen as he tried to multitask.

Looking over at Evan, Seth asked softly, "But what if one Tiny purposely endangers the life of another? Or if some refuse to acknowledge your rules? They respect Louis as a father-figure, but will they be led by someone they consider their equal – *or less?*"

Although he knew the questions were being directed at his assistant, the Professor turned around in his chair. "They are all good kids," he remarked softly but defensively. "They've grown up with Louis as their role model. They haven't seen violence or evil; they don't need harsh consequences or a long list of rules."

Seth frowned. "But Jesus said that all manner of evil thoughts come from our own hearts. We don't need to *see* wrong behaviour to act it out. It's just part of our fallen human nature."

Recognizing the point, Evan considered, "We didn't teach them to steal or hit each other, or rebel against authority – yet those things have happened easily enough on their own."

Leaning back in his chair, the Professor disagreed. "Such a view leaves Christians feeling demoralised and in a constant state of guilt," he argued.

"That *is* possible," Seth acknowledged, walking a few steps closer to the Professor, "especially if we lack faith in God's willingness to forgive us, or if we doubt that His love is *specific to us* and focus only on our own unworthiness. Then you're right, then we could implode with despair. But, if we realise where evil comes from, we are better equipped to fight the battle, and our appreciation for God's graciousness will be much deeper."

"Is God *gracious?*" the Professor questioned with a wry smile. "That's not the God I read about in the Old Testament."

"Have you read the Old Testament?"

"Only parts of it," he admitted. "But I've certainly read what others have said about Him. He wiped the whole world out, even the animals! He endorsed genocide. He valued *one* family of people over everyone else but He often annihilated thousands of Israelites when He lost His temper. He..."

"I suggest you read Psalm seventy-eight," Seth interrupted quietly, coming even closer to the Professor so his voice wouldn't startle any Tinys. Having found a helpful book on Christian Apologetics, Seth felt better equipped to take on such arguments. "Psalm seventy-eight summarises God's relationship with the nation of Israel," he explained. "To understand God's *judgment,* you need to first appreciate His *great love.* You see, the Jewish nation didn't choose God, *He chose them* because of His relationship with their fathers. He delivered them from being slaves in Egypt. He revealed His supernatural power in astonishing ways to them, like never before. He demonstrated His ability to provide food for millions in the wilderness *every day* for forty years. He gave them wise laws that would keep them safe from sickness, disease and oppressive behaviours."[4]

"*Wise* laws?" Jacques interrupted with disdain. "You call getting stoned to death for disrespecting your parents *a wise law?*"

Seth replied quietly even though he was no longer near the dome. "Sir, there is no record of that law ever being carried out. Same with an eye for an eye, or a hand for a hand. Those laws were there to demonstrate what God thought of the sin and make everyone aware of the *maximum* penalty that was deserved. For some punishments, a monetary fine could be substituted..."

"Still – did a disrespectful child deserve to die?"

"If you read that law through carefully, you will see this was a last resort," Seth answered. "It was only put in place if the parents had exhausted all other means. It was for an older son or daughter who was completely rebellious, refused to listen and had given themselves over to worthless living and drunkenness. And it was *the parents* who had the option of giving their son up to the elders of the city – not the other way around."[5]

"It's very severe!"

"The Mosaic Law was given to a nation that had been slaves in Egypt for 400 years. They didn't choose God – God chose them.[6] He met this rough group of people where they were at with all their hard-heartedness and social customs, intending to gradually bring them to Christ.[7] God knew He had a better covenant coming for those who would willingly align their lives with His in the future."[8] Pausing a moment, he asked, "Professor Lemans, have you ever compared the

---

[4] Deuteronomy 4:1-8; 7:12-15; 1 Timothy 1:8-10
[5] Deuteronomy 21:18-21
[6] Deuteronomy 4:32-27
[7] 1 Timothy 1:8-10; Galatians 3:21-24; Mark 10:2-9
[8] 1 John 3

Old Testament to the Code of Hammurabi, which was a Babylonian Code of Law around this time?"

"No."

"It's worth taking a look," Seth encouraged. "Hammurabi inscribed that he was making very good and fair laws for his people, but his laws were often *much more* severe than God's."

"But your God told the Israelites to wipe out entire nations, so that they could take over their land."

"God executed His justice in overthrowing nations that had become entirely perverse," Seth defended. "He says in Leviticus eighteen that if Israel didn't wipe out those nations the land itself would have vomited them out. That land had been promised to Abraham four hundred years earlier, but God didn't give it to Abraham *then* as the inhabitants had not yet reached such a perverse state. The Jewish people wandered as pilgrims and endured bondage as slaves until God determined the nations in possession of the promised land had become so wicked that His judgement was required."

Shaking his head, the Professor was not convinced. "The God of the Old Testament is not someone I would look to, should I need moral guidance in my life. He's *jealous!* How petty! He's vengeful..."

"But God is jealous in a protective way, like a good husband," Seth protested. "He loves us and doesn't want us to be seduced by foolish things that will ruin our happiness and take us away from living forever with Him. Real love and jealousy go hand in hand."[9]

"Does the theory of natural selection establish any better example?" Evan inquired softly, walking over to join the discussion.

---

[9] Copan, P. *Is God a Moral Monster,* pg. 34-40

"Natural selection is one hundred percent amoral," the Professor admitted quietly, "but it doesn't make claims to be *the* moral authority."

"I do agree that natural selection is amoral," Seth nodded. "The concept of natural selection is based on selfishness and is devoid of compassion. It cares nothing for the suffering of anyone involved, or any emotional responses they might have – but according to the theory, benefits itself in a physical way at the expense of all others. Isn't that true?"

"It's called 'survival of the fittest' for a reason," Jacques acquiesced.

"So, how did humans 'evolve' kindness? Or self-sacrifice? Or compassion? Where do these amazing qualities come from? Who started it and why?"

"I don't know," the Professor acknowledged with a shrug.

"Fair enough," Seth nodded evenly. "And what kind of morality do you hope you will see in Paradise?"

"I hope they will act on the basis of love and servant leadership, putting each other's needs above their own," he stated. "And I have seen some remarkable examples of this in the last year. Louis has done everything he can to make his world a better place. During the fire, both Louis and Zahir risked their lives to save Ponce. Most of the Tinys did what they could to help. I see wonderful, caring friendships developing among them and..."

Evan had been fairly quiet during this exchange. Piping up, he added, "I agree, Jacques. Louis has been an exceptional leader all the way through, and that's one reason he is so in awe of Jesus Christ."

With a frown, the Professor argued, "Louis learned everything he needed to know from the servant leadership course... don't forget that. *If* Jesus was an actual historical figure, I'd agree that he had some good things to say and he did set a fine example, but I'm sure he got his ideas from other compassionate humans who evolved the same type of morality."

"But we have to accept Jesus as either a truth teller, or a complete fraud," Seth pointed out. "Jesus didn't claim to be 'just a good man', he claimed to be the *only source of truth*[10] and the *Son of God.* He said he learned everything from *his Father - God.*[11] He didn't speak his own opinions.[12] He encourages us in the Bible to be merciful and kind, because God, *our Father*, is merciful and kind.[13] Jesus didn't try to be better than the God of the Old Testament, Jesus showed us who God really is."[14] Folding his arms across his chest, the redhead pointed out, "Many people today are misrepresenting the God of the Old Testament and unfairly distorting His Laws. But don't forget that Christian morality made the world a better place. Nations who based their morals on Christian ethics gradually transformed Western civilizations from the darkness of oppression and tribal warfare to a time of great accomplishments and compassionate freedom."[15]

Folding his arms together, the Professor argued, "Yes, but Christians also started brutal wars, promoted slavery and oppressed women! Think of the Crusades!"

"True, people have struggled with how to *implement* God's rules," Seth explained. "Their harsh or lax implementations have sometimes created a bad reputation for God's laws which were intended to save lives, minimize hurt and establish order. I don't see God's truth as the problem – *human implementation* of that truth is where we go wrong. Too many feel that *'the end justifies the means,'* but that isn't

---

[10] John 14:6-7; Acts 4:11-12
[11] John 5:19-37
[12] John 14:9-11
[13] Matthew 5:44-48
[14] John 14:7-11
[15] Vishal Mangalwadi. *The Book that Made Your World: How the Bible Created the Soul of the Western World.* 2011

Scriptural. Viciously forcing people to convert was never condoned by God and doesn't bring about the willing devotion that He desires." Raising his eyebrows, Seth prodded, "Professor Lemans, who do you think has done more harm in the world – Christians or Atheists?"

"Christians for sure," the Professor replied without hesitation. "It's not just the Crusades that took many innocent lives, think of the Inquisition!"

Seth nodded. "And we could argue about who was worse – the Christian Crusaders and the Inquisition which slaughtered millions of people, or Twentieth Century Atheistic regimes like Stalin and Mao that wiped out *tens* of millions. But to debate this wouldn't actually prove anything, as those instigating the crimes may not have been acting upon their core beliefs."[16]

Jacques looked at him with a quizzical expression.

"Well, Jesus told his followers that those who take up the sword will *perish with the sword,*"[17] Seth explained. "He never encouraged his followers to force others to believe, like the Church did in the Crusades and Inquisition. Instead, we are commanded to forgive, to suffer ourselves to be defrauded, to do good to those who do evil to us. The Christian Crusades and the Inquisition were not motivated by *the teachings of Christ,* but by power, greed and misplaced zeal."

Evan agreed. "It makes sense to say we need to look at the foundational principles to see which worldview encourages true caring and compassion, and which one leads to selfishness and a lack of regard for the sanctity of human life."

Pondering the discussion, the Professor wasn't as antagonistic as he had been in previous conversations with Seth. He appreciated the answers the two young men were giving even if he wasn't ready to

---

[16] Scott Hahn & Benjamin Wiker. 'Answering the New Atheism' 'The Problem of Morality.' Emmaus Road, 2008, 2019. Pg.95
[17] Matthew 26:52; Luke 6:27-36

admit it. A digression was therefore in order! "It is somewhat of a mystery that compassion and kindness evolved," he acknowledged. "Yet, you are saying that our hearts are *full of evil*, so compassion and kindness is a mystery to Christians as well!"

"Fair point," Seth conceded with a smile. "Evil comes from our hearts since the fall,[18] but a moral conscience and goodness was implanted into us by God at the very beginning.[19] He created us in *His image* and called us *'very good'* on the sixth day. He wants us to be like Him." Finding Luke chapter six on his phone, Seth read, "'Jesus says, *'But love your enemies, and do good, and lend, expecting nothing in return, and your reward will be great, and you will be sons of the Most High, for he is kind to the ungrateful and the evil. Be merciful, even as your Father is merciful.'*" Looking up, Seth said, "The goodness you see in people is from God.[20] Jesus encouraged us to follow *His Father's example*. God hasn't changed!"

"I don't agree," Jacques argued as a smile crossed his face. "If there was anyone like Jesus around today, I'm sure, as Dawkins says, he would be so impressed by scientific progress and reason, he'd be a moral atheist."[21]

Evan and Seth looked at each other with surprise.

"A moral *atheist?*" Seth clarified, frowning. "I don't think so - not the man who came to do His Father's will,[22] who *spoke* His Father's word[23] and stated plainly that God was *his* God![24] Jesus wasn't a better God, he is the perfect manifestation of God."

---

[18] Genesis 6:5-6; Jeremiah 17:9-10; Mark 7:21-23
[19] Romans 2:14-16
[20] Exodus 34:5-7
[21] *Atheists for Jesus* – An essay by Richard Dawkins, 2006
[22] John 6:38; 5:30; Matthew 26:39
[23] John 8:28
[24] John 20:17

With a shrug, the Professor's eyes twinkled. He did enjoy stirring Seth up. However, when it came to discussing controversial subjects, he had met his match. Seth also welcomed debates. Returning to their discussion on morality, the young redhead added, "Many scientists have become so proud of their ability to discover and harness the laws of the universe that they think that purpose, ethics and morality can also be discovered through logic and science. The world is in a mess because we have discarded God's standards and we can't agree on what our own should be. Natural selection can't *evolve* morality - it's *opposed* to morality. Only a Being much greater and wiser than ourselves, who wants the best for us, has the authority to determine right from wrong."

Seeing some action within the dome, Evan walked closer to peer in. He whispered, "Hey, look what Odin has!"

Getting up from his chair, the Professor strode over. Seth hurried to look in. In his carrycart, Odin was proudly pushing a big, shiny red gem to the store.

"He found one of the treasures!" Jacques exclaimed softly. "The first one!"

"But not the best," Evan smiled.

"What's the best?" Seth asked quietly, looking up at his friend.

"The sun-catcher," Evan whispered. He pointed to where Odin had been digging. "If he digs a little closer to the trench on the right side of the hill, he'll find it. He's getting very close."

The storekeepers were outside as Odin approached. Nancy and Milan were playing with Rusty, throwing apples for him to run and catch. Often the friendly dog ate the apple, and occasionally he brought it back in his mouth. Stopping their game, they looked up when Odin swaggered over.

"Look what I found!" he boasted. "This beats all trades!"

In awe, Milan ran to get some water to wash off the gem. Once it was clean, it sparkled a brilliant red in the sunshine.

"You found a treasure all right!" the slim storekeeper agreed in amazement, examining the large gem that he could barely lift. "Everyone has been hoping to find it. Others will be willing to trade a lot for this."

Wiping his hands gleefully, Odin declared, "Well, I'd say this beauty is worth at least a month or two of free meals and maybe a haircut. I'm sure it will also pay back for any inconvenience I've ever caused."

"What do you mean by 'it will pay back for any inconvenience'?" Nancy inquired.

"Well, like my latest science experiments that went poorly," Odin explained, shuffling back and forth on his feet. "If I trade this in, then I've paid back for everything that *everyone* blames me for."

Nancy and Milan shared a look. "It *is* special," she murmured to her helper.

"Others will trade highly for it," he agreed. "Whatever you think, Nancy."

Standing up straight, Nancy folded her arms across her chest and made her best offer. "I'm willing to trade four weeks of free meals. But I can't say this pays for the damage you've caused. That's another issue and that's not for me to decide."

Odin stood his ground. "Six weeks, a haircut, and I don't have to do anymore work."

"A haircut for sure," Milan bargained with a wry smile, "two weeks of meals and no more work."

"But that's not our decision," Nancy protested. "We should ask Uncle Louis about the work part."

"Milan's deal sounds good to me," Odin chuckled. "Take it or leave it."

The storekeepers looked at each other and shrugged. Odin turned and strode off to the forest.

"Well, there goes his self-inflicted consequences," the Professor remarked softly with chagrin. "I guess the stone staircase remains unfinished."

"And who will haul the water and supplies back and forth?" Evan queried.

"I suppose we should be happy he showed remorse for two days," Jacques said sadly, shaking his head. "One bright gem and he thinks he's made up for all the harm he's brought on the others."

"Ironically the gem isn't even his," Evan mused. "It belonged to you, Jacques. You hid it there. All he did was find it!"

A Secret Message

Chapter 10

When all the dressings had been changed later that morning, Uncle Louis motioned for Aimee to come over. "Anything I can get for you, Uncle Louis?" she asked, walking over cheerfully. A very clean Lily had brought him his breakfast several hours ago, and now she was sitting beside Ponce holding his hand and reading a book about a family camping adventure. The small, freckle-faced girl was bravely persevering to read even though there was a very bad smell in the room. Zahir had gone back to sleep.

"The father hastily set up the tent," Lily read, "'while thunder echoed all around and the skies turned an ominous grey. Suddenly, his youngest son called out to him...'

"Did you know," Lily suddenly interjected, "that in the big world a guy marries a girl and they have children. Why don't *we* have fathers and mothers? Or get married? Or have babies?"

"Our world is not quite the same," Uncle Louis chuckled.

"But can we get married? Can I marry Ponce?"

Ponce was half-asleep, but his eyes opened wide. "Married?" he asked. "What are you saying, Lily?"

Uncle Louis nodded. "Yes, you could get married if you are very sure about each other."

"Why do we have to be sure?"

"Because marriage is a promise to care about someone for your whole life," he told her.

75

Smiling at her injured friend, the brown-haired girl exclaimed, "I will *always* love Ponce!"

"You and me, Lily," her friend mumbled dreamily, closing his eyes. The lunch bell sounded from the store.

"I'll be back later!" Lily said, kissing the hand she was holding.

Once Lily had gone and both patients were slumbering, Uncle Louis reached into the pocket of his dressing gown and pulled out an envelope. "I want you to go somewhere very private and read this," he whispered to Aimee. "If you are confused by anything, you can ask me secretly when everyone else is asleep. Do you understand?"

Intrigued, Aimee took the envelope, wondering what the message could possibly be about. She felt something small and hard inside, that moved when she tilted the package.

Kenzie and Vahid entered the room and picked up the urinals. "Okay, girls out," they said. "Time for the male nurses to take over."

Aimee left and closed the door.

She heard Uncle Louis say, "I think we may all need a good wash today."

Running out into the clear, sunny air, Aimee breathed it in deeply. Even though the windows were always open in the Caring Centre, the smell had been steadily worsening.

Holding on to her envelope, Aimee saw Lily was still talking to Odin. He had just brought up a pot of clean water and left it in front of the mansion. "Thanks for the water," she called out, wondering why he hadn't brought it up all the way to the Crisis Room. "And that stair pathway will be so helpful once it's done," she added gratefully. "Thank you, Odin."

Lily smiled. "Yes, I can get to the store so much faster now," she agreed. "And stairs are especially good when we have to use the outhouse in the middle of the night!"

"It's the last pot of water I'm bringing," he told them proudly.

"What?" Aimee asked, stopping in her tracks.

"I found a precious treasure in Mining Hill," he shrugged. "I've traded it in for everything I've done wrong. No one can blame me anymore for anything. You'll have to find some other *slave* to carry water and finish the staircase."

"But you were doing such a great job," Aimee protested earnestly. "Why wouldn't you want to finish your work and feel a sense of accomplishment?" she asked. "Couldn't you do just three more steps? And we need those pots of fresh water every day to keep our patients clean and healthy."

"Find another slave," Odin smiled, turning around. "I'm free."

Disappointed, Aimee parted company with the others, taking the path to the lake, while Lily ran to the store. She knew someone would likely volunteer to bring water and carry the used materials back to the train. But she was discouraged that Odin's attitude had soured once again.

Not particularly hungry, and eager to read the secret letter, Aimee wasn't concerned to miss lunch. Sanaa was always bringing food up to the mansion in between meals. "Good friends are reliable like that," she thought.

Down by the water, the young nurse observed that the waves were just beginning to roll in. The beach seemed so lonely and forsaken. Walking out on the pier, she reflected sadly, "All the surfers are in the Caring Centre." Dangling her legs in the cool, refreshing water, the young lady with the wavy, copper-brown hair opened her envelope and looked inside. She saw a strange metal shape and a single piece of folded paper. Pulling out the note, she read, "To Aimee. From the Professor and Evan."

Her deep blue eyes grew large in astonishment. Never would she have dreamed that the Professor would write a private letter to her! He was the Mastermind of Paradise!

With great anticipation, she opened it up. It was a long letter!

"Dear Aimee," she read. *"Now that Uncle Louis can no longer communicate with us, we are giving this important assignment to you. Please be very careful who you share these details with. If you can, keep it a secret unless we tell you otherwise. The communication device you will need to operate is a powerful and potentially dangerous tool. It can educate you in many good ways, but if used wrongly, it may cause harm. We feel you will be responsible to use this tool in a positive and helpful way. This is one very important reason we have chosen you."*

The message carried on telling her how to find the secret cave where all the communication would take place. She was told to take the key out of the envelope and not to lose it or tell anyone else about it. The key would unlock the door of the cave and turn everything on. When she got inside and closed the door, she would find a large black rectangular device on the wall. She was to push in the side button and look for a white dove symbol on the screen and press on it. Then she was to touch Evan's name for a video message.

Aimee swallowed hard and looked around. With such fervent requests for secrecy, she hoped she wasn't being watched! Thankfully, no one else was in sight, as most had headed to the store for lunch. Carefully, she read the letter over a second time. She had often wondered about the window in the cave and just how Uncle Louis communicated with the Professor. It was a mystery, and she was very excited to discover how it all happened. "It's not just a regular window," she considered, looking at the details in the Professor's letter. "It's a 'device.' It has to be turned on! It's a powerful tool and a source of information. What is this thing? What is a *'video'* message? And they've chosen me! Why me? This is so, so strange and yet very special!"

With a rush of euphoria, Aimee tucked the letter back into the envelope with the key, determined to make her discoveries right away. From the lake, she walked stealthily around the back of Rainbow Hill, as she had been told, keeping well-hidden in the trees. She was surprised that a number of the trees had fallen on the hill, and it was annoying to climb over them all. In the valley between the two hills, she walked back and forth a couple of times before seeing the faint pathway that led toward a large rock. Sure enough, the rock moved easily, and the key worked. She entered a dark room as the door closed behind her and she felt for the lever. It worked! A light came on. The large, black, rectangular device was easy to spot, but it didn't look much like a window. She couldn't see through it at all. Feeling around the edges, she eventually discovered the long, narrow, side button. Exerting some force, she managed to push it in. To her great surprise and wild delight, the whole box lit up with glowing colours. There were many symbols to choose from, and one was a white bird. She pushed on it. Up came a small picture of Evan, just as she remembered him from the nursery! His blond hair stood up in a wild fashion, just as it had before. There was also a picture of an older man with only a partial grey beard. Beside his face, were the words, "The Professor."

"What?" Aimee said with astonishment. "This is the Professor?" She studied him carefully. He looked wise and kind, but not particularly powerful. "This is *the Mastermind of Paradise?*" she marvelled.

When she pushed on Evan's name, the screen lit up and he stood motionless in the window! She saw the little white triangle on his face that she had been told to touch. Trying it out, she was astonished when Evan began to speak!

"Hi Evan!" she exclaimed excitedly, but Evan just kept on talking as if he hadn't heard her. Perplexed, Aimee listened to his message.

The tall young man with the blond spiky hair explained everything, using his own phone to show her how to send messages or make phone calls, and telling her what it would look like should she receive a message from them.

"We would like you to come here every night when the others have gone to bed," Evan said, "or sometime during the day when everyone is occupied elsewhere. We don't want you to draw any unnecessary attention to what you are doing. Message us every day with the nursing report on all the burn victims. Call us anytime if you have concerns. If Paradise needs supplies, let us know and we'll put them on the train and send it in the morning."

"Okay," she replied. "I will."

Evan didn't seem to hear her. He ran his fingers through his hair awkwardly, as though he were wondering what to say next. Then he added, "Well, that's enough for today. We'll take you through a few other features next time. Goodbye, Aimee."

The picture stopped moving. Evan stopped talking. The white triangle appeared on his face again.

"So, maybe that was a video message," Aimee thought to herself, admiring all the other colourful symbols on the screen. She looked around the room. It had a little desk in one corner with a messy pile of papers spread out on top and project instructions pinned to the walls. A chair was positioned in front of the phone. At the back of the room was a table covered with a long cloth that hung all the way to the ground. Fascinated, Aimee could hardly wait to come back. The floor was quite dirty near the table and Aimee looked around for a broom, but she couldn't see one.

"Well, I should try to give the Professor a report," she thought, pressing on the round circle with his face. The picture came up in a large square and she pressed on the symbol that Evan had showed her in his video. Immediately, music began and the screen became larger.

Then the Professor's face appeared, only he was smiling and moving right away without any triangle to press!

"Hello, Aimee," he said gently.

A little frightened, Aimee said, "Hi. Um... I'm Aimee."

"Yes, I know," he smiled. "I've been hoping you would call. I'm the Professor. How are your patients?"

Aimee sucked in her breath. The Professor was really talking to her! He could hear what she said! He was asking her questions! Once Aimee got over her initial feelings of intimidation, the conversation went well. She told him all he wanted to know about her patients and their wounds.

"The next couple of days will be difficult," he warned her. "We are worried about infection setting in. You must monitor their temperatures and let us know right away if anything changes. We can send in stronger medication if there are problems. You can call me or text me anytime – day or night."

He encouraged Aimee to try a few different messaging options, just to ensure she knew how to use the system. When everything was sorted out, they both said a friendly goodbye.

"He's nice," Aimee thought with a smile. "I think I like him. He reminds me a little bit of Uncle Louis. He's just a lot younger."

Leaving the cave, Aimee locked the door tightly and rolled the fake stone back into place. "Now, how can I keep the key safe?" she wondered. Her dress didn't have a pocket. A small rock lay close by. It seemed like a good idea to hide the key under it so that it would always be there when she came back. Carefully positioning the key under the rock, she left it there and ran to the shower. She knew it was very important for anyone who went outside the Caring Centre to wash themselves well before they came back in, which meant she was now showering several times a day. A huge pile of towels had come in on the train, and had been stacked nearby. When she was finished, she hung her wet towel on the clothesline to dry.

Making her way back up Rainbow Hill, Aimee met Charley, Vahid, Tina and Yu Yan near the clearing. To her surprise, they were taking down the solar lights. When she asked about it, Charley told her that Uncle Louis had asked for the lights to be strung outside the mansion, especially around her big window, so that the nurses could see in the dark.

"Oh, that's a great idea!" she smiled. "Thank you!"

By the time Aimee reached the house, her dress and hair were nearly dry. Looking at the time on the clock, she realised it was mid-afternoon, and almost time to change the dressings again and give out the medications. Washing her hands carefully, she brought the materials into the room. The sun was streaming in through her big window, but Zahir and Ponce were sound asleep and tossing restlessly. She could hear the other nurses across the hall talking to the beach boys.

Uncle Louis looked up and whispered, "Did it work?"

Running over to his bedside, she kneeled down. Quietly, but with astonishment, she told him, "I saw Evan and he told me what to do, and then I talked to the Professor! I actually talked to him! He's... he's very nice."

"Good girl," Uncle Louis sighed happily. "Now if something happens to me, you can take over."

With an anxious frown, Aimee asked warily, "What do you mean, Uncle Louis? I need you here."

"The Professor has chosen you," he told her.

"Why?" she inquired.

Squeezing her hand, Uncle Louis breathed deeply. His lined face was filled with deep emotion. "Because he feels he can trust you, Aimee. Make sure you always treasure that trust," he whispered. "It's very important for the safety of everyone in Paradise that the Professor can trust someone to tell him the truth and to do what he asks. Do you understand that?"

Aimee nodded fervently.

"Good," he sighed. "I believe you will do your best."

Zahir cried out in his sleep, and for a moment, Aimee and Uncle Louis were distracted. He and Ponce looked quite flushed.

"I have something special to tell you," the older Tiny said softly. Not knowing how long he had left, he felt it was important for Aimee to understand her relationship with the Professor. "You see," he said, "in the real world - the Professor's world - people do get married, just like Lily was saying. A man marries a woman and they have children."

"Really?" Aimee clarified eagerly, her eyebrows raised.

"Yes," he nodded. "After my heart attack, when I was in the emergency bed, the Professor told me that you and I... well, we are his real children."

Aimee looked bewildered.

"We weren't born in a normal way," he explained. "It's complicated, Aimee. But had things been normal, you and I would be brother and sister. The Professor is our father, and his wife - who died young - is our mother."

This was astonishing information. For a moment or two, Aimee was completely overwhelmed by the concept.

"But... what about everyone else?" she begged. "Where did they come from?"

Uncle Louis shrugged. "Somehow the Professor was able to incubate children from other fathers and mothers. I'm not exactly sure how," he told her. "He didn't tell me where everyone else was from."

Aimee was reeling with all she had learned. "What does this mean?" she asked.

Shifting slightly against the pillows, Uncle Louis smiled. "It means that you and I are more responsible than anyone else for what happens in Paradise. The Professor expects more from us. We have to make sure that Paradise stays happy and beautiful, because that's what our father longs for."

Nodding, Aimee took a deep breath. She remembered thinking that the Professor and Louis looked similar. "Do I look like my mother?" she wondered curiously.

"When I'm gone," Uncle Louis continued, "you will be one of the next leaders of Paradise. You will have to think about what is best for everyone, not just what is best for you. It is very important to keep this perspective. And Aimee," he cautioned, "don't tell any others about this special relationship you have with the Professor, or they may become jealous. You must keep it a secret."

It was all a little frightening. Aimee wasn't sure she was ready to think about what was best for everybody else and to keep so many secrets!

"Nothing can happen to you, Uncle Louis," she whispered, covering his hand with hers. "You have to stay with us. I couldn't be a leader without you!"

Uncle Louis smiled and squeezed her hand.

Zahir cried out again.

"Go help him," Uncle Louis encouraged. "I am worried about him and Ponce. I had the guys give us sponge baths, just to keep us all clean. Infection is a deadly thing."

Looking up at the clock, Aimee could see it was time for the pain medication to be given out. She squeezed the dose into a cup and took it to Zahir. His face was red and sweaty. He barely opened his eyes and he wasn't responsive to her request to drink. Laying her hand on his forehead, she realized that Zahir felt abnormally hot. Taking the long thermometer out from under Ponce's bed and following the instructions that had been sent in, she inserted the nib under his arm. Uncle Louis watched anxiously.

Counting slowly to sixty, Aimee checked the number. "Zahir's temperature is a little high," she relayed to Uncle Louis. "Should we be worried?"

"Write it down and we'll keep a close eye on him," Uncle Louis assured her. "Make him drink some more and then... well, you know what to do, right, Aimee?"

Looking over, Aimee understood that Uncle Louis wanted her to go to the cave and give a report. She nodded. Writing down Zahir's details she tried to give him the balanced salt solution. But Zahir shook his head, refusing to drink or open his eyes.

"He doesn't want any," Aimee reported.

Speaking with a stern voice, Uncle Louis said, "Zahir, you have to drink if you want to get better. Force yourself, my boy."

Realizing she had to insist, Aimee held the cup up to his lips, and tried again. "Please, Zahir," she begged firmly. "Please drink this. You need to get better."

Reluctantly, Zahir drank, but he still didn't open his eyes. Gradually, Aimee coaxed him into drinking a lot, but not everything.

Yu Yan arrived and they both struggled to get Ponce to drink as well. He was sleeping soundly, and his temperature was also over 38° Celsius. After they had forced both patients to drink, Aimee, Tina and Yu Yan did the afternoon rounds, caring for all their patients, taking their temperatures, and recording all the details.

Tina called out for more ointment, so Aimee brought her some.

Damien and Lema were sitting up and playing chess in Georgia's old room. Taking the tub of ointment, Tina rubbed it into Franz' leg wound.

Sanaa, Vinitha and Diya were crowded around the players and talking excitedly about Odin's new treasure in the store. "Now we know it's true," Sanaa was telling the others. "There really are treasures in Mining Hill! The red stone is so shiny and beautiful!"

Looking over at Aimee, she said, "Wait till you see it! You'll be amazed! Light passes right through it…"

"I'm going to trade for it," Diya insisted.

There was a crestfallen look on Sanaa's face. Out of all of them, Diya could always make the best trades. Being the only seamstress, her clothes were always in high demand.

Lema looked over at Sanaa, "When I'm out of here, we'll have to go digging!" he sang out.

"Yes, we will!" Sanaa laughed, clapping her hands excitedly. "I wonder what other gems we'll find."

"I'm in," Franz said.

"Me too," Diya agreed, sewing sequins on to a shirt, as she kept one eye on the chess game.

"Ah, you'll just stand there telling everyone else what to do!" Franz retorted. "If you get the red gem, why would you need more?"

Diya tossed her head haughtily. "If you actually listen to me, *you* might find the treasure!"

Vinitha looked up shyly. "Have you seen Odin's haircut?" she asked everyone.

Aimee was surprised. "Really?" she asked. "He got his hair cut?"

Nodding, Vinitha relayed, "He wanted it short and it looks really good on him."

"This I will have to see," Aimee exclaimed.

"Check mate," Damien laughed, closing in on Lema's king.

"No way!" Lema protested. "Let me check the rules!"

But it was a fair win, and the game was over.

Diya cheered loudly for Damien.

Watching the others interact, Aimee was confident there were no concerns to report with the beach boys; their temperatures were normal, their eyes were bright and lively and all their wounds were healing fast.

Skepticism

Chapter 11

Walking around the Rainforest Biome late that Sunday afternoon, the Professor spent some enjoyable time with Rachel and her young son, Jordan, as they tended to the animals. Having been stripped of many of his professional duties by the Ethics Committee and on his summer break, Jacques had more time on his hands than he was used to. Since it was the weekend, Rachel had brought her five-year-old son in to see where she worked. The young boy was enthralled with the monkeys and the reptiles, but not entirely sure about the jaguar, saying to his mother, "He has mean eyes."

Passing by the library, the Professor was surprised to see Evan and Seth sitting at a table, deep in discussion. For a moment he hesitated and then he noticed that his big, framed portrait, which had hung over the doorway ever since the Biome had opened, had been taken down.

Swallowing hard, he nodded glumly to himself. He was being marginalized in every area of the Greenville University where he had once been held in high esteem. In anticipation of a negative outcome at the upcoming Tribunal Hearings, his portraits were being removed. Distantly, he heard Evan say, "What evidence is there, aside from the Bible, that Jesus truly existed?"

The Howler monkeys started up a roaring chorus.

Glancing over in his direction, Evan was surprised to see the Professor standing in the hallway. "Hey, come join us," he called out warmly.

Feeling rather dejected, Jacques was in the mood for a stimulating conversation. With a smile he jested, "Who's decision was it to put those monkeys so close to the library?"

Evan laughed, and then explained to Seth that the Professor had planned everything. "But it makes a good first impression when people enter the main doors," he assured his mentor, noticing the sadness in his eyes.

Once the Professor was seated and the monkeys had settled down, Evan told him, "I just asked Seth *your* question about whether there is evidence for a historical Jesus."

Seth smiled and nodded at Jacques. Having just read a few pertinent articles, he was longing to share what he'd learned. "So, you want to know if there is evidence *outside* of the Bible that Jesus existed?"

"Seems a fair question to me," the older scientist replied wearily, resting his arms on the table.

"What would it take to *convince* you?" Seth asked.

The monkeys started up again. Looking dubious, Jacques paused to consider his answer and then spoke loudly, "If you could show me twenty independent, non-Christian accounts of Jesus' life within the First Century that he lived, then I'd likely believe."

"Nothing less than that?"

"Probably not..."

"Do you need twenty accounts to verify that Plato existed?"

"No... we have his writings..."

"You also have *Jesus' words* recorded by his closest friends."

"But that's in *the Bible* – which we have good reason to doubt for many other reasons."

"Well, first of all," Seth answered, "I just have to say this - healthy skepticism is good because it keeps us from being duped by lies, and there are a lot of lies in our world today. *Radical* skepticism, on the other hand, which rejects *reasonable* evidence and demands proof beyond any possible doubt can actually conceal our determination not to believe. We can even fool *ourselves* by this type of reasoning."[25]

For a moment the roaring monkeys were so loud that the conversation paused. Looking at his phone, the Professor saw that it was six-thirty. "Feeding time," he said dismissively. "Once Rachel and Jordan bring those monkeys their food, they'll settle down."

Seth smiled at Evan. They had been introduced to the cheery, young, dark-haired lad who was proudly helping his mom.

Looking over at Seth, Jacques assured him loudly, "Okay, if you can give me twenty independent, non-Christian accounts, I will believe."

"If I showed you those tonight," Seth called out over the noise, "would you be *happy* to see the evidence, or," he smiled kindly, "would you quickly think of some other reasons to keep doubting?"

The noise ceased almost instantly. "That's a little unfair," Jacques protested. "I suppose since you can't show me *twenty* accounts, you are calling my request *'radical skepticism'?"*

Seth shrugged. "Well, what if you said to me, 'The Bible can't be proven true unless I can interview the authors?' Would you call that healthy skepticism, or asking for the impossible? Can the writings of Plato, or Isaac Newton be proven genuine through personal interviews with the authors? If the evidence we demand to see would invalidate *all* other ancient writings, then we aren't making fair requests."

"I didn't ask to interview the authors," Jacques stated defensively, having never thought of himself as a 'radical skeptic' before.

---

[25] Ferrer, H.M. (2019). page 121.

Reluctantly, he revised his demand, asking, "Okay. Can you show me *any* independent, non-Christian accounts of Jesus within a hundred years of his life?"

"I can," Seth nodded confidently. Pulling up an article on his phone,[26] he said, "There are at least four non-Christian, independent accounts that are verifiable. Showing him the information on the screen, he pointed them out, "Tacitus, a Roman historian writing around 115 - 200 C.E., mentions 'Christus' who was executed by Pontius Pilate and from whom the Christians derived their name."

Scrolling down, he added, "Josephus, a Jewish historian who was born a few years after Jesus was crucified was considered by most Jews a traitor because he worked with the Romans... and he was not a Christian. He had no ulterior motive to support Christians in his writing. Yet, in his historical account - *'Jewish Antiquities'*, he mentions that James was the brother of 'Jesus-who-is-called-Messiah' and speaks of him teaching the people and being crucified by Pilate.

The Professor quietly considered the accounts as Seth read, "Lucian of Samosata, a Greek satirist, living in 115 -200 C.E. wrote, *'The Passing of Peregrinus.'* His writings clearly show that he was not a Christian as he derided those who *'having convinced themselves that they are going to be immortal and live forever, the poor wretches despise death and most even willingly give themselves up.'* Yet, he refers to the believers as 'Christians', who 'worship the man who was crucified in Palestine because he introduced this new cult into the world'."

Scrolling down, Seth added, "Pliny the Younger, who knew Tacitus and was a Roman governor, speaks of Christians singing hymns to Christ as a god."

---

[26] Michael Gleghorn. *Ancient Evidence for Jesus from Non-Christian Sources.* https: www.bethinking.org

"So that's four," Seth stated, "Tacitus, Josephus, Lucian and Pliny."

Scanning the online article, the Professor could see that it had proper citations and references. "That's *four,*" Jacques repeated flatly. "They are all writing within two hundred years after Jesus supposedly died." With a slight twinkle in his eye, he suggested, "Perhaps by then the Christian fables had integrated into society so much, that people just referred to them as we would Santa Claus. You know that there's no *archaeological* evidence that Jesus existed."

"Jesus wasn't wealthy," Seth argued dismissively. "His purpose wasn't to establish monuments, or even own a house. And he only spent three days in the tomb of another man... there was no time or need to engrave his name on the rocks. However," he said, looking directly at the Professor, "there *is* physical evidence that Roman crucifixion was occurring at this point in history. When historians want to verify a historical account, they check that the details are in accord with the practices of the time. They check that the recorded names of government officials match with other historical records of the same time period – which they do in the Gospels. They check that recorded occupations match the local customs of the time period – which they do in the Gospels. Geographical descriptions, the food, coins, measurements, agricultural practices, animal industry, places of worship and social norms all are in keeping with what is known of this time period – and the Gospel accounts. All the details recorded by Matthew, Mark, Luke and John display this type of accurate, 'insider' information... and nothing is out of place."

"Oh lá lá! The writers obviously did some careful research," Jacques acknowledged with a grin. "That's why their lies spread so well."

Seth and Evan exchanged glances. In the distance they could hear the macaws calling out in the bird sanctuary.

"Rachel has made it all the way around," the Professor smiled. "They'll be heading home soon."

"Lies, eh?" Seth reflected. "Our entire calendar system is based on the life of Jesus Christ. That's quite amazing *if* he never existed."

Jacques smiled.

"Did you know," Evan interjected, "that of all the classical, ancient works, the New Testament has by far the greatest number of surviving copies? Most ancient works have a dozen or so copies and that's all. Homer's Iliad has the second most surviving reproductions – nearly two thousand. But there are *twenty* thousand New Testament manuscripts!"[27]

"That doesn't surprise me," the Professor replied evenly. "A lot of people were duped, and they all wanted a copy. The New Testament radicalized people. People were so sure it was true that they made crazy decisions, but all truth is subjective..."

"Is that a *true* statement?" Seth prodded.

"What do you mean?"

"Is the saying, *'all truth is subjective'* true or false?" the young man argued. "If *all* truth is subjective, then your statement cannot be verified."

Jacques began shaking his head.

"Don't get me wrong," the red-haired student continued, "I believe there *is* subjective truth, like our own personal preferences. You may feel blue is the best colour, and that may be true for you, but not for me – because I love green. But Jesus' life, death and resurrection are based on *real historical events*, and therefore they are *absolute truth* – not subjective."

---

[27] J. Warner Wallace. *When It Comes To Ancient Texts, The More Copies We Have, The More Confidence We Have.* 2016. https: coldcasechristianity.com

"If I can't study it through my five senses then it can't be proven true," the Professor debated, enjoying the argument.

Having read such sentiments in the Professor's book, Seth had done his investigation and found answers to the challenging questions. With a smile he retorted, "But yet you are trusting your *own reasoning* - which you can't study with those five senses, to be a reliable guide in determining the truth! According to your worldview, your brain evolved to help you *survive,* not to *determine the truth.*"[28]

Nodding, the Professor chuckled. Seth wasn't an easy push-over and he had some valid points.

Evan had also thought these matters through since Seth had put him on the spot about 'missionary work' in Paradise. He piped up, saying, "Let me explain one of the most powerful proofs that I found as strong evidence that Jesus truly existed and rose from the dead." Looking at the Professor he asked kindly, "What might motivate someone to make up a lie and promote it all over the world?"

"Fame? Pride?" the Professor suggested. "If someone published a lie on social media that the whole world believed, they might feel quite proud of themselves."

In agreement, Evan continued, "So, some might tell lies to get fame, make money, obtain power or gain some other pleasures for themselves. Lies are often told to avoid painful consequences. In fact, our world is overwhelmed with 'fake news' and lies," he said, shaking his head in dismay, "to the point where we hardly know what to believe anymore. But think about this, the early Christians were *persecuted* for those beliefs they promoted. Most of the disciples lost their *lives* because they chose to keep preaching a resurrected Messiah, regardless of the violent threats they received. Many early Christians were martyred - crucified, fed to lions, hung, beaten,

---

[28] Ferrer, H.M. (2019). Page 136.

mocked and shamed.[29] They had to leave their homes, sometimes their families, give up jobs and status, and they didn't stand to gain *anything* material in this life.[30] In the Gospel accounts, Jesus clearly warned them ahead of time that anyone who wanted to follow him had to *'take up their cross'*[31] to do so. As I see it, there is only one powerful reason that people will refuse to recant under threats of losing everything – and that is, if they feel that the truth they profess is absolutely certain and so valuable it must be shared with others."

"*Ça alors!* Why would anyone want to bring such a terrible fate on others?" Jacques frowned.

"Because their hope is for a *'better resurrection'*," Seth replied.[32] "They were looking forward to *eternal life* in the future with Jesus."[33]

"And that's why Christians become radicalized," Jacques reasoned anxiously. "That's why the Bible is *so* dangerous. People lose their focus on the here and now and will do anything for some fanciful vision that may never come true."

Seth groaned.

"Maybe," the Professor conceded, attempting to be fair, "the disciples were confused and thought that Jesus had died, when he didn't. Perhaps they didn't mean to promote a lie, they just thought they had witnessed a miracle that didn't really occur..."

"So, he was taken off the cross and put in the cave *still alive?*" Seth queried.

Jacques nodded.

Looking at the distinguished scientist dubiously, Seth followed through with the suggestion, "And then three days later, completely

---

[29] Hebrews 11:34-38
[30] John 15:17-23; Acts 8:1; Romans 8:35; 2 Corinthians 11:25-31; Revelation 6:9-11
[31] Matthew 16:24-27
[32] Hebrews 11:35
[33] Hebrews 11:33-40 and 12:1-2

healed from being beaten, tortured, crucified and thrust through with a spear, Jesus wriggled out of the linen wrappings, moved the heavy stone and overcame trained soldiers? Is that *possible?"*

Jacques shrugged.

"Even if the disciples got past all the guards Pilate had set in place, and managed to *carry him* out of the tomb," Seth argued, "how could he have fully recovered only three days later? Even if they had access to antibiotics, that would be incredibly fast healing! Whether he was miraculously healed or resurrected, both would involve God's supernatural intervention."

Recognizing the improbability of the situation, the older scientist tried another tact. "So, maybe just the New Testament is valid?"

Seth shook his head slowly. "Jesus himself recognized the authority of the Old Testament," he explained.

"How?"

Giving examples, Seth listed, "He directly quoted from it to defeat his temptations to sin. At the end of the Gospel of Luke, he quoted from 'the Law and the Prophets' in order to prove to others that he was the true Messiah. He said that his role was to *'fulfil'* the Law and not to destroy it. Many times, when he was teaching, he said, *'It is written'* or *'Have ye not read,'* in reference to Old Testament Scriptures."[34]

Jacques pondered the list silently.

Rachel and Jordan had finished feeding the animals and called out their goodbyes from the doorway.

The three debaters waved cheerily and said goodbyes of their own.

Jordan was excited. "The jaguar ate his steak in one bite," he told them, astonished. "But he left the grapes."

---

[34] Luke 4:1–12; Luke 24:25–27,46; Matthew 5:17–19; Matthew 11:10; 21:13; 26:24,31; Mark 7:6; 9:12–13; 14:21,27; John 6:31, 45; Matthew 15:4; 19:4–9; 12:3–5; 22:29–31; Mark 12:10,26; Luke 6:3

"He might come back for dessert later," Jacques chuckled.

"And the mommy monkey wouldn't share her apple!"

"Good thing you have a nice mommy," Evan quipped.

Jordan nodded and reached out for his mother's hand.

"I'll be waiting to hear about the patients," Rachel called out.

"I should hear soon," Jacques assured her, looking quickly at his phone in case he'd missed a message, but he hadn't. They all waved again and the Khalids departed, hand in hand, for home.

Returning to their discussion about whether or not Jesus had endorsed the Old Testament, Evan had a few more things to add. "Jesus spoke of God creating Adam and Eve as though this were an established fact,"[35] he noted. "In fact, Jesus referred to many Old Testament people, like Noah and Lot, David, Jonah, Abel and Zechariah.[36] Never once did he insinuate that they were myths.

"He even spoke with Moses and Elijah in the transfiguration,"[37] Seth added. "If we think that Jesus taught a different God, it's more likely that we simply don't understand the Old Testament correctly."

"Perhaps," the Professor acknowledged slowly. "But I find it really hard to understand or even *like* the God of the Old Testament!"

Looking up kindly, Seth said, "You know, sometimes we dislike people because of what others have said about them, but when we actually get to know them ourselves, we may discover the rumours are wrong. They may become our best friends. I think it's the same with God. Many past events have been taken out of context and spun in the worst ways possible, without giving the whole story."

Nodding, the Professor admitted this could be true. He had never read the whole Bible from cover to cover – only small sections here and there.

---

[35] Matthew 19:4-6
[36] Luke 17:26-30; Matthew 12:3; Matthew 12:39-41; Luke 11:50-51
[37] Luke 9:28-36

"Remember what you always told us in class," Evan encouraged. "*Follow the evidence wherever it leads.*"

Jacques chuckled, knowing he had often added, "It doesn't matter how fantastic your theory is, if it doesn't hold up to experiment, if it doesn't match the evidence you discover – then it's not viable. Throw it out and start again. Science doesn't progress by holding onto *established theories* but by following the evidence."

Internally, he pondered, "Are there documented proofs I am refusing to consider because I want to cling to my favourite hypothesis? Have I become a *radical skeptic*, refusing reasonable evidence?" The conversation had given him plenty to think about. Rising from the table he thanked the young men for the interesting discussion and headed back to his office. He hoped he would soon get a report from Aimee.

Chapter 12

$\mathcal{A}$s prearranged, Evan and Seth went out for dinner that evening after their chat with the Professor.

Sitting down in a private booth for two, right next to a big screen TV, Evan noticed a 'Breaking News' banner headline. "Hey, look at that!" he said.

Seth read, "A Special Report Tonight on the Tinys Right After the Six O'clock News."

"Paradise has made the headlines," the redhead exclaimed. "It's all-over social media."

"I know. Donations and cards are pouring in," Evan nodded. "We aren't quite sure what to do... although the Professor is facing heavy fines for his unethical use of reproductive material. He is appreciative of the assistance toward keeping Paradise running."

A young waitress approached their table. "Can I get you anything to drink?" she asked politely.

Both of them asked for water and were ready to order. The half chicken dinner with fries and sauce was within their meagre student budgets.

"How are the burn victims?' Seth asked, once the waitress had taken their order.

"The next two nights will be crucial for Zahir and Ponce," Evan fretted. "Apparently, this is when infection generally sets in, and it's critical to get the meds just right."

"How will you know if you've got them correct?"

"If their temperatures start going up, the doctors will recalculate the antibiotics. No one has ever treated someone so small."

"So, I suppose the new nurses will be checking their vitals?" Seth nodded. "Can someone communicate with you now that Uncle Louis is confined to bed?"

Evan explained the whole situation and the way they had taught Aimee to use the phone. He also told him about the Khalids' willingness to do anything for the Tinys, and all the medical supplies they had donated.

A beep sounded on his phone and he took it out to look at the message. It was his friend, Jim, asking how things were going.

"Sorry, Seth," Evan apologized, putting the phone down on the table and choosing to respond later. "We're waiting to hear from Aimee tonight. Hopefully, she'll give us a full report."

"I know a lot of people are asking this question," Seth prodded, "but does Dr. Khalid feel confident that *everyone* will recover?"

Evan looked over at Seth's concerned face. "There are no guarantees," he said soberly. "We're waiting to see how the boys pull through in the next few days. Louis's prognosis is poor, since obviously, surgery can't be done, and his heart attack damaged a lot of the muscle."

"I'm really sorry to hear that," Seth replied in dismay. "Louis pushed himself to the limit to save Paradise, and now he is just going to die... and that's that? Can't we give him something more?" With a desperate look on his face, he appealed, "Evan, is there any way we can share the message of salvation with him?"

Evan smiled at his younger friend. "Seth, I invited you to dinner tonight because I have something very important to tell you! You won't believe what has happened in this last week since the fire. I could have just sent you a message, but this news is worth a fine-dining celebration! I believe your prayers were answered."

Astonished, Seth looked up. "Really? How?"

As they waited for their chicken dinners to arrive, Evan filled him in on the particulars. He told him about Louis' discovery of the Bible online weeks before the fire, and of his insistence while in the Emergency lab, that he be allowed to have 'God's Book' in Paradise. "Louis feels that *his prayers* were answered!" Evan exclaimed. "He is determined to do a search for truth and find out whose book he agrees with more – the Professor's or God's. If you still have that small copy of the Bible, Seth, I'm actually *allowed* to send it in!"

Seth's green eyes were wide with wonder. Trying to process everything Evan had told him, he clarified, "So, Louis has already discovered the Bible... *online?* And Professor Lemans has *agreed* to allow God's Book to enter Paradise?"

Evan nodded happily.

The young student was overjoyed. "This is definitely worth celebrating and thanking God! And yes, I have a Bible!" he exclaimed. "And I've already marked in some key cross-references and notes, just in case an opportunity came up."

Evan explained the details. "Louis promised he would share the Bible only with those in the Crisis Room for now, and that he would also read the Professor's book to them." Continuing on, he explained the whole discussion that had taken place between the Professor, himself and Louis. He even showed Seth the messages Louis had typed on his phone.

"Unreal!" Seth smiled. "I would never have dreamed it could happen this way! I would love to meet Louis. What an amazing guy he is! I'll bring the Bible to you early tomorrow morning."

"Here are your meals," the waitress said, handing them both overflowing plates of food - mostly fries. "Let me know if you need anything else."

Both men thanked her and then Seth suggested they say a prayer. Bowing their heads, he prayed earnestly, "Our Heavenly Father, we thank you for our lives and the privilege of calling you our Father. We thank you for this good meal, our health, and our friendship; we know that all good things come from You. We are thankful that You found a way to enlighten Louis even before we prayed! And we are astounded at this remarkable opportunity for Your Word to enter Paradise. Please bless the Tinys with the opportunity to find Your precious salvation." In a more sober tone, Seth begged, "We ask now for direction in determining how to care for the Tinys. All life originates and is sustained by Your power. None of us can exist without Your life-giving spirit breath, and you care for us all, no matter how small or insignificant we may be. Please save Zahir and Ponce from infection. We live in an age when science has overreached its boundaries and tinkered with Your creation in ways that surely bring grief to You. For the Professor to take Your gift of life to those who are made in Your image, and miniaturize them to bring glory to himself is truly wrong. Please forgive him this wrong. Please help him to give You the glory as the wonderful Designer, Creator and Father that You are. In the name of our Lord Jesus Christ, Your Beloved Son, we pray. Amen."

Silently, the two science students began eating their meals. Evan was deep in thought over Seth's prayer. He had never considered apologizing to God for what he and the Professor had done. Yet, he had been feeling very uncomfortable ever since he realised it was wrong to modify human life in such a drastic way. Had they tried to bring glory to themselves by misusing their knowledge? Yes... he had to admit, he had desired to see his name emblazoned across social media and in exclusive scientific research magazines. Such personal revelations deeply disturbed his conscience.

The silence extended uncomfortably for a few minutes as they munched on their fries and dipped their chicken into the delicious sauce. "And God is *my Father*," Evan pondered inwardly. "I belong to Him. He notices me... maybe He even *loves* me. Have I disappointed Him by what I have done? Have I misused my abilities in altering the lives of others who are 'made in His image'?" The tall researcher was filled with anxious regret and he stopped eating.

"I'm sorry," Seth apologized. "Evan, I should have talked to you about this first. While I was praying, I just felt the urgency of the situation with Zahir and Ponce in critical care and I was strongly moved to ask for God's forgiveness."

Evan nodded, sitting back in his chair. In a remorseful tone, he agreed, "You're right, Seth." With a sigh and a shake of his head he added, "I know you're right. What we've done with Paradise is wrong in God's eyes. I fully admit it. These little people could have become regular human beings had we not shrunk them down. At the time I thought it was a fantastic experiment to be involved with, and I thought it would be really fun for them. I didn't fully think about how short their lives would be, or that they might hope for something more... or that we were trying to bring glory to ourselves!"

Seth looked up sadly.

With remorse, Evan confessed, "I was wrong to get involved with this. I suppose I should also pray and personally ask God for forgiveness?"

"We need to set things right," Seth agreed. "God will forgive those who sincerely repent and desire to change."

"I'll pray when I get home," Evan promised. "I get it now." Wiping his mouth with his napkin, he laid down his fork. He had completely lost his appetite. With a sigh, he pleaded, "But, Seth, I'm in too deep to get out of this. I have to see this project through to the end. I can't abandon the Tinys... or even Professor Lemans. They need me."

"They certainly do," Seth agreed. "What's already done can't be undone. You *are* responsible for their lives."

Nodding, Evan relayed wistfully, "I should tell you that I've been experimenting to try to find a way to change the Tinys back to a real human size."

Looking up with astonishment, Seth exclaimed, "Really? Is that even possible? How would that even work?"

Shrugging his shoulders, Evan replied, "I've seen it happen randomly with a sunflower and a whole group of butterflies and moths that we sent into the dome. I know it's possible... somehow. I've been experimenting with fish eggs, but so far... no success. I've spent hours and hours trying find a way to undo our mistake."

Seth sighed. "Evan, I feel that a lot of the damage humans have done to God's creation can only be undone by God Himself," he said. Considering this for a moment, the redhead suggested, "If it is God's will that His creation is brought back to Him, then maybe you should pray for His wisdom to guide you. Perhaps all of this should be simply left in our Father's hands."

This was a new thought for Evan. He looked long and hard at Seth. "I'll do that," he said remorsefully. "Tonight, I'll pray for forgiveness and ask for God to guide me... guide us..."

A 'bing' sounded on Evan's phone. It was a report from Aimee. She had sent a WhiteDove message to both the Professor and his assistant. Still sitting at the restaurant table, Evan read it to Seth, *"Zahir and Ponce have elevated fevers of 39° C. They have slept almost the whole day and are still too sleepy to open their eyes or hear me talking to them. It's been very hard getting them to drink the medicine.'"*

"That doesn't sound good," Seth frowned.

Evan texted back right away. *"Ensure they drink all their medicine, however long it takes. Try dipping cloths in lukewarm water and placing them on their foreheads and chests to get those temperatures down. Let us know in a few hours if it's still rising."*

A response from the Professor came in right after his, saying much the same and requesting an immediate video call with her.

Looking up at Seth, Evan relayed soberly. "Well, we did expect elevated temperatures today and tomorrow. Hopefully we can monitor this carefully and keep their fevers under control."

Seth looked at him with a troubled expression.

Minutes later, the special news report on the large TV screen in the restaurant caught Evan's attention.

"We're all on the edge of our seats hoping that Zahir and Ponce will have a favourable recovery," the female reporter was saying. "Professor Lemans has informed us that Dr. Farouk Khalid and Dr. Mark Montgomery, two of Greenville's finest doctors, are working closely with him to assess the medical needs. The next two days will be critical for the burn victims' recovery. Nurse Aimee has been educated on how to use a Smartphone and they are all waiting to hear from her this evening. She has been asked to report on their vitals every day. No doctor has ever studied or medicated a Tiny before. It's all a bit of guessing-game... although these doctors are basing their estimates on much more knowledge than I'll ever have!"

As other patrons in the restaurant craned their necks to see the TV screen, the co-reporter nodded. "Or most of us," she added. "Dr. Khalid trained at a prestigious hospital in Israel and has been working at the Greenville University Hospital in the Cardiac Ward for the past eight years. His wife, Dr. Rachel Khalid, is the head animal doctor at the Biosphere. Dr. Mark Montgomery is our resident specialist who has developed a highly successful burn treatment formula right here in Greenville, which has gone world-wide! All three have contributed greatly to our community and scientific research."

"And now," the other reporter announced, "in case you haven't seen it already on social media, we have actual footage of the shocking catastrophe that happened only days ago in Paradise." Across the screen came a video of the fire. Many of the Tinys were lined up, passing water pots to the front-line firefighters. Zahir and Louis' heroic effort to save Ponce had been captured, but the video ended abruptly.

"That's when I told them all to leave," Evan remarked ruefully to Seth.

Commenting on the injured victims and heroic medics, the reporters displayed a few older pictures that the Professor had sent in from happier days. One picture, which had already gone viral the week before, was from the first celebration in Paradise. Wearing her white celebration dress, Aimee was singing with Zahir, and a large group of Tinys stood around them.

Smiling, the reporter elaborated, "I'm sure most of you have heard the beautiful love song created and sung in Paradise, trending now across social media. Aimee is the female singer here in the white dress. Tragically, her handsome duet-partner, Zahir, was one of the most severely injured in the fire after risking his life to save a fellow Tiny. Unfortunately, Zahir is likely to have permanent scarring across his face and limbs. Not only did Zahir and Ponce suffer in this incident, but Uncle Louis, as he is affectionately called, had a near fatal heart-attack in his efforts to help the young men. According to Professor Lemans, Aimee's immediate assistance and successful CPR brought him back to life. At this moment, nurse Aimee and four other Tinys are caring for the injured in a makeshift hospital. The doctors have sent in an important list of instructions for them to follow."

Evan and Seth exchanged knowing glances.

"Where did she learn CPR?" the male reporter asked.

"Apparently, Uncle Louis taught her," the other reporter smiled.

"How does he know all these things?"

"Believe it or not, they are connected to the Internet inside the dome. Uncle Louis can Google anything!" she added with a laugh.

Closing the story, the female reporter appealed to her audience. "I'm sure that we all are cheering for Uncle Louis, Zahir and Ponce to pull through these critical hours! In the meantime, the Paradise attraction at the Greenville Biosphere will not be open to the public until further notice. And sadly, as we've been reporting in the last few days, Professor Lemans has been stripped of his tenure and is facing huge fines for his unethical conduct in this experiment."

Evan sighed, knowing that he was also complicit in all that had gone on and wondering if his own career might be affected. What troubles lay ahead? "It doesn't matter," he told himself, "I'm a part of this and I'm seeing it through to the end."

The announcer went on to discuss an outbreak of a deadly 'new' disease that was making inroads among a certain demographic of the population. There were already five hundred cases in Canada!

"I don't fully understand suffering," Evan remarked to Seth. "Do terrible things just happen by chance and God looks the other way, or does He actually bring suffering upon our world?"

Sitting back in his chair, Seth reflected thoughtfully on the question. "Both can be true," he replied. "We're told in Ecclesiastes, that 'time and chance' happens to all.[38] Our world is a living, dynamic planet and sometimes we get in the way of the inbuilt forces of nature. God hasn't promised to protect us from every danger – but He has promised to bring us back to life if we put our trust in Him."[39]

"But sometimes God *will* bring suffering?"

"Yes," Seth nodded. "We live in a cursed world because of sin.[40] In the past God has brought fire, disease, pestilence, strong winds, even a *global flood* to punish those who rebelled against Him.[41] And He has promised He will use these forces to judge our world.[42] We are in the 'last days' before Jesus returns and, for the most part, our society has rejected God's standards and the purpose that He has for His creation."[43]

---

[38] Luke 13:1-5; John 9:1-3; 11:1-44
[39] John 5:21, 25-29; 1 Corinthians 15:42-56
[40] Genesis 3; Romans 8:18-25
[41] Genesis 6-7; Genesis 19; Exodus 7-11; Job 38:22-23; Psa. 135:6-12; Isa. 45:6-7. See also Benson, T., "Stormy Wind Fulfilling His Word". (1983) CSSS.
[42] Ezekiel 38:18-23; Zechariah 14:1-12; Luke 21: 2 Peter 3:3-13; Rev. 16:15-21

Evan mused over the answer. "So sometimes we suffer for our own decisions, or the decisions of our society, and sometimes we are subject to time and chance?"[44]

"And sometimes our sufferings might even be for the *benefit* of others, like Job, or Jesus,"[45] Seth added. "Suffering actually has a very important purpose, it's not necessarily a punishment. As the Apostle Paul says in Romans five, *'...we rejoice in our sufferings, knowing that suffering produces endurance, and endurance produces character, and character produces hope...'* Suffering can produce strong character and strengthen our relationship with God. It isn't intended to make us bitter and turn away. It is part of God's plan to test if our relationship with Him will withstand adversity."[46]

Evan looked at him thoughtfully and nodded. "And I suppose suffering can help us develop empathy for others," he added, thinking of various instances where he had seen this happen in Paradise. "Maybe it also helps us value what we have more highly."

"Speaking of valuing our gifts," Seth reflected, "would we appreciate God's willingness to forgive and His merciful heart if we've never experienced the shame and disgrace of failure? And would we see the need to share this mercy and kindness with others?"[47]

With a downcast expression, Evan said, "I wish I could help Jacques see all this. Sadly, he's chosen the bitter route."

Seth sighed deeply as he collected his used napkin and utensils on his dirty plate. "Unfortunately, some view God as a genie in a bottle," he remarked. "Our Father in Heaven isn't there only there to grant all our wishes and provide us a comfortable life – like Professor Lemans is trying to do in Paradise. When we're feeling happy, it's easy to have

---

[44] 2 Timothy 3:1-5; Isaiah 24:5 (whole chapter); Genesis 9:9-17; Romans 1
[45] Job 42:7-16; Isaiah 53; Romans 5:6-11
[46] Deuteronomy 8:1-18; 1 Chron. 28:9; Jer. 17:9-10
[47] Luke 7:38-48; 1 Timothy 1:12-16; 1 Corinthians 15:8-10

faith that He exists. But when bad things happen, even believers can quickly begin to question if God is real. Yet, He purposely chooses to test our commitment and see if we will truly love *Him* with all our heart even when things are tough,[48] or if we are only in love with His gifts."

---

[48] Deuteronomy 8:2-19; Hebrews 12:5-15; 1 John 3:16-24; 5:1-5. See also, Pople, J. *"To Speak Well of God – An Exposition of the Book of Job,"* (2009), page 26, 28.

A Long Night

Chapter 13

*I*n the night, Aimee woke up to the sound of Uncle Louis' voice. He was calling for her. She sat bolt upright in bed. The night air was always cooler than during the day. Pulling on the long, white nightshirt that Diya had made for her, Aimee noted that the bed beside hers was empty. She didn't have time to wonder where Lily might be. Running out of the room, she could hear groaning. Kenzie met her in the dark hallway. "Zahir and Ponce are really unwell. I don't know what to do," he expressed anxiously.

Rushing into the room, Aimee was thankful for the solar twinkle lights that had been tied up around her big window. In the soft lighting, she could see that Zahir and Ponce were tossing restlessly and moaning.

"Aimee," Uncle Louis directed. "Feel their foreheads."

She placed her hand on Zahir's head. "He's burning hot!" she exclaimed. Quickly, she assessed Ponce. She took their temperatures. They were both at nearly 40° Celsius. Taking their pulses, she also noted that their heartrates were up and they were breathing quickly.

Uncle Louis called her to his side. "You know what you need to do," he whispered. "Send a message. Relay their temperatures. Explain that Zahir and Ponce are hallucinating and feverish. No doubt they are fighting infection. I believe these young men need stronger medication." With an unusual urgency to his voice, Uncle Louis implored, "Hurry, Aimee!"

Kenzie looked over curiously. Sensing that this was a crisis, Aimee fairly flew out of the house. It was dark. It was hard to see in the forest as she climbed down Rainbow Hill, but Aimee was thankful for the stairs Odin had set in place.

"I can't lose them!" she kept telling herself all the way to the cave. "I can't lose them!" She found the key under the rock, opened the door and turned on the light. Quite distraught, Aimee sent an urgent message to the Professor and hoped with all her heart that he would reply.

Within ten seconds, there was an answer. "I'll contact the doctor immediately. Take some cloths, dip them in lukewarm water and lay them on your patients' chests and foreheads. Give them another dose of pain medication and force them to drink more fluids. This will help cool them down. Then wait by the store for the train. We'll send stronger antibiotics."

Locking up the cave, Aimee quickly showered and made her way back up to the Caring Centre. She passed on the instructions to Kenzie and helped him find cloths. They picked up the wash pot that still had plenty of water and took it into the room. Once they had laid wet cloths on both the patients, Kenzie tried to get them to drink. Aimee stood up to leave.

"Where are you going *again?*" Kenzie asked, looking desperately at Aimee. "Please stay and help me."

Pausing, a look of anguish passed over her face. "More medicine is being sent in," she explained quietly. "I have to wait for it to come in on the train."

"How do you know all these things?" he implored.

Looking over at Uncle Louis, Aimee wasn't sure how to respond. She didn't want to be dishonest.

"She's talking to the Professor, like I used to do down in the cave," Uncle Louis said quietly, taking the liberty to include Kenzie in the secret. "Please keep this to yourself."

111

Astonished, the young man didn't know what to say.

Aimee fled through the dark forest and across the meadow to the train tracks. When it began to rain, she sat under the veranda of the store. A long time passed by. She yearned to be back in the Caring Centre, where she could see how Zahir was faring and do something to help, even if it was only to hold his hand.

"But I'm thankful that Kenzie and Uncle Louis are with him," she assured herself. "Even if Uncle Louis has to stay in bed, he knows what to do. I must wait here for the medicine."

Sitting out in the cool darkness, Aimee had plenty of time to reflect. While she was distressed for all three of the patients in her room, her heart was wrapped around two of them in particular. Both were her main source of comfort and reassurance. Both gave warm hugs, encouraging remarks and kind smiles. Life in Paradise would not be the same without them. She knew that just as she had watched Zahir's dog grow old and die, she was watching Uncle Louis fade away. Losing Uncle Louis would be terrible enough! Losing Zahir... well, the thought of losing Zahir seemed impossible to bear.

"He saved Ponce's life," she agonized. "It would be so unfair for him to lose his own just because he was kind. And Zahir is still so young. And... and..." Sobs burst out as Aimee bent over with her face in her hands. The courageous actions of her friend during the fire had completely won her heart. "I *love* Zahir!" she cried out. "I love him more than anyone else!"

Tears rolled down her face, as her mind went back to the dark night when she had stood on Rainbow Hill and sung the saddest song of her life. She sobbed harder as she remembered Zahir joining her and turning her sad song into one filled with comfort and joy. He had brought light into the darkness. In her mind, there was no one else quite so special!

Almost half an hour went by very slowly as Aimee sat under the shelter of the veranda, impatiently waiting for the train and reliving old memories. She was thankful she had put on the long white shirt, so she could wrap it around herself in the cool night air. Huddled in the folds of cloth, while the rainmaker passed over the roof time and again, something became very clear in her mind. There were two people in Paradise that she couldn't bear to lose, and she certainly couldn't bear to lose them both at once. "Even if Zahir *always* belongs to Georgia," she sighed, "I will be thankful just to have him here in Paradise. He gives the best smiles. He says the kindest things. I may never give him another long hug, but I will always appreciate his friendship." With longing eyes, she looked toward the train tunnel. "Please send that medicine in quickly!" she begged no one in particular. "Please let it work!"

Finally, the train came in. Little did the young nurse know how much turmoil and deliberation had gone on in the middle of the night on the other side of the glass. She didn't know that Farouk and Rachel Khalid had risen from a sound sleep, called Dr. Mark Montgomery and made numerous calculations with him on the phone. Then Rachel had stayed back with Jordan, while Farouk had driven to the hospital, where he packaged and labelled the stronger antibiotics in the tiny bottles. The kind-hearted doctor had then driven across to the Biosphere, met the Professor in the parking lot, been ushered into the Paradise Room, spoken careful instructions that Jacques had written down in tiny, legible form, and was now standing outside the dark dome beside the Professor, looking in with great anxiety. Deliberating softly with one another, they were trying to determine whether it would be best to bring the burn victims to their side of the world in the morning, or not.

Aimee only knew that the train had arrived. When she rolled open the door of the first car, the lights came on inside, which helped her to see everything. Picking up the tall eye-dropper bottles, she saw from the labels that there were two of each type of medication. Placing the extras on the ground beside the tracks, she gathered one of each new bottle and the written instructions. Two was all that she could carry.

Running across the dark field, Aimee crossed Rainy River. Usually, it was just a dry riverbed, but since it was still raining, it was knee-high. She saw little rabbits scamper away and her deer friends watching her from the woods. But she hardly acknowledged the animals. If they were hungry, she knew they could always go to the store and eat from the compost pile. Important lives were at risk, and at that moment she could hardly think about anything else; she even forgot to shower.

Kenzie was putting more damp cloths on the patients' heads and chests trying to cool them down when she re-entered the softly lit room. With great relief, he ran over to take the big bottles from her arms. Zahir and Ponce were still restless and moaning.

Uncle Louis called out softly, "That's my girl!"

Standing by the window, Kenzie and Aimee read the instructions in the soft light. "I am so thankful for these lights!" she said, and he agreed. Together they measured out the dosages. Aimee held the cups while Kenzie filled the dropper and squeezed it out into each one. Picking up Ponce's cup, the weary male nurse took it to him.

With the medication, Aimee sat down on the chair between the two burn patients. She called out softly to Zahir, but it took a louder attempt to wake him. When his eyes fluttered open, he didn't even recognize her. He seemed to be in the middle of a nightmare, and called out, "No, no, please don't! Don't fry me! No, no! Not Freddo! Not Freddo!"

With a sad smile, Aimee wondered what terrible things were happening in Zahir's nightmare. He thrashed violently around almost knocking the medication out of her hand.

Kenzie had finished giving Ponce his dosage, so he dashed over to hold Zahir's flailing arms down by his side. Gradually, they helped him drink the new antibiotics and some painkiller too. Seemingly oblivious to their presence, Zahir swallowed mechanically. Then it was time to administer the protein formula and more water, all the while restraining their hallucinating patients.

Once the doses had been given out, Kenzie yawned and rubbed his eyes. He hadn't had any sleep all night. Aimee said, "I can take a turn with them, if you like. I'm wide awake."

"Thank you," he nodded gratefully. "Even an hour or two would be great. Just wake me up if you need any help." Exhausted, he collapsed into the extra bed.

After changing the wet cloths on her patients, Aimee settled on the chair between them, taking both their hands and hoping with all her heart that the medicine would soon take effect.

"Freddo! Freddo!" Zahir called out in distress.

With deep compassion, Aimee assured him that Freddo was okay.

Near dawn, the young men began to relax. Their foreheads became cooler to the touch. Ponce fell into a sound sleep. Aimee turned her full attention to Zahir. He wasn't thrashing around as much as before.

Hopeful melodies welled up inside her heart. She didn't want to wake anyone, so she kept her voice soft and low. *"I want to see you in the morning,"* she sang, just barely above a whisper, *"alive, awake and well."* She hummed quietly, as she thought of the next line. *"May the sun brighten up your face and give me good news to tell."* Tears welled up, as she continued, *"I'd like to see some recognition when you open up your eyes. And most of all, I want you to always stay alive."*

Repeating the song once more, Aimee began to feel very tired. Not wanting to leave her patients while they were dangerously ill, even if they were now both sleeping peacefully, she curled up on the sofa, wrapping herself in a spare blanket. One last line came to her and she quietly murmured the words, *"Because without you, I don't think I... would... survive."*

The Lady in White

Chapter 14

Slowly, Aimee became aware of her surroundings. Little birds were singing in the trees and squirrels were chattering away. Sunlight was filling the room, while smells of ointment and unpleasantries wafted past her nose, and then she heard a faint groan. With a start, she came to and sat bolt upright on the pink couch in the Caring Centre.

Zahir's blue eyes were alert. "Did you stay in here all night?" he asked wearily.

"Zahir! You look so much better!" she cried out with astonishment. Jumping up from the sofa, she ran over. Taking the damp cloth off his forehead, she felt his temperature. "You aren't burning up!" she announced ecstatically. Wide-eyed, she looked over at Uncle Louis.

Having been awake for a while, Uncle Louis cheered, "Oh, that is very good news, indeed!"

"Why was he burning up?" Ponce asked fearfully, confused.

"You both had fevers," Uncle Louis replied. "You were fighting infection and you became far too hot. Thanks to Kenzie and Aimee, you're doing much better this morning."

Lethargically, Zahir reached over and clasped Aimee's arm. "Thank you, Nurse Aimee," he said gratefully. "And you too, Kenzie," he nodded at his friend.

"I had so many strange, scary dreams," Ponce mumbled, peeling off the cloths on his chest. "But there was also this beautiful lady in white, who sometimes turned into a butterfly." He smiled, looking over at Aimee in her long, wrinkled shirt. "She was singing a really pretty song."

"Nice," Zahir mumbled wearily. "Mine were just scary. This nasty creature was trying kill me and Freddo. I kept trying to save my dog, but..." he paused to catch his breath. "Come to think of it," he reflected thoughtfully, "that creature had a gigantic frying pan..."

Aimee laughed. She sat down between her patients and reached for Zahir's good hand. Seeing him alive and talkative generated immense joy and relief. She wanted to dance around the room and sing her song again, but instead she teased kindly, "Maybe you're feeling guilty for all those poor fish you've caught?"

Ponce laughed.

"Could be." Zahir's eyes were smiling. He squeezed the hand that was holding his.

Uncle Louis piped up, "I also heard the Lady in White," he said, his eyes twinkling. "And I think she got her wish this morning." Looking over at Aimee, he winked.

"Me too," Kenzie piped up quietly, picking up the bottle of pain medication.

"What? You all heard a song, and I missed out?" Zahir mumbled. Looking slowly over at Kenzie, Ponce and Uncle Louis, he then turned back to Aimee. "How did it go?"

But the others couldn't remember the details, and Aimee didn't think Georgia would appreciate the song being sung again. Her housemates would soon be getting up. With a teasing expression, she just smiled at her dark-haired patient.

"So, was there a song, or not?" he begged.

Aimee shrugged. "You and Ponce were imagining all sorts of strange things," she laughed, patting his hand.

Georgia poked her head in to greet the patients before heading to the store. Her eyes glanced around the room. Wet cloths were still on

Zahir's chest. A bowl of water sat on the floor, and new bottles of medicine crowded the side table. One nurse was sitting very close to the dark-haired patient. "Was it a rough night?" she asked tentatively.

"They were very feverish," Aimee told her. "I was really afraid they weren't going to make it."

"Seriously?" Georgia questioned, her green eyes narrowing. "It was that bad? Is that why you're holding Zahir's hand?"

Blushing, Aimee felt guilty, even though she had convinced herself that her needy patients required extra care. Zahir let go and she stood up to walk away.

Kenzie frowned.

"It's like you're taking advantage of this situation and *stealing* my man," Georgia protested angrily. "I have to go and cook every day in the kitchen, and you're sitting in here holding hands with Zahir!"

Uncle Louis smiled. "Holding hands is an important part of the healing process," he informed the angry blond. "Aimee is just being a good nurse. She holds my hand too."

"Mine too," Ponce piped up.

"Don't be so hard on the nurses," Kenzie argued. "Aimee's only doing the job she's been *asked* to do."

Nevertheless, rather mortified, Aimee decided the handholding had run its course. Ponce and Zahir were no longer in such desperate pain. She didn't want to upset Lily and Georgia needlessly, since that was 'hurting' them. A little shaky, she turned away and began folding the blanket on the sofa. Georgia had accused her of *stealing!* There were only two rules in Paradise – no hurting and no stealing... was she guilty of breaking both? Even Uncle Louis' principle, to *'do unto others as you would have done unto you,'* didn't seem clear in this situation. Who was she to think of first?

In a soothing voice, Georgia offered, "I'll come hold your hand, Zahir, when I'm done serving breakfast. I love you," she called out cheerily.

"I love you too," Zahir responded with a dutiful tone. There was no doubt that the two still shared a special relationship.

Georgia smiled at him, glared jealously at Aimee, and left the room.

Voices called out from the next room, "Hey, what about us? We need some handholding in here! We're in *so much* pain! Who loves us?" There was a chorus of laughter across the hall, but Aimee didn't smile.

Charley and Milan brought in a large, heavy package that they had carried all the way from the train. It was wrapped in brown paper with Uncle Louis' name in bold letters. Vahid followed with a smaller package in the same brown paper.

"You can leave those here by my bed," Uncle Louis smiled, pointing to the window seat beside him.

"What are they?" Vahid queried. "They feel like schoolbooks." With a chuckle he asked, "Do Zahir and Ponce have to do school up here with you?" He winked at Ponce, and Ponce groaned.

"They are books that I am studying," Uncle Louis told him. "If either one is accurate, it may become a school lesson one day."

Rather shaken, but trying her best not to show it, Aimee began her rounds of pain medication with Kenzie. Glumly, she decided the pink sofa would be the best place to sit when talking to her patients. It was far enough away that handholding was not an option. She didn't want to face another jealous reaction from Georgia.

Healing

Chapter 15

After all the bandages were changed that afternoon and the medicine doled out, Zahir and Ponce soon fell sound asleep again. Their temperatures remained steady, just a little above normal, and the smell was dissipating. Georgia came up with a book, but seeing the young men were having another nap, she decided to go across the hall and play games with the beach boys and Sanaa instead. Chess was becoming quite popular and so were card games.

Aimee slipped out to give another report down in the cave. Thrilled to share her good news with the Professor, she hummed the new song that she had sung to Zahir. To her surprise, she met Lily in the forest.

"Where are you off to?" Lily demanded suspiciously.

"I'm just enjoying the forest," Aimee laughed, immediately feeling uncomfortable with half-truths.

"Of course," Lily nodded merrily. "Write some songs while you're walking around!" She tossed her head back proudly. "See you later when you're finished talking to the Professor."

"The Professor?" Aimee echoed, pretending to be surprised by the remark. "Talking to him?"

"We know that's where you're going," Lily shrugged. "It's obvious that Uncle Louis can't talk to him anymore. And somehow the train keeps coming back and forth with all the right supplies."

"I'm not sure where you are getting these ideas from," Aimee said.

"I'm just not sure why *you* were chosen," Lily admitted, "unless it's because you're one of the nurses."

Alarmed that her secret was already out, Aimee walked through the darkest part of the forest, climbing over a few more fallen trees. Carefully, she found her way to the cave and took the key from under the rock. Once inside, she turned on the light and closed the door. There were dirty streaks on the phone. The letter she had received from the Professor was upside down and she was sure she had left it right side up.

"Has Lily... or someone else been in here," she wondered anxiously, "or did I leave this mess?" She used the cloth that was on Uncle Louis' desk and wiped the screen. "I'd better keep this key with me," she decided. "Maybe someone saw me put it under the rock."

Pressing the WhiteDove app, and making a videocall to the Professor, Aimee sat down on the chair. It didn't take long for him to answer. Eager to share her good news with him, she told him all the details of the long night. Having been anxiously awaiting a message from her ever since he woke up early that morning, Jacques was overjoyed to hear that both patient's temperatures were almost normal.

"They were alert and talkative this morning," Aimee recalled, clapping her hands together joyfully, "and now they are both sleeping soundly again."

Wildly thankful for the good news, Jacques didn't tell her that he had stood with the doctor deliberating anxiously for an hour in the night, slept on the cot in the lab and been unable to concentrate on anything else since he woke up. "This is wonderful, wonderful news!" he rejoiced, relieved that the patients could remain in the dome. "I'm so proud of you, Aimee. You followed the instructions well, and I'm very thankful that you messaged me when there was a problem."

Aimee was grateful for the new medication and formula. "I'm so, so happy the guys are better!" she exclaimed. "I couldn't bear to lose them!"

"I couldn't either," he smiled pleasantly. "You have some very special Tinys in your care."

Aimee nodded enthusiastically. Then she remembered her conversations with Lily. She told the Professor what Lily had said and also relayed that Uncle Louis had let Kenzie in on the secret.

Jacques was concerned. He pondered the matter. "Once the others have figured out that you are communicating with me, there's not much we can do to keep it a secret," he said with resignation. "Just try your best not to draw attention to this privilege. I don't want the others to react jealously towards you or find a way to use the phone inappropriately themselves. Please be sure to keep that key with you at all times!"

Nodding meekly, Aimee didn't admit she had been leaving it under a rock. But she told herself she had to be much more careful from now on.

Showering before heading back to the Caring Centre, Aimee held tightly to the key. She begged Diya for a long piece of ribbon and her housemate tossed her one of the many that she had hanging on pegs. Privately tying it around her neck, Aimee hid the key under her dress.

Another evening passed quickly as the four nurses changed dressings, cleaned wounds, monitored temperatures and gave the correct dosages to each patient. Aimee was thankful when Vahid arrived and it was time for bed. Kenzie left yawning, and Tina dashed off shortly after.

"I hear last night was rough?" Vahid said to Aimee outside the room.

She nodded wearily. "I am *so* tired!" But she went over the new instructions and showed him the bottles of medicine that they were now to use.

Vahid was eager to take a turn. "Get some sleep while you can. I'll take care of them all," he said.

Lily was already in bed when Aimee came in, and she mumbled good night to her. Aimee fell asleep almost instantly. However, in the middle of the dark night, a strange noise woke Aimee up. It was a heavy rumble that reverberated up and down her spine. Not only was the rumble intense, but she could feel a warm circle of pressure on her lower back. Turning over, she felt a heavy body slip off with an annoyed 'meow.'

Aimee could hardly believe that a cat had been sleeping on top of her! Ever since Ripple had begun killing small animals and birds, like Colours, cats had become the one and only animal Aimee did not like. However, she grudgingly picked up the sleepy, very large cat. It was dark and hard to see, but Aimee knew by its size that it had to be Yu Yan's pet, Mia.

"Why are you here again, Mia?" she whispered, as she quietly took her downstairs. "And why would you choose to sleep on me of all the people in this house?" Putting the cat outside, Aimee said softly, "Go home to Yu Yan. That's your girl." Then she tiptoed back upstairs to Lily's room.

However, when she climbed back into her bed, she realized that Lily was not beside her; her bed was empty. "This is strange," Aimee thought, recalling that Lily's bed had been empty the night before when she'd awoken to Uncle Louis' urgent call.

As Aimee contemplated Lily's absence, suddenly a noise at the window startled her. The silhouette of a head appeared, and Aimee sat up wide awake. As the petite girl climbed through the window, Aimee recognized her roommate.

"What are you doing?" Aimee asked, bewildered.

"Oh, it's just the easiest way to get in," Lily whispered. "I had to visit the outhouse. I didn't want to wake anyone up."

"Easiest way?" Aimee clarified wearily, lying back down. "You must be a good climber."

When the light of dawn spilled in the next morning, Aimee looked over immediately to see if Lily was still there. Sound asleep, her roommate's dark hair overflowed her pillow. Dirt was in her hair. The copper-haired nurse observed her friend carefully. There were also muddy streaks on Lily's elbow.

Rolling over, the petite girl opened her eyes. "You're always up so early," she moaned.

"What were you doing last night?" Aimee inquired curiously. "Did you roll down the hill?"

"No," Lily flushed. "Why?"

Following Aimee's eyes, Lily looked at her arm. She saw the streaks. She sat up and saw the dirt on her pillow. "Come to think of it," Lily replied hastily. "I fell. It was dark last night and hard to see."

"True," Aimee nodded. "It was." With a laugh, she added, "Do you have any cuts? I can fix them up for you."

Lily shook her head with a smile. "No, I'm fine, thanks. It was a soft tumble. I didn't realise I got so dirty. It was dark, you know."

As Aimee pulled on her clothes, Lily added, "I really appreciate how well you are looking after Ponce. I'm so glad he's getting better. He says you're a very good nurse."

With a smile, Aimee said, "Thanks Lily. I *love* this job."

A Luna Moth

Chapter 16

ringing in the protein formula the next afternoon with Yu Yan, Aimee was feeling grateful that she had been asked to be a nurse. She had now given two positive morning reports to the Professor and he had happily passed on the news. The young nurse didn't know about Twitter and Instagram, but they were lighting up with reposts across the social media chain, with thousands of likes and loves piling up. So many people across the world were hoping the burn victims would pull through.

Kenzie came running up the stairs to check on the patients and he stayed to help. Ponce and Zahir had been sleeping on and off all morning, and now they needed their pain medication and antibiotics. While Kenzie measured the doses into cups and the girls gave them out, Aimee began humming a tune.

"It's the Lady in White," Ponce teased, who had taken to calling her this ever since the night of the fever.

Bringing Uncle Louis his special formula, Aimee noticed he was lying on his side reading one of his new books – the biggest book, which he'd propped up against the window seat. "Are you going to read it to us?" she asked him curiously.

"At some point," he said quietly, aware that Yu Yan was still in the room, and the Professor had limited the investigation to a specific five.

Aimee continued to hum her catchy melody. All the patients now readily accepted their portions, and no longer did they have to force anyone to drink. Kenzie placed wet cloths on all the bandages so they would be easier to remove. He brought in some clean wipes for the girls to use and picked up the bottles of medicine to take back out to the hallway.

Sitting down to unwrap the moistened gauze on Zahir's lower leg, Aimee added some words to her tune, *"A little medicine here,"* she smiled, singing, *"A little formula there. We'll put on some ointment and wrap you with care."*

Zahir laughed and then winced as the gauze came away from a sensitive spot.

"I'm sorry," Aimee apologized.

Ponce vocally expressed his pain as Yu Yan was a little too hasty with one bandage. "You'll wrap us with care!" he called out. "What about the *unwrapping?* That's what hurts the most!"

Yu Yan gave him a look of reproach. "I'm trying my best," she exclaimed.

"Be glad it's not me," Kenzie called out cheerily, as he brought in the ointment and clean gauze for each of the nurses. The night before he had tried to help remove the dressings and Ponce had overreacted numerous times.

"Yeah, you are definitely the worst," Ponce teased, "but, it was your first try. I'll give you that."

Laughing, Aimee picked up a sterile saline wipe, and began to wipe the long weeping wound on her patient's lower leg. Continuing with her song, she added, *"You'll go out of here feeling all brand new. Cause here is where we love to look after you."*

Zahir looked over at Ponce with a wry smile. "Is this the White Lady's song?" he asked.

"No, no," Ponce replied, shaking his head. "There was some line about hoping you would always stay alive."

"One day you'll sing that song again, right?" Zahir encouraged.

"It's too bad that you only dreamed about being fried for dinner," Aimee bantered, applying the ointment. "It was your friend who dreamt about a lady in white."

Zahir looked perplexed. Aimee felt that was just as well, since Zahir was still Georgia's 'claim.'

She took off the bandages on his arm. Underneath, yellow pus oozed out around the newly formed scab. It smelled bad. Her face wrinkled instantly.

Raising his head from the pillow, Zahir looked at the sore with a look of disgust. "I feel *so* sorry for you!" he remarked dismally as Aimee wiped the pus away. "This is such a gross job! You must wish that you could go back to working in the kitchen. I wouldn't want to be assigned to this messy, smelly work!"

"Don't feel sorry for me," she protested earnestly. "I wouldn't trade jobs with anyone!"

Raising his head, Zahir frowned, "Really? Why not?"

There were at least two reasons that Aimee could have given. One was safe and easy to say, and one was quite difficult in a crowded room where a revoked rule still held sway in her mind, and she wasn't sure how her words would be received. She chose the safe remark. "I once caused the loss of life," she reflected sadly, thinking of Rosa, "and now I've found a way to save lives. This means way more to me than cooking food."

With a shrug, Zahir lay back on his pillow and closed his eyes. "We all need to eat to live," he replied flatly. "Cooking food is also an important way to keep people alive."

Aimee looked up from the wound and smiled, but Zahir's eyes were closed. Kenzie picked up the bottles of medicine to take back to the hallway.

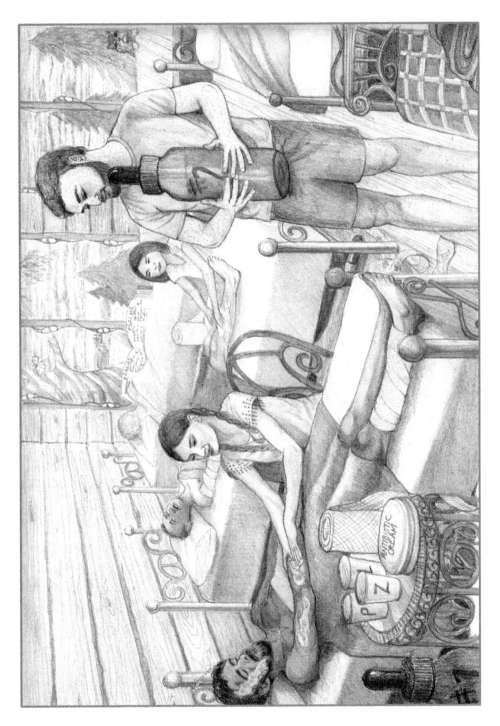

"You could ask Kenzie to do this messy part," Zahir murmured.

Aimee stopped what she was doing and looked up with a tragic expression.

Opening his eyes, Zahir saw the look. "Or not," he relented. "You're doing a great job, Aimee. I just feel badly for you. I'm... *rotting!*"

A pale green moth flew through the window. A cat bounded in, with its eyes on the moth. No one had noticed that Mia was so close by.

"Oh no you don't," Aimee called out, trying to catch the cat. "No killing in here!"

The cat jumped on Zahir's bed. Uncle Louis called out instantly, warning of cat scratches and infection to uncovered wounds. Zahir was quick to react, trying to avoid the cat's paws. Kenzie sat the medicine bottle down and dashed in, scooping Mia up in his arms before she could walk on any of Zahir's open sores. With haste, he took the animal outside and ran down the hill for another shower.

As the patients relaxed, Aimee cleaned everywhere the cat had touched. The moth found a resting place high on the wall.

"A Luna moth," Uncle Louis exalted, happy that it was resting near him. "And this one is the right size."

"I loved my ride on the Luna moth," Aimee recalled dreamily, coming back over to rub ointment on Zahir's wounds. The ring around his neck was almost healed. It was now a thin, strangely pinkish line. "That night is one of my *favourite* memories."

For a few minutes everyone recalled the day, nearly two months ago, when the moths and butterflies had grown to a gigantic size. Aimee had been the first to get the ride of her life. The twinkle lights that now hung in the Crisis Room window had attracted the moth at night.

"That was one incredible ride," Zahir murmured. "Skimming over the water was exhilarating, like nothing I've ever done before or since."

"We were all so worried you were going to end up in the lake," Aimee recalled.

Zahir chuckled and then winced as Aimee tried to gently remove the dead tissue from the oozing sore on his face. The long wound on his face was always the most sensitive. "It was a little worrisome," he agreed, "but that only added to the thrill!"

"I wish I'd gotten on," Uncle Louis reflected. "It did look fun."

"Me too," Ponce added. "Only I knew nothing about it. I didn't even see it happen."

Chuckling, Uncle Louis said, "You were likely deep in the North Forest. You can't see much when you're hiding away in dark dens."

"Yeah, yeah," Ponce nodded ruefully. "There are lots of things I wish I could change... lots that I *will* change..."

Speaking more seriously, Uncle Louis asked, "How does a moth begin life? Do you remember the book we read?"

"As a baby moth?" Ponce suggested, as Aimee picked up the bottle of ointment nearby.

Uncle Louis shook his head and gave them all a detailed description of the early developmental process.

Trying hard not to flinch when Aimee applied the ointment to his face, Zahir clarified, "So, caterpillars don't have wings?"

"No," Uncle Louis replied. "They don't look anything like a butterfly or a moth. Caterpillars are quite ugly, but they change into these beautiful creatures through a process called 'metamorphosis.' Remember this - it doesn't matter what we've done in our past, we can all be transformed into something better."

Suddenly, the Luna moth flittered over and came to rest on Ponce's arm. Aimee stopped attending to her patient and stared in amazement. The moth fluttered its wings gently, but it didn't move. It was so close!

Ponce stayed as still as he could, restraining himself from hollering even when Yu Yan removed the wet gauze from his arm.

"All caterpillars do is eat," Uncle Louis told them, as they marvelled at the exotic creature. "They eat and eat and get bigger and bigger, until they know it's time to change. Then they wrap themselves up in sticky thread cases called 'cocoons,' and their bodies completely break down into a liquid substance. Over a number of days, that liquid substance is transformed into this new gorgeous creature with wings. It's almost like they... *die* and then they are brought back to life as something better... much... *much better.*"

Looking over, Aimee noticed a peaceful look on Uncle Louis' face as he closed his eyes and leaned back on his pillow.

"That's remarkable!" Zahir exclaimed, watching the Luna moth slowly flap its pale green wings.

Aimee nodded. "I've never heard of one kind of creature turning into another."

With a smile, Uncle Louis opened his eyes and nodded. "When butterflies and moths are released into Paradise, they have already gone through the caterpillar and metamorphosis stage. You don't see the ugly stage; you only see the beauty."

The lovely, pale green Luna moth flapped its wings harder and rose into the air. It flew back out the window.

"Wow! That was incredible," Ponce marvelled. "I'm so glad it chose to land on me."

For a moment, all the Tinys watched the moth fly away until it was out of sight. Having finished caring for Zahir, Aimee picked up her supplies and walked over to help Yu Yan.

"Uncle Louis," Zahir said with a little hesitation, "Did the Professor find a way to make dead people come back to life?"

Glancing over curiously, Uncle Louis replied, "No, he has not."

"But he brought you back to life," Ponce pointed out. Then as Aimee began to unwind the bandage on his leg, he suddenly wailed, "Ouch! Ouch! That's stuck! Oooh, that hurts! Be gentle!"

Aimee looked over at Uncle Louis with a smile. She applied another wet cloth to the gauze and waited for the area to moisten.

"The Professor didn't bring me back to life," Uncle Louis smiled.

"But Kenzie says you were... dead," Zahir remarked slowly.

Sitting down in the middle chair, Aimee helped Yu Yan clean Ponce's oozing sores. Trying her best to avoid causing pain to their very sensitive patient, Aimee listened carefully.

Uncle Louis glanced briefly over at Aimee, and then he asked the dark-haired young man. "Do you remember our First Aid class, Zahir?"

With a short laugh, Zahir looked at Ponce with amusement. "The one where this guy helped you demonstrate?"

Ponce smiled. "Hey, I was *so* helpful that day!"

Nodding, Uncle Louis agreed. "Yes, Ponce, you were. It was one of your better days."

"What?" Ponce retorted, but then he laughed.

"I taught all of you CPR that day," Uncle Louis recalled. "Aimee listened and learned well. When I had a heart attack during the fire, Aimee did what she needed to do and saved my life."

With a quick gasp, Aimee looked over.

"Was I breathing when you found me Aimee?"

Slowly, Aimee shook her head.

"Did I have a pulse?"

She shook her head again.

"So," Uncle Louis deduced. "I was technically 'dead.' But Aimee pumped my heart and breathed air into my lungs and according to the doctor, I was already breathing again before I was put on the train."

With a twinge of regret, Uncle Louis said, "I never thanked you, Aimee. I came back in here and there was so much happening that I've forgotten to tell you how grateful I am that you wanted to learn CPR. You learned well, and you came quickly to my rescue. Thank you, Aimee."

A pink flush spread over the young nurse's face.

From the bed beside her chair, Zahir reached over and patted her back. "Saving lives seems to be your thing," he said kindly.

"Thank you," Aimee said, smiling with embarrassment. Needing a moment to herself, she gazed up at the clock. "Oh," she said, "It will soon be time for the protein formula. I'll just get it for everyone. Don't worry, Ponce, I'll be right back."

Hopping up, Aimee rushed into the hallway where most of the bottles were kept. With one hand on the wall, she held on to her moon necklace while she tried to regain her composure. Hearing that she had saved Uncle Louis' life was overwhelming. Aimee needed to come to terms with it all. She did recall that Uncle Louis had been breathing again before he was put on the stretcher, even though his eyes had stayed closed and he had remained unconscious.

"I can hardly believe that such a simple technique can save a life," she thought breathlessly. "I'm so thankful that I helped Uncle Louis before anyone else." Then recalling Georgia's insistent demand to care for Zahir, she admitted reluctantly, "Perhaps I owe that one to her."

In the room, she heard Zahir speak up, "Thanks for saving my life, Uncle Louis. I would have been burned a lot worse if you hadn't rolled me over and put out the fire."

"Lema helped a great deal, too," Uncle Louis recalled. "I'm so thankful he acted quickly to drench you both with water.

Aimee heard Ponce speak up. "Well... since you're all talking about saving lives," he began hesitantly, but very sincerely, "Zahir... thank you for saving mine."

"You're most welcome," Zahir replied.

Coming back to the doorway, Aimee looked in with a smile. Zahir's Shining Moon necklace still hung forlornly on his bed post.

"I know most of the guys would have just let me go," Ponce admitted, as Yu Yan finished unwrapping his wounds. "I probably didn't deserve to be rescued, but thanks... thanks... for caring."

Zahir reached over and gently punched Ponce on his shoulder. "I'm sure you would have done the same for me," he replied.

"Yeah," Ponce nodded. "Yeah..." But he had nothing else to say.

Tears welled up in Aimee's eyes and she had to stay in the hallway for a few moments longer, trying to wipe them away. When she finally returned to the room, she could hear Uncle Louis encouraging Ponce to move his elbow and keep his scars flexible.

"It's so important to know how to care for people," she realized. "And there are many ways to save a life!"

Riding Waves

Chapter 17

Out in the hallway, early the next morning, Aimee picked up the pain medication. She heard a lot of commotion coming from the young men in Georgia's room. When she peered in from the doorway, Lema and Damien were having an arm wrestle on one of the beds. Franz was cheering Lema on. "Come on, come on," he called out. "You can beat him!"

Surprising Damien with a sudden burst of strength, Lema brought his friend's arm down. He and Franz whooped and hollered.

"One for you," Damien laughed. "Three for me."

Aimee stood in the doorway. "I don't think any of you need pain medication this morning," she observed with a smile.

Immediately, they all began to grimace in pain and look like they were ready to faint.

"Ah, come on, beautiful nurse," Damien pleaded, with a teasing grin in her direction, "we need a little more caring in this room." Holding out his hand, he begged. "How about some kind attention here?"

Aimee laughed and blushed against her will, but she didn't step forward. While the handsome Damien still had more of an effect on her than she liked to admit, she was now well aware that charming manners and dashing good looks weren't enough to build a happy, committed relationship. His lustre had faded.

Generally, Tina and Yu Yan attended to the beach boys once Aimee had given them their early morning pain medication and she knew they would soon arrive. Looking at the healthy scabs the young men were eager to show her, she said, "It looks to me like you're all ready to go back to the beach, but Uncle Louis needs to check. He might think differently."

"Yes, the beach!" Lema cheered. "Go-karting! Surfing! We need to get out of this room!"

"I don't know," Damien suddenly pondered with an impish grin, lying back lazily on the pillows. "I'm kind of keen on beds. I didn't realize they were so comfortable."

"Ah, but it's not the same," Lema argued. "You can hardly hear the water from here, or the loons, and the air isn't nearly so fresh."

"You definitely can't see the stars," Franz added, "or feel free."

"I've been sleeping better in this bed than I ever did in a hammock," Damien responded, "and I hear everything through the windows just fine." He turned to Aimee with a smile, "Do I have to be injured to stay in the Caring Centre?"

"Yes, you do," she said firmly. "Georgia will want her room back eventually."

He frowned and lifted his fingers toward his healing wounds. "Maybe I'll have to scratch these itchy scabs!"

"Don't you dare," Aimee warned in a teasing fashion. "You could get them infected."

"Exactly!" he laughed. "More meds, full service, and a soft bed! Ah, this is the good life!"

Tina and Yu Yan's voices were coming through the windows. "Your nurses will soon be here," Aimee smiled, turning to leave. "No pain medication for you."

"Then we definitely need some handholding," Damien teased.

All the beach boys laughed.

Aimee was relieved to exit their room. As she walked down the hall, she overheard Zahir talking with Uncle Louis. She could hear distress in his voice. "I don't think it's like that."

"I don't have any experience with this," Uncle Louis was saying quietly as she drew close to the doorway, "and you can't really have a private conversation in this crowded room, but once you're out of here, you should talk... openly... honestly..."

Zahir groaned. "The last time was *brutal.*"

"Words aren't as meaningful as actions."

"I don't know, Uncle Louis," he responded dismally. "I'm okay with the way things are. I'm a wreck. I hurt all over. I don't even like my own thoughts right now... I just can't deal with any more pain. I don't want to *give it...* or take it."

Realizing this was a private conversation, Aimee began humming a tune so they would all know she was returning. She wondered who Zahir needed to talk to. "What was the 'last time' that 'was brutal'?" she asked herself. "Is Zahir doubting Georgia's love for him?" The comments the beautiful blonde had made right after the fire were rather brutal, but they weren't *the last...* "Perhaps he was more hurt when she said she wouldn't come in because of the smell?" Defensively, she thought, "Poor Zahir!"

Walking into her old room with the bottle of pain medication and a spoon, Aimee was surprised to see that Zahir was holding the large, grey-striped cat. Still bandaged, his wounds weren't in danger of infection.

Ponce looked up at her wide-eyed.

"Mia is in here *again,*" she complained in a teasing way. "How long has she been here?"

"All night, I guess," Zahir replied gravely, his eyes listless as he patted the cat. "She was sleeping on me when I woke up."

Aimee didn't admit to her own cat encounter.

137

"Cats are killers!" she remarked derisively, measuring out a spoonful of the pain medication. Ever since her pet bird had been eaten by Ripple, Aimee was distrustful of the whole species.

Cuddling it closer, Zahir disagreed, "This one is very fluffy and warm. She wouldn't hurt a thing."

"She's huge," Aimee argued merrily, giving Zahir his dosage. "I'm sure she could take down a dog!"

Her patients laughed. Zahir's eyes brightened a little and Aimee smiled.

"Feel how soft she is," he said.

"She's a cat," Aimee stated flatly, picking up some used bandages from the floor. "She's hunts small animals and... *birds!* Plus, she's not supposed to be in here when you have open wounds."

"Listen to her purr," Zahir encouraged, with a slight smile. "Isn't that such a relaxing sound? I don't think Mia has ever killed anything... not squirrels, or rabbits, certainly not *dogs!*"

Laughing, Aimee couldn't resist the appeal. She reached out and patted the cat. Mia was soft and she eased into the patting and purred even louder.

"Okay," Aimee relented graciously, "I'll like one cat... but only because she's still innocent." Picking her up, Aimee added, "But for now she has to go back outside."

Zahir looked forlorn when Aimee took the cat. Taking it outside, she coaxed it to head back to the meadow. Then she walked back up the stairs and washed her hands carefully in the soapy water before re-entering the room.

Later that afternoon, Georgia and Lily came in to read to the patients. With their hair still wet from the mandatory shower, the two girls dragged in the book and laid it against Ponce's bed. Georgia sat down on the chair in between the two patients.

"It smells better in here today," the pretty blond girl observed happily. "I can deal with this." Positioning herself close to the dark-haired patient, she said cheerfully, "Oh good, this chair is on the *right* side."

Aimee looked over with a quizzical expression. The chair was actually on the left side of Zahir.

Lowering her head down to look at the patient from the level of the mattress, Georgia smiled, "From here you look just like your old self, Zahir! Once all those scabs fall off, I'm sure you'll be right back to the way you were!"

Kenzie quickly walked out of the room.

Aimee glanced over to see a dark look cross Zahir's face.

Sitting back up, Georgia looked curiously at Zahir. She leaned over and frowned. "Is there something wrong with your eye?" she asked.

"I hope not," he answered wearily.

Suddenly alarmed, Aimee drew closer. "Which eye?" she asked, and then she noticed the cloudiness.

Zahir put his hand over his left eye and stared out the window with his right. "There is a dark spot," he admitted despairingly. "I keep hoping it will go away."

Immediately, Uncle Louis and Aimee wanted to know all the details. Kenzie came back in and listened carefully as Zahir explained that he had just started noticing a small dark spot in his vision.

"It looks kind of weird," Georgia stated in a matter-of-fact way. "I can't believe *no one else* has noticed," she added with a reproachful glance in Aimee's direction.

The thought that Zahir might have another injury and more pain to endure distressed Aimee greatly. She couldn't bear Georgia's blunt assessments of her patient, or the implication that the nurses weren't doing a good job. On the verge of tears, she rebuked her housemate sharply. "How can you say that? Zahir has enough to deal with! He doesn't need to be told that his eye looks *weird!* That's just... *mean!*"

"It's okay, Aimee," her patient pleaded. "You all need to be completely honest with me. Just tell me the truth."

It was one thing to deal with Georgia's taunts and the heart-wrenching news that Zahir had another injury, but to have her favourite patient imply that she wasn't being honest added to the hurt. Folding her arms across her chest, the young nurse's face flushed red.

"I wish you had listened to me, Zahir," Georgia protested regretfully. "You should never have gone into that fire!"

Zahir swallowed hard and closed his eyes.

"Aimee," Uncle Louis called out sharply, before the copper-haired nurse could react. "Come here, I want to show you something."

Walking indignantly to the other end of the room, Aimee heard Kenzie lash out. "If he had listened to you, he wouldn't be able to forgive himself now. And that would be worse!"

Ignoring the remark, Georgia began telling the patients that she'd found a new exciting adventure to read.

No one replied.

Reaching the elder Tiny's bedside, Aimee looked back to see Georgia ruffling Zahir's dark, curly hair, "Come on, Zahir, don't look so serious!" the tall blond teased as she picked up his hand. "I'm here with you," she laughed. "I *love you* regardless of how you look. Come on," she coaxed, "where's your smile?"

"What are we reading about?" Zahir asked flatly.

"It's all about a boy who was stranded on the ocean for many days," she told him excitedly. "He escaped from a burning ship with a very large dog. It's kind of like our flood and fire experiences mixed in together."

Georgia began reading. Lily held Ponce's hand and listened.

Uncle Louis had his own big book open. He pointed eagerly to some of the words and Aimee knelt down beside him and read them silently. She didn't know who had written the book or was giving the message. All she knew was that the words had a quiet, calming effect on her distressed and resentful heart. *"Love your enemies, do good to those who hate you, bless those who curse you, pray for those who abuse you. To one who strikes you on the cheek, offer the other also, and from one who takes away your cloak do not withhold your tunic either. Give to everyone who begs from you, and from one who takes away your goods do not demand them back. And as you wish that others would do to you, do so to them."*

She reread them a few times to herself, as Uncle Louis stroked her hair gently. "There's a better way," he whispered.

"What is this book?" she begged curiously.

"I'm going to tell you soon, very soon," he replied quietly, "but I thought you needed this now." He smiled and whispered, "Remember, *'as you wish that others would do to you, do so to them.'*"

Nodding glumly, Aimee looked up at Uncle Louis. Had she followed his advice earlier, she wouldn't have said things in the past that she regretted, things she had still not made up for. She recognized that having an angry tiff with Georgia in front of Zahir was not going to make anyone feel better. She sighed and patted his arm. "Okay," she agreed.

Aimee could not have explained the calming effect of the words she had just read. Had the French psychologist observed the interchange from the other side of the dome, she might have pointed out to Jacques Lemans that this was a step toward the state of 'well-being'. Don't just listen to yourself – *talk* to yourself. Instead of allowing her to be tossed to and fro with turbulent emotions and distorted views, Uncle Louis had encouraged her to master powerful feelings with guiding principles.

Seeing that Kenzie had started cleaning the floors, Aimee got up to organize the supplies. As the others listened to Georgia's story, she looked out at the tumultuous lake and thought to herself, "Maybe my feelings are like those waves. Some are good and fun to ride, and some are just... destructive... to everyone." She recalled how the surfers had called Odin a 'rolling tumbler' - a wave that looked good but tossed them hard headfirst and left them feeling regret and despair. As she took out the empty bottles of medicine and placed them by the stairs, she reflected unhappily, "And they called *me* a 'whoosh,' and... well, sometimes I do fizzle out way too soon." In the hallway, she tucked all the used bandages in the pots to be taken out to the train. Picking up the jar of washing water, she took it outside to dump on the grass. Vahid had brought in a clean supply that morning. Marching back up the stairs, she thought, "There are waves that aren't worth catching – like today – jealousy and resentment. I'm glad Uncle Louis stopped me before I said things that would have made everyone upset. Maybe those are 'rolling tumblers!'"

Coming back into the Caring Center the young nurse looked out the big windows to see a smooth, glassy wave holding its peak all the way in. "The beach boys would like that one," she thought. With a smile she remembered the thrill of riding a good wave in, even though she had only ever caught them near shore. Glancing over at the three patients in the room who were doing so much better and recovering well, she held up her head and told herself, "And then there are some waves, like compassion and...*love*, that can give us the power to help others in wonderful ways. Those are the waves that bring joy."

Diya brought in clean blankets and took out the used bedding. Vahid walked up the stairs bringing another pot of fresh water and taking out the used supplies. He had volunteered to take over Odin's job. Tina and Yu Yan stretched out on the spare bed, enjoying the story.

At the far end of the room, Uncle Louis was still facing the window, reading his new book. Sweeping the floor, Aimee was intrigued, wondering what other wise words of advice the book might hold. The older man was deeply absorbed in it for hours on end. When was he going to share it with all of them and why was he waiting?

Mia popped back in through the window and headed for Zahir. Since all the open wounds were covered back up, Uncle Louis wasn't concerned. "Just don't let her touch your face," he warned, as the cat curled up on the young man's chest and looked up at him contentedly with adoring eyes.

While Georgia continued reading, loud purrs reverberated through the room as the scarred patient stroked the animal's head. Still not completely ready to forgive 'killer cats,' Aimee did love to hear them purring.

The words that Uncle Louis had pointed out to her began to affect her conscience. The recognition that she wanted to ride waves of compassion and love began to make an impact. Aimee had never made amends for telling Georgia that she 'hated' her. As the minutes ticked by, the copper-haired nurse realised there *was* a better way, a way that might help make peace, and please Uncle Louis.

When Georgia reached the end of the chapter and paused to turn the page, Aimee was standing nearby. In a pleasant tone she spoke up, "I just want to say thank you for telling us about Zahir's eye," she said kindly. "Now we'll know to watch it carefully. Maybe there is something we can do to help him."

The blond-haired storyteller looked up in surprise, without any appreciation for the gracious acknowledgment Aimee had made. At that very moment, a loud shout came from across the hall. Franz had beaten Damien in chess and was celebrating his victory.

"I'm so tired of being in here!" they heard Damien call out despondently.

"Sore loser!" Lema teased. "Come on! You beat me all the time!"

Damien ran into the Crisis Room. "Uncle Louis," he begged desperately, "How much longer do we have to stay in here? I love the nights, but I *hate* the days! I want to surf! I need to get out of here!"

Rolling over, the older Tiny asked to see his wounds. Remembering the advice Rachel had given him before he had returned to Paradise,

Uncle Louis was pleased to see dry scabs. With a smile he said, "You can leave, as long as you keep yourselves clean. But no surfing until those scabs come off, which might take a couple more days. If you're in the water for too long they will get soft and you may get an infection. And if you have any bleeding or pus, you need to come back and have the nurses check you over."

"So, we're free to go? Night and day?"

"You are, as long as you're *careful.*"

"He said *no* surfing," Franz complained.

"Just a couple more days," Damien clarified. "There are other things we can do!" Leaping up, he shouted out joyfully. "Let's go! Rosa's Hill, here I come!"

Uncle Louis frowned. "Um, maybe that's not a good idea either, just yet. You might scrape those wounds and get dirt in them."

"Come on, Uncle Louis," Damien argued. "We've never fallen out of the go-karts. We'll drive carefully." Looking over at the girls, he said, "Hey, why don't you all take a break and come with us?"

Still holding Zahir's hand, Georgia looked up with interest. "I'm reading right now," she replied, "but I'll come after dinner tonight."

"Me too," Lily smiled. "I haven't done anything fun for *so long!*"

Ponce pouted, but Lily didn't notice. Lema and Franz were standing in the doorway looking in with eager anticipation.

Damien extended the invitation to Tina and Yu Yan, and they agreed to come. It had been nearly a week since the fire when all their regular activities had ceased.

Diya appeared with an armful of clean bed sheets and a new pair of swim shorts for Damien, since his other ones had been singed.

"Let's get Diya to come!" Lema chuckled.

Addressing the pretty, dark-skinned girl, Damien said, "Diya, you don't know what you're missing. You sit in here sewing all day and never have any fun. You've got to try it. Pick any one of us for your driver, and we'll give you the best ride."

It was actually the first time anyone had put pressure on Diya to join in. She was always so committed to sewing, with so many orders to fill, that no one thought of encouraging her to participate.

Looking up with a pleased expression, Diya said, "I wouldn't mind trying it, as long as I have a safe driver."

"Pick me or Lema," Damien suggested with a mocking glance in Franz' direction. "Franz has only one speed and it's way too fast!"

An argument ensued, but eventually Diya said she would try all three and see who she thought was the best.

Looking over at Aimee stacking the bedsheets in a neat pile on the couch, Damien smiled. "What about you, Nurse Aimee? You need to do something exciting too. You must be bored out of your mind in here. I know you're not afraid of go-karting anymore. Why don't *you* join us after dinner?"

Aimee shook her head. "Thanks for asking," she replied evenly, "but I have lots to do in here." In all truthfulness, the Crisis Room was exactly where she wanted to be.

"Everyone but the whoosh then," Damien grumbled. "Well, that's fine. See you girls after dinner! I'm out of here!"

Hollering excitedly, the beach boys exited the Caring Centre.

"Don't listen to his names," Zahir mumbled as Georgia turned the page for the next chapter. "Don't let it bother you."

Aimee looked up appreciatively as she collected the dirty dishes, but deep inside the name did bother her. "There's some truth to it," she sighed, setting the bowls down in the hallway for the kitchen crew to take back.

Georgia spoke up. "Damien isn't trying to be mean," she said defensively. "He makes up names just like you sing songs. He calls me Gorgeo," she giggled.

Zahir prodded, "Aimee, what do you mean there's truth to it?"

She explained, "A whoosh is a wave that fizzles out just when you think it's going to be good." With a shrug she admitted, "Sometimes I give up too soon."

"You *are* afraid of a lot of things," her blond housemate agreed.

Zahir frowned and Aimee held her tongue.

Rolling over in his bed, Uncle Louis gave Aimee a smile of encouragement. Seeing that Tina and Yu Yan were looking bored, he addressed them, saying, "You girls have done an excellent job caring for everyone. With the beach boys leaving, I think it will be best if you resume normal life and are available *outside* for any other injuries. Kenzie and Aimee can handle the rest of us in here from now on."

Looking up gratefully, Kenzie smiled.

Tina and Yu Yan didn't wait for the story to be over; they were happy to leave. Georgia began the next chapter, but seeing the patients were struggling to stay awake, she excused herself to go make dinner. "There's so much work in that kitchen *every day!*" she complained. Glancing in Aimee's direction she taunted, "I'll be so glad when you go back to your old job. I haven't had *any time* to work on my books or my paintings!"

Aimee nodded, but she didn't commit. For now, she was very happy with her new assignment.

Standing up, Georgia begged Uncle Louis, "Can I please have my room back tonight? It's not needed anymore, right?"

Kenzie looked over at Aimee. "Want to help me switch the beds around?" he asked.

The copper-haired girl nodded, and the two nurses headed off to clean up Georgia's room. Leaving the adventure book behind in the hall, the tall blond said a loving goodbye to the sleepy Zahir and ran off to collect food from the garden. It was nap time in the Caring Centre.

Treats

wo hours later the three extra beds that were no longer needed had been stored neatly in a spare room downstairs. The sheets were washed and hung to dry, and Georgia's bed was back in its former position. The Caring Center now consisted of one room, two nurses, three patients, and the occasional cat.

Peeking into the room and seeing that nap time was over, Aimee sat down on the couch. Mia was purring on Zahir's chest, Ponce was exercising his elbows and Uncle Louis was once again on his side, facing the window. It looked like he was asleep until his arm moved to turn pages in the big book. Lately, it was his favourite position.

Eager for some conversation, she asked her patients, "What do you want to do the most when you are all better?"

"Fishing," Zahir replied instantly. "I miss early morning fishing."

Ponce laughed. "Lily says we're getting married," he said. "Sounds like a great plan to me."

"Plans are good," Zahir agreed, as he stroked Mia's soft fur with his good arm. "We need some sort of a purpose for life. Otherwise, every day just comes and goes and before we know it our lives will be over."

Uncle Louis looked over with interest. "What kind of a plan do you have in mind, Zahir?"

"I don't know," he sighed. "It just seems like there should be something more. I don't really know what's missing."

Looking over with empathy, Aimee saw the dark brooding look in his dull blue eyes. Something was bothering him, and she didn't know what it was or how to ask.

"I might have a purpose for you," Uncle Louis told him.

"Really?" Zahir looked up with interest.

"I'm going to tell you about it tonight after dinner," he promised.

Ponce had been thinking about his own plans and he piped up dreamily, "I'd like to make the North Forest a place that everyone can enjoy."

"That's a grand vision," Uncle Louis encouraged. "What do you have in mind?"

"I think I'll call it the Fun Forest," he replied happily. "I'd like to have rope swings and bridges in between the trees. I want the girls to enjoy it as much as the guys. What do you think, Aimee?" he asked. "Would you come if we built swings and had bridges to walk on?"

"That sounds like fun," she agreed.

As they discussed other ways to change the North Forest into an activity centre for girls and guys, they heard a loud series of crashes in the distance. "What was that?" they all asked.

"Something fell over," Ponce said.

Aimee told him about the tree outside Lily's room.

"Maybe Odin is taking down some of the burnt trees," Ponce suggested.

Satisfied with his suggestion, Uncle Louis was giving some tips on how to support the tree bridges, when Sanaa and Lema came up the stairs with dinner.

"Look what we're having today!" Sanaa exclaimed, giggling merrily. There was a plate of fried fish in her hands.

Zahir's face lit up.

"I caught it myself!" Lema boasted, carrying the other plates, "and Georgia fried it. She's getting really good in that kitchen."

"Thank you!" Zahir said with delight, as Sanaa handed him a plateful. "I've been *dreaming* of fried fish!"

"And there are more treats," Sanaa laughed, as they divvied out the fish to everyone. "Georgia decided to put strawberries in the salad and mmm, it's good. You're going to love it!"

"Yes!" Lema cheered, bringing in the bowls of salad. "And Lily mixed some oil and honey together and sprinkled it all over... *and it is tasty!*" Clapping his hands together, and making his limbs move in ways that he and Sanaa had perfected, Lema danced around the room.

"This fish is amazing!" Zahir exclaimed, savouring the tasty morsels. He glanced over at Lema. "You have no idea how much I appreciate this!"

"Or maybe I do..." the tall, black Tiny laughed.

"I'm not so sure about the strawberries," Ponce grimaced, looking at his bowlful, "but if Lily was in on this, then I guess I'd better like it too." He chuckled.

After two painful arm movements, he groaned, "It hurts so much to feed myself."

Aimee came over to help Ponce eat, even as Uncle Louis reminded him about the importance of moving his arms often while his wounds healed. "I'll do one, you do one," Aimee suggested, bringing a forkful of salad to his mouth.

With a groan, Ponce munched on the salad and took the fork to slowly pick up the next mouthful.

Lema sat down to talk to his friends and inquire about their injuries. Having not had the opportunity to tell him before, they both thanked him profusely for the buckets of water that he dumped on them in the fire. Without him, they knew their injuries would have been much worse.

With a smile, Lema appreciated their gratitude. They shared recollections of the ordeal for a while.

When there was a break in the conversation, Sanaa looked over at Aimee excitedly, clapped her hands together and said, "Guess what? Today when the train came in, *guess* what was on it?"

As Aimee helped Ponce with his meal, she tried to think of things, but nothing she suggested was correct.

"Lots of *birds!*" her friend laughed, clapping her hands and wiggling her hips. "Lots of them! So many lorikeets that I couldn't count them all. And bluebirds and cardinals."

With excitement, Aimee looked out the window. In the sky she could see colourful birds flying around the orchards. Flocks of birds! "Yes!" she cried out joyfully. "Oh, I'm *so* glad!"

"And rabbits," Lema chuckled. "Five new little rabbits. And lots of butterflies, bees and fireflies. There were even two more bats since the others completely disappeared. Can't miss mango blooming season."

Ponce had finished his salad, so Aimee ran over to give Sanaa a hug of joy.

"I miss you!" Sanaa exclaimed, hugging her back. "I hardly see you anymore."

"I miss you too," Aimee replied.

"I will personally ensure that all the cats have collars!" Sanaa promised her friend. "We don't want any more dead birds!"

Zahir plucked Mia's collar. The bell tinkled. "Mia's good," he announced.

Uncle Louis was laughing. "Aimee," he smiled, "I want you to take a well-deserved break. Go feed the animals with your friends and see what is new. There will be time to fix up your patients when you get back."

"Really?" Aimee said, looking all around. "But it's almost time to change the bandages."

Zahir had his mouth full of salad, but he nodded in agreement, and Ponce said he would be fine until she had returned.

When Zahir had swallowed, he encouraged, "Go have fun and then you can tell us all about it." With an affectionate chuckle he added, "But please come back. We need you."

Flashing a grateful smile in Zahir's direction, Aimee ran outside with Sanaa and Lema. She spent a glorious hour spotting new birds in the trees and finding baby rabbits at the compost pile. Lema helped her bring back a carrycart of compost treats for the deer and squirrels on Rainbow Hill, while Sanaa chatted about all the goings on. It had been well over a week since she had last fed the animals. Her friends took a seat on the bench swing to watch the deer finish off their treats while Aimee quickly showered and changed her clothes. Re-entering the Caring Centre she gave a glowing report to her restless patients.

The New Books

Chapter 19

*A*fter only a few rounds of go-karting that evening, Kenzie returned early to see how the patients were faring. Still a little wet from the shower, water droplets glistened in his brown curly hair. With at least two to three showers a day, the nurses had never been so clean!

Looking around, Uncle Louis was pleased to see that the four Tinys in the room were the exact group the Professor had suggested could take part in the investigation. He was confident that all the other Tinys were enjoying evening activities and wouldn't be back until dark. They had at least two precious hours.

"Take a seat, Kenzie," he encouraged. "I have something to share with the four of you."

Kenzie looked over at Aimee who was sitting on the couch. She patted the seat next to her. "There's room," she smiled.

When everyone was settled and looking at him expectantly, Uncle Louis began, "I have two new books that I am allowed to only read with the four of you. We have a mission to sort out truth from error, so that we can then share truth with the others here in Paradise. The Professor has reluctantly given the five of us permission to investigate, but that's all. For now, we will keep this a secret and read only when we are alone together. Is everyone okay with that?"

"This is a good time to do it," Kenzie nodded enthusiastically. "Evenings are a fun time for the others, at least until it gets dark. No one else will be here but us."

"And the days are lengthening." Uncle Louis replied, looking up at the new clock on the wall. "It's been light until eight-thirty lately."

Looking over at Kenzie and Aimee, Uncle Louis asked, "You both don't mind staying here in the evenings and missing out on all the fun?"

Kenzie and Aimee shared glances and nodded eagerly. A secret mission was exciting to at least four in the room. Aimee was already intrigued by the new book.

Ponce sighed. "Is this like school?"

"Don't worry," Louis assured him. "It *is* like school, but I won't be upset if you fall asleep."

"Good," Ponce sighed, "because I'm *way* too tired for school."

"What is it about?" Aimee begged, eager to begin.

Having the attention of the others, Uncle Louis asked, "Have you ever thought about where life came from?"

"The Mastermind of Paradise?" Aimee answered, frowning just a little.

"The Professor made us, didn't he?" Kenzie asked.

Uncle Louis looked at them steadily. "This is our mission," he said. "We need to find out *who* or *what* made us. The answer to this question greatly impacts our sense *of purpose*, our morality, and our hope for life after death."

"*Is* there life after death?" Zahir inquired earnestly.

Uncle Louis saw the angst in the questioner's blue eyes. He quickly pondered that of the five Tinys in the Crisis Room, only one was without a 'near-death' experience. Rather than reply directly, he said, "I have two books. One tells us that we are alive by chance. All the plants, animals and people that we see here in Paradise were randomly generated, with no purpose or design. It all just happened without a plan or a planner."

"But that doesn't make sense," Zahir interrupted. "Obviously, the Professor designed us very well."

Pausing for a moment, the older Tiny answered slowly, "The book that I'm telling you about was written by... *the Professor.* You see, the Professor didn't make us; he only made our lives *possible* by taking life from his world and miniaturizing it. He believes that everything in his world happened through wonderful coincidence, even though he knows how much research and thought he put into building Paradise."

Wide eyes looked over at Uncle Louis with astonishment, and then disappointment set in as they realised the implications.

"But if life just happened by chance, then it's not likely we can get it back," Aimee reasoned sadly. "Who would give it to us?"

"Yes," Kenzie agreed. With astonishment, he asked, "Why did the Professor *miniaturize* us?"

"He feels Paradise is a much happier place to live in than his own world," Uncle Louis replied.

"But if the Professor had to work so hard to make Paradise," Zahir reflected, still considering the issue, "then someone had to *make* the Professor's world."

Uncle Louis smiled, "So, the other book I have was written by a Being called God, who claims He made the Professor's world, the landforms, the universe and *all life* – the people, the animals, the birds, the plants - *everything.* He also promises that He can bring us back to life if we die."

"God?" Zahir questioned, his good eye lighting up. "Well, that sounds more hopeful. Why have we never heard of God before?"

"That's a question we will need to answer," Uncle Louis acknowledged, "but first we need to read both books and sort out which one holds the truth."

"The Professor is okay with this?" Aimee clarified nervously.

"Somewhat," Uncle Louis nodded. "He has agreed to this reluctantly. That's why he wants us to keep this discussion private until we've made a decision about which one is true."

They all nodded but Ponce was already drifting off to sleep.

"All right," Uncle Louis said, "which book should we start with?"

Everyone voted for the one that involved a purposeful designer and a hope for life after death.

Uncle Louis asked Aimee to read the first chapter.

"In the beginning," she read, *"God created the heaven and the earth."*

"What is the *earth?"* she asked.

Uncle Louis had explored many of the chapters in Genesis and the Gospel accounts before the fire. From what he'd seen on the Internet, he was able to explain that the earth was the 'big' world, an enormous round ball with large bodies of water and vast expanses of land. He told them that the whole sphere floated in dark space. Paradise was only a tiny speck situated on the huge planet Earth.

Ponce piped up drowsily, "Hey, you're finally telling us about the *big* world."

"Maybe you don't want to fall asleep just yet?" Uncle Louis chuckled.

"No way! I'm wide awake now," Ponce insisted, sitting up in his bed.

Aimee read on, *"The earth was without form and void, and darkness was upon the face of the deep. And the spirit of God moved upon the face of the waters. And God said, "Let there be light, and there was light."*

Astounded, Aimee blurted out, "Did this God just speak words and it happened? How powerful is He? Is this for real?"

"That's what we have to determine," Uncle Louis smiled.

Excited, Aimee read on and on. They discovered that the dry land was called Earth and that God claimed to have made all the plants and trees!

Then she read, *"Let us make man in our image, after our likeness. And let them have dominion over the fish of the sea and over the fowl of the air, and over the cattle, and over all the earth, and over every creeping thing that creeps on the earth. So, God created man in His own image, in the image of God He created him; male and female He created them."*

It was an astonishing thought. "People are made in the image of God?" she exclaimed. "He has made us *like* Him?"

Kenzie pondered the idea. "If Vinitha used clay to make the image of a sunflower, then it would look like a sunflower, right?"

"It would indeed, Kenzie," Uncle Louis nodded.

"Then do we look like God?"

"What do you think, everyone?"

"Well," Aimee pondered as the setting sun began to cast rays of light into the room, "if this book is true, then it sounds like it's telling us that we must look like the one who made us." Tingling with excitement, she said, "We wouldn't survive without the Professor looking after us, so maybe God looks after His world in the same way. Maybe this God is the *Mastermind* of the Professor's world and the Professor doesn't even know it."

Uncle Louis nodded. "It's worth an investigation, isn't it?"

"I don't know," Ponce remarked warily. "If the Professor doesn't believe in God, then why should we?"

"That's a good question," Uncle Louis acknowledged.

Zahir was troubled. "But you say the Professor is a very intelligent man, so why wouldn't he know about God?" he challenged. "This seems too important for him to miss!"

"That thought has kept me awake many nights, Zahir," Uncle Louis admitted wearily. "So, we are going to read the Professor's book as well. He is certainly very intelligent and has had years of research and education – far beyond what any of us can ever hope for. And he is a good man, whom I love dearly. However, the promises and the guidance that I read about in the Bible seem to be what I've been searching for. But, if the Professor says something is wrong, I am very hesitant to tell anyone otherwise. This is the reason I need all of you to help me decide what is true."

Bewildered, Zahir looked over at Uncle Louis. "Have you not had anyone to talk to about this?" he asked compassionately.

"No," Uncle Louis sighed heavily. "This has been a distressing and yet exhilarating discovery. I'm so thankful to be able to share it with the four of you."

They read on to learn that God had made the first man from the ground and breathed into his nostrils the breath of life. Molded dust had been energized by God's spirit, creating a *'living soul.'* [49]

"So, it's God's breath of life that makes things come alive," Zahir considered. With a smile he asked, "Did He do CPR on us?"

Uncle Louis chuckled. "There are some similarities," he considered.

Aimee, who was sitting beside the Bible, spoke up. "There are some notes written beside that verse," she said. "The first one says, 'Job thirty-four, verses fourteen and fifteen.'"

Uncle Louis pointed out the tags on the edge of the pages that marked each separate book by name. While Aimee looked for the passage, the older man explained that the Bible was a collection of many books, penned by many writers who all claimed to be recording the words of God.

---

[49] Genesis 2:7 (KJV) 'soul' – Hebrew (Strong's H5315) 'nephesh' – 'a breathing creature, animal, vitality, soul, beast, body, breath, creature, appetite, fish, person, etc.'

Finding the passage in Job, the copper-haired nurse read, *"If He should set His heart to it and gather to Himself His spirit and His breath, all flesh would perish together, and man would return to dust."*

"So, this spirit can be given and taken away," Kenzie observed. He looked over at Uncle Louis. "And you say that God can give it back again?"

"There are four more references in the margin," Aimee piped up. Following the second pencilled-in passage, she turned to Psalm 146, and read, *"Put not your trust in princes, in a son of man, in whom there is no salvation. When his breath departs, he returns to the earth; on that very day his plans perish."* Reading the comment scribbled in beside the verse, she added, "It says here that 'plans' actually means 'thoughts.'"[50]

"Hmm," Zahir pondered. "That's like the reverse of the first passage. We lose our breath; we go back to dust and our thoughts end. Are there anymore notes?"

Aimee followed the passages in order. The last one stirred excitement. John chapter six said, *"And this is the will of Him who sent me, that I should lose nothing of all that He has given me, but raise it up on the last day. For this is the will of my Father, that everyone who looks on the Son and believes in him should have eternal life, and I will raise him up on the last day."*

"That's more like it!" Zahir said excitedly, sitting up in bed. "We will be raised up... on the *last day*... somehow... What is *eternal* life? When is the last day? Who is making this promise?"

Uncle Louis answered two of his questions, "Eternal life means never dying again. The person making this promise is Jesus, God's Son." He sighed, "This book is so big. I want to read it to you all at once, but I've also promised to read the Professor's book."

---

[50] Hebrew (Strong's H6250) 'eshtonah' – 'thinking: - thought'

"We've got to read about Jesus!" Zahir pleaded. "It sounds like he is the one who will give life back to us if we die."

"Yes, we do need to read about Jesus," Uncle Louis agreed. "Especially since he is now *my* new role model. I would encourage all of you to be like Jesus."

Recalling that Zahir had once said that he wanted to be like Uncle Louis, Aimee looked up and caught her friend's eye. They shared a smile.

Having already taken an hour reading God's Book, Kenzie volunteered to read a chapter from the Professor's. After only two pages, everything they had just learned was turned upside down. Instead of a plan and a purpose, a designer and a guardian, the Professor explained the universe had randomly come into being by chance explosions, fabulously incredible and very timely mutations, and the survival and reproduction of the fittest at the expense of the weak. It was a nasty beginning with no care or concern for life or those with reduced capabilities, but a mad, amoral rush for the selfish betterment of each individual. Instead of portraying God as a merciful Being who encourages everyone to rise to His level by caring for one another and living by His standards, the Professor labelled 'God' as a mythical character who took sadistic pleasure in obliterating people in fits of anger, inflicting suffering and burdensome rules, punishing the victim instead of the perpetrator... the accusations went on and on.

Kenzie continued to read the Professor's words, *"The universe we see and study has the exact features we should expect if it evolved without any purpose or design, but rather came together through remarkable, random occurrences that led to the increasing complexity of life."*

"No purpose?" Zahir repeated despondently, lying back down. "But how can anything that functions well just happen without a

plan? Our boats and our go-karts all required planning, a lot of experimenting and careful work."

"I agree," Uncle Louis piped up. "And our miniature world required years of planning, research and design on the Professor's part. It didn't just come together on its own. I remember the daily reports he gave me. It was an intense effort!"

As Kenzie continued to read, he came to a section where the Professor referred to various fables about the beginning of life, saying, *"In reference to the book that has beguiled many in the past, it would be an exaggeration to state that the Bible is evil. Instead, it is a bizarre compilation, as you would expect from a ragtag group of authors, composed of many violent and immoral tales. Some are idealistic and perhaps comforting like a good fairy tale, while other accounts are so unbelievable that it is a wonder anyone has been foolish enough to think they could occur. For instance, whenever has one man's voice parted the depths of the sea in the middle of the night, so that millions of people could walk across dry ground to the other side? Anyone with a high school education can appreciate that such a scenario is well beyond the forces of nature, as are many other similar accounts of 'miraculous' occurrences recorded in the Bible. It is obvious that these stories have been fabricated in order to elevate 'God' to the realm of the supernatural, which has misled so many naïve followers to believe he was worthy of worship and submission. However, to be fair, centuries of revisions, translations and attempted improvements have, no doubt, caused these stories to evolve fantastically beyond the original accounts. We have no idea if what we read today is even close to the original manuscripts."*

"Oh," Zahir said, sounding deflated. "So, what we just read in Genesis may not be the actual words of God... *even if He's real?* The Bible has been changed over and over?"

"Those are the questions we need to answer," Uncle Louis replied. "Is this accusation against the Bible based on true facts, or is it perhaps... an exaggeration?"

"I'll write it down," Aimee offered, running to get her nurse's journal and a pencil.

When they finished the Professor's first chapter and had written a few more questions, Aimee remarked, "This is not a happy book. I don't feel excited to read it. I feel disappointed and sad."

"Me too," Zahir agreed.

"Kinda depressing," added Ponce, who had managed to stay awake.

"I promised I would give you the opportunity to hear both sides," Uncle Louis smiled. "There must be some reason the Professor has such a negative view of God and the purposelessness of life. We need to hear him out."

"Maybe he explains it later on in the book," Kenzie piped up. "This is only the first chapter."

Outside the sky was darkening and a beautiful sunset was glowing across the lake. They could hear several Tinys swimming in the water. Laughter rang out across the hills. Around the window in the Crisis Room, the solar lights came on automatically, illuminating everyone with a soft glow.

"I suppose the others will be coming home soon?" Uncle Louis considered. "Maybe we should stop there for the night."

"Please, can you just read about Jesus until they start coming in?" Zahir begged.

"Why don't we take a quick break," Kenzie suggested. "I'll get the three of you ready for the night, and then we can read for as long as it's possible?"

"Sounds great," Ponce agreed wearily. "I'm *so* tired! I just want to sleep."

Kenzie's idea was adopted. Aimee left the room to watch the sunset outside, while Kenzie helped the patients walk around, stretch their sores and get ready for the night. Hoping to sit on the swinging bench, she was surprised to see that Sanaa and Lema were already there.

"You're not go-karting tonight?" she asked.

"No," Sanaa replied sheepishly, "We were just enjoying the view."

For a moment Aimee wondered if they had overheard their book reading discussion. She decided not to ask, thinking, "I hope they *have* been listening. I wish I could invite them in."

There was another loud crash in the forest. "It sounds like Odin is busy in the Fun Forest," Aimee stated with a smile, sitting down on the deck beside her friends. "Maybe he's making something good."

Pairing Off

Chapter 20

ointing to the list on the Student Information System that same evening, Evan was eager to show the Professor his final marks. He had an average of ninety-one percent.

"*Oh là là!*" the Professor smiled, clapping Evan on the back. "You're that much closer to your master's degree."

"Yes, I am," Evan agreed, as they both walked over to the dome. "Perhaps only one more semester to go."

"And then you can do research for the Greenville University, right?" the Professor pleaded. "I need you here as long as this project continues."

"I'm fully committed," Evan assured him as they stood side by side in front of the large terrarium. They glanced intently at one another. The Professor couldn't imagine running Paradise without Evan's assistance, and Evan knew he could never leave the Tinys until the project had come to an end. They were both staying.

"Have you made any progress with the fish eggs?" the Professor inquired, walking slowly around the lake toward Rainbow Hill.

"No, I've given up," Evan said quietly, but then he knew he had to explain. "You see, Jacques," he said hesitantly, "I'm not interested in this type of genetic manipulation anymore. We both realise our Paradise project isn't ethically sound because it is a social experiment based on personal motives... even though we hoped it might benefit the human race at the start. That's why we've had to keep it hidden and why we now face serious consequences for our actions. Over the past few months, I've become convinced that what we've done was morally wrong in God's eyes. I feel guilty for my involvement even though I didn't fully realise at the start that it was wrong to tamper with God's creation. I've apologized to God and asked for His forgiveness... "

"What are you saying?" the Professor remarked in dismay, even as he felt a twinge of conscience himself. "Evan, how far will this go? You're getting mixed up with very delusional ideas."

"I'm letting the evidence lead me."

"Evidence!" the Professor retorted.

Having watched a scientific documentary the night before, Evan felt he had another appeal to make to his mentor. "Macro Evolution is not science," he pleaded. "It is a *theory* of history.[51] Creation is also a theory of history. There may be scientific facts put forward to support both theories, but in the end, evolution and creation cannot be experimentally proven or repeated. Therefore, I would argue that Macro Evolution is *not* true science. Let's face it, Jacques, you can't breed Cocker Spaniels and get back to wolves because there's no genetic information left to revert back to the wild. It has to be reintroduced. You and I both know that mutations do not *add* new, useful information to DNA, information can only be *lost.*"

"With enough time, I'm sure that good mutations do occur..."

"Enough to account for the vast variety of life we see all around us?" Evan argued. "And how did so many species survive while waiting for the next mutation to be beneficial and functional? Jacques, think about it. There's remarkable forethought and anticipation in nature. There are systems in place to *repair* and protect every organism from accidents, disease, bacteria and viruses! Can evolution

---

[51] "Dismantled – A Scientific Deconstruction of Evolution"
https://Creation.com

– a blind, random, unintelligent force - anticipate the need to repair, and create internal defenders? Everything we study speaks to an intelligence far beyond any human ability..."

"The supernatural," Jacques muttered, unwilling to show the deeply disconcerting effect that such arguments were having on his mind. "I don't believe in the supernatural."

For a few minutes they both silently walked around the dome, observing the beautiful world they had put together. They saw Kenzie helping Ponce down the stairs toward the outhouse. Zahir was walking slowly behind but on his own. Suddenly, Evan noticed a large swath of trees that had collapsed on the far side of Rainbow Hill. "What happened to all those trees?" he said in alarm.

Coming to his side, Jacques looked in with astonishment. "I have no idea," he replied. "It looks like someone chopped them down!"

"Who would do that?"

They both looked in closely. "No, no," Evan observed. "Their roots are still attached. Either they were pushed over, or they *fell* over."

"It is the steep side," the older scientist deliberated. "I'll do some research. Maybe they aren't getting enough sunlight, or nutrients." Looking in more closely, he asked, "They weren't chewed on by the deer, by any chance?"

But there was no evidence they had been damaged by anything.

"More wood for Zahir to carve when he's back on his feet," Evan smiled.

Carrying on around the dome, the young scientist noticed that Sanaa and Lema were digging deep into the ground on Mining Hill. "Looking for treasure," Evan remarked with a smile. "Now that everyone has seen the ruby, there may be a few more attempts."

"They are in the right spot," Jacques nodded. "I hope they find it."

"Are we still planning to open up to the public in May?" Evan inquired.

I'd really like to," Jacques nodded, looking in on the North Forest which had lost most of the pines. "As soon as the burn victims recover, and the charred debris from the trees have been cleaned up we should open the Viewing Tunnel to the public." Reflecting thoughtfully, he added, "You know, it's rather strange, but the publicity surrounding the fire and the heroic rescue has raised so much compassionate interest in the Tinys that the Governing Board messaged this morning to give their condolences and ask how things are going. They even asked if we needed any financial help!"

"That's amazing!" Evan nodded.

"It is!"

With a sudden frown as he observed the forest, the Professor queried, "Where are Odin and Franz?" Outside the glass greenhouse, the sun was beginning to set and the brilliant colours reflected off the water. "I haven't seen them in hours," he murmured thoughtfully. With a smile he added, "You know, they haven't been complaining or causing trouble lately, and Odin *almost* completed the stairs before he found the gem. I'm slightly optimistic they are changing... for good."

"I hope so," said Evan, "I really hope so!"

Looking around the terrarium, the two scientists noticed that new targets had been set up in the North Forest in the large, cleared area where the fire had destroyed many of the trees. The young men weren't anywhere to be seen.

Noticing a stash of long, straight sticks behind a tree, Jacques inquired, "What are those?"

Evan gazed in. "Arrows?" he said with surprise. Then he pointed. "Look over there. They've made some crude bows as well! How did they come up with bows and arrows all on their own?"

Running quickly over to his desk, the Professor came back with his binoculars. "And those arrows look sharp!" he exclaimed.

Anxiously, Evan agreed. "I would almost consider those to be... *weapons!*"

"Oh lá lá! We'll need to monitor the situation. Hopefully they are up to something useful."

Evan groaned. "I'm not betting on that!"

They could see Nancy and Milan taking kitchen scraps out to the compost pile beside the store. Rusty was following behind. The deer were running down the hill in anticipation of tasty delights. A bell tinkled as Ripple attempted to pounce on something in the bushes, but she came up disappointed.

"Putting bells on the cats was a great idea!" Evan remarked.

The Professor agreed. "Hopefully the rodent and bird population won't be decimated so quickly this time."

Coming around Mining Hill, they saw Charley and Yu Yan sitting on the steps of the farmhouse chatting, while Bojo kept a watchful guard against small intruders. Tina and Vahid were cleaning out the chicken coops.

Suddenly, Sanaa and Lema hooted and hollered loudly. Looking over, the two scientists saw they were leaping excitedly around a large object which they had pulled out of the ground.

"Is it the suncatcher?" Jacques exclaimed hopefully.

Brushing off the dirty, glass dewdrop, the two Tinys were ecstatic. It was indeed the suncatcher! Long rays of evening sunlight sent rainbows dancing in all directions.

The loud, happy cheers drew the attention of several other Tinys, who left their activities to race up the hill and see what their friends had found.

In no time at all, Nancy, Milan, Vahid, Tina, Charley and Yu Yan had gathered on Mining Hill and were helping to lift the large crystal into a carrycart. With a lot of lively chatter, the heavy gem with the long, jeweled chain was wheeled down the hill.

"I wonder what they'll trade it for?" Evan mused.

"It's the best one that we buried," the Professor replied. "Maybe they'll get a few months of free meals?"

But the gem didn't go to the store. To the surprise of the scientists, Sanaa and Lema told the others that the gem should be something everyone should share. "Let's put it up on Rainbow Hill," Sanaa suggested merrily. "Then we will always have rainbows up there that all of us can enjoy."

The others applauded her idea. Outside of Paradise, the scientists clapped quietly too. "I love her spirit!" Evan whispered.

"Interesting," the Professor noted quietly. "Odin found a gem and felt it paid off all his misdemeanors. He walked away, days after causing that fire, thinking he owes nothing more to anyone and he didn't even finish the staircase! Sanaa and Lema find the most valuable gem and want to share it freely with the whole group. They ask for nothing in return..."

Pondering an analogy, Even reflected, "We gave them those gems and all they had to do was dig them up." Looking at the Professor sideways, he bravely decided to share his spiritual thoughts. "In a way," he mused, "it's kind of like God's gift of salvation... don't you think? Some aren't even interested in the offer and feel it's too much effort to go digging. Some only think of how they might benefit themselves, while others want to share it with everyone."

"Evan," the Professor called out disapprovingly, "you are spending *too* much time with Seth!" Nevertheless, he considered the idea as they observed the large group of Tinys march the prized gem across the meadow. Emma, the golden retriever was lying in the sand, watching her master. In the setting sun, Vinitha and Damien were carrying a surfboard over to stack in Zahir's creative wooden holder, which now held about ten sleek boards.

"I don't see the need to make any promises," they heard Damien say to Vinitha. "What difference does it make? We'll stay together as long as we both want to stay together."

"But it would be *so fun* to get married," Vinitha was protesting. "And then you could come live in my house with me."

"Why do we need to get married just to stay in the same house?" Damien laughed.

"Because that's what everyone else is doing," she replied.

"Who says we have to be like everyone else?" he argued. "If you want me to stay with you, I'll come stay with you. I'm not so keen on hammocks anymore."

"But is it right?" she questioned.

"There's no rule about it on the board," he shrugged. "I'd say we can do whatever we want."

"I'd like to make promises first," she insisted.

"Really?" the surfer retorted disdainfully. "What difference does it make?"

Vinitha struggled to give an answer. She didn't seem sure of herself, but she was emotionally distraught.

On the other side of the glass, the Professor observed, "It seems like most of the Tinys are pairing off in one way or another."

Evan wasn't pleased that the Professor thought it was okay for the Tinys to pair off in serious romantic relationships without making a commitment to each other. "I think you should encourage them all to get married before they begin sharing houses," he remarked.

"On what basis?" the Professor frowned. "It's certainly not the norm in our world anymore."

"On the basis of caring about each other's feelings," Evan protested. "You want a world with minimal suffering and 'no hurting.' The Tinys need to understand that a full romantic relationship requires loyalty through the good and bad times, and a real commitment to each other. If romantic relationships are treated lightly... or *selfishly,* the *worst* kind of hurt can result.

"I think the no-hurting rule is good enough," the Professor replied. "I don't want to make any other rules."

Evan said no more, well aware that he was only the assistant, but he strongly hoped that lovely, shy Vinitha was not going to be badly hurt. In the last few days, he'd noticed the attractive, charming surfer was thoroughly enjoying his sessions with Georgia and Diya, while Vinitha worked alone on her pottery. Somehow Damien always managed to make his lessons full of frolicking fun and lots of laughter. It was a good strategy for keeping his students engaged, but Evan hoped that one guy wasn't going to captivate more than his fair share of the ladies. They were already short one girl.

Walking around to Rainbow Hill, the tall student assistant saw that the shiny gem in the carrycart was now at the top of the clearing. He heard the Tinys deliberate over where they should hang the treasure.

"Get out your phone, Evan," the Professor urged quietly. "We should record this."

A large Eucalyptus overhung the edge of the clearing and Lema volunteered to climb the tree and wrap the chain around its branches. However, the others felt Lema was too heavy and volunteered Charley in his place. Aimee came running over to watch the proceedings.

Nervously, the young farmer climbed the tree and skirted along the extended branch. The chain was long, and those on the ground attempted to throw it up and snag the hook on the branches. Finally, it caught. Bit by bit, with Charley's guiding hands above, they managed to pull the gem up on the chain until it hung high in the tree. Reflecting in the setting sun, the swinging crystal distributed beautiful colours on everyone's faces and clothing. Aimee was delighted. Sanaa and Lema were enthralled by the bright reds and purples. Clapping their hands and dancing in and out of the reflections, they soon had the whole group singing a happy chant.

On the other side of the dome, Evan stopped recording and lowered his phone. He chuckled softly. "We need to record some more of their shows," he said. "Sanaa and Lema win the prize for the most upbeat music."

"We could play their music in the Rainforest Biome!" the Professor suggested. "It would be perfect!"

170

Evan agreed.

"Treasure Discovered in Paradise!" Evan mused. "How's that for a video headline?"

"Great idea," Jacques replied eagerly. "Let's put that up on our website. We need a good news story."

Walking over to the computer, the two scientists could hear the laughter and shouts as the Tinys ran around in the rainbow lights. They shared a happy smile.

Confidential Information

Chapter 21

*A*s the sun slid from view and darkness settled in across Paradise, the rainbow lights stopped dancing on the Crisis Room walls. Aimee showered and joined Kenzie to administer the last daily dose of medicine. Zahir was anxious about his eye, as the dark spot was growing. The nurses could see it was noticeably cloudier. Uncle Louis quietly indicated to Aimee that she should tell the Professor.

After everyone had been given their medications, Uncle Louis started to read Matthew chapter one. In the softly lit room, his voice was quietly reassuring. One by one, he went through a long list of fathers and children! Looking at several pencilled-in references, he shared with them that Jesus was the son who had been promised to both Abraham and David.[52] On his mother's side, he was a direct descendant of the forefathers, and God through His Holy Spirit power had miraculously caused an egg in Mary's womb to develop into a son without any human father.[53]

Not having ever seen animals give birth, or humans for that matter, Uncle Louis had to explain the process that occurred in the 'big' world, which then became a lengthy discussion.

---

[52] Abraham - Genesis 12:1-3; 22:15-18; Galatians 3:16;
David – 2 Samuel 7:12-16; Luke 1:26-35; Revelation 22:16
[53] Luke 1:35

Once they were back on topic, Uncle Louis shared the notes Seth had written in the margin. "Jesus was not the *only* miraculous birth in the Bible," he read. "Adam was formed from the dust without any human parents.[54] Eve was formed from his rib. Sarah and Elizabeth had children long after it was possible for them to conceive. God's incredible power to create a human being isn't confined to normal human reproduction."

They had barely started into the account of the wise men coming to seek the newborn baby when Zahir and Ponce drifted off to sleep. As much as Zahir wanted to listen to the story of Jesus, the burn victims were still in the recovery stages and sleep was essential.

When he saw the two young men had drifted off, Uncle Louis stopped reading. "I guess that's it for tonight," he said with a chuckle.

Kenzie wanted to have a closer look at the new gemstone, so he ran outside to check it out.

Seeing that the other two patients were sound asleep, Uncle Louis motioned for Aimee to come over. He was counting his days carefully, not knowing how many he had left. There were a few things he wanted to make sure the next leader of Paradise understood. He hoped they would get a chance to visit the cave together, but it was still a big undertaking for him to even walk around for five minutes on a flat surface. The cave was so far away...

Eagerly, Aimee came over and knelt beside his bed. "Are you feeling okay?" she asked with a loving smile.

"I've been waiting for a good time to talk to you alone," he whispered, his white hair glowing in the soft light beside his bed.

"Oh?" the young nurse said, a little surprised.

"Aimee," he said in a serious tone, keeping his voice low. "You know I only have a little longer with you all?"

---

[54] Adam - Genesis 2:7; 1 Corinthians 15:45-49; Eve – Gen. 2:21-23; Sarah - Genesis 17:15-19; Elizabeth - Luke 1:5-20

"Uncle Louis, I don't want to talk about this," she said sadly, reaching for his wizened hand.

"Neither do I," he replied, clasping his hand firmly around hers, "but there are things that you need to know. When I'm gone, you need to carry on educating everyone in Paradise the best way you can. You see, Aimee, we live in a tiny dome. The phone is a source of information that extends far beyond us and will help you discover many things. Outside of Paradise, where the Professor and Evan live, is a vast world of humans, all big like they are. Their world – the Earth – is full of beauty, with enormous mountains that are much, much grander than anything we have here! They have massive lakes and oceans, and thousands more varieties of plants and animals than we enjoy."

Aimee's eyes were big and round as she tried to absorb all this astonishing information.

"You'll see it on the phone," he told her. "It looks enticing. You'll wish you could visit their big world in person. You'll start feeling that Paradise is very tiny and confined. But," he warned earnestly, "we can't survive in their world. Paradise is perfect for Tinys, but if we were to try to leave Paradise, we would die in less than an hour."

"But you were gone for a day and a night," Aimee pondered.

Uncle Louis pointed to the oxygen tanks that still lay near his bed. "I had a special mask to wear so that I'd get enough oxygen," he told her. "Without that on constantly, I would have died."

"But then how do they live in it?" Aimee begged.

"Their world was made for them and our world was made for us," Uncle Louis told her. "Enjoy what you can learn about the big world, but don't become obsessed with getting there."

"I won't," Aimee promised sincerely. "I love Paradise! I don't want to leave it."

He squeezed her hand. "I'm sure you will use the phone very wisely. Learn from it. You can discover anything you want to know, but just remember that not everything is *true... or good."*

"Really?" Aimee looked up with surprise. "How will I know what is true and what isn't?"

"Compare various answers. Don't believe everything you see or read. Look for real evidence and choose what can be proven," he told her. With a pause, he added, "Sometimes I've been fooled, so I try to always keep my mind open to the possibility that I could be wrong."

In the soft, radiant lighting, Aimee looked at him with anxious concern. If Uncle Louis wasn't always right... she was certain she would mess up... often!

"But, Aimee, there's something else I need to tell you," he continued.

"What's that?"

"In the Professor's world, there are people who enjoy unhealthy and destructive behaviors."

Aimee looked at him with bewilderment.

Uncle Louis nodded gravely. "The Professor has a blocker on the phone in Paradise," he explained. "If you see a dark screen that says, "Website blocked" you will know you have stumbled onto something promoting unhealthy and inappropriate behaviour. However, not everything can be blocked. If you see things that make you feel uneasy, or you know that you wouldn't look at them if anyone else was around, then make yourself turn away. Shut them down. A part of you may want to search for more – but trust me, sometimes curiosity can destroy your happiness. Don't allow those dark images inside or they will darken your life. I've learned this myself. There are things I've read and watched that I regret with all my heart. Good things are easily forgotten but bad images and information are much harder... maybe even impossible to block from your mind once you've let them in. Use the phone as a helpful tool, but don't ever let it have power over you. Live your life in the real life around you, stay active, keep busy, get outside, enjoy your friendships here in Paradise – these are the things that will keep you happy."

Alarm was filling Aimee's eyes. "I'm not sure I understand," she said warily.

"Don't worry," he assured her, squeezing her hand lightly. "You have a good sense for what is healthy and what isn't. Hold on to what you know."

"Uncle Louis," Aimee said, anxiously, "what will I do when I don't have you to talk to? I don't know if I can handle all this responsibility on my own."

He nodded. "You will be able to talk to the Professor and Evan."

She sighed, "But they aren't here with me in Paradise," she lamented. "Uncle Louis, you must hang on. I need *you!*"

"I am trying my best," he said with a smile. Then turning serious, he knew it was time to talk about her future. "It will be helpful to have a good friend," he told her. "At some point, Aimee, you might decide you want to marry. And if you make that decision, choose a Tiny who is honest, loving and kind. You will need someone to help you to sort through the truth and lies, right and wrong. There is so much to sort through and it's always better to make these decisions with a trusted friend. "'Two are better than one,'" he quoted in a paraphrased fashion. "'If the one falls, the other can lift him up.'"[55]

Aimee nodded sadly. She was quite sure she wanted to choose the one who *had* lifted her up at her darkest moment, but that someone loved someone else.

Uncle Louis squeezed her hand comfortingly.

Just then, Kenzie came running up the stairs. He didn't know he was interrupting a private conversation and he was anxious to share what he had seen. Barely keeping his voice to a whisper, he told them

---

[55] Ecclesiastes 4:9–10

about the dew-shaped gem and how it was still glittering in the moonlight. "It's such a beautiful treasure!" he exclaimed quietly, glancing at the sleeping patients. "I'm so glad they hung it close by! Now we all can enjoy it."

Excited to see for herself, Aimee rose to her feet. "I'm going to look too," she said. "And then I need to talk to the Professor."

Marriage

Chapter 22

*A*s Aimee and Kenzie attended to their three patients the next morning, one of them was asking questions about the things he'd heard the night before.

"That was a lengthy list of parents and children," Zahir remarked to Uncle Louis. "How long has the big world been around?"

"That list of generations goes back four thousand years from when it was written," Uncle Louis told Zahir. "And we are living about two thousand years since Jesus was born."

"So, there's been around six *thousand* years of history?" the young man calculated. "And our lifespan is about five or six years?"

Uncle Louis nodded, explaining that people in the big world often lived to over eighty or ninety years.

As Aimee helped Kenzie loosely wrap new gauze bandages around Ponce's leg, their very vocal patient exclaimed, "That's just not fair. They get to live *so* much longer than us!"

"Living for any time *at all* is a precious gift," Uncle Louis reminded him. "What you need to consider is how you will *use* the gift you are given – not whether you get as long as someone else."

"How's your eye?" Kenzie asked Zahir.

"No better," he answered.

Aimee looked down sadly. Late last night she had told the Professor about the dark spot, and after he had conferred with Dr. Montgomery,

178

he had relayed that nothing could be done. He felt the heat of the fire had likely damaged Zahir's vision, and it was very possible that he would go blind in that eye.

Georgia and Lily popped in to say good morning on their way to help with breakfast. "How are you today, Zahir?" the tall blond girl asked kindly.

"Awake and alive," he smiled.

"I might not be in to read to you this morning," she apologized. "I'm going to try to surf for the first time today. Damien said to come when the water is calm."

Zahir nodded. "Have fun," he said flatly.

Aimee glanced up to see a dark look cross his face. "That hurt," she thought.

"I love you so much!" Georgia called out as she turned to leave.

"I love you too," Zahir replied without emotion.

"I'll be back soon, Ponce," Lily called out with a big smile. "And I love *you!*"

"You're the best," Ponce sang out. "I'll be waiting *right here,*" he told her, and then he chuckled to himself.

Later that morning when Sanaa and Georgia brought breakfast to the Crisis Room, Lily and Vinitha tagged along. The four young ladies were freshly showered and having an animated conversation when they reached the front door. Overhearing her friends as she and Kenzie cleaned up, Aimee was intrigued.

"It was so beautiful!" Lily exclaimed. "She was in a fancy white dress with flowers in her hair, and she had a beautiful bouquet of roses in her hand. You see, the girl who is getting married is called 'the bride' and her man is called 'the groom.' A really good singer sang pretty songs as the bride walked up to her groom who was waiting for her, and then everyone stood up. They made a promise to always stay together and then he... *kissed her!*"

179

"And this is called 'marriage'?" Georgia clarified. "They make a promise to *always* stay together? They *both* make the promise?"

"Ooh, I like this!" Sanaa cheered, clapping her hands.

Aimee was very curious as to where her petite roommate was getting such information. It almost sounded like Lily had seen a wedding happen, not just read about it in a book. But maybe it was a book with lots of pictures... or ... *had Lily been in the cave?*

As the girls ran up the spiral staircase, bringing a breakfast of strawberry mash buns and fruit salad, Aimee walked into the hallway, to organize the supplies. She questioned her roommate, "I heard you talking about... *marriage,* Lily. Where are you getting these ideas from?"

For a moment, the petite girl went very white. She nearly dropped the bowls of fruit salad that she was carrying. Then she recovered herself. "Oh, it's just a book that I've been reading."

"A book about marriage?" Kenzie asked as he came out the door to get another bottle of antibiotics.

"Yes," Lily replied. "This is what people do when they really love someone. They promise to *always* stay together, and they have a celebration. Some people even have a big cake."

Vinitha's dark eyes were dreamy. "I would love to do that!" she sighed.

With uncharacteristic sharpness, Kenzie replied, "Then don't get talked into anything less."

"What do you mean?" she asked.

"Choose someone who believes in promises," he told her bluntly, "just like you do." Picking up the antibiotics he walked quickly back to the patients.

Having overheard their conversation, Aimee looked up at Vinitha with empathy. She saw the sadness in her eyes. They both knew Damien did not like rules or promises.

Georgia took the buns to the patients.

Lily had more to share. "And they give each other rings to remember the promise," she added, "and everyone comes to watch their wedding. Their best friends put on special dresses and stand beside them holding flowers!"

Sanaa danced around the hallway, singing, "A promise. A promise. I love it! I love it! I'm going to do it!"

"If you make someone a promise, you *can't* change your mind," Lily reminded her.

"Ooh, I won't change my mind," Sanaa laughed. "Lema is mine forever!" She took the fruit salad from Lily.

"It does sound beautiful," Vinitha reflected, still holding her bowls. "If two people promise to stay together," she reasoned, "then I guess that means that marriage is just a special relationship for *two*... not three, or four...?" She looked over at Georgia uneasily.

"Yes," Lily nodded with delight. "Just *one* guy and *one* girl sharing a house together."

Vinitha was lost in thought as Georgia returned and collected the bowls of fruit salad from her.

"And I love Ponce's cabin," Lily smiled happily. "I'll miss the big mansion, but I like little houses too." She looked up in Aimee's direction with a smile. "Then you can have my room all to yourself."

The new ideas were swirling around in Aimee's head - marriage, making a promise and not changing your mind, leaving the girls, sharing a house with a guy. This all sounded far more serious and life-changing than Sanaa's rule had been. "I'd like to see this book," she said curiously, looking over at Lily. "Can you please show it to me?"

"Oh... I'll see if I can find it," Lily frowned.

To herself, Aimee thought, "Maybe I'll Google 'marriage.'"

As the other girls ran off outside, Aimee walked into the Crisis Room carrying the protein formula and balanced salts. Ponce and Zahir were looking at each other with the same sort of curious surprise that Aimee felt. Uncle Louis was smiling but Kenzie was not.

"What was that all about?" Zahir queried with a chuckle. "Are the girls making new rules again?"

"This one may be a good idea," Uncle Louis laughed. "Making a promise to stay faithfully committed to the person you choose to love protects both partners from a lot of hurt and pain. At least with marriage, this is a 'rule' understood and agreed to by both the guy and the girl, and if it's a public promise, then everyone else knows about it too – which is also very important."

"But if you're promising to be with someone for the rest of your life," Aimee reflected anxiously, "then... you want to be very sure you are making your promise to the right one."

"Well of course!" Ponce laughed. "I know Lily is the one for me!"

Aimee was not listening. "What if," she continued wide-eyed, "the one that you love marries someone else and you can never get them back?"

Kenzie looked over quizzically.

"Yeah," Ponce agreed. "That would be sad! If you make a promise, it can't be broken... right? Promises can't be broken?"

Kenzie shrugged, responding to the previous question. "You can always try for second-best, I guess," he said in a matter-of-fact tone.

"I would *hate* to be someone's *'second-best,'*" Zahir murmured.

Uncle Louis rolled over and chuckled. "Second-best is better than no best at all. In a committed, caring relationship, second-best may eventually become the best."

Suddenly, Aimee noticed that Zahir was trying to wipe away tears. Kenzie ran over to hand him a cloth.

"What is wrong with me?" Zahir questioned, forcing a laugh. "I have no idea why this keeps happening. It's *so* embarrassing!"

Seeing that Kenzie was looking after Zahir, Aimee excused herself and ran outside. Her patients were clean, well-bandaged and all the medication had been given out. She needed time to think through this new concept and do a little research on her own.

Research

Chapter 23

Running through the forest to the cave on that grey morning, Aimee heard another series of crashes fairly close by. She stopped in her tracks and listened fearfully. "What is going on?" she wondered. There was another crash and this time she saw two trees fall over on the far edge of the forest. "Trees are falling down quite frequently," she observed. "Why?" Instead of heading down the hill, she dashed to the edge of the forest and looked down the steep side. At least fifty trees had fallen over and their roots – *very small* roots, were sticking up in the air. "Oh dear," she thought. "I must tell the Professor about this!"

Racing back to her usual pathway down the hill, Aimee quickly made her descent to the shady valley between the hills. Two more crashes were heard before she rolled the large, fake stone out of her way. Pulling out the key from under her t-shirt, she opened up the door. Closing it quickly behind her, she turned on the phone and sent the Professor a text. "Trees are falling down in the forest," she typed. "I saw at least 50 down and I heard a few more crashes before coming inside. Most of the fallen trees are behind Rainbow Hill on the steep side, where hardly anyone goes. Is this a problem?"

Waiting for his reply, Aimee hastily Googled 'marriage.' Everything Lily said was true. There were pictures of girls in white dresses, videos of weddings, advice and even articles discussing whether or not marriage was a good idea. Watching a couple of videos, the young nurse was astounded. It all looked so beautiful and romantic, just as Lily had described! "She must have been in here," Aimee concluded. "How dumb of me to leave the key under that rock!"

Putting aside all the thoughts and questions about marriage, Aimee chose to explore other questions she had from the books they had read with Uncle Louis. She was very curious about Planet Earth. Just to see what would happen, she touched the microphone on the Google search. Evan had told her this was something she could use. Instantly, a white screen came up with the words 'Listening...'.

Aimee tried speaking to it. "What does Planet Earth look like?"

Dark space images came up instantly, with a glowing blue and green sphere, looking like a precious gem in the vast darkness. To her amazement, an unfamiliar voice spoke to her, saying that Earth was the only planet known to harbour life. Seventy percent of earth's surface was water – a fundamental element for the existence of life. She could see from the rotating sphere that this proportion was true.

"It's so beautiful!" Aimee exclaimed. "Is this the world the Professor lives in? And the earth just hangs in the air!" she considered. "How is that possible? How does the water stay on it? Some of the water is completely upside down."

With delight, Aimee's spoken questions led her to find out that the sun is constantly pulling the earth toward itself, but the earth is moving sideways so fast that it circles the sun, and doesn't fall into the burning star. When she asked why water stayed on the round earth, some of the answers were very complicated. The word 'gravity' kept coming up, but the concepts were difficult for her to understand.

"I can't make anything just hang in the air like that," she thought, astounded. "This God must have power and intelligence beyond anything we've ever seen. How could this planet... this universe just happen accidentally?"

As she continued her investigation, she discovered pictures of the moon, the seas, the multitude of life in the ocean, the mountains, the rivers. She was breathless, astonished, and fascinated. It was just as Uncle Louis had told her. It looked very enticing. Suddenly, Paradise seemed rather tiny and confined."

A reply came in from the Professor. "No, trees falling down is not normal. I am aware of the problem, but I'm not sure what is going on. I'll do some more research. Please warn everyone not to walk around on that side of the hill for now. If a tree fell on someone it could hurt them quite badly."

"I will warn everyone," Aimee replied.

Another message came through from the Professor: "Aimee, how are things going today? Are your patients doing better? Are their temperatures normal? How are they feeling about their injuries? Is Uncle Louis any stronger? Has he said anything about his heart? Is he staying in bed? Are you coping okay with your new job? I'm sorry for so many questions. All of you are on my mind most of the day. ☺ ♡ "

With a smile, Aimee answered all his questions with fairly positive replies. She liked the little smiley face and the blue heart that the Professor had added to his message.

"How did he do that?" she wondered. With some investigation, she discovered the smiley face in her message box, clicked on it and then realized there were *hundreds* of icons to choose from. Overjoyed with all the options, she sent back five happy smiley faces, many colourful hearts and a hand wave.

The Professor returned a happy face with tears coming down. He was so thankful he had put Aimee in charge of the critical care patients. He was very relieved that it hadn't been a mistake to return Zahir and Ponce to Paradise, and he loved his little daughter!

Staring at the emoji, Aimee wondered, "Is he laughing, or crying? Or maybe he's laughing so hard, he's crying!"

185

After they said goodbye there were other things that Aimee was eager to research. Remembering that Genesis chapter one had claimed that man was formed from the earth, Aimee asked, "Is man made from dirt?" The answers varied. Some articles agreed that human beings were made from thirteen elements found in the earth's crust, while others argued for star dust. It was confusing to sort through several contradictory arguments. However, most agreed that human and animal bodies turned back to dirt when they died.

She asked about the Garden of Eden and looked at various locations where people thought it might be. Most agreed it once existed somewhere in the Middle East near the Tigris and Euphrates rivers. Some felt that a global flood had destroyed the previous typography of the earth.

"A global flood?" she pondered briefly. "What's that all about?" But there was an even more pressing question to consider. "Who is God?" she asked.

Google readily answered her question, providing links to many sites. Aimee read and read for quite a while. A lot of the descriptions used words she had never heard of before, like 'omnipresent' and 'omniscient'. Typing in those words, she found out that "God is present everywhere at the same time," and "God knows everything." Countless articles came up on the topic of God. The more she read, the more she became convinced that God was a well-known Being or concept that was very prevalent in the Professor's world.

"Why have we never heard of God before?" she asked out loud.

Many links came up to sites answering what would happen to those who had never heard of God, but nothing answered the particular predicament of the Tinys.

"So, Google has limits," she observed with a smile. Out loud, she asked, "What is the Bible?"

This time, Google produced a multitude of articles to read through. Some links suggested that the Bible was not really from God, other links were certain that it was from God. Her head began to hurt. "Oh, I wish Uncle Louis were here with me!" she moaned. "This is way too confusing to sort through on my own! I need a friend."

Turning everything off, she left the cave and ran to the shower. It was nearly time to give out the next round of medications.

Criteria

Chapter 24

*E*van dropped by to ask the Professor a question in the Greenville University. Having heard that Jacques had appointments in the science lab with two students who had failed the final exam, he walked down the hall, expecting the interviews to be over. However, the Professor was still conferring with one last student who was loudly arguing his case. It had been a difficult exam and marks were low across the class. Even though the exam had taken place a few weeks earlier, it had taken a while for the final term results to be posted and a date set to discuss the impact this would have on course selections for the fall. Needless to say, the current crisis in Paradise had left the Professor a little behind in his teaching responsibilities.

Seth and another student who had only just barely passed the exam were having an animated discussion just outside the lab door. Evan heard words like 'Jews', 'God said' and various other religious terms. "He's at it again," he marvelled. "Seth is certainly not afraid to share his beliefs."

"How did you do on the course?" Evan asked awkwardly, as he drew near.

Rolling his eyes, Seth shook his head dismally. He relayed that even after some last-minute tutoring, he had failed the Professor's exam and consequently the course by only a few marks.

"I'm sorry," Evan apologized. "You spent too much time tutoring me last semester."

Seth shook his head. "No way, that was great! I just needed to study more."

The other student was still pondering the conversation he had been having with Seth. "There's no way that antisemitism is on the rise," he scoffed. "If anything, minority groups are better protected than anyone else in our world."

"There were three articles about it yesterday," Seth told him.

"The Jews are always complaining about every little thing that happens to them," the other student argued. "They are no more persecuted than any other race."

"They are God's 'chosen' people," Seth shrugged, "which brings great privilege and heavy responsibility. And because God has singled them out, many people are jealous. This hatred is going to build up until 'all nations' come against Jerusalem..."[56]

The second interview terminated, and the belligerent student walked out of the room mumbling under his breath, "Good thing your teaching career is over!"

Having overheard Seth's remarks, the Professor looked towards the door. He prodded, "God's *chosen* people? That's just one more reason to think twice about having faith in such a Being. I don't like or trust a 'God' who plays favourites!'"

Seth looked over in surprise. "What do you mean?" he asked.

"What kind of God singles out one race of people above all the others? How unfair is that?"

"Do you really want to know, Sir?" Seth inquired with a genuine tone to his voice.

The Professor was curious to hear Seth's answer, yet he maintained his tough stance. "All I know," he stated firmly, leaning

---

[56] Zechariah 14; Joel 3

against the door frame, "is that a Being who shows such favouritism based on race is not someone that I would choose to worship."

For a moment, Seth hesitated. The other student said a polite goodbye and headed toward the main doors. Evan raised his eyebrows in response to the Professor's challenging remark.

"He didn't choose Abraham because of race," Seth began, frowning. "He chose him because he was one of the rare individuals who believed God and trusted Him.[57] God was able to work with a man like that and develop a family who would choose to walk with Him. He wasn't looking for a pure bloodline. God wanted to develop a family who would share His values and promises with the rest of the world. Throughout Biblical history, many Gentiles who believed in God joined themselves to the Jewish people and became included in their lineage."[58]

"So, are you saying that all Jews have this faith - this *blind desire* to believe without any evidence?" the Professor challenged, raising his dark eyebrows.

Clarifying one word, Seth said, "'Faith' is 'persuasion based on evidence' – solid evidence. That's the Biblical definition in Hebrews eleven."

"If I read *your* translation of it?"

"No, if you look up the meaning of the word 'faith'."[59]

The Professor shook his head with amusement.

Undaunted, Seth answered his previous question. "The promise of salvation was never intended to be limited to Abraham's natural family," he stated with an engaging smile. "Right back in Genesis,

---

[57] Genesis 15:6; Romans 4:3,13-25; Genesis 18:18-19

[58] Tamar – Matthew 1:3; Rahab – Matt. 1:5; Ruth – Matt. 1:5

[59] Hebrews 1:1 'Faith' – Greek word 'pistis' (Strong's G4102) – 'persuasion, that is, credence; moral conviction. 'Evidence' – Greek word 'elegchos' (Strong's G1650) 'proof, conviction, evidence, reproof'

God said that *'all nations'* would be blessed through Abraham and his seed.[60] Anyone who chooses to have the same faith in God as Abraham did, and to believe in the Messiah – the *most* important descendant of Abraham - can be included in God's family. Anyone who believes can become a *spiritual* Jew and inheritor of the promises. Read Galatians three, or Romans eleven," the young man encouraged.

"Then what makes the Jews God's *chosen* people?" Professor Lemans argued, as he absentmindedly scrolled through a lengthy list of messages on his phone. "If anyone can become a Jew... then why specifically favour the race?"

Meeting Evan's curious gaze, Seth took a moment to reply. "Okay, it's like this," he said, "there are two separate things here. One is that the offer of salvation - *forgiveness and eternal life* - is open to anyone from any nation who chooses to have faith in God and believe in the Messiah.[61] The second is that *because* God made individual promises to Abraham, the Jewish family is the one that God has set up to be a witness for Him to the rest of the world.[62] And most of the time they have been *unwilling* witnesses..."

"Witnesses?" the Professor asked, looking skeptical. "How?"

Evan raised his eyebrows; he was intrigued.

Seth was happy to explain. "Well, for instance, the return of the Jewish people to the land of Israel, after being scattered throughout the whole earth for nearly two thousand years, is a miracle that everyone can see. Read Ezekiel chapter 36 to 39 and you'll have evidence that the Bible is divinely inspired. What other book could accurately predict the history of one nation with such specific detail, three thousand years ahead? And we are right in the middle of it all

---

[60] Genesis 12:3
[61] Galatians 3:7-9, 25-29
[62] Isaiah 43:1-15; Ezekiel 36; 39:7,21

coming true! The return of the Jewish people is all in preparation for the return of Jesus Christ."

It was easy to see that Seth was getting rather excited about his testimony, and Professor Lemans loved a good debate. "Perhaps the Jews have read these prophecies and are just making it all happen," he surmised, looking up with a patronizing smile.

Evan cocked his head, waiting for Seth's reply.

"If it was an easy history to enact and orchestrate, that might be a possibility," Seth admitted, "but Professor Lemans, most prophecies concerning the Jews have come to pass *against all odds*, against their own will, and involved many other nations. Some of the prophecies accurately predicted the Jews would be driven from their land and scattered throughout the world.[63] That happened in AD70 – against the Jewish will. The Jews fought against the Romans with all their might to *stop* this from happening. Other prophecies predicted terrible treatment from other nations, horrible suffering, mockery, hatred, and fear. Who would want to bring about a *fulfilment* of those prophecies? And in order to fulfil them, it required other unbelieving nations to cause the abuse."

Seeing that the Professor was still engrossed with his phone, Seth lowered his voice, "Just think, Professor Lemans," he encouraged, "when Israel became a nation again in 1948, as God accurately said they would in the last days[64], they were immediately vastly outnumbered and attacked on all sides by hordes of Arab nations with an overwhelming barrage of weapons. The world didn't expect the Jews to survive. Many agree that Israel's victory in the War of Independence was miraculous!"

---

[63] Deuteronomy 28:64-67; Leviticus 26:27-39; Nehemiah 1:8; Jeremiah 9; Zechariah 7:8-14; Luke 21:20-24
[64] Ezekiel 37:21-28; 38:7-16

"Terrible treatment for a chosen people," the Professor scoffed. "I sure wouldn't want to be *chosen!*"

"They only received these punishments when they turned their backs on God," Seth explained. "God clearly laid it all out ahead of time in the Old Testament. If they obeyed His laws, He would elevate them and bless them. If they disobeyed, God warned them about the punishments they would and *did* endure. However, the Jewish people are not any different than the majority of human beings in all other nations today. *Most* humans choose to follow their own way and turn their backs on God... regardless of the warnings He's given to all of us."

The Professor had heard enough. "I've got things to do this morning," he told Seth flatly, sliding his phone back into his pocket, "and I still need to discuss a few things with Evan."

"That's fine," Seth nodded. With a sad look on his face, he added, "I'll miss you in September when I give Biotechnology another go. I might have failed your course, but you are a great teacher. I've enjoyed your classes." Turning to leave, he nodded goodbye to Evan.

As Seth headed toward the main doors, the Professor's shoulders drooped. He was going to miss teaching. He would even miss his debates with Seth, but he knew he deserved such consequences for overstepping ethical boundaries.

Following the Professor back into the lab room, Evan didn't react even though he disagreed. Instead, in a pondering fashion, he queried, "You know, I've been thinking a lot about the future of Paradise. If something were to happen to Aimee, what criteria do we have to choose the next Tiny for communication purposes? Or, what if she can't handle the responsibility on her own? Will we just put all the Tinys' names in a hat and pick one out? Or do you have a list of requirements to guide our decision?"

As the Professor stacked the papers on his desk, he was still thinking about his discussion with Seth. Absentmindedly, he replied,

"Well, obviously we want to choose someone we feel we can work with who is responsible and trustworthy and can handle the temptations of the Internet. Louis and Aimee both want to do the right thing and aren't easily pulled in a wrong direction."

"Anything else?" Evan prodded.

With a shrug, the Professor added, "We also need someone who respects us and wants to receive our guidance and direction." Reaching for his leather bag, he added, "And most definitely I would choose someone who has a genuine care for others and puts their needs above his own... like Zahir... *or Kenzie.*"

"So, I suppose Odin won't meet that criteria?"

Jacques scoffed. "I can't believe you're asking me that, Evan! There's no way *you or I* would choose a Tiny who would damage Paradise just to see whether or not we'll respond." With a skeptical look he inquired, "What are you setting me up for?"

Evan was smiling. "And I know you wouldn't choose Damien... or the other beach boys?"

"No," he smirked. "They are too busy surfing to take notice of what's happening anywhere else."

"What about Charley?"

Looking up, a sudden anxious look passed over the Professor's face. He asked, *"Ça alors!* Evan, why are you asking me about all these Tinys? Is everything okay with Louis? Is Aimee all right?"

"For sure. As far as I know," Evan replied. "I'm just curious to discover your criteria for choosing a leader. After all, we didn't have a choice with Louis, and we are very fortunate he has been such a wise, caring, patient leader. It's rather remarkable in every way."

"Louis did take a very helpful course..."

"Would that helpful course change Odin into a good leader?"

The Professor laughed. "No, I think not. One would need to start with the desire to be a good leader in order to benefit from the course."

"What about Sanaa?"

"She has a lot of good qualities," the Professor agreed. "She's very thoughtful, positive, occasionally selfless, and takes leadership initiative easily enough, but..."

"She hasn't sung songs of thankfulness at night..." Evan smiled.

"True," the Professor nodded, grateful that Evan had said it. "But I really don't see why we need to decide this now," he argued.

Evan smiled. "Alright, we don't," he agreed. "But I heard your conversation with Seth, and I wonder if you are being true to your own good judgment?"

With a look of surprise, the Professor chided his assistant, "What do you mean? Is that what you wanted to talk to me about?"

Avoiding the direct question, Evan answered, "I thought you were hard on Seth," he explained, "and I feel you are being unfair in your criticism of God. Obviously, God would choose to work with an individual who believed and trusted Him and wanted to please Him in every way! Isn't that the reason you have chosen Aimee over Franz? If some of Abraham's family also showed these same good characteristics, would it not be fair for God to choose them to carry on the special relationship with Him?"

"But not all Jews show those characteristics," the Professor argued. "Rachel, for instance, doesn't even believe in God."

"True," Evan replied. "And those who don't, don't have a special relationship with Him, outside of being *unwilling* witnesses that God's word is truth – as Seth explained. I'd say it is entirely fair for God to choose to extend His blessings through the Jewish people to the whole world, based on the foundation of the promises He made to His friend Abraham. It's something that I believe you would do yourself."

The Professor sat down in his chair with a sigh. "Evan, did you come here for a Bible discussion?" he asked skeptically. "Or to sort out the criteria for leadership? I've got to meet Rachel in an hour to make a decision over the ailing polar bear. If you have something important to say, get on with it."

Taking a chair on the other side of the desk, Evan brought up his real reason for coming. He had a question concerning RNA polymerase, and he knew the Professor would have the answer.

Although the Professor had a busy schedule ahead of him, he was always willing to help his assistant with any scientific questions. A half hour quickly slipped by as they worked through the issue together.

Rachel's Text

Chapter 25

*L*ying in bed that night, the Professor scrolled through his messages. So many had been coming in, that he and Evan had set up a weekly blog to give all the facts. Everyone wanted to know how Zahir and Louis were doing. Many asked about Ponce. Some pleaded for pictures and sent donations, while others wanted to know when he would do another interview. The latest video he had posted, of the Tinys hanging the rainbow suncatcher, was going viral.

"Paradise has attained world-wide status based on *suffering,*" he murmured to himself. "How can this be? I thought happiness would be the selling-feature, but instead it was Zahir's compassionate rescue and the terrible injuries he incurred."

Gazing out his open window to the full moon that was rising above the leafy trees, he considered several unexpected events that had taken place since he had begun his experiment. "There have been some major upsets," he thought to himself. "The flood, my daughter's depression, the girl's rule, the dangerous science experiments... the fire..."

Setting his phone down on the night table, he thought about the fire. It had all happened so fast. Over the last nine days, he had been insanely busy trying to deal with the impact of such a catastrophe. "Yes," he admitted to himself, "it was *a catastrophe...* purposely started by three of my Tinys. It wasn't 'an act of God'... it was *arson!* Unbelievable!"

"And now," he thought, "Louis wants to read the Bible! How is it that *my* son, my wonderful, responsible son suddenly developed this yearning for something more? I tried so hard to keep his life free of false hopes and restrictions, and ironically, he is prepared *to give up everything* to search this out."

A beep on his phone, caused him to look over. There was a message from Rachel. He picked it up wondering if she had any news. He read,

> "The DNA results came back today. Zahir IS OUR SON!!!!! I am ecstatic! We are both so excited and very much in love with that brave young man! Farouk and I want to thank you so much for involving us in this project and allowing us to do this test. We are with you one hundred percent!
>
> Is there any way possible for us to talk to Zahir, once he's better, even if it's only a WhiteDove call? We would love to meet him and be a real part of his life.
>
> And we love his name! Farouk says you chose well! Is it possible for me to suggest a Jewish middle name, just to acknowledge my part in his ancestry? Jordan, being our firstborn, is the namesake for Farouk's side. I would love to give Zahir the name of my father, Haniel. It is also his grandfather's name."
>
> Thank you! Thank you! Thank you! With love from all of us!"

Happy tears were flowing down Jacques' face when he reached the end of the text. He was overjoyed that Zahir was a Khalid. Ever since Rachel had told him of her donation, he had hoped this would be the case. Knowing that the Khalids were grateful to have a son in Paradise was deeply satisfying. Their friendship was very important to him.

He pondered Rachel's request. "They want to speak with Zahir," he thought soberly. "Of course they do. But to do so means granting Zahir Internet privileges. That will be easy enough if he and Aimee are teamed up to communicate with me, but if she chooses Kenzie, and Zahir is with Georgia, then I'll have a group of *four*. Such a scenario is possible... I suppose... just less workable."

For many reasons, Jacques longed for Zahir to be his daughter's best friend. "If I could choose any of the Tinys to be my son-in-law," he mused, "I would pick the dark-haired young man with valour, intelligence, his mother's blue eyes and a kind heart."

Reading the message one more time, the Professor curiously Googled the new name addition - 'Haniel.' To his shock and deep consternation, the majority of baby name sites gave the meaning as, *'God is gracious!'*

All the Tiny's names had been carefully chosen by the Professor eighteen months ago, to represent their cultural heritage. He had tried his hardest to avoid any association with the God of the Bible.

"What do I do?" he asked himself as sweat broke out on his forehead. "Rachel is begging for a small input into Zahir's life, as any mother would want, but Zahir has become the Tiny that has attracted the attention of the media more than any of the others. This new name opposes everything that I've said in the past!" He pondered the dilemma anxiously. "I'm sure that Rachel would love for his middle name to be acknowledged, but if someone discovers the meaning, the press will have a field day!" Shuddering, he rubbed his face in his hands. Then with sudden curiosity he sat up in bed and reached for his phone. "Zahir Haniel Khalid," he thought, saying it out in full to himself. "I wonder what his last name means?"

Looking it up, he had his answer in a few seconds. Khalid meant 'eternal, immortal, to last forever'!

Putting all the meanings together, he said to himself, "Light in a dark place – God is gracious, eternal, immortal, to last forever." For a moment he was too astonished to move. The message was the complete antithesis to his own! A heavy chill went down his spine. His hands shook as the phone dropped onto his lap. "*Ça alors!* How could this happen?" he asked himself. "I thought I had barred God from my world. How can this message be living right inside Paradise?"

Then he recalled one more thing: "Louis is now reading God's Book to that young man and my daughter!"

It all seemed so outrageously ironic, as though a power greater than himself had reached down and taken over the controls! For a long while, he lay still, staring out the window, watching clouds pass over the moon, as his thoughts churned deep inside.

"Perhaps," he fretted at last, "God *is* at work in *my world.* Perhaps He is at work... *for good.* What if He truly answered Louis' prayers? What if He saved the Tinys from the destructive fire that could have wiped them out? What if God is working in Paradise to... *save* my family, not to harm them?"

Tossing and turning, he pondered this new perspective. Sleep seemed a long way off. Reaching over to his night table, he switched on the light and picked up Seth's 'Ten Reasons to Believe in God.' The article had lain untouched on his bedside table for weeks. He perused it once again less sceptically than he had before.

"I'm going to look into this more carefully," he promised himself with a wry smile. "I will do a full investigation as any good scientist should. I will research the other side. And I will *follow the evidence wherever it leads.*"

Two Trees and a Lie

Chapter 26

*A*fter dinner was over the next evening, loud shouts and laughter echoed from Rosa's Hill. Eagerly, five Tinys gathered together in the quiet, peaceful Crisis Room. Many rainbows had danced on the walls in the afternoon sunlight, but now only a few faintly shimmered. The sun was just beginning to set.

Kenzie walked over to the large Bible that lay on the window seat beside Uncle Louis' bed. With the solar lights on all night, the older Tiny was never in complete darkness and could read as much as he wanted, day or night. The beach boys didn't really like the glare in the sky, but they understood the special circumstances.

Uncle Louis had decided it would be best to try and read one chapter from Genesis and Matthew each night. While Zahir longed to know more about Jesus, Uncle Louis knew from his own investigation that it was important to first understand what had happened at the very beginning of the world. As directed, Kenzie opened the Bible to the second chapter of Genesis and took his turn to read.

Zahir settled back attentively on his pillow, Ponce closed his eyes, and Aimee made herself comfortable on the sofa.

Finding the place where they had digressed the night before, Kenzie started reading about God planting a garden in Eden with lots of beautiful productive trees, rivers, animals and treasures of gold and precious stones. Man's first job was to be a gardener.

With a chuckle, Kenzie remarked. "This reminds me of Paradise!" He read the next few verses, "The LORD God took the man, and put him into the Garden of Eden to work it and to keep it. And the LORD God commanded the man, saying, 'You may surely eat of every tree of the garden, but of the tree of the knowledge of good and evil, you shall not eat, for in the day that you eat from it you shall surely die."

"So, there were two special trees," Uncle Louis pointed out. "A Tree of Life, and a Tree of the Knowledge of Good and Evil. The man was clearly told not to eat of the second tree."

"What is a Tree of the Knowledge of Good and Evil?" Aimee asked.

"We will need to read the next chapter to understand," Uncle Louis replied.

Kenzie continued, reading God's words, "It is not good that the man should be alone; I will make him a helper fit for him."

"The man was all alone?" Aimee questioned. "I wonder why God only made one human at first?"

They read on, discovering that God brought all the animals to the man who gave them names, but Adam didn't find a 'helper' that was suitable for him from among the animals.

Curiously, they continued the story.

"Wow!" Aimee marvelled after Kenzie read the next few verses, "God actually took a rib out of the man to make a woman. I wonder why He didn't just make a girl from the dust, like He made the man?"

"Good observation," Uncle Louis praised. "God made both the male and female animals from the dust, but He must have intended for humans to have a much closer, unique relationship. The woman was formed from the man's side. She was part of him."

Kenzie read the next part quietly, *"Then the man said, "This at last is bone of my bones and flesh of my flesh; she shall be called Woman, because she was taken out of Man." Therefore, a man shall leave his father and his mother and hold fast to his wife, and they shall become one flesh."*

After a few moments of complete silence in the room, Zahir spoke up. "Wow. How special is that?! Two become one. This sounds like... well, very much like the marriage concept that Lily was talking about."

"Yes," Uncle Louis agreed with a chuckle. "And notice that God allowed Adam to experience a period of loneliness so that when Eve was created from his side, the first man fully appreciated God's special gift. And maybe he felt some pain after the surgery – there was sacrifice involved to gain this gift."

Kenzie pondered the concept. "Adam said Eve was *'bone of my bones,'* ... a man and a woman are to become 'one flesh.' This sounds like a very serious commitment – a promise that can't be broken, just like Lily said."

"A lifelong decision," Zahir agreed.

"You are both listening well," Uncle Louis praised. From his prior research, he added in some points that he'd gleaned online. "Here in the beginning, we see what God truly wanted for His creation - committed family units living as faithful stewards of the earth and enjoying a full relationship with their Creator in a beautiful garden. Sin destroyed this peaceful state, but God has been slowly working with our hard hearts to bring us back to a true Paradise in the future."

Aimee wasn't quite sure what to say. "It's kind of strange that everyone is talking about weddings, and then we read about it in this book," she observed.

"Yes, it is," Kenzie nodded thoughtfully. "Although, I don't see anything about songs, or flower bouquets, or fancy dresses," he chuckled.

"I told Lily that wasn't necessary," Ponce piped up.

Since his eyes were closed, everyone was surprised that Ponce was still awake. Uncle Louis smiled.

Laughing, Aimee remarked, "I tried looking for the book Lily was talking about, but I didn't find it." She wished she could share the information she had Googled, but then she would have to explain about the phone.

Kenzie had noted another interesting feature in the verses he'd read. "Why don't *we* have mothers and fathers?" he asked, looking at Uncle Louis.

Uncle Louis did his best to explain how the Tinys had developed in the Professor's laboratory, from the minimal knowledge he had himself. "The Professor didn't 'make' you," he reiterated. "He took life that was already in existence and gave it the conditions to grow."

"But, then we must have parents somewhere?" Zahir puzzled. "Are they Tinys like us? Where do they live? Will we ever get to meet them?"

Uncle Louis didn't have all the answers and couldn't share everything that he knew. Instead, he discussed marriage a little more, based on what he had gleaned from the Bible before the fire. He explained how a man and a woman were to commit to live together, forsake all other romantic interests and become their own family unit.

"This is actually really helpful," Zahir confessed, sounding relieved. "We've all grown up with boys on one side and girls on the other. I wasn't sure if it was right to change that arrangement. But it seems that marriage is something which God intended for the people He made." With a light laugh, he added, "God says it's not good for a man to be alone! I think I like this book. I like it a lot."

There were smiles all around. However, to their great surprise the third chapter began with a crafty serpent questioning Eve.

Aimee wanted to know what a serpent was.

Uncle Louis laughed, saying that he was grateful that the Professor hadn't put any serpents in Paradise. He then asked for a piece of paper and a pencil, and the copper-haired nurse ran to get her journal for him to use.

Once he had the supplies, Uncle Louis drew a picture of a long, tubular creature with evil eyes and a forked tongue.

"Oh, that's creepy looking!" she said. "I don't think I'd go near anything that looked like that."

"Not even if it talked to you?" Zahir teased.

"Well," Aimee considered, "I guess it would be rather intriguing to hear an *animal* talk."

Kenzie read what the serpent said, *"Did God actually say, 'You shall not eat of any tree in the garden?'"*

"But that's not true," Zahir piped up. "God said there was only one tree they couldn't eat from."

Aimee questioned, "Is it telling a lie?"

They were pleased that Eve set the serpent straight. But then, the serpent insinuated that *God was lying!* He told Eve that the punishment for eating from the tree wouldn't actually be death, and that God was trying to keep them from becoming wise like the Creator Himself! *"You will not surely die,"* the serpent said, *"For God knows that when you eat of it, your eyes will be opened, and you will be like God, knowing good and evil."*

"This is confusing," Zahir murmured. "Is the serpent choosing to tell a lie? Or is it passing on its own wrong ideas?"

"Maybe the serpent is right," Ponce suggested with a wry grin.

"I don't know," Aimee replied nervously, "but I sure hope Eve doesn't listen. I don't like this serpent."

Reading further, they discovered that Eve *was* fooled by the lie, and thought she'd try the beautiful fruit. And not only that, but she gave some to her husband.

"Oh no," Aimee said anxiously. "They are both going to get in trouble. They only had one rule to keep."

Kenzie raised his eyebrows, "And the consequences of disobeying God's rule *is death!* I'm surprised they would risk it!"

With a smile, Uncle Louis asked, "Do you think they appreciated what death really was? Had they even seen death?"

Everyone looked at each other, remembering their own innocence before Rosa's accident. Aimee had to close her eyes and take a deep breath. She would always feel guilty for foolishly causing such a serious accident.

Thinking it through, Kenzie pondered the answer to his own question, "So maybe the consequence didn't seem so terrible, since it was beyond their experience..."

"But if God is really God, the Creator of us all, including the Professor," Zahir reasoned anxiously, "this makes me think that *we* need to know if God has made rules for *us*. What if we are disobeying important rules that God has recorded in His book because we don't even know what they are? What if there are harsh consequences to disobeying those rules?"

They read on with trepidation, as God questioned his first two children who were hiding amongst the trees. Adam and Eve responded with feeble confessions and laying blame on others.

"So, the man blames his wife, and the woman blames the serpent," Zahir smiled.

"It's always great to have someone to blame," Aimee laughed.

Kenzie observed, "I suppose it's good that they both eventually admitted to eating the fruit."

"True," they all agreed.

They were pleased to read on and discover that the serpent was punished first, after he had lied to Eve. Kenzie read God's words to the serpent, *"Because you have done this, cursed are you above all livestock and above all beasts of the field; on your belly you shall go, and dust you shall eat all the days of your life. I will put enmity between you and the woman, and between your offspring and her offspring; he shall bruise your head, and you shall bruise his heel."*

Looking at one another in confusion, the Tinys didn't completely understand the serpent's punishment. Uncle Louis explained that 'offspring' meant 'a person's child or children.'

"There are some notes in the margin," Kenzie called out, looking at them carefully. "It says that 'enmity' means 'the state or feeling of being actively opposed or hostile to someone or something – hatred.'"

Aimee tried to summarise the concept. "So, women will hate serpents, and their children will always fight with serpents..."

Thinking deeply about the Bible passage, Zahir asked, "But why will *the children* crush the head of the serpent?" he wondered. "Why wouldn't Adam kill it himself?"

"I would have smashed it!" Ponce boasted. "Just like we did to that big black spider!"

"Yes, you would have!" Aimee agreed. "So, why didn't Adam?"

"And why would the serpent be bruised on the head, but the offspring bruised on the heel?" queried Kenzie.

Ponce was enjoying the discussion. "Sounds to me like the serpent got stepped on," he replied.

No one had any better suggestions, so they read on. The woman's curse seemed a lesser punishment than the one put on the man. But it involved pain in childbearing!

"Hmm, so having a baby is painful," Aimee considered sadly for a moment, but then she decided with a smile, "I'd still want to have one. Imagine... a *baby* Tiny! It would be so cute!"

Reading over Adam's curse, the Tinys wanted to know about thorns and thistles.

Uncle Louis had investigated this himself, so he did another drawing, with rather exaggerated sharp prickles extending from a nasty-looking plant.

"I'm so glad we don't have thorns in Paradise!" Aimee exclaimed.

There was some discussion about God replacing Adam and Eve's fig leaf clothes with the skin of an animal. Uncle Louis explained that an animal would only be skinned if it was dead, so this would have been the first death Adam and Eve would have seen. "Blood had to be shed," he added sadly.

"Why?" Aimee asked with tragic eyes.

"Well, because God had already told them that if they disobeyed, they would die and return to the dust," Uncle Louis explained, thankful that he had looked into this when he had still had access to the cave, "but they didn't actually die that day, although the process had begun. They lived for many, many years. Instead, something had to die in their place to remind them of what they deserved themselves. And then God forgave them."

When they reached verses twenty-two to twenty-four, the copper-haired nurse was dismayed. "So, Adam and Eve got sent out of the garden so that they wouldn't eat of the Tree of Life and *live forever!*" She sighed, "Uncle Louis, if this book is real, does that mean that there is no more hope of living forever? Was there once a way that became lost?" Sadly, she remarked, "I don't know if I like this book..."

Uncle Louis chuckled. "You've only read a few chapters," he said. "The Bible is a very big book and it's all about salvation."

"What is salvation?" Zahir asked.

"Salvation is the way to forgiveness of sins and being right with God," he smiled. "It's the way back to the garden."

"Forgiveness... of sins?" Aimee questioned. "What does that mean?"

"Well, sin is going against God's rules,"[65] he explained. "From what I've read in the Bible, people who have done something wrong admit their mistake to God and if they are truly sorry, God doesn't give them what they deserve. He chooses to forget what they did. It's like they never did it in the first place."

---

[65] BDB definition for 'sin'. (Hebrew 2398) 'chata' – "to miss the way, go wrong"

208

Aimee's eyes flew wide open, staring at Uncle Louis. Could she be forgiven for causing Rosa's death? Would God forgive her? "The Bible is about forgiveness?" she asked, enthralled.

Uncle Louis nodded. "Maybe we should take a break here," he said. "It's getting dark outside. Kenzie, perhaps you can take the guys outside for a little stretch and exercise, and then we can do a chapter of the Professor's book?"

Zahir and Ponce left their beds to follow Kenzie. Ponce still needed a shoulder to lean on as one of his burns was over his knee and painful to stretch, but Zahir's wounds did not affect any joints. Gradually, he was getting up more often and moving around on his own.

The Professor's Perspective

Chapter 27

When the guys had left, Uncle Louis called Aimee over. "Are you still blaming yourself for Rosa's death?" he asked kindly.

Kneeling down beside his bed, Aimee burst into tears.

"You poor girl," he said compassionately, stroking her hair. "I saw it in your face! Yes, God can forgive you. You shouldn't be carrying so much guilt. What you did was not intentional, and you are truly sorry. Look, why don't you take some of these questions that have come up tonight and run down to the cave. Give the Professor a report on how everything is going, and then see if you can call Evan. He might have better answers for you than I do."

"Right now?" she questioned, wiping her tears away. "But I love our evenings when we all read together. How about I go when everyone falls asleep?"

Uncle Louis smiled and patted her head. "You are a special girl," he said. "I'm so glad you are my sister! I love you, Aimee."

There were some quizzical looks in Aimee's direction when the guys came back up to the Crisis Room. Leaving Uncle Louis' side, Aimee wiped her tears on a cloth and sat back down on the sofa with Kenzie.

In a quiet voice, Kenzie said, "Uncle Louis, I should just let you know that Sanaa and Lema are outside on the bench. They are often in that spot at this time of night. They may overhear..."

"That's okay," Uncle Louis nodded. "I've been asked to limit who is in the room with us, but nothing was said about who may be outside. But thank you for telling me, Kenzie."

Picking up the other book, Uncle Louis read the title of the second chapter, *"The Evolution of Morality.'* Let's see what the Professor has to say."

Within the first two pages, the four young Tinys became very confused. They had learned from the Bible that God created man 'very good.' Uncle Louis had explained that it was man's disobedience in partaking of the 'Tree of Knowledge of Good and Evil' that led to an ongoing inner struggle between serpent-like thinking and a 'very good' conscience implanted from the beginning by the Creator. In the Bible, God had clearly defined morality by giving His laws and setting the standards of 'holiness.' He knew what was best for His creation to thrive. Serving others and caring for the oppressed and underprivileged was an important foundation of all the laws of God, because this was the character of the Creator Himself.

However, in 'Faith or Fact – An End to Delusion,' there was no higher intelligence guiding life, or authoritatively defining right from wrong. Since evolution was simply a chance occurrence, improved by many helpful mutations coming together at just the right time, then who had any authority to say what was right or wrong? If life was all about the survival of the fittest and the extinction of the weakest, then 'morality' in evolutionary terms had neither example nor a written code on which to build. This was acknowledged by the Professor, with a quote from Charles Darwin, the founder of evolutionary thought. "With savages, the weak in body or mind are soon eliminated; and those that survive commonly exhibit a vigorous state of health. We civilised men, on the other hand, do our utmost to check the process of elimination, we build asylums for the imbecile, the maimed, and the sick; we institute poor-laws; and our medical men exert their utmost skill to save the life of everyone to the last moment. There is reason to believe that vaccination has preserved thousands, who from a weak constitution would formerly have succumbed to smallpox. Thus the weak members of civilised societies propagate their kind. No one who has attended to the breeding of domestic animals will doubt that this must be highly injurious to the race of man. It is surprising how soon a want of care, or care wrongly directed, leads to the degeneration of a domestic race; but excepting in the case of man himself, hardly anyone is so ignorant as to allow his worst animals to breed." [66]

Reading it over twice, Uncle Louis asked the Tinys what they thought of the quote. Some of the concepts were foreign and he had to explain several words.

Zahir spoke up with concern, "So, if we all just evolved, then he's saying that it's better that the weak die off, and the strong reproduce?"

"That is the logical outcome of the theory of evolution," Uncle Louis agreed. "Only the strongest and best of the race should have children, and they should produce many children. The weak, on the other hand, should be excluded from breeding, and left to die off as they will..."

"That kind of thinking could lead to really selfish behaviour," Kenzie remarked.

"Now," Uncle Louis pointed out, "the Professor does not agree with Darwin's logical outcome, and goes to great length in this chapter to encourage us to be kind and unselfish, but on what basis? The chance 'god' doesn't give us a helpful example to strive to follow. If evolution is all about improving the species by the survival of the

---

[66] Darwin, Charles. *The Descent of Man,* pt. 1, chap. V, pg. 168

fittest and elimination of the weak, on what basis should humans extend compassion or help to those who are suffering? The Professor explains that it is logical for us to be kind to those related to us, but he struggles to explain how we could have evolved compassion for strangers or enemies. On what basis would anyone give his life to save those who are weaker or less worthy?"

Ponce's eyes flitted open for a moment, and then he closed them quickly.

The chapter went on to list examples of God's genocide and indiscriminate killing in the Old Testament. The Midianites were massacred, the inhabitants of Jericho put to the sword, even many of the Israelites whom God was leading into the 'Promised Land' were killed by plague or venomous snakes when they complained and rebelled against God.

This was disconcerting for the Tinys, hearing about such horrendous events for the first time. In his book, the Professor had remarked, *"The Old Testament is full of violence and destruction. In the process of 'delivering' his favorite people from slavery, the Old Testament 'god' obliterated the peaceful nations all around. Women, children and the elderly were butchered by his 'chosen' race, who then greedily took over their houses, livestock and farmlands. Yet, this same 'mighty' god wipes out thousands of his own chosen people for very understandable weaknesses - like complaining when they haven't had any meat to eat for months on end. How can anyone trust or admire such a vengeful, unpredictable, wrathful being? When superstitions and myths abounded in ages past, certainly this god fit in well with all the other strange tales of immoral, supernatural beings wreaking havoc on mankind. But in our Modern Era, where morality has evolved to a much kinder and humane level – these tales are appalling! In the 21st Century, we can easily perceive that this is not a being we want to hold up to our children as an example to follow!"*

Since no one in the room, aside from Uncle Louis, had read about God leading Israel out of Egypt, they were unable to comment on whether God was acting fairly or in fits of unprovoked anger.

"However, it seems to me," Uncle Louis pondered, "that the Professor's alternative view isn't any better than the one he is condemning. Didn't he say that evolution is all about the strong fighting to survive and selfishly taking the best for themselves?"

Feeling rather shocked by the accusations they had just read, the other Tinys remained silent.

Having already looked at many of the cross-references that Seth had written in the margins and even a number of pencilled notes, Uncle Louis was open to a different perspective than his father's. "I don't think God *unfairly* wiped out the *'peaceful'* inhabitants of Canaan. It says in Genesis... maybe chapter fifteen, that God didn't allow Abraham or his descendants to take the Promised Land for four hundred years until the wickedness of the people in the land required His intervention."[67]

Looking up the Genesis passage, Uncle Louis found a note that had written in the margin that he remembered had been helpful. Pondering it, he relayed, "It says here that God warned the people of Israel that if they engaged in the sinful practices of the people of Canaan, they too would be 'vomited out of the land,'[68] and in fact they were," he remarked, reading on. "Hundreds of years later, when they rebelled against God's standards of holiness and began behaving just like the other nations, God brought destruction on them and scattered their survivors all over the earth."[69]

He stopped and looked closely at the handwritten notes. "This also says, 'that any individual from the land of Canaan who showed

---

[67] Genesis 15:12-16
[68] Deuteronomy 9:1-7; Leviticus 18:19-30; Leviticus 20:22-27
[69] Ezekiel 36:16-20; Isaiah 64:6-12; Luke 13:34-35; 21:20-24

faith in God was saved – like Rahab and her family,[70] or the whole Gibeonite clan.'"[71]

Having been listening intently, Zahir spoke up, "It seems to me, that if it's true that God created and sustains the life of this world, then obviously He should get to make the rules. And if life comes from Him, then it's something He can freely take away if people despise Him."

Kenzie agreed. "The Professor writes as though he thinks he is far better than God." Looking in Uncle Louis' direction he asked, "Is that true?"

Uncle Louis sighed. "I don't know. I don't think he would state it like that. But I do feel he's bitter against Him... even though he doesn't even believe He is real... it's all rather strange to me."

After so many deep concepts to consider that evening, the patients were struggling to stay awake. Both were asleep by the time they reached the end of the chapter.

"Good night, fellows," Uncle Louis said affectionately. "We'll read some more tomorrow. Matthew chapter two will have to wait."

---

[70] Joshua 6:17–25; Hebrews 11:31
[71] Joshua 9

215

The Plan of Salvation

Chapter 28

An increasing din of voices and laughter signalled the return of Aimee's housemates that evening. The young nurse left the mansion to make her way down to the cave. As usual, Kenzie stayed in the Crisis Room with the guys, in case anyone needed help during the night. Quietly slipping through the forest, Aimee heard another crash of trees. It was becoming a common occurrence. Most of the trees on the steep hillside had toppled over.

There were a lot of questions that Aimee hoped Evan would be able to answer. First, she chatted to the Professor. He had also done some research.

"I found out why the trees are falling over," he told her with a sad smile.

"Why?" she asked.

"It turns out that trees need the wind to help them develop strong root structures and strengthen their wood."

"Wind? What is wind?"

"In our world we have plenty of wind," he told her. "The air blows around us. On some days the blowing air is pleasant and cooling, but at other times it can be destructive, cold and irritating. I thought you would all enjoy Paradise better without the wind, so I didn't put any in."

Aimee still wasn't sure she knew what wind was, but she asked, "Will all the trees fall down without it?"

"Possibly," he admitted. "So, I'm going to gradually increase the force of ventilation, hoping that it's not too late. Be prepared to see waves on the lake any time of day now, and find that your hair is blowing all over the place. At night when everyone is asleep, I'll program one hour of heavy blowing. Then if trees fall down, at least you'll all be safe inside your homes."

Smiling, Aimee tried to imagine life with wind.

The Professor asked her to visit the store the next day and see if Nancy and Milan needed anything aside from the usual shipments. "And how is the book supply?" he asked. "Have Georgia and Lily read all the new books to the patients?"

"They haven't come to read in the last few days," she relayed. "Georgia is taking surfing lessons and Lily is making a surprise for Ponce in the Forest. He has big plans to make it a Fun Forest, so she's talked Franz and Odin into helping her make something that Ponce will love. I'm not sure what it is."

"So, Georgia is not coming in to read?"

"No."

There was smile on the Professor's face that Aimee didn't understand. He asked, "Are you feeling rather bored in the Crisis Room? What do the patients do all day?"

"We talk when the guys aren't sleeping," Aimee told him. "And they sleep a lot! Sometimes, Uncle Louis reads to us from the two books that you allowed to be sent in... but only when no one else is around."

"Right," he nodded with interest. "And what do you think of the two books?"

"The one fills me with hope and the desire to be a better person," she said.

"And the other?"

217

Aimee faltered. She wasn't sure how honest she could be. There was an awkward silence.

"I suppose the other may use a lot of scientific terms that you don't understand?"

Nodding, Aimee was thankful for his input.

"You can ask me about anything that you don't understand."

"Thank you," she said, forcing a smile.

The Professor told her about some of the games he had sent in that Ponce and Zahir might be able to play now that they were healing. Then he asked about Uncle Louis. "Does he get up and walk around at all?"

"Oh yes," she said. "Kenzie makes all of them get up and stretch a few times each day. Uncle Louis walks around the room and sometimes he walks down outside to the patio. Ponce and Zahir now use the outhouse on their own. Walking up and down the hill gives them a lot of exercise!"

There were many other questions, which Aimee answered as best she could.

Once the Professor had said goodnight, Aimee called Evan.

Two faces came up on the video. Evan was sitting beside a red-haired young man in a room with many chairs and they both had Bibles on their laps. Several other people stood behind them talking to each other. She saw a verse written across the back wall.

"Aimee, this is such a surprise," Evan exulted. "I'm so happy that you're calling *us*."

Aimee wanted to know who Evan was with and where they were, so he introduced his friend, Seth, and explained they were in a church building, and had just finished a Bible class on the book of Romans.

When Evan asked why she was calling, Aimee explained they had been reading from the Bible. She relayed some of the questions they had.

"I'm going to let Seth answer your questions," Evan smiled as he stood up with the phone and walked into a quieter room. "He's been reading the Bible a lot longer than me."

Seth followed his friend with his Bible in hand. With a laugh he said, "But I'd love to hear *your* answers for Aimee. Go ahead, Evan."

"No, you'll explain it much better than me," he protested.

Smiling, Seth shrugged his consent. He replied to Aimee's first question from the Bible. "Being made 'in the image of God'[72] is unique to human beings," he told her. "None of the animals were made in God's image. No doubt this means that we resemble the outward form of God and His angels, but I believe it's even more than this. Humans have the ability to reason on a much higher level than anything else in creation. Adam and Eve were made 'very good,' and Romans chapter two tells us that we have an inbuilt conscience to help us determine right from wrong. God created the world with precise laws and rational order, and He gave us intelligent minds that can search out His complex formulas and *'think His thoughts after Him.'*[73]

Nodding, Aimee's eyes were wide open. "Then God must view us as a very *special* part of His creation," she reasoned, thinking this was a great contrast to the Professor's view that man evolved from apes. She liked Evan's friend with the bright red hair. He had an engaging smile.

"He does," Seth agreed earnestly. "And God had an amazing plan in mind when He first created human beings. It was to fill the earth with those who not only are in His image, but who also *choose* to think and act like Him, in order to 'fill the earth with His glory.'[74]

---

[72] Genesis 1:26 – 27 - "image"– Hebrew 6754 – Strong's definition – "to shade; a phantom, that is, (figuratively) illusion, resemblance; hence a representative figure, especially an idol: image, vain shew." See also 1 Corinthians 11:7

[73] Johann Kepler, 1571 -1630

[74] Numbers 14:21; Psalm 72:19; Revelation 21:22-27

God's name is Yahweh, which means 'I will be who I will be'. He wants to adopt[75] a family who choose to reflect His moral likeness, so He can share His incredible Divine nature with them.[76] So, Yahweh, our Father in Heaven started with a beautiful creation," Seth smiled, pointing to the creation pictures on the wall.

Aimee was enthralled.

"Planet Earth is a witness to our Father's marvelous intelligence and creativity, and His ability to extravagantly provide for all the needs of every creature He created. If you think Paradise is beautiful, the real world is a thousand times better... even a million times better!"

"It is!" she agreed in amazement, gazing at the breathtaking scenery on the posters and recalling her own discoveries on the Internet.

"But the first man and woman didn't appreciate God's plan or His love for them," Seth continued with sadness in His voice. "They chose to listen to a crafty, lying serpent instead."[77] Pausing, he asked, "Was everything that the serpent said, a lie?"

"Not completely," Aimee pondered.

Seth nodded. "The most convincing lies are those that combine truth and error. Sometimes lies sound good, but there can be a little twist that is wrong and often hard to catch. Did the serpent portray God as someone to be trusted?" he asked.

"No," Aimee replied. "The serpent made it sound like *God* was the one who was lying in order to keep good things from them."

"Exactly," Seth nodded. "And, instead of trusting God who was trustworthy, and loved them completely, and had done everything to give them an amazing existence, Adam and Eve trusted the lying

---

[75] Romans 8:12-17; Galatians 4:1-7; Ephesians 1:3-6
[76] Revelation 14:1; 22:4; 1 John 3:1-11
[77] 2 Corinthians 11:3

serpent – who had done nothing to *earn* their trust - and they ate the forbidden fruit." He showed Aimee a picture of the story that hung on the Sunday School wall. The snake looked even scarier than the one Uncle Louis had drawn.

Continuing, Seth said, "Because they chose to see God as a liar trying to keep good things from them, and despised the love He had shown, the world became cursed with evil and death." He then asked her another question. "But what did God promise concerning the serpent?"

"He said Eve's children would crush the serpent's head."

Seth smiled and nodded. "Yes, God's message of salvation begins with the very first sin," he told her. He explained that God has established the principle that sin requires death,[78] but forgiveness is possible through death of another,[79] and in the Old Testament this provision was made through lambs, goats and cattle – in anticipation of the real sacrifice Jesus would make. [80] In response to the very first sin, God put an animal to death to clothe Adam and Eve with its skin. However, this sacrifice was tied into the promise in Genesis chapter three that God would ultimately bring salvation through one of Eve's descendants, or children, who would overcome the curse and provide the way to live forever.[81]

It was all adding up to the same message that Uncle Louis had shared, and Aimee was beginning to put it together.

"Do you have any idea who the most important descendant of Eve might be?" Seth asked.

With a frown, Aimee thought it over. "Well, Uncle Louis says that he wants to be like Jesus Christ..."

---

[78] Genesis 2:16-17; Romans 6:23; 5:12-14
[79] Leviticus 17:11; Hebrews 9:22
[80] Hebrews 9:11-28; 1 John 1:7; 1 Peter 1:19-21
[81] Romans 5:8-21

"Jesus is the one!" Evan cheered, hoping Seth's detailed explanation wasn't going too deep for the young Tiny.

"He stepped on the serpent?"

Evan and Seth looked at each other hesitantly.

After a pause, Seth encouraged, "Aimee, there's more to this than just people trying to kill serpents, or 'snakes,' as they are commonly called."

"Snakes," Aimee repeated thoughtfully.

"It's like this," Seth told her. "Because the serpent was the first to lie and lead someone to sin and ultimately death, the serpent represents the temptation to sin. When we feel the pull inside to try something that is forbidden, it's like having the serpent speaking inside of us.[82] If we listen to it, we will sin. God says that all sin is worthy of death."[83]

"Any sin?" Aimee said in a small voice.

"Yes," Seth replied kindly. Seeing the anxious look on her face, he smiled, "Don't worry, Aimee. God knew we all would need His plan of forgiveness and salvation!"

Turning to another poster, the redhead explained, "Jesus Christ was God's Son, and he lived a perfectly sinless life. He never gave in to the serpent-like thinking inside him.[84] All his life he stepped on the 'head of the serpent,' rather than allow his own fleshly thinking to persuade him to go against God. Jesus' goodness provoked so much envy and hatred in some people that he was put to death by the very people he was trying to save. But Jesus remained sinless to the end, putting that tempting voice to death once and for all on the cross.[85] He likened his own death to a brass serpent on a pole.[86] As a mortal,

---

[82] James 1:13–15
[83] Romans 6:16–23; 1:28–32; 8:13
[84] Hebrews 4:15–16
[85] Hebrews 2:14–18
[86] John 3:14; Numbers 21:4–9

dying human being, Jesus 'in every respect has been tempted as we are, yet without sin.'[87] When he rose from the grave, God gave him immortality – God's sinless nature[88] – and he will never be tempted by serpent-like thinking again."

Evan pointed to a picture on the wall with three crosses on a hill, and then one that showed an empty tomb.

"Are there Bible pictures all over the walls?" Aimee asked.

Seth smiled. "This is the Sunday School room," he said. "We have a lot of pictures in here." He gave her a quick tour of the decorated room with many pictures and shelves full of books. A table and ten chairs sat in the middle.

"That looks like a good place to learn," Aimee smiled. Then she reflected on what Seth had said. "When someone is given im... immorality..."

"Immortality," Seth corrected with a smile.

She struggled to pronounce the word. "Then they are *never* tempted again?"

"Exactly," Seth nodded. "When God gives us *His* nature,[89] we will no longer feel the impulses to do wrong. That will be a wonderful day of freedom for all of us![90] That is when we will finally be able to fully enjoy Paradise." He smiled and waved dismissively, "Goodbye, human nature!"

Aimee mulled it over.

Building on the concept, Seth said, "Because Jesus faithfully gave up his life in obedience every day, God accepted his sinless death as a sacrifice to redeem us[91] and give everyone an opportunity to live

---

[87] Hebrews 4:15

[88] 1 Corinthians 15:42-57; Hebrews 5:8-9

[89] Philippians 3:20-21; 1 John 3:1-4; 1 Corinthians 15:49; Rom. 8:29; James 1:13

[90] Romans 8:18-31; Acts 3:19-21

[91] Isaiah 53; 1 Peter 2:24; Romans 6

forever if they confess their sins, ask for forgiveness and are baptised into the name of Jesus Christ."[92]

Aimee was trying to understand, but there was a lot of new information in Seth's explanation. She looked at him wide-eyed.

"That's a lot to take in..." she said hesitantly. "I really don't understand why Jesus had to die."

Seth tried again, "There is a chapter in the New Testament that explains this very well," he said. "You might want to show this to Uncle Louis. It's in Romans chapter five."

While Seth was finding the passage, Evan piped up. Since he was new to the Gospel message as well, he had struggled with the same concerns only a few weeks before.

"I understand your question, Aimee," he said. "This is how Seth explained it to me. God makes laws – fair laws. Our entire universe is based on unchanging, steadfast, calculable laws, that we can measure, depend on and make our plans around. God said that sin brings death.[93] It's a law. But, in his *mercy,* God made a provision that one day He would have a Son who would be willing to give up his life on a daily basis[94] as well as on the cross to save everyone afflicted with this mortal, fleshly condition... including himself.[95] God has promised to forgive the sins of everyone who chooses to identify and believe in that Savior's sacrifice.[96] Death is what we all deserve, and Jesus was *willing* to be our Savior.[97]

---

[92] John 3:14-18; Romans 8:31-39; Galatians 3:27-29; Acts 2:37-39; Rom. 6:1-14
[93] Genesis 2:17; Romans 6:22-23; Romans 5:12-21
[94] Luke 9:22-23
[95] Hebrews 2:9-18; 5:1-9:
[96] John 3:16-18
[97] Leviticus 17:11; Hebrews 9:11-28

"Okay, I see," Aimee said, remembering her discussion with Uncle Louis. "So, you are saying that this is all linked into the very first sin, when an animal died instead of Adam and Eve?"

Evan clapped in an encouraging way. "Yes, exactly," he praised. "Just as God covered Adam and Eve in the skin of a sacrificed animal, God will cover us by His Son's sacrifice.[98] They confessed their sin and God forgave them. They lived for hundreds of years after this sin, and likely had to repent, confess and ask for forgiveness many times over."

Agreeing with Evan's remarks, Seth said, "Here's what the Bible says in Romans chapter five. *'Therefore, just as sin came into the world through one man, and death through sin...'*" Pausing, Seth explained, *"*That's speaking of Adam and his sin. Sin and death came into the world because of Adam."

He continued to read, *"And so death spread to all men because all sinned. Therefore, as one trespass'* - Adam's trespass -," Seth interjected, *"'led to condemnation for all men, so one act of righteousness'* – Jesus giving up his life – *'leads to justification and life for all men. For as by the one man's disobedience the many were made sinners, so by the one man's obedience the many will be made righteous... so that, as sin reigned in death, grace also might reign through righteousness leading to eternal life through Jesus Christ our Lord."*

"What is this 'grace' that reigns?" Aimee asked.

"Grace is a beautiful gift that isn't deserved," Seth told her. "Even though God holds firmly to His laws as a good Father, He provided this plan of salvation because He loves us and wants us to be saved."[99]

Trying to bring it all together for Aimee, Seth found a chart on the wall, that he showed her with his phone. Pointing to each little picture

---

[98] Leviticus 4:20, 26; Romans 4:6–8; Romans 8:6–21
[99] 2 Peter 3:9; 1 Tim. 2:3–4; Ezekiel 18:23; 33:10–11; Titus 2:11–14

he explained, "Jesus is the 'offspring' or the 'child' of the woman... the promise to Eve," he told her. "Through God's Holy Spirit power, Jesus was miraculously born by a mother without a human father and therefore he is called the Son of God.[100] Jesus was obedient in all that his Heavenly Father asked him to do. He never disobeyed God. Jesus crushed the serpent's head - he destroyed the serpent by overcoming the voice of human nature in his life and willingly putting it to death on the cross[101] - which for him was like a temporary bruise on the heel that lasted only three days. Because of his faithfulness and implicit trust in His Father, all of us have been given grace. We are gifted the opportunity to find the way back to forgiveness and salvation – the way to live with our Creator forever."[102]

"So, there *is* still a way to the Tree of Life," Aimee smiled happily.

"Yes," Seth nodded. "There is definitely a way back. Keep reading through Genesis. You will find out about the man Abraham to whom God first preached the *Gospel message,* as we're told in Galatians three. The promises that God made to Abraham are the foundation of all the promises in the Bible. And," he paused thoughtfully, "I'd also recommend that you also take some time to read about the primary descendant spoken of in those promises [103] - the Messiah - Jesus our Saviour."

"There is a lot to read," Aimee reflected. "So, God made promises to people about Jesus... long before he was born?"

---

[100] Luke 1:35
[101] Hebrews 2:14-15; Hebrews 5:8
[102] Revelation 22:1-5
[103] Galatians 3:8-16

Seth nodded. "Yes, throughout the Old Testament, God promised a son who would bring salvation. He promised this son to Eve,[104] to Abraham[105] and even King David."[106]

"And Jesus was the son of them all?"

"Yes, they were all related in a family line.[107] Today we call this family line the Jewish people. Many other people are in this family line, but only some were given this specific promise."

"We started reading the book of Matthew," Aimee told them.

"Excellent!" Seth replied. "Keep it up. That's exactly what I'd recommend."

Aimee left the cave later that night still a little confused but also excited to find out more about God's promises. The charts and pictures had been helpful. "There *is* hope for life after death!" she rejoiced. "There is forgiveness for our sins! And immortality means no more human nature! I love this message!"

---

[104] Genesis 3:15
[105] Genesis 22:14–18
[106] 2 Samuel 7:12–16
[107] Matthew 1:1; Galatians 3:16; Acts 13:22–23; Romans 1:1–3

Awards

Chapter 29

Having been on the new antibiotics and protein formula for over two weeks, Zahir and Ponce were improving quickly. Their wounds were closing over and forming scabs, and now Uncle Louis and the nurses had to keep reminding them not to scratch, regardless of how itchy those scabs were becoming. At Aimee's request, new anti-itch cream came in, to be applied whenever it was needed. With some of the wounds no longer covered by gauze, the patients often applied it themselves.

Two and a half weeks after the fire, Ponce and Zahir were able to walk around the house and even sit outside if they avoided the sun. Zahir's right eye was steadily worsening, but he could still see fine with the other. He often remarked how much he appreciated the ability to see and that he never wanted to lose this gift!

Uncle Louis insisted the two patients stay near the Caring Centre. "You still need to be reminded to drink every couple of hours and take all your medications," he told them. "You still need to be very careful to keep everything clean and dress those wounds with antibiotics. When your scabs come off on their own, you can move back to your own homes."

Often in the afternoons, when it was time for Kenzie and Aimee to pass out the medication and rub ointment and anti-itch cream into the wounds, Ponce and Zahir would rest in bed, listening as Uncle Louis read through the records of Genesis. Even Ponce enjoyed hearing the stories as a gentle breeze blew through the windows. Most afternoons the patients would eventually fall asleep. They were still abnormally tired as their bodies continued to heal.

With Seth's advice in mind, Aimee had been taking careful note of all that God had promised Abraham. She had made quite a list: a great name, becoming a great nation, so many descendants they couldn't be counted, nations and kings coming from him, and all nations blessed through him and His descendants. She was curious to hear that the land of Canaan, from the Nile to the Euphrates River, was promised to *Abraham* and his descendants *forever.*[108] "Why?" she wondered. "Why would they all want that same piece of land?" She had looked it up online and it was just a tiny stretch adjoining the Mediterranean Sea. "And if they are to receive it forever, I guess they will be raised to live forever! Well, I like that."

When the patients fell asleep that afternoon, Aimee coaxed Kenzie and Uncle Louis to read through Galatians three, like Seth had recommended. To their great surprise, they had discovered that Jesus Christ was Abraham's most important descendant! With astonishment they read, *"For as many of you as were baptized into Christ have put on Christ. There is neither Jew nor Greek, there is neither slave nor free, there is no male and female, for you are all one in Christ Jesus. And if you are Christ's, then* you are *Abraham's offspring, heirs according to promise."*

"So, these promises relate to Abraham and Jesus!" Uncle Louis exclaimed. "And if we're baptized into Christ, then we will also inherit them..." Following a few more notes in the margin, they examined Hebrews eleven, and Acts chapter seven, to see that Abraham had never received *any* of those promises in his lifetime but had complete

---

[108] Great Name & Nation — Genesis 12:1-2; 17:5-6;
Many Descendants — Gen. 15:4-5; All Nations Blessed — Gen. 12:3;
Land Forever — Genesis 13:14-17; 17:7-8

confidence that their fulfillment would be in the future - in the future with Jesus! [109]   A number of passages written by hand on the page linked to Isaiah two, and eleven, Ezekiel thirty-six and thirty-seven, and Zechariah fourteen, and helped them to visualise the special promises God had given for the land of Israel in the future. It would be a place where the whole world would come to learn of God and worship the Great King!

Vahid suddenly burst into the Caring Centre with a large brown paper package. "Special delivery for you, Uncle Louis," he said, bringing the envelope to him. "I'm sorry we didn't bring it this morning. Somehow, it was taken into the store by accident."

Sitting on the window seat beside the older man's bed, Kenzie and Aimee looked over curiously.

"Just so you know," Vahid relayed. "There's a big pine tree across the stone stairs."

Uncle Louis looked over at the nurses. "A tree on *this side,*" he said with concern. Almost all the trees on the steep side of Rainbow Hill had fallen over, but it was rare for them to fall in other places. "Last night that wind blew so strongly!" he recalled. "I do remember hearing a loud crash."

Aimee nodded.

Zahir and Ponce opened their eyes.

"There's a saw in my house," Zahir murmured sleepily. "It's hanging by the front door."

"Thanks," Vahid replied.

"I'll help you," Kenzie offered, jumping up.

Uncle Louis was reaching into the brown envelope. "There's a bunch of medallions in here!" he marvelled. Pulling out a list of names, he looked over at the others. "We will be doing another awards

---

[109] Acts 7:2-6; Hebrews 11:8-16,39-40

ceremony," he announced cheerfully. "A new Courage Celebration is in order."

Glancing over at the curly, brown-haired nurse who was heading toward the door, the older Tiny said, "Kenzie, while you're out there, please tell everyone that after dinner tonight, we'll gather outside the mansion and give out these medals. There were many brave actions during the fire."

"I'll do that," Kenzie agreed. Getting up, he ran off with Vahid to find the saw and spread the news.

When dinner was over that night, all the Tinys gathered outside the mansion. It was a grey evening, but a lovely breeze was blowing, and the trees around the house were swaying softly in the wind. It was strangely beautiful to see them moving. Although the new suncatcher was whirling around, there was no sunshine to reflect.

Kenzie and Vahid brought Uncle Louis down to sit on the swinging bench and handed him the brown envelope. Zahir saw the older Tiny shiver and so he made his way back upstairs to grab a blanket, which was gratefully accepted.

Taking his place beside Ponce who was standing against the wall of the house, the two patients stood together, still bandaged in a couple places on their limbs. However, most of their wounds were now healing well with dark purple scabs.

There were several complimentary remarks given when Odin arrived. It was the first time Aimee had seen his new haircut and she was impressed. The wild, unkempt Tiny looked far more respectable. Looking over at Vinitha, she gave her a smile. "Great job!" she praised.

Once all the Tinys had gathered around, Uncle Louis began with a speech, "As you know, the Professor has sent in some special tokens of acknowledgement for the valiant actions of many during the fire. Most of the time, here in Paradise, everything goes smoothly, and life has been very easy for us. But occasionally we have had some terrible events which have tested our responses. Certain Tinys have demonstrated remarkable courage and compassion at those times, and the Professor believes you deserve special recognition for this. Taking out the Shining Moons, Uncle Louis laid them out on the table in front of him. Some were attached to gold chains, and some were not. One by one, he named the recipients of those four shiny, silver moons. Kenzie, Damien, Lema and Sanaa had all shown extra fortitude to fight the fire and rally the others to help. Lema was singled out for saving the lives of Zahir and Ponce, since he had fearlessly endured the heat to put out the flames on their hair and clothes. Now the proud possessor of two moon medallions, Lema expressed his gratitude with a happy celebration dance. Damien who had also come dangerously close to the fire was quite pleased to now have a Gold Heart *and* a Shining Moon and proudly showed them off to everyone. Sanaa rejoiced as well, when she received hers. Kenzie quietly slipped his on without much ado.

Tina, Yu Yan, Kenzie and Vahid were all given small silver double hearts for their "Compassionate Care of the Injured."

Milan, Vahid, Charley, and everyone who didn't already have a gold chain, were given silver necklaces with a Circle medallion, for "Persistent Effort in Adverse Circumstances." Even Odin, Franz and Ponce were given the Circle medallion.

Damien was incensed. "That doesn't make any sense!" he remarked indignantly. "They started the whole disaster, and yet they get a medal for grudgingly helping us less than half of the time?"

"They definitely don't deserve it!" Lema grumbled.

Uncle Louis wasn't entirely sure he agreed with giving the instigators rewards, but his role was to support the Professor as much as possible. However, he did feel it laid a foundation for what he hoped all the Tinys would learn one day. To the whole group he said, "It is important to face up the to the consequences of our actions, and I think these three young men have done that." Then he added, "And it is important to show true forgiveness when people make mistakes, because we all want forgiveness when we act foolishly." Looking at Odin, Franz and Ponce, he quietly encouraged, "Remember to show this same kind of mercy to others. If you forgive others, you too will be forgiven. There's not one of us that doesn't need forgiveness."

Then Uncle Louis pulled out a gold star much like his own and a gold heart. All eyes were drawn to it. "While all of you showed courage to fight the fire and the Professor is *very* pleased by the response that everyone gave, there is one young man who stood out above the others, risking his life and enduring much pain to save someone else."

Before Uncle Louis said another word, all the Tinys looked over at the dark, curly-haired young man with the long purple wounds. Holding out the two medallions, Uncle Louis said, "Zahir, you well and truly deserve the Finest Star and the Gold Heart."

Zahir stepped forward and took his rewards politely. "Thank you," he said. He looked like he wanted to say more, but then he shook his head and retired back to the wall.

For a moment, Uncle Louis covered his face with his hands. Many of the Tinys were putting on their necklaces and comparing their medallions, thinking that the ceremony was over. But it wasn't. Uncle Louis reached into the package one more time.

He pulled out another Gold Heart. "Aimee, he said, choking up slightly. "This is for you. You also saved a life, in fact, in the last few weeks, you've saved three. Thank you for your love and compassion to those of us who were in need."

The emotion in Uncle Louis' voice brought tears to Aimee's eyes. She stepped forward to receive her reward, but first she gave Uncle Louis a hug. The hug led to more tears between both.

"Come on, come on," Damien called out with distaste. "Don't get all emotional. It's just a necklace."

"It's more than a necklace," Zahir disagreed, holding his medallions in his hand. His chain still hung upstairs on his bed.

"What do you know, Scar Man?" Damien muttered.

"The Lady in White definitely deserves this recognition," Ponce smiled graciously.

Zahir and Kenzie nodded, but no one else understood who 'The Lady in White' was or cared to ask.

Odin got up to leave. "Well, finally, I have a necklace," he laughed loudly. "Even if the rest of you still don't seem to understand that I was just trying to help out. I was only trying to break us all free from this cage. I didn't mean for it to turn out the way that it did!"

"Do it again, and you know what will happen!" Damien threatened fiercely.

With caution in his voice, Uncle Louis asked, "What will happen?"

"They say they'll drown me!" Odin called out, lumbering off toward the unfinished staircase. "But I won't be going down without a fight!"

"Are you serious?" Uncle Louis asked, looking at Damien with deep disapproval.

"If no one else is going to stop him, I will!" Damien replied savagely, folding his arms across his chest and standing tall.

"And I'll help," Lema piped up. "We've had enough of all the trouble he's caused."

Sanaa looked distraught. Taking her friend's arm, she whispered something in his ear.

Uncle Louis called Odin back and launched into a full discussion with the whole group. He asked them about their feelings concerning retribution, forgiveness, consequences and who had the authority to carry out justice. Many voices were raised and dissenting opinions given. There was an underlying angry frustration that Odin, Ponce and Franz had not faced adequate punishment for their harmful disruptions and were not curtailed by any fear of what might happen in the future should they cause harm once again. Some of the girls were fearful that Odin and Franz might cause another disaster. Damien kept insisting that if no one else was going to stop the troublemakers, then he would. Charley and Vahid were on his side. Lema was perturbed. Odin and Franz boasted that if anyone tried to mess with them, they would be sorry. Ponce and Kenzie tried their best to reconcile the two groups and make peace, while Uncle Louis protested that it was never right to take someone's life, regardless of what they had done. He told them all firmly that those decisions were to be left to the Professor.

"Are you joking?" Damien retorted angrily. "Leave it to the Professor? The Professor *rewards* fools for throwing a few buckets of water on a fire that *they started?* How can we trust that he'll ever stop these troublemakers from harming us again? They keep getting away with it! What if someone had lost their life in that fire? Would the Professor still send in medallions to honour their *'persistent effort'?"*

"I wasn't trying to harm anyone," Odin reiterated. "I was trying to help you all go free. But if anyone tries to mess with me," he chuckled, "don't think I'll go down easy."

Zahir had not said a word as he listened to the arguments rage on all side. Uneasily, he made a suggestion, "I think we need a few more rules with clear consequences..."

"Like what, Scar man?" Damien raged. "Are you going to get Aimee to write another board and tell us all to keep *our cats in at night?"*

The intensity of the argument was too much for Uncle Louis and he began getting heart pains. Seeing him clutch at his chest and grimace, Aimee ran behind the bench swing and put her hands on his shoulders.

"Guys, we need to stop this," she begged earnestly. "We don't want Uncle Louis to have another heart attack. How about we all think these matters over for a week and then offer fair suggestions that we think will work. Let's talk about it later when we've all calmed down."

There were loud grumbles and complaints, but everyone could see that Uncle Louis was in pain. Odin and Franz departed toward the

North Forest, and Damien ran off to the lake, which was now ablaze in the setting sun. With some hesitation, Vinitha got up and followed the handsome surfer.

It had been a heated argument without any real satisfying conclusions. Uncle Louis' chest pains began to subside after Kenzie brought him his medication and Aimee rubbed his tight shoulders. Zahir sat down on the bench beside the older man and kindly reached over to hold his hand. The others stayed in place, hoping to enjoy some time with their beloved uncle. It had been a long while since Uncle Louis had sat with the whole group. The farmers and storekeepers didn't want to leave while he was still upset.

Closing his eyes and taking some deep breaths, Uncle Louis was thankful for Aimee's relaxing massage and Zahir's firm hand. He hoped he had persuaded the surfers that drowning uncooperative Tinys was not an option or a viable threat. After witnessing such a deep divide, he was now fully aware how difficult it was going to be for anyone to guide their peers in the same way that he had. Being so much older and the parent-figure among them, he had established a respectful relationship to varying degrees. Once he was gone, he worried it might not take long for groups to form that would hate and oppose one another, unless... *unless...* a higher authority of a different kind could be established. He desperately hoped he could set this in place before his time was up.

Another loud crash sounded, and they all looked up. A beautiful pine had fallen near Zahir's house.

"I loved that tree," the dark-haired patient remarked glumly. "I need to get better and figure out what to do with all this wood."

Justice

Chapter 30

On the other side of the glass, two researchers were making journal entries. "Trees are falling all over Rainbow Hill," the Professor jotted down. "We have begun production of new seedlings that we'll ask the Tinys to plant in a couple months."

Looking up, he whispered to Evan, "This was certainly an oversight on my part. I should have researched the negative effects of a wind-less world. The information is all there online. Stress is required for strong roots to develop."

Evan nodded. "I never thought to investigate either... oh well! There will be quite a mess to clean up if they keep falling at this rate. And we should keep an eye on the carbon-dioxide levels as well. Losing so many trees will affect our ratios."

"True!" Jacques ran over to check the data on his computer system. He finetuned the program to keep everything in balance.

Coming back, they witnessed the Courage Celebration begin and then the terrible disagreement that broke out among the Tinys. They were horrified to hear the deep bitterness and threats against those who had started the fire.

"I didn't realise there were such strong feelings against Odin and Franz," the Professor remarked quietly, with his pen in hand.

"I believe some have lost faith in our ability to handle the troublemakers," Evan surmised. For a moment the tall, blond scientist was lost in thought, and then he stood up straight with a keen look on his face. "This is it!" he said.

"This is *what?*"

"Don't you see?" Evan whispered excitedly. "A God of love with no sense of justice would be a weak, powerless God... ineffectual to hold back the forces of evil.[110] You want to show love and kindness to all the Tinys because you are a very loving man. But not all people, not *all Tinys* are like you. Some have a strong pull toward destruction and harm – and they will only restrain their evil desires under harsh threats and consequences."

"But Odin and Franz have improved a great deal," Jacques argued quietly. "I think kindness is helping to change them for good – even if it isn't happening as quickly as we'd like."

Evan sighed. "I'll keep hoping."

Damien began his rage against the Professor's decision to reward the instigators for helping extinguish the blaze."

Jacques was alarmed by what he heard. Curiously, he asked, "Do you feel that our decision to reward the instigators provoked this outburst?"

"Somewhat," Evan mused. "But I believe not punishing the troublemakers is really what provoked this backlash. The lack of clear consequences for those who purposefully harm their environment or human life is creating fear in the other Tinys. They don't feel we are reliable guardians of their world, so some want to take justice into their own hands."

For a few minutes they watched anxiously as Uncle Louis clutched at his chest, and Aimee put an end to the heated discussion. With

---

[110] Miroslav, V. "Free of Charge:" (2006), pages 138-139.

Kenzie and Zahir's help, the elder Tiny was stabilized, while Damien bolted in one direction, and Odin and Franz stalked off in the other.

Jacques sighed glumly. In his mind he recalled the freewill constraint triangle. Seth had said, "You can pick two of the three. If God wants to give us freewill and allow *everyone* to live, unfortunately the world is not going to be a completely loving and happy place..."

He turned to Evan, "But without Louis' help," he asked, "how do we force Odin or Franz to cooperate with *any* consequences that we might put in place?"

"We have a problem..." Evan agreed thoughtfully. "Paradise will function well if *everyone* is loving and caring toward each other, but when anger, resentment, jealousy and hatred begin to fester, like it is now, if we don't have good rules in place and lay out clear consequences for misbehaviour – we may have a civil war on our hands."

"Oui! I think Zahir made that observation."

"He did and it's a good one," Evan stated, "but Zahir lacks the proper authority to carry it out. Let's not kid ourselves, none of the other Tinys will have the same authority among their peers that Louis did. We're throwing potential leaders into a volatile situation that could pit Tiny against Tiny. Even if we crown a King and Queen, the others will have no reason to accept their new elevation... unless..." he pondered thoughtfully as an idea came to him. "Unless *you and I* begin interacting with all of them on a regular basis. Maybe they will respect us."

"That is a good suggestion, Evan," Jacques praised. "We may need to interact with all of them if anything happens to Louis. We may need to change our model..." Realizing that his assistant was hastily scribbling copious notes, the older man stopped and watched curiously. Evan filled one whole page of his journal.

"Whatever are you writing in there?" the Professor inquired.

239

Looking up with his pen poised in the air, Evan smiled. "Jacques, this has been so helpful to me," he said. "I've struggled to understand how God could ever be angry against His creation, or take harsh vengeance on those who disobey Him, but now I think I see it. Without a powerful God who promises one day to bring evildoers to justice and to punish those who have lived their lives against His laws, what incentive is there for humans to curtail selfish desires?[111] A God who truly loves His creation won't allow evil to take over His world or go unpunished *forever.* And a world where everyone is allowed to do whatever is 'right' in their own eyes, would be a frightening place to live. It's not Paradise!"

Thinking it all through for a moment, the tall blond assistant added anxiously, "In fact, *this* is the world we are beginning to see in society today. Human beings are losing their moral compass. Individuals are promoting various 'rights and wrongs' and it's nearly impossible for everyone *to agree* on moral standards. Sure, we all agree that murder is wrong, but what about abortion, euthanasia... or even gender issues? In our world, those who protest the loudest get their way. There is little fear or respect for authority anymore – we are heading toward chaos. I hope with all my heart there *is* a God in Heaven who will intervene, stop the evil and establish order as Seth insists that He will."

With a frown, Jacques was surprised by Evan's heartfelt gush of words. "You got all that from one discussion?" he laughed. "I jotted down 'Damien has set himself up as an authoritative leader based on intimidation and harsh threats. Perhaps he needs a course on servant-leadership.'"

"I'm sorry, Jacques," Evan apologized, watching Vinitha argue with the blond surfer on the beach. "I suppose these questions have been on my mind, so it hit home to me in this way. Don't you see?

---

[111] Ecclesiastes 8:11; Isaiah 26:9-10; Romans 2:2-12

God's 'wrath' isn't an unpredictable, uncontrollable action of an abusive Father or capricious King.[112] He clearly lays out His laws ahead of time, tells us the consequences if we disobey, and patiently waits to intervene until it is absolutely necessary to save His creation from mankind's abuse. Until the door is shut,[113] His grace is there to forgive and protect any who turn to Him for guidance and salvation. This is what a 'Good God' is."

"I don't know, Evan," the Professor replied with a frown, even though he was very happy to see so many Tinys still gathered around Uncle Louis outside the Caring Center. "I think you're switching to the other side awfully fast. However, I do like your idea about us interacting with the Tinys on a regular basis. You're quite right that some sort of authority figure needs to back up Aimee and Zahir... *or Kenzie,* if that's who she chooses. Let's think this through carefully."

---

[112] Psalm 78; Isaiah 63:7-14; Hebrews 3:7-19
[113] Matthew 25:1-13; Luke 13:25-30

A Wedding Song

Chapter 31

On that grey, troubled evening a substantial breeze blew across the top of Rainbow Hill, and without the sunshine everyone felt a little chilled. Zahir walked into the house and brought down a stack of blankets. Several Tinys were thankful to wrap themselves up, as Zahir tucked a warm comforter around Uncle Louis. Once again, the dark-haired patient took his seat close beside the older man on the swing. Aimee continued to massage the ageing Tiny's shoulders, sensing it was helping him to relax.

For a few minutes everyone sat in silence recovering from Damien's emotional outburst. Since the fire and the accident almost three weeks ago which had changed so much in Paradise, some, like Charley, Nancy and Milan had not had much interaction with Uncle Louis. After the heated argument they weren't in the mood for fun on the hill.

"There were no rainbows today," Sanaa said sadly, looking over at the suncatcher.

"I've been enjoying them in the Caring Centre," Uncle Louis remarked. "They are usually the best around mid-afternoon."

Glancing around the group, Uncle Louis asked, "So, what else has been happening in Paradise? I feel so out of touch. Has everything been okay at the store?" he asked Nancy.

"Yes," she smiled. "Milan has taken over your room, just to keep everything safe at night."

"Good decision, Milan," Uncle Louis nodded.

"We're learning how best to shear the sheep," Vahid spoke up. He laughed, "It sure will be a lot easier if Kenzie is there to help us the next time."

Tina giggled. "Yes. Charley and Vahid had to sit on the sheep's legs, while I cut off the wool."

For a while, Uncle Louis talked to the farmers about their new woolen products, and then Georgia spoke up. "I'm going to make a new book," she said excitedly. "Damien asked me to do one about his surfing shows."

Uncle Louis nodded quietly. "Not the fire?"

"Oh no," she shuddered. "That was far too scary! I don't want to remember anything about it!"

Kenzie piped up, "Maybe Vinitha will do a book on the fire. All those heroic actions shouldn't be forgotten."

Georgia and Kenzie exchanged resentful looks.

After some whispering in the corner, Ponce announced, "Lily and I are getting married! That's exciting news!"

Throwing her arms around Ponce, Lily nodded. "As soon as Diya makes my dress," she exclaimed.

"I might have it done by next week," Diya promised.

Nancy came over to Milan and raised his hand in the air. "We're getting married too," she said proudly.

Milan smiled up at her. "Diya will be busy," he said.

"I've already started your dress as well," the gifted seamstress promised Nancy, "since you traded the beautiful red gem."

"Thank you," Nancy smiled.

Lily rolled her eyes. She had only traded five tickets to the Fun Forest, which hardly compared!

"I'll do your hair, girls," Georgia offered.

"That would be lovely," Nancy said.

Yu Yan spoke up quietly, "And Vinitha and I will make you each a flower bouquet."

The girls clapped eagerly.

"Just remember, everyone," Uncle Louis pleaded. "Making a promise to love someone for the rest of your life won't always be easy. This is a commitment to look after each other and think of your partner first, through good times and bad."

"Of course," Ponce smiled. "Lily *always* puts me first."

Knowing Ponce was joking, Uncle Louis smiled.

Turning to Aimee, Lily pleaded, "Will you and Zahir sing a song for us? A wedding song?"

Swallowing hard, Aimee glanced briefly over at Zahir. She felt this was going to be an awkward, emotionally disconcerting task.

Zahir looked alarmed. He frowned and then he shrugged. "We can try," he said.

"I'll play the music," Georgia offered. She looked up at Zahir, "We've already made a lot of beautiful melodies. They only need some words."

Zahir nodded. He didn't look enthused.

"Make it a good song," Nancy smiled. "I want you to sing at our wedding too."

Lema and Sanaa had been deliberating in the corner with plenty of giggles and laughter. Suddenly, they both stood up and Sanaa clapped her hands with excitement. "And we're going to get married, too!" she cheered and then she broke out into a happy dance. Lema clapped along, and spontaneously began to sing. Sanaa chimed in.

Everyone looked at each other with amazement. It was the beginnings of a beautiful song and the words were very fitting for a wedding!

Aimee laughed. "I think Sanaa and Lema should do the song!" she suggested.

245

"Two songs will be fantastic!" Ponce smiled. "You can both do songs! But my nurse – The Lady in White – has to sing at our wedding, and she sings best with Zahir."

Kenzie smiled. "Hey, Vahid," he called out, "let's bring the xylophone up here. Then Zahir can practice."

Without hesitation, the two ran off toward the store. Sensing they might need help, Charley ran after them. While the others filled Uncle Louis in on their daily lives, answering questions about mango production, the bats, the bees, the honey supply, and many other practical matters, the xylophone was hoisted up the hill and positioned under the veranda of the Caring Centre.

Damien and Vinitha rejoined the group, hand in hand. The tall blond surfer seemed to have calmed down.

Everyone turned to Zahir in eager anticipation, hoping to hear some beautiful music. Thanking Kenzie and Charley, the dark-haired man with the deep purple scars stood up from the swing, left his new medallions on the table and headed over to the instrument. With some hesitation, he picked up the mallets and tried out a few tunes. However, his right arm was stiff, the music was flat and it lacked his usual flair. Discouraged, he put down the sticks. "I'm just not... feeling it right now," he apologized heavily. Turning to Ponce he said, "Sanaa and Lema sing really well."

Georgia picked up the mallets and began playing the songs which she had helped create. "Come on, Zahir," she encouraged. "What about this one?"

"It sounds beautiful," Damien called out. "You're the best at this, Gorgeo!"

Looking down, Zahir didn't respond as he made his way back to the bench swing.

"Or maybe this," the pretty blond girl said, trying something else, but she just couldn't inspire the musician.

Aimee wasn't in the right mood either. As the deflated musician sat back down on the swinging bench close by, there were no melodies welling up inside her heart, just anxious, jealous thoughts. She couldn't imagine singing a wedding song with Zahir about love and special relationships if Georgia was included.

Trying one more tune, the beautiful blond looked up with exasperation. "What's wrong with you?" she rebuked Zahir. "These are so pretty. You liked them before. You *only* have to think of some words. How hard is that?"

When Zahir didn't answer, Georgia tossed the mallets aside and burst out, "You aren't the same anymore! In fact, you are *so* different – I don't even *know* who you are."

Aimee swallowed hard. She wasn't sure where to look.

Kenzie spoke up. "That's not fair, Georgia," he protested. "Zahir is the same good man he's always been. A few scars don't change who someone is!"

"Well, I've had enough of this!" Georgia retorted angrily, running off to the stone stairway.

"Time to go-kart," Damien called out with an amused smile as he looked around at all the bewildered Tinys. "We can get in a few runs if we go right now." With the blond surfer heading to the stairs, most of the Tinys followed. They had enjoyed a chat with Uncle Louis, were dismayed by all the drama, and needed a fun escape.

Zahir walked off into the forest and Kenzie ran after him. Bewildered, Aimee took a seat on the swing and was thankful that Uncle Louis patted her hand.

"All in all, that was a rather rough evening," Uncle Louis murmured. Laying her head on his shoulder, Aimee agreed.

"And to think it all started with an Awards Ceremony," he sighed.

A Willing Sacrifice

Chapter 32

After spending a long hour apart, the group of five re-gathered in the Crisis Room that evening. Reading time with Uncle Louis was a welcome diversion to the unsettling arguments that had soured the celebration ceremony.

Bringing Zahir's medallions up to the room, Aimee placed them on the medication table. Light from the setting sun reflected off the new gold heart, but the dark-haired patient wasn't looking. He was staring out the window in despair.

With deep compassion, she asked, "Are you okay?"

"I can't see out of my right eye at all," he complained, turning his head to look at her with his left. "But," he sighed, "I guess I should be thankful that I can still see with the other."

"I'm so, so sorry, Zahir," she replied sadly, not knowing what else to say. She longed to give him a hug but held back. While it seemed that his painful relationship with Georgia might be falling apart, she wasn't quite sure it was over.

Realising that anything on his right side was not easily seen, Aimee picked up the medals and walked in between the two patients. She began slipping each one on to the chain that still hung around his bed post. "You have a lot of medals here," she reminded him gently, pointing to each one of the three, "You've been honoured for kindness, courage, and selflessness in *saving* a life. These are *all* the most important ones. You have some really special treasures."

248

The discouraged patient shook his head sadly and closed his eyes. "Those aren't my treasures. They may be very kind gifts from the Professor, but real treasures don't leave wounds around your neck."

Uncle Louis looked over compassionately. "Actually, sometimes they do," he encouraged. "Sometimes the best treasures are only found through a great deal of pain and self-sacrifice."

Keeping his eyes closed, Zahir frowned. "I can't take *any* more pain," he said despondently. Tears began to flow and he angrily wiped his face.

"Now you're finally sounding like a normal guy," Ponce joked. "I thought I was the only one who couldn't handle pain!"

A slight smile hovered across Zahir's lips, but he didn't open his eyes. "What if I lose sight in my other eye?" he asked nervously. "What if I can't see at all?"

Uncle Louis was quick to assure him that only the right side of his face had been affected by the heat. "There's no reason to worry you'll lose sight in your other eye."

Zahir didn't seem at all comforted. He put his hands over his face.

Appreciating Zahir's distress, Uncle Louis chose to read what he thought would be most helpful. "Tonight, I think we should launch right into Matthew," he suggested. "We're so close to the end. Let's just finish this story."

While Uncle Louis read about the last week of Jesus' life, Kenzie and Aimee tended quietly to the wounded patients. Working closely together, they had established a little routine and knew what the other needed without a word. Kenzie measured the dosages and passed them to Aimee who took them to the patients. If she saw a bottle of medication or formula was nearly empty, she would go to the hallway and bring in a new one. There were three separate doses for each burn victim and one for Uncle Louis. When all had been given out, they passed wipes and ointment back and forth as Kenzie worked on Ponce's deepest wounds, and Aimee cared for Zahir. To anyone sitting back and observing the situation, the nurses had become a highly efficient team who worked well together.

As they cleaned the wounds, Uncle Louis called their attention to one particular verse that he felt was pertinent to the distressing evening they had endured. *"You know that the rulers of the Gentiles lord it over them,"* he read, *"and their great ones exercise authority over them. It shall not be so among you. But whoever would be great among you must be your servant, and whoever would be first among you must be your slave, even as the Son of Man came not to be served but to serve, and to give his life as a ransom for many."* [114]

"Did you all hear that?" Uncle Louis asked.

Everyone nodded.

"This is servant leadership from the best example who has ever walked this earth," he told them. "We lead best by serving."

As they listened to the parables about the return of Jesus and his reaction to the preparedness of his servants, or lack thereof, both patients began to relax and Zahir's gloominess subsided.

Some of the scab was breaking up around the edges of the wound as Aimee cleaned her patient's arm, and she was surprised to see bright pink skin underneath. "Maybe it's not completely healed," she pondered.

When she was done, Aimee took her usual seat on the sofa. Kenzie, however, took the chair in between. He rested his hand kindly on Zahir's good arm.

His dark-haired friend smiled up him and relaxed against the pillow. "You're ministering to the sick," he chuckled, repeating the words that Uncle Louis had just read. "May you enter into eternal life."[115]

---

[114] Matthew 20:28
[115] Matthew 25:31-46

Kenzie laughed. "Thank you," he said warmly, patting Zahir's arm. "May we all!"

In a reflective tone, Uncle Louis mused over the reading he had just done, "Whether this book is true or not, I really love God's Son, Jesus," he said. "His teachings are easy to understand and so compassionate, and they just make good sense."

Aimee agreed. "His rules aren't made on a whim that only serves half the people..."

"Exactly," Uncle Louis chuckled.

Zahir looked over at the older man by the window. "Uncle Louis," he said kindly. "I understand why *you* love Jesus. Just like you, he didn't sit back and demand that other people look after him. His life was about caring for others, healing them, feeding them, and teaching them helpful advice that would make their lives better. That is how you've led us."

Uncle Louis smiled. "Thanks, Zahir," he said warmly. "I have tried to lead like this, but I never had such Divine wisdom to pass along." With a chuckle he contemplated his own life. "Ironically, since the Professor insisted that I learn and practice servant-leadership," he mused, "he taught me about Jesus Christ even before I knew his name. Now with what we've learned, we have a much higher reason to serve those around us in this same way. Remember, good leadership isn't dominating other people by fear and forcing their cooperation. Good leadership involves service – listening to people, having empathy for their feelings, healing them with your words or actions, persuading them with logical arguments and real evidence, building up your community and showing the right way by how you act. Remember that – *'example'* not intimidation. Force and threats may bring compliance for a time, but it doesn't change hearts. Always desire to save lives, *not destroy*.[116] And remember that the only one who can

---

[116] Luke 9:56

251

truly save any of us is Jesus Christ through the way that his Father provided.[117] So, if we want to *save lives* and change hearts, we must *lead* everyone to the Son of God."

There were nods all around. While they were all in agreement, some privately doubted their own abilities.

"A few miracles would be nice," Ponce considered with a grin. "Just think, if you were Jesus, you could heal our wounds instantly."

Zahir agreed.

Uncle Louis nodded. "Well, the rest of this story goes far beyond servant leadership. Let's keep reading."

While the sky grew dark and loons called out to each other on the peaceful lake, the solar lights cast a soft glow throughout the cozy room. A few fireflies flitted in and out of the open windows.

Riveted to the terribly sad story in the last few chapters of Matthew, Aimee hugged her legs on the pink sofa. Her eyes were fastened on Uncle Louis as he read the dramatic record. The religious leaders had become enraged with Jesus' popularity and his incredible healing powers from God, which they lacked. They were appalled at his words that openly contradicted centuries of their revered, man-made traditions. Jealousy and anger brought them to a point where they were blind to their own ungodly behaviour and failed to see the horrendous injustice of killing a man who had *never sinned* and who had compassionately healed the sick and wounded. They were terribly envious when Jesus claimed he spoke words that were *directly* from God. The rulers considered *themselves* to be God's chosen ones, yet God wasn't showing these wonderful powers through them. Instead of seeing their own error, they foolishly decided that Jesus must be an imposter!

The four Tinys listened to the sad account, hearing that Jesus was increasingly distressed by the terrible plight God had warned him he

---

[117] Acts 4:12

252

was about to endure. And yet, after tearfully begging God to find another way, Jesus accepted God's plan for his life, saying, "Not as I will but as You will." [118]

With horror, the four Tinys listened as Uncle Louis read about the betrayal by a close friend. With vivid imaginations, they saw the kind healer forsaken by all his friends when he needed them most, tried unfairly in a court of law that should have protected him from such injustice, and then when he stood bloody and wounded in front of hundreds of people whom he had compassionately helped, those very same people cried out for him to be put death!

Aimee wiped away tears as she listened. She felt for the disciple Peter who was greatly confused when Jesus gave himself up to be treated as a criminal, and losing faith, wasn't brave enough to admit his relationship with his very best friend. Denying he knew Jesus three times, Peter felt devastating grief when Jesus turned and looked his way! She well remembered what it had been like to receive a look of loving disappointment from Uncle Louis.

The elder Tiny explained crucifixion to them all, filling their hearts with dread as they imagined the terrible pain of nails being driven through one's hands and feet, and then all of one's weight hanging upon those wounds.

But the story didn't end in despair. Smiles broke out on all their faces when Uncle Louis read the last chapter about Jesus' resurrection! Wide-eyed and happy, Aimee imagined herself as one of the women heading out early in the morning to wrap Jesus' dead body with spices, only to discover that he wasn't in the empty tomb. Instead, an angel in shiny white clothes declared that Jesus was alive! She could imagine Mary's joy when she saw her Savior standing in

---

[118] Matthew 26:38-42

front of her and fell down at his feet. Jesus had been restored to life and was the first to receive God's gift of immortality.[119]

A loud snore disturbed her vision. Ponce had fallen asleep.

"I've read all four accounts of Jesus' life," Uncle Louis said, "and each one has unique details that are interesting to piece together to give us a fuller picture. In the Gospel of John, one of the disciples doesn't believe Jesus is actually alive again, until he sees the print of the nails in his hands and the scar on his side."[120]

"Jesus still had wounds after he was raised?" Aimee frowned.

"Yes," Uncle Louis smiled, glancing quickly over at Zahir. "Giving his life for the whole world left Jesus a marked man. I'm sure God could have taken those marks away when He raised him up, but perhaps they were left to remind everyone of the price Jesus paid to give us salvation. If the Gospel records are true, we only have this amazing hope because Jesus Christ was *willing* to give up his life for others."[121]

Pondering his words and relating them to the experiences they had all endured, Aimee echoed, "Jesus was willing to die for others... and so were you, Uncle Louis – you almost died trying to save Ponce and Zahir." Hesitantly, she turned to the dark-haired man with the long purple scars, "And you, Zahir," she said, swallowing hard. "You almost died to save Ponce."

Glancing quickly in Ponce's direction to ensure he was still asleep, Zahir shook his head unhappily. In an anguished whisper he protested, "There is a big difference between what I did, and what Jesus did. I ran to *help* Ponce, not give up my life for him." Darkly, he murmured, "I thought it would be a quick fix... I'd lift the burning beam off his back, drag him out and be done. I had no idea I would be

---

[119] 1 Corinthians 15:20-23; Colossians 1:18; Revelation 1:5; Acts 26:23; Philippians 3:21; 2 Peter 1:4; Romans 8:29
[120] John 20:24-29
[121] John 10:17-18

burned." His voice broke. "Or how painful burns would be, or how much it would change *everything...* or... maybe... I wouldn't have tried."

Still sitting beside him, Kenzie squeezed his arm. "You would have tried, Zahir... even if you knew you would suffer. I know you."

In the soft light, Aimee could see the anguish come over Zahir's face. "I don't know that I would have, Kenzie! I don't know!" he grieved. "Don't think so highly of me!" And then he began to sob. "No, I would *never* have paid this price! *Never!*"

Aimee couldn't bear to see Zahir so distraught. Running over, she kneeled down by his scarred arm and took his hand in both of hers. Zahir sobbed and sobbed as though his heart would break, while his two friends on either side tried their best to comfort him.

Ponce woke up with all the noise and wanted to know what was going on. In a low voice, Uncle Louis tried to explain that Zahir had been touched by the story they read.

Having finally vented some of the deep personal distress he had been holding back, Zahir apologized with embarrassment. "I'm sorry," he said, choking on another sob, "I can't believe I'm crying about silly scars and one blind eye. I shouldn't be so upset about this! I *hate* these thoughts! I should be thankful that we are *all* still alive. I should be thankful that I can still see!" Fervently, he expressed, "Those are precious gifts that I still have!" But then he broke down crying again.

Kenzie patted his arm. "I get it," he assured his friend lovingly. "You paid a heavy price."

With a heart full of compassion, Aimee rested her face against the scarred arm.

In a sleepy voice, Ponce asked, "Are you talking about the fire?"

Reaching over, Kenzie patted Ponce's hand. "Yes," he said, "don't worry, Ponce. Zahir will be okay."

"I'm sorry, Zahir," Ponce begged. "I'm sorry I ruined your life..."

Zahir choked up again.

"No, no," Kenzie corrected, "Don't say that, Ponce. Zahir's life is not ruined!"

"But this is all my fault," Ponce cried. "I'm sorry, Zahir. Now your girlfriend is mad at you, and you don't look the same... and..."

Trying to console Zahir and keep Ponce from making things worse, Kenzie held the arms of both patients. "Just remember," he interrupted, "Zahir is *still* the same good man he's always been. Scars don't change who someone is on the inside."

Aimee longed to say something comforting, but everything that came to her mind she dismissed. She longed to say, "I still love you, Zahir," but that seemed too forward. To say, "I still like you," wasn't nearly strong enough. She longed to say, "I still think you're handsome," but again she wasn't sure how that comment would be received. So instead, she just held his hand, kept her face against his arm, and was very thankful that Kenzie was carrying the conversation.

Finally, Zahir turned to look at Uncle Louis, and murmured quietly, "What I wanted to say... *before I lost it...*" Again, there was a catch in his voice, and he had to close his eyes for a second. Persevering, he choked out, "This Jesus that you've read about, knew everything *ahead* of time! He told his disciples that people would despise and reject him and put him to death! A death of torture![122] And he *willingly* gave himself up. He chose to go through with it! I could never have gone in knowing what lay ahead!"

Aimee shuddered.

"This *is* incredibly inspiring leadership, Zahir," Uncle Louis agreed. "I don't have that kind of courage either... but I know that Jesus is the leader that I want to follow."

"You both have way more courage than I do," Kenzie admitted.

---

[122] Matthew 17:22-23; Luke 9:22; 24:6-8; Psalm 22; Isaiah 53

"Or me," Aimee added meekly, thankful to say something, "and I *love* your honesty, Zahir!"

The distressed patient squeezed her hand, but he spoke with despair, "What? My honesty that I'm not the courageous rescuer you all hoped I was?"

Aimee looked up past the dark eye that could no longer see, into the one that was filled with grief. "No, I love your desire to be truthful," she clarified, "even if we might think less of you. That's what I love."

Zahir didn't answer, but he held her hand tightly.

For a while, they all reflected on what they were learning and the strong pull it was having on their heart. Looking out into the black night, they heard the loons call out again and laughter down by the water.

In a quiet voice Zahir added, "It must have been so humiliating for Jesus to have hung on that cross, naked in front of those he loved, shamed... helpless... *rejected*... dying with thieves."

"But he knew in his mind that he had done the right thing," Uncle Louis encouraged. "He knew he was suffering for the benefit of others. Jesus told his disciples, that there is no greater love than to lay down your life for another. Don't forget that, Zahir. If Jesus had thought of his own life first and turned down the opportunity to save the world, he would have escaped the physical pain, but been filled with deep mental anguish for the rest of his life."

Ponce spoke up quietly, "Do you wish you had let me die?"

"No! Of course not!" Zahir protested earnestly as the tears flooded down his face again. "Don't *ever* say that!"

"But isn't that what we're talking about?" Ponce argued. "Are you sorry that you helped me and ended up a mess? Do you wish you'd listened to..."

Uncle Louis interrupted. "Ponce, what we are trying to do is relate to Jesus' sufferings.[123] We're trying to empathize with his feelings when he gave his life for us," he explained. "So, for instance, Ponce, how do you think Zahir would feel if you turned against him now after he saved your life?"

"What?" Ponce protested earnestly. "Why would I do that? I would never do that!"

Still holding Zahir's hand and sitting on the floor beside his bed, Aimee looked over with a quizzical expression. She wondered why Uncle Louis was asking this question. Ponce had been quietly supportive of Zahir ever since the fire. While he often fell asleep when they were reading and mostly talked about the amazing adventure centre he hoped to build in the forest, Ponce didn't complain nearly so much about fairness. A gentle change had taken place – one that involved deep gratitude.

"I'm not saying that you would, Ponce," Uncle Louis said kindly. "In fact, I *believe* you wouldn't. But in trying to appreciate Jesus' sacrifice, which was on a much greater scale than anything any of us will ever give, I'd like to consider our reaction to such great love."

Ponce nodded.

"So, imagine," Uncle Louis explained, "that after Zahir endured so much pain to save you, you decided that you wanted nothing to do with him. Maybe you might say that Zahir hadn't helped you at all, or that you could have rescued *yourself* from the fire. How do you think that would make Zahir feel?"

"But I wouldn't say that!" Ponce fretted.

"Zahir would feel devastated!" Kenzie piped up, still holding on to his friend's arm. "And I'd feel devastated for him! He would feel like his sacrifice was all for nothing."

---

[123] 1 Peter 4:12-13

Uncle Louis nodded. "Exactly! Even if you were someone who really didn't mean to make such a painful sacrifice, you would feel very hurt if it wasn't appreciated. So, think about Jesus. He *willingly* chose to suffer for us. He knew the torture and suffering he'd have to endure, and he did it anyway, because he had compassion on us - *sinners.* So, how will Jesus feel if we don't value his sacrifice, or if we say that we don't need him? Or that we can look after ourselves? How will Jesus feel if we don't *change* our lives because of what he did?"

Aimee understood the powerful point. She pleaded, "What does Jesus want us to do, Uncle Louis?"

Uncle Louis looked over at the guys. "Anyone have an answer?"

Kenzie pondered the matter. "Well, Jesus talked a lot about repentance and forgiveness..."[124]

Nodding, Uncle Louis agreed. "So, if the Bible is true, then we have been called to stop living for ourselves and to ask for forgiveness. In other places we are told that we need to commit our lives to Jesus in baptism."[125]

"Do you think the Bible is true?" Kenzie inquired.

"I'd like to do a little more investigation," Uncle Louis sighed. Looking over at Aimee with a hopeful expression, she immediately understood what he meant. Uncle Louis wanted to get to the cave.

Anxiously, she considered that it was a long way to walk up and down the hill, and lately he hadn't ventured any further than just around the house. She hoped he could get strong enough to go, and then she began to wonder what she could do to make such a trip possible. She could see how much he wanted to make one more trip.

---

[124] Matthew 4:17; Mark 1:14-15; Luke 13:1-5
[125] John 3:5; Acts 2:38; Acts 22:16: Romans 6:1-14

A Poor Reaction

Chapter 33

*L*ate the next evening as Aimee and Kenzie looked after their patient's wounds, Uncle Louis read a chapter from the Professor's book. The purple scab was crumbling away on Zahir's arm, exposing large new patches of bright pink skin below. It looked a little odd against his dark olive tone and Aimee was worried that he wasn't going to like the results. Looking up, she saw that Zahir was gazing at his arm with a troubled expression.

Kenzie was wiping Ponce's leg. "These scabs are coming off!" he announced happily. "How exciting is this! You guys will be back to your old selves soon and free to go home!"

Uncle Louis rolled over with a smile. "I'm so pleased! This is great news!" he said.

Ponce began asking exactly when he could leave the Caring Centre, but Zahir was silent.

As she cleaned her patient's facial wound carefully with the sterile wipe, large sections of the softened scar tissue came free. "The scabs are coming off your face as well," Aimee smiled.

Zahir nodded warily. Removing the dead skin, Aimee applied the special ointment that the Professor had sent in. The bright pink discoloration on her friend's dark olive-skinned face was very noticeable. Glancing quickly over to Ponce, she noted that the pink skin on his arm blended in better with his reddish, bronzed tone.

Under the scabs, the new skin was also distorted and wrinkled. The scar had badly marred Zahir's appearance on the right side of his face, all the way from his beard to his hairline, and sadly, his blind eye had clouded over. Aimee had always hoped that once the scabs came off, Zahir would look the same again... but he didn't. Knowing he was going to be very upset with his appearance, tears of sympathy welled up in her eyes.

"What's wrong?" her patient asked anxiously.

"Nothing's wrong," she replied, forcing a smile. "You have a nice pink glow. It's healing well."

"I'd like to look at myself," Zahir said suddenly. "I want to see for myself."

Feeling nervous about Zahir's response to his appearance, Aimee didn't meet his gaze. "Sure," she said, stopping the treatment.

Getting up, Zahir walked into the little room with the sink, the hard chair and a mirror. Aimee looked over at Uncle Louis and Kenzie with trepidation. The older man closed his eyes and sighed deeply. They all waited breathlessly, but they didn't hear any reaction. A whole minute went by. Aimee nervously twisted her hands together. She looked up at Kenzie again.

"Do you think Zahir's okay?" he whispered.

Aimee stood up and walked into the small room. Zahir was standing at the sink with his head down. Tears were falling from his eyes. Drawing close, she embraced his arm with deep sympathy. "It's okay," she said kindly, unable to stop her own tears. "You're still *you!*"

"No, it's *not* okay!" he protested angrily, pulling away. "I look horrific! My face is a mess. I don't even recognize *myself!* This *is not me!* No wonder you're crying! How can you say it's okay? You're not being honest with me, Aimee! You're not!"

261

Never had Aimee seen Zahir so angry. "Just leave me alone," he begged, sobbing. Pulling further away, he covered his face with his hands. "I'm sorry, Aimee. Please go... please just *go!*"

For the first time ever, the copper-haired nurse felt that she had failed Zahir. He had never told her to go away before. Had she done a lousy job healing his burns? Was she a bad nurse?"

Returning to the room, she couldn't hide that she was crying. Uncle Louis looked up with compassion and Kenzie came over and gave her a quick hug. Even Ponce looked up sadly.

"Don't worry, Aimee," Uncle Louis said softly. "He's just in shock. Give him time. He'll get over this."

Unable to speak, Aimee nodded and bolted from the room.

Twilight was settling in as Aimee ran out of the house and into the forest. A tree fell close by as she headed straight to the control cave, but she didn't turn to look. Pulling out her key, she unlocked the door and turned on the light. She barely remembered to close the door behind her. Then she went over to the phone and turned it on. With tears streaming down her face, she messaged the Professor. "The scabs are coming off," she wrote, wiping her eyes frequently, "and Zahir's skin looks very pink underneath. It's wrinkled and stands out and looks quite different than it did before. His blind eye has turned cloudy. Zahir looked at himself in the mirror and was very upset, even angry. Did I do a bad job looking after him? Did I do something wrong?" With her heart breaking, Aimee added several very sad emojis to her message.

She sent the text. While she waited for a reply, she decided to investigate burns.

"Ok, Google," she said, and the screen immediately lit up. "Burn victim," she said. Several articles and pictures came up on the screen. She scrolled through them. It was reassuring for her to see that many people had scars after major burns and some were far worse than Zahir's. She read articles about treatment and realized that unless skin grafts were done, most burn victims ended up with very visible scars. Googling 'skin graft', she quickly understood that such an operation required abilities way beyond basic nursing care.

Music sounded from the tall, thin black box, and Aimee realised the Professor was video calling her! Accepting the call, she was happy to see his face. "Are you okay, Aimee?" he asked.

Bursting into tears, she explained what had happened when Zahir had looked in the mirror.

"I am so proud of the way you have looked after Zahir and Ponce," Jacques praised with a catch in his voice. "Had you not followed the instructions carefully, they may not be alive today. You kept them from dangerous infection, and they have healed so well."

"Thank you," she said, wiping her face with her hand.

"There will be scarring," Jacques informed her. "Unfortunately, scarring is a sad but very *normal* consequence of burns. The ointment you are using may diminish the scarring a little over time, but it won't go away. The best nurse in *my* world could not stop Zahir from scarring, and likely no one could have saved his eye. You did well, Aimee!" he praised. "It will be hard at first for him to accept that this is his new appearance. Once he realizes that all his friends still love him regardless of his looks, he will stop feeling so upset. Give him time and lots and *lots* of understanding."

The Professor asked if she had investigated burns online, and Aimee told him she had seen images.

"Look up the 'emotional impact of burns,'" he suggested, "and you will see that there is often a lot more to the healing process than just the physical wounds. Zahir and Ponce will go through emotional challenges as they re-enter normal life. It may not be so hard on Ponce as his wounds aren't across his face. But they both will need friends to reassure them again and again, until they adjust. It may take some time and patience, Aimee. This may be the *most* challenging part."

"I'll look into it," she promised.

"Do you feel up to this?" he asked kindly. "Do you feel you have enough support?"

"Uncle Louis has been so helpful," Aimee nodded. "I'm so thankful he is with us! And Kenzie is Zahir's best friend." She told him about the tearful outburst the night before and how well Kenzie had handled the situation.

"So, Zahir was upset because he regrets helping Ponce?" the Professor clarified.

Aimee nodded.

"Poor Zahir," Jacques empathised. "This is all hitting him hard. I can understand his feelings. Odin or Franz should have helped. They were the ones who started that fire. Ponce was their buddy."

"We had a good discussion about it," Aimee began tentatively. "We were reading that Jesus gave his life for the world and God left the scars on him so that everyone would remember what he did."

Nodding politely, the Professor wasn't sure what to say.

"Zahir started crying," Aimee relayed, "because he said that if he knew all the pain he'd have to go through, then maybe he wouldn't have rushed into the fire. He was amazed that Jesus knew exactly what he had to endure, and he still chose to give up his life to save others."

"Interesting," the Professor responded flatly, not wanting to enter a religious discussion with his beloved daughter... not when she had so much to deal with already. "Well, just call on me if you need any more help," he smiled. "Sometimes challenges like this are very hard for the caregiver... *not just the patient.* You may need to talk it through frequently."

Tears welled up in Aimee's eyes.

"I love you, Aimee," he said tenderly. "You are doing everything I hoped you would as a nurse. Just persevere, Darling. Everything will get better in time."

"Darling?"

264

"It's just a kind name for someone you love."

Aimee had not realised there were kind names as well as hurtful ones. She liked Darling. "Should I call you... Father?" she asked.

"I would love to hear you say that," he smiled, "and Dad would even be better."

Smiling, she tried it out. "Goodnight... Dad," she said.

"Goodnight, my Darling," he smiled. "Hang in there."

The kind name was almost like getting a hug. When they had disconnected, she sat happily for a moment, contemplating the amazing privilege of having a real father. Then, she took his advice and read an article on the emotional impact of burns. After a few paragraphs, she realised that all the mental turmoil Zahir was struggling with was a natural part of the healing process. One article concluded by saying that the emotional impact could be greatly lessened by the presence of loving and supportive friends and family.

"It's going to take time," she told herself, "but one day Zahir will laugh and sing again. In the meantime, I want to be one of his loving and supportive friends. I will try my best to lift him up, just like he did for me."

There were muffled sounds outside the cave door. She heard Lily's voice. "She hasn't come to bed yet. I think Aimee's still in there."

"And the light is on," Franz whispered.

"No fair," Odin replied, adding in several strange words that he said in a rude manner. "This is *our* time. She can't take it all!"

"Shush!" Lily said. "She'll hear you."

"I *am* in here," Aimee called out loudly, "and I *do* hear you! And I'm doing an important investigation. None of you are supposed to be in this room!"

Some muffled laughter rang out and there were scurrying noises as the three Tinys ran off.

"Oh no," Aimee thought. "They *have* been coming in here. This is why Lily gets up in the middle of the night! She must be taking my key when I'm sleeping. But they can't get in without it! They won't get in again!"

Before she left, she wrote another message to the Professor telling him what she'd overheard, confessing her foolish decision to put the key under a rock, and promising that from now on she would always keep it around her neck.

Speak Up

Chapter 34

From the phone, Aimee knew it was past midnight when she made her way back to the Caring Centre. She showered in the room beside the outhouse and walked up the stone stairs on Rainbow Hill. The wind was blowing strong, and she glanced from side to side nervously, hoping that the trees wouldn't topple over on her. She was very surprised to meet Kenzie near the clearing. Sitting on the top stair in the dim moonlight, his face was lined with worry.

"Aimee, where have you been?" he asked anxiously. "You stayed away a long time!"

Just in case anyone else was listening, she replied in a hushed tone, "I've been talking to the Professor. I've been in the cave."

He nodded. "That's what Uncle Louis thought," he said. But then he chided, "Aimee, you shouldn't have run off. You have no idea how badly Zahir feels."

Swallowing hard, Aimee bit her lip. "I'm sorry," she said. "I was really hurt. I needed time to think. I needed to talk things over with someone."

Standing up, Kenzie put his hand on her shoulder. "You can talk to me, Aimee," he pleaded, "and sometimes I might need to talk to you as well. This is hard on both of us!"

She nodded sadly.

"I think we've done our best to heal the burns," Kenzie continued emotively, "but I feel for Zahir... inside... *inside his mind.* I can't imagine looking in the mirror and not recognizing myself. He used to see a reflection that any guy would be proud of and now he sees a face that he doesn't want to claim. It must be really hard to have done the right thing and then be damaged for the rest of your life. It must be devastating when the girl you once thought loved you tells you that you stink, and is repulsed by your looks and rarely comes to see how you're doing. Instead, she's hanging out with a guy who..." Kenzie ended his lengthy outburst mid-sentence.

Aimee nodded sadly as the wind blew the loose strands of her hair around. She knew there were other things that Kenzie could add, and it was unusual for him to speak so passionately. "It must be *so* hard," she agreed. "I learned a lot tonight. Apparently, Zahir's scars are normal. We didn't do anything wrong, Kenzie. And it's also very normal for people with major burns to go through a lot of negative emotions and tears as they heal. It may go on for weeks."

"Really?" her friend replied, thinking through the new information thoughtfully. "So, this is *normal,*" he considered with relief. "I think it will help all of us to know that – Zahir included."

Remembering the Professor's words to her, Aimee added, "And also dealing with all the patient's emotions can be really hard on the care-givers."

"Yeah, it is!" Kenzie agreed. "It hurts to see my friend so down, and I don't always know what to say." With a deep sigh, the curly-haired nurse pondered how they could help. Looking at Aimee again, he said, "So then, we need to help him get his confidence back. I'd say, he comes first right now... not our feelings... not anyone else's feelings..."

Aimee looked up. "What do you mean?" she asked.

"You can't take off like that when your feelings get hurt," he chided a little harshly. "He's going to say things he doesn't mean. Zahir is trying to deal with thoughts he doesn't understand... and he hasn't worked through. We need to stay balanced for him."

"I'm sorry," she said. "I'll try harder."

With a probing expression, Kenzie asked, "Are you still worried about Georgia?"

Bowing her head, Aimee admitted, "Yes, I definitely don't want to upset her again."

"And where has Georgia been lately? Has she been caring for him?"

Aimee shook her head slowly.

Shifting uncomfortably, Kenzie sighed, "Aimee, if you really care about Zahir, this might be a good time to tell him. There's no rule, Aimee. He hasn't made promises to anyone, and Georgia has demoralised him." With a smile, he said, "I'd say you should stop hiding your feelings. I can see them, but Zahir can't. Don't tell him anything that isn't true," he cautioned. "Kind words that aren't real just hurt worse in the end. But if you have something true to say, then speak up."

"With everyone in the room?" she asked anxiously.

With a laugh, Kenzie looked relieved and gave her a quick hug. "Of course! We'll be cheering for you!" he smiled. "Come on, let's get some sleep before the morning comes."

Following her friend into the mansion and up the stairs, Aimee could hear Uncle Louis reading. *"... I praise you, for I am fearfully and wonderfully made. Wonderful are your works; my soul knows it very well. My frame was not hidden from you, when I was being made in secret, intricately woven in the depths of the earth. Your eyes saw my unformed substance; in your book were written, every one of them, the days that were formed for me, when as yet there was none of them..... "[126]*

In the softly lit room, Uncle Louis was on his side reading from the Bible, while Zahir was sitting up in bed, his head and arms resting on his knees. Ponce had been asleep, but his eyes fluttered open when Aimee walked in. Kenzie stood in the doorway.

"The Lady in White is back," Ponce mumbled wearily.

Aimee walked around the bed to the chair between the patients. She was relieved to see a calm, serene look on Zahir's face. It was a very different expression from the one she had left. Whatever Uncle Louis had been reading had soothed his troubled spirit. Hesitantly, she reached for his hand and sat down beside him.

"I'm sorry, Aimee," he said.

"You aren't mad... at me... anymore?" she implored.

"I was never mad *at you*," he replied earnestly, squeezing her hand. "I was mad at life, at circumstances, but certainly not with you." With a kind smile, he added, "If I ever say, 'go away' again... *which hopefully I never will...* it only means that I need a few minutes to pull myself together. I don't like to be seen with floods of tears coming down my face. I'm sorry. Please don't take it personally."

For a moment, Aimee considered giving him a hug. She sensed it would be received well, but Ponce was looking over curiously, and Uncle Louis and Kenzie were close by. Then Ponce winked. Aimee stood up; the atmosphere just wasn't quite right.

"Okay, just 'a few minutes' next time," she nodded, laughing. Turning to head to Lily's room, she said, "Good night, everyone."

"You've been the very best nurse that I could ask for!" Zahir added.

Looking back at him, many things went through Aimee's mind that she yearned to tell her patient. However, even with Kenzie's recent

---

[126] Psalm 139:14-16

271

encouragement, it wasn't easy to give vent to long-repressed feelings while three sets of eyes looked on.

With a teasing smile in Ponce's direction, Aimee praised, "Tears are better than hollers, anytime."

"Hey," Ponce jested. "But at least I get it all out! Zahir tries to keep the lid on everything... but it's going to burst through one way or another."

Zahir had to laugh. There was a lot of truth to Ponce's bantering.

Aimee said a second goodnight and headed off to Lily's room.

Words

Chapter 35

*A*hh, that sun is lovely," Uncle Louis sighed the next morning, breathing in the fresh air that was flowing through the room. With the eyedropper in his hand, Kenzie squeezed out the older Tiny's portion of formula and Aimee took it to him.

"I think we should all get outside today," the copper-haired nurse smiled, handing her elder brother his cup.

Bringing over the wipes and the ointment, Kenzie set them down on Zahir's bed for Aimee, and began to clean Ponce's wounds. The scabs were still coming off. As the two nurses worked on their patients, Uncle Louis told them what he could see out the window. Deer were nibbling the grass, lorikeets were chatting noisily in the big tree nearby, squirrels were jumping from one branch to another, and two more trees had come down in the forest. Uncle Louis had even heard them fall in the middle of the night.

On her way to make breakfast, Georgia popped in to say good morning. Her apologies to one particular patient tumbled out anxiously. "I'm sorry for what I said yesterday. I shouldn't have been so upset about the song." Suddenly, noticing the discolouration on Zahir's face, she looked over at Aimee with a frown. "Why is Zahir turning pink?" she asked. "Have you been following all the instructions carefully?"

"Very carefully," Zahir replied.

Resisting the urge to lash out, Aimee kept her voice even. "He's actually healing well and so is Ponce," she smiled. "It's quite normal for burn victims to have scarring."

With resignation, Zahir looked down at his arm and sighed. "Pink's my new colour. I'm just thankful to be alive."

"He's had an excellent nurse," Uncle Louis informed Georgia. "The scarring isn't Aimee's fault."

"Well, I still love you, Zahir," Georgia reassured him. Forcing herself to smile at Aimee, Georgia added, "And you *have* been a good nurse. I don't know how you put up with all that mess and smell. I sure couldn't."

Kenzie's remarks in the early hours of the morning echoed in her mind as Aimee's face flushed red. Zahir was looking down and she couldn't read his expression, but she knew the words must hurt.

"Will he *always* have those scars?" Georgia questioned, watching Aimee take some ointment from the round container and rub it on his pink, wrinkled skin. "Or will that stuff you're putting on make them go away?"

Aimee swallowed hard. Defensive anger flowed through and gave her the courage she needed. Her voice wavered, but she spoke up for the young man who had already been through so much. "You know, when I see these scars," she said to Georgia, "I remember the courage Zahir had to save Ponce's life, even though he put himself in danger." Tears welled up in her eyes as she turned to her patient. "I'm so proud of your scars, Zahir. I hope they *never* go away."

"Me too!" Uncle Louis added.

Ponce and Kenzie agreed.

Zahir sighed deeply. He looked up at Aimee with sincere appreciation and then his eyes flooded over.

Georgia tossed back her long blond hair. Her green eyes glittered angrily at the copper-haired nurse. "I might not be in to read today," she told Zahir in a rather miffed tone. "Surfing lessons are on the big waves this afternoon. I'm so nervous and excited! But... I do love you!" she proclaimed earnestly.

Aimee missed the look of distain that was directed her way, since she was handing her patient a dry cloth to wipe his face.

Looking out the window as he hastily wiped his eyes, Zahir nodded, but he didn't reply. Georgia repeated her words of affection louder.

"Georgia," Zahir pleaded quietly. "I don't want to hear any more *meaningless* words. If you don't mean it, don't say it."

"Of course, I mean it!" the blond argued.

Struggling to stop his streams of tears, the dark-haired patient spoke gently, "I don't want to hurt your feelings, Georgia, but this is not working for either of us. I'm not interested in half-hearted relationships, and I know you won't be either." Turning his head to look up at the blond beauty, he begged, "Please don't say those words to me... again. It hurts more than it helps."

In a huff, Georgia whirled around and fled down the stairs. Zahir clamped the cloth firmly across his eyes and held it in place.

Kenzie looked over and smiled.

Hope filled Aimee's heart.

Uncle Louis cleared his throat and began talking about how much he would love to eat an apple. "And a bouquet of flowers would be lovely as well," he added. "I haven't seen flowers for so long. I wonder if the sunflowers are ready for picking..."

Rubbing the anti-itch cream into Zahir's arm, Aimee looked over at Uncle Louis with a smile. "I'll go to the store when I'm done," she promised happily. "I'll bring back some apples for everyone, and yes, let's get outside today!" she added.

Once the scars were attended to and the medications given out, Kenzie led the three patients through their morning stretch and exercise program while Aimee cleaned up the old bandages. As usual, one trip up and down Rainbow Hill to the outhouse and shower finished the session off for the two young men.

Aimee took a break to walk over to the store, talk to some of the other Tinys and pick up apples and flowers. Vahid and Charley were dragging dead trees over to the farmland. They had already collected twenty-one, and a pile of sawed-off branches lay nearby.

A loud discussion was taking place in the store as Aimee walked in.

"Just try it!" Odin was saying, holding a plump, pale carcass by its two legs.

"But that's disgusting," Nancy pleaded, as Milan tried to keep his eager dog from investigating the new aroma. "Look, it's bleeding! I can't put a dead chicken in the oven! We use the oven for food, not dead things."

"You fry *dead* fish in a pan," Franz argued. "What's the difference?"

Nancy tried to argue that they fried fish *fillets* in a pan, but she stopped mid-sentence, seeing the point.

Damien walked in with the farmers.

Vahid noticed the dead bird immediately. "Where did you get that chicken?" he inquired with alarm.

"It paid a visit to the Fun Forest," Odin chuckled. "Franz has a good shot."

"My first try with the new bow and arrow," Franz boasted, "on something living, that is."

"You *killed* one of our chickens?" Vahid exclaimed in disbelief.

"What happened to all its feathers?" Charley cried out, horrified.

"You don't eat the feathers," Odin smirked. "It's the meaty part that tastes so good."

"How would you know?" Vahid shouted. "Don't you dare touch another one of our pets!"

"Or what?" Odin asked, bemused.

Not having an adequate response, Vahid looked over for help from his farmer friends.

"Or you'll answer to us," Charley replied, motioning to himself and Vahid. "Both of us and likely Kenzie too!"

"And me!" Damien piped up, crossing his arms and standing tall. "Look here, you Rollin' Tumbler," he said, using his derogatory term for Odin, "touch those chickens again and you'll have a ride out in the lake that you'll never forget."

Pretending to be frightened, Odin said, "Oh, I'm so scared! And what about Franz? Will you dump him in the water too? I'm sure he's really worried about swimming!"

Lema piped up, "Touch those chickens again and we'll give you some firsthand wave education. You'll find out what a real Rollin' Tumbler is!"

Odin didn't reply. For a brief second he looked fearful. Then he said, "Remember, *we* have bows and arrows. We *killed* a chicken!"

Damien's eyes narrowed. "Are you threatening us?"

"You threatened me first," Odin scoffed, "even though Uncle Louis told you to stop it."

"You're asking for trouble," Damien told him. "You might get it sooner than you think. If no one else is going to do anything to stop you from causing harm, then I will!" He glared at Franz. The wiry young man was much smaller, but they had been friends for a long time. "Don't touch the chickens!" he said flatly.

Franz tossed back his stringy hair. "One was fun," he said proudly. "There are lots of other things we can practice on."

Rusty lunged forward again, finding it hard to resist the fresh bare meat dangling from Odin's hand.

Milan grabbed his dog around the chest and spoke to him sharply. Then looking up at Odin, he declared, "We aren't cooking the chicken here. Chickens are *pets* in Paradise, and they don't belong to either of you! Take it away and make sure the dogs don't get it."

"You need to bury it deep!" Charley called out. "Or we will."

Using words that sounded crude and mean, Odin complained that burying the chicken was a terrible waste.

The other Tinys looked at him blankly, confused by his language.

Damien frowned. "I don't know what you're saying. You talk strange!"

In a rage, Odin threw the chicken on the floor. He turned around and stomped off.

Rusty lunged forward eagerly, pulling Milan along the floor.

Quickly, Charley picked up the dead carcase. "I'll bury it," he said.

Vahid shook his head in dismay, "We'd better build higher walls with all those dead trees so the chickens can't get out. I didn't realise their lives were in danger!"

Lema and Damien left. Aimee talked to Nancy and Milan for a while, finding out what supplies were needed. She returned to the mansion with flowers, apples and the worrisome tale of a dead, naked chicken.

Her patients were outside in the shade under the veranda, learning how to play cards with Lily, Sanaa and Lema. Uncle Louis was sitting on the bench swing. The apples were gratefully accepted by everyone. The story concerned everyone except for Ponce, who found it so hilarious that he couldn't stop laughing.

"You need to get better, Uncle Louis," Aimee pleaded. "Damien is still threatening to take Odin out in the water. What if he actually drowns him? And Odin is saying strange words and threatening to use weapons. They'll listen to you, Uncle Louis, but they'll never listen to anyone else."

Zahir looked up anxiously as he laid down a Jack of Spades.

Sanaa groaned and decided to pick up the card.

"He won't really drown him," Lema piped up. "I won't let him. But he may give Odin a good a scare and that's what Odin needs!"

Uncle Louis spoke up. "Remember, we can only set an example, listen, empathize, educate and speak in a persuasive way. We can't force anyone to comply, and we won't win everyone over. And we certainly cannot take the life of another. The Professor will ensure that things don't get out of hand."

Lema didn't seem convinced, but Sanaa was giving him a look that had a restraining effect.

Coming outside with the chess set and seeing that everyone else was occupied with their card game, Kenzie asked Aimee if she wanted to learn how to play. Neither of them had tried it before, but following the instructions in the box, they had fun figuring it out.

Later that afternoon when they were back up in the Crisis Room, getting their medications, which had nearly run out, Zahir asked Uncle Louis, "Can you please read more to us? From God's Book, preferably," he smiled.

"Would you like to hear another story?"

"A story sounds great!" Ponce chimed in, relaxing on his bed.

Uncle Louis began reading in Exodus, about a terrible time in Israel's history, when they were enslaved in Egypt.

While the two nurses went through their well-established routine, a fresh breeze blew through the room, and little rainbows danced all over the walls. Uncle Louis basked in the warm sunshine near the big window. Even Ponce was enthralled to hear about baby Moses being rescued by the Egyptian princess and brought up to live in the palace. Eventually, he slumbered off to sleep while Zahir fought valiantly to keep his eyes open. Healing was still taking a toll, even though it was nearly complete. Almost three weeks had passed since the fire.

As she gathered the used wiped and bandages into a pot, Uncle Louis stopped reading. "Aimee," he said quietly.

Aimee looked up. Kenzie walked into the room with another pot to collect used supplies. Zahir's eyes fluttered open.

With a laugh, Uncle Louis said, "Okay, this is for all three of you, then," he smiled. "If you're feeling anxious about how Paradise will run without me here, I believe this book may be the key to making everything a lot easier."

"How?" Zahir asked anxiously.

Kenzie and Aimee stood still to listen.

"Well, if it's true," Uncle Louis prefaced, "this book provides the impetus to *self*-governance for everyone. If God is *our* Creator and so powerful that He can bring universes into being, then He is an authority far higher and mightier than *anyone* here in Paradise. You won't have to go through heated debates trying to determine right from wrong; God has already laid it out for us. When we believe that we have a Creator, who is watching over all – not just when we are visible outside our houses, but who even knows the thoughts that pass through our minds[127] - this will be a powerful motivator for everyone to live right and *think* right. It will help to stop wrong actions before they even get started!"

"But how can we convince the others that they need to care about God?" Zahir asked.

Thinking it through, Uncle Louis answered, "Only by sharing the message, just like I've shared it with you. Just think, if everyone chooses to follow Jesus' example, Paradise could be an even better place than it has been in the past. The Bible is full of encouragement to treat each other kindly and to put others before ourselves."

The three Tinys liked his vision.

He sighed, "However, we still need to fully determine if the Bible is true – and you may have to do this without me... But if it's true, then the key to helping your world be the best it can be is to share this hope with everyone and live by this example."

---

[127] 1 Chronicles 28:9; Psalm 139:1-18; 1 Kings 8:39; Jeremiah 17:10; Acts 1:24; Hebrews 4:12-13

A Window of Good and Evil

Chapter 36

*D*inner that night was enjoyed outside the Caring Centre on the stone patio. Lily, Sanaa and Lema brought extra food and stayed to enjoy it with those in the mansion. Lema had kindly pushed up a carrycart of fruit scraps and leftover bread to the girl's yard, knowing that Aimee would be delighted to feed it to the animals. Everyone had a blanket around their shoulders as the breeze whipped their hair around.

Kenzie had been visiting the farmers and he returned with a wide cream-coloured scarf in his hands. "Look at this everyone," he said proudly. "Vinitha made this from the sheep wool. She has been making all kinds of beautiful things. Feel how warm this is!"

Taking it around to everyone, they all tried it on with pleasure.

"Vinitha is so clever," the curly-haired nurse exclaimed. "She's even going to try colouring some of the wool with raspberry juice."

"I'll trade for one," Aimee smiled, wrapping herself in the cozy scarf. The large blankets they had been using were rather cumbersome.

"Me too!" Sanaa piped up. "I'd like a coloured one!"

Kenzie was pleased. When he sat down to eat his meal, Sanaa and Lema told of things that had been happening in the gardens. They were picking apples every day. A bat had landed in Sanaa's hair one night and Lema demonstrated her reaction, which everyone thought was funny.

"Did you hear about Damien and Georgia?" Lily asked.

"Hush," Ponce said quietly, his eyes darting over to Zahir. "Not now." Before anyone could ask questions, he begged Lily to tell them about the new construction in the Fun Forest. The bows and arrows were of great interest. Some felt they were dangerous, others thought it sounded fun.

As they discussed the daily happenings, Sanaa told them she was keeping an eye on the mango tree and hoping the fruit would be ready in a week. She was also elated that rainbows could be seen down in the gardens late in the afternoon.

While Uncle Louis rocked comfortably back and forth on the bench swing, the others laughed and joked around the stone table. Once she had finished eating, Aimee got up to feed the animals. Zahir joined her. The squirrels and birds were already helping themselves to the scraps in the cart. The dark-haired man with one bright blue eye tried to whistle to the squirrels. Due to the tightness on the right side of his face, it took several attempts before he managed to make the familiar noise. However, it had been a long time since the squirrels had heard the sound. They perked up and chattered at him, but they didn't come running. The deer, eager for treats, saw the apple cores, and eagerly waltzed over.

Gradually, the sun fell below the horizon and twilight set in. Ponce asked if he could go back to his home for the night, and Uncle Louis agreed that he was well enough. So, he and Lily meandered off happily, hand in hand to the stairs. Sanaa and Lema took the path to the beach. Once the cart of scraps was empty, Zahir walked over to sit with Uncle Louis again on the bench swing. The dark-haired patient didn't seem to feel the same urgency to return to his house.

Panting hard, Vahid came running from the clearing in distress. "Kenzie," he wheezed. "Can you come to the farm for a bit and help us out?"

Looking up from the stone table where he had been sitting, Kenzie said, "Sure. What's the matter?"

"It's Vinitha," his friend blurted out. "She... she found out..." With an anxious glance in Zahir's direction, he ran over and whispered something in Kenzie's ear. A pained look came over Kenzie's face.

"She's just really upset," Vahid explained to everyone else. "Kenzie always knows what to say to people. Can he please come with me for a while?"

"Let's take tonight off from reading," Uncle Louis suggested. "Feel free to go, Kenzie. I think we can all manage tonight."

With a grateful nod, the two farmers dashed off together.

Sitting beside Uncle Louis on the sturdy bench swing he had crafted months ago, Zahir talked to the older Tiny about some of the things they had read. Both were of the opinion that so far, the Bible was more convincing than the Professor's complicated treatise against it. While she patted the deer, Aimee enjoyed listening in.

As the loons cried out to each other down on the lake, Paradise gradually became a peaceful place. The darkness descended, the breeze blew gently, the pets were called home, and many Tinys went to bed.

Zahir left to visit the outhouse.

Uncle Louis watched Aimee trying to coax a squirrel to take a leftover strawberry top from her hand. Having already gorged itself, and no longer used to receiving nightly handouts, the squirrel was hesitant to come any closer. The older man desperately wanted to get to the cave. He could feel that his days were numbered, and he didn't have much time left. His heart had been beating in an erratic fashion the last few nights, although he hadn't told anyone. Yet, he knew there was no way to get down and back from the cave without

283

someone on either side. He felt that both Kenzie and Zahir would be of great assistance to help his sister lead Paradise, but the last instructions from the Professor had indicated she was to choose *one.* Having been confined to the Caring Centre for almost three weeks, he had been unable to discuss anything further with his father.

Fairly confident that he understood Zahir's feelings after a recent talk, Uncle Louis wasn't absolutely certain he knew Aimee's. He had observed that she and Kenzie worked very well together and had formed a close friendship, but he also suspected she cared deeply for Zahir. From his bed by the window, the older man had noticed the incredible dedication, some very loving looks, and the quickness to shield one patient in particular from pain of any kind. Yet, he did wonder if the reactions he had witnessed were motivated by Aimee's compassionate heart or true love. While he was hesitant to push a relationship together that was still fragile and fraught with misunderstandings, Uncle Louis was longing to get to the cave and have one full night of investigation. He needed to be certain that the Bible was true. Feeling a few more irregular beats in his chest, he wondered if this might be his last opportunity.

Aimee looked up from feeding the squirrel and asked, "Are you doing okay? Do you need a drink?"

Uncle Louis motioned for her to join him on the swinging bench. When she was seated beside him, he asked quietly, "Do you think you could take me to the control cave tonight?"

"I can try," she said hesitantly. Helping Uncle Louis get down the hill wouldn't be so difficult, but she had no idea how she would get him back up.

"I'd really like to do some research on the Internet about the Bible, and I'd like to do it with you," he said, trembling a little from the cooling temperature, even with a blanket wrapped all around him. "I feel this is something that we need to sort out together," he pleaded, "and I'm not sure how much time I have left."

"If it takes us half the night to get there, I'll do my best," she promised. Taking off the new woolen scarf that Vinitha had made, she wrapped it around his shoulders. "This is so warm," she smiled.

"Aimee," the older Tiny said hesitantly, "if something happens to me, which it will soon, I feel that leading Paradise may be too big a burden for you to carry alone. Is... is that how you feel?"

"Yes," she sighed, leaning close and wrapping her hands tightly around his arm. "That's why you must hold on, Uncle Louis. I need you!"

"If you could choose another Tiny to share this responsibility with," he said thoughtfully, "someone to help you to make the important decisions, who would you choose?"

Aimee sighed and looked away, but she didn't hesitate long. "Zahir," she admitted.

A huge smile spread across Uncle Louis' face. "I thought as much," he replied, "but I didn't want to presume. Do you feel you can work with Zahir and that he will help you to make good decisions?"

For some reason, which she didn't fully understand, Aimee choked up with tears. "Yes," she sobbed. "I do. Please ask Zahir."

Uncle Louis put his arm around her shoulders. "I thought you'd choose Zahir," he assured her, "although... Kenzie might be a very close second?"

They shared a smile. "Kenzie is *very* nice. He would be a great second choice," she agreed, wiping her tears away, "but he's... he's not Zahir."

"Okay... that is true," Uncle Louis chuckled, sensing the deep feelings behind the simple statement. He felt he had his answer. "Then I'm giving you permission to ask Zahir to come with us tonight. I'll need both of you to help me get up and down."

"Really?" Aimee clarified with astonishment. "*I*... should ask him?"

They both saw a tall silhouette enter the clearing.

285

"Go, ask Zahir to join us," he encouraged.

Standing up, Aimee was all smiles. "Thank you!" she said gratefully. "Thank you, Uncle Louis!" Although he was her brother, Uncle Louis would always be his name.

Running off, Aimee met Zahir in the clearing.

"Is everything okay?" he questioned with a frown.

She nodded, bursting with happiness. "Uncle Louis and I are going to talk to the Professor," she said quietly, "and we want you to come with us."

"Me?" Zahir whispered incredulously. "You're asking *me?* You're going to talk to... *the Professor?* In the secret cave? Why? What is this all about?"

"Please come," Aimee assured him softly. "You'll understand when we get there. Besides, I need your help to get Uncle Louis down the hill."

It wasn't an easy descent. Even with Aimee and Zahir on either side of Uncle Louis, he was dizzy and breathing heavily all the way down.

"How will we get back up the hill?" she asked.

"I don't know," the older man replied, uneasily.

"You're doing so well, Uncle Louis," Zahir encouraged. "Just one step at a time. We'll make it. Rest when you need to. There's no hurry."

Reaching the bottom of the hill, Uncle Louis sat down wearily on the last step. Zahir and Aimee rested on either side of him until he was able to catch his breath. Eventually, they pressed on and he stumbled to the cave entrance.

Aimee pulled out the key from around her neck. Having heard voices the night before, she made sure no one was nearby before unlocking the door.

Entering the cave, Zahir looked around curiously. Aimee closed the door behind them. Uncle Louis turned on the phone.

"We might need a couple more chairs," the older man mused regretfully. A whole night of investigation will be hard to take standing up. "Do you think you can run back to the mansion and bring a couple down?"

Aimee and Zahir quietly hurried back through the forest to grab two chairs from the girls' mansion. Taking a backway up the hill, they had to climb over several fallen trees.

Once they had collected the chairs, they decided to take the stairway down. They were almost to the bottom, when suddenly Zahir stopped in front and turned around. Aimee nearly ran into him. Hesitating, in the shadowy woods, he asked, "Aimee, why did you ask *me* to come with you and Uncle Louis?"

Aimee's face flushed bright red, but it was too dark to notice. On the spot and unprepared, she stumbled to find reasons... *safe* reasons, "Because... you are the one I'd choose," she said hesitantly. "I know I can trust you and that you will be a good leader..." She paused.

With a sigh, Zahir's shoulders slumped. He nodded his head. "Well, thank you," he said uncertainly. "I appreciate it... but, what do you mean by 'good leader'? Is this about *leadership*... in Paradise?"

"Yes."

"Then I'm not the best choice," he said firmly.

"Why not?"

"Aimee," he pleaded with an edgy tone of bitterness, "I know you said you loved honesty – but things are worse than you think. I'm really not who I used to be... or... who *I thought* I was. Aimee, I actually *regret* being kind... to Ponce! How can I regret saving a life? I find myself feeling intensely angry, jealous, resentful, and crying when I have no idea why. I hate these feelings, but I can't get rid of them. How can I be a leader? I'll hurt people's feelings... maybe even *yours* again. And what if I become completely blind and become a burden on... well, everyone? You should pick Kenzie – steady, reliable, faithful Kenzie. For so many reasons, Aimee, you should pick him."

"Zahir," Aimee protested, "what you're feeling is normal..."

"This is *not* normal!" he exclaimed with dismay.

"I did some research..."

"You did? How?" he challenged.

Around them, the wind came strongly through the trees. Warily, they both glanced up at the swaying branches.

"You'll find out how to research if you come to the cave," Aimee begged. Earnestly, she tried to explain, "Zahir, apparently what you're feeling is normal for someone who has gone through permanent physical injuries. Anxiety, depression, regret – it's all a part of healing on the inside. It won't always be like this. Your feelings will settle down. You'll recognize yourself again."

Sounding even more discouraged, he reaffirmed, "I still think you should choose Kenzie."

Aimee hesitated. It was the perfect moment to tell her anxious friend exactly how she felt. No one else was around to make things awkward. Love was the most important reason she was choosing him over Kenzie. However, Zahir was not speaking in his usual kind, reassuring way. The bitterness and frustration in his voice undermined her confidence. Even though she was trying to encourage him to remember that he was healing, she was thrown off by his negative reaction to her request. She had fully anticipated he would be grateful for this special opportunity to be on a secret mission with her, but instead he wanted to pass it off to another guy! If he loved her, why would he encourage her to choose Kenzie? It just didn't make sense.

Unsure of herself, Aimee's head and heart failed to come to a consensus. The wave of doubt had hit hard and she faltered. Once again, she opted for 'safe' answers.

"I'd like to choose *you,*" she said uncertainly. "Please come tonight, Zahir. Please see what this is about before you make a decision."

Reluctantly, Zahir moved forward, but Aimee's heart sunk. "He really doesn't want to do this," she reflected sadly, following him down the hill. As they hurried quietly through the valley between the two hills, carrying the chairs and dodging swaying tree branches, she struggled to understand it all. "Is there something special between us," she wondered, "or am I just imagining what I want to believe? Oh, what is Zahir thinking? Does he just lack confidence, or is there something that I don't know about? Maybe he would still rather be with Georgia... or someone *else!*" As they reached the cave door, she tried to reassure herself, "Once he sees how exciting this is, he'll want to be involved. I'm sure we'll eventually work things out between us."

When they got back, the older Tiny let them in and thanked them. "Someone has definitely been in here," he frowned as they set the chairs down beside the other. Looking at Aimee, he said, "The screen is covered in fingerprints and the floor is very dirty. Have you made sure the key is always with you?"

Aimee shook her head meekly. She explained about hiding it under a rock, and relayed the conversation she had overheard between Odin, Franz and Lily.

"Well, that explains it," he said regretfully. "From now on..."

She showed him her ribbon necklace. "I know," she nodded. "I always keep it around my neck now. I make sure I pull my blanket right up to my chin. I don't know how Lily gets the key off without waking me up."

Uncle Louis frowned. It didn't seem possible to him either.

Alarmed by the evidence of intruders, Uncle Louis didn't notice that his potential successors looked very glum. Turning back to the black screen on the wall, he asked Aimee to explain the phone functions to Zahir, which she did in a flat, mechanical way. The older Tiny had to point out a few that she didn't know. Finally, he asked Aimee to call the Professor.

Aimee selected a video call.

"Let's meet the Professor," Uncle Louis smiled.

In an instant, the Professor showed up on the screen and he was looking right at them.

Zahir's bright blue eye opened wide. Awestruck, he was fixated with the screen. It wasn't a still picture; the Professor was moving around and looking at them as though he were right with them in the cave. And even though he was the 'Mastermind of Paradise', there on the rectangular screen, he didn't appear much bigger than a regular Tiny.

"Hello," Jacques said cheerfully. "Louis, I'm so glad to see you again! You look really good! And you've got a crew with you tonight," he observed with a pleased expression.

Uncle Louis nodded. "Aimee and I made a decision to include Zahir," he told him proudly, knowing how much this would mean to his father. "I would never have made it to the cave tonight, without their help – one on each side. And Aimee would like to have a trustworthy friend involved in this process. It's a very big responsibility."

Zahir looked over at Aimee with a tinge of alarm but she didn't meet his gaze. Instead, she was questioning if she had made the right decision. She knew Kenzie would have been fully supportive. "Maybe this shouldn't be about who I love the most," she pondered. "Maybe I should have chosen the one I work best with..."

"I'm so pleased to see you all," the Professor rejoiced, with a nod of approval in Uncle Louis' direction. Looking at Zahir directly, the Professor said, "You are a courageous young man, Zahir. I'm very pleased that you saved Ponce's life when others would have let him die. And you've healed well. Your scar looks terrific."

Still not his usual self, Zahir was completely overwhelmed. Everything was so astonishing to him that he hardly knew what to say. Nodding, he flushed dark red and managed a polite thank you. Unconsciously, his hand reached up to touch his facial wound.

290

Turning his attention to Aimee, the Professor smiled, "Aimee, you've excelled at nursing. You've saved lives as well."

Aimee's response was much the same.

"Those who show they can serve well are given even bigger opportunities," he smiled. Looking kindly at the oldest Tiny, the Professor said, "Uncle Louis has been a wonderful leader of Paradise. I'm sure you will both agree."

Aimee and Zahir both nodded enthusiastically. Aimee put her arm around Uncle Louis' shoulders and smiled up at him.

With a deep sigh, the Professor added, "You know that Uncle Louis is not in good health. Sadly, his time with you is limited."

Burying her face in Uncle Louis' shoulder, Aimee did not want to talk about this.

"It's okay, Aimee," Uncle Louis said softly, putting his arm around her and pulling her close. "We all know this is the case. We must think about the future."

Wiping his eyes, the Professor continued sadly. "For things to function in Paradise, there must always be someone who can communicate with me," he explained kindly. "Sometimes there are emergencies, and someone needs to message me right away. Sometimes you need special supplies, or just some advice."

The younger Tinys nodded thoughtfully.

"So, this is how you always just 'know' things," Zahir remarked, looking over at Uncle Louis.

With a smile, he said, "It is."

"I'm choosing Aimee to communicate with me," the Professor stated, looking at her directly, "and I'm *very happy* for Zahir to be included as well. I can see that the two of you will make a good team. You've both shown an interest in serving others and caring for their needs. You've both appreciated Uncle Louis' fine example and I have no doubt you will follow his methods. Being leaders of Paradise means putting others' needs above your own. You need to think about what is best for Paradise, even if it may not be what is best for you personally. Serve to lead; lead by serving."

It was a high calling and at that moment both team members felt rather uncertain about their future together.

Unaware of their inner doubts, Uncle Louis spoke up, "Perhaps you could give them the same message you gave me," he said. "Maybe you could tell them about the Internet."

"Yes," the Professor agreed, looking at the younger Tinys. "This black box on the wall," he began, "is a very powerful tool. You can ask this phone any question you like, and it will give you many detailed answers. However, not all the answers are true and some are completely false. You need to be very discerning in your investigations. Research carefully, compare answers and talk things over between yourselves. You will discover many helpful, eye-opening materials. You will learn more than you ever thought possible. You will be able to experience my world - to see it and to view it in action. But, always keep in mind that the Internet is to be used as a tool to *help and benefit* others in Paradise. Never use it to harm *yourselves* or anyone else."

With a quick glance, Aimee looked over at Zahir. She couldn't wait to see his reaction to all the things she had seen on the phone. It was truly a direct window to the Professor's world.

"How can it harm someone?" Zahir asked cautiously.

The Professor acknowledged his question, "What you see may cause you to become discontent with Paradise. There is a lot of poisonous material on the Internet. This poison can make all other enjoyable aspects of life seem dull and boring. It's a poison that lures you to keep coming back for more even though you know it is making you feel terrible about yourself and sapping you of the ability to enjoy life's simple pleasures."

The younger Tinys shared a brief, anxious glance.

Nodding at their wary response, the Professor had a little more to say, "If you come across images or videos that make you feel uncomfortable, shocked, or ashamed, or frightened," he told them, "have the wisdom and self-control to turn it off. If you know you wouldn't look at something if Uncle Louis was sitting there beside you, it is likely poisonous material. Don't look at things like that. Make a decision to always, *always* avoid this dark, intoxicating venom. It's been put online to lure you in and destroy your spirit, don't give it power over your mind."

Frowning, Zahir spoke up. "Please explain poison and venom," he requested. "I've never heard of those before."

With a chuckle, the Professor nodded kindly. "Of course, you haven't," he smiled. "In my world poison is something that is used to make others very sick, or even kill them. You remember the spider that entered Paradise by mistake?" he asked.

Aimee and Zahir both nodded their heads.

The copper-haired girl was thinking about the serpent in the Garden of Eden. "His *lie* was like poison," she thought.

"Well," the Professor told them, "venom is the poison that a spider might inject to kill its victim."

"A spider or a snake," Uncle Louis interjected.

"Could that spider have *killed* Rosa and Lily?" Aimee exclaimed.

"Yes."

"Scary stuff," Zahir replied, a little dazed by all he was learning.

Uncle Louis told the Professor about the worrisome signs that someone had found their way into the cave.

"That isn't good," the Professor agreed. "Evan and I will look into it. I'm pleased that Aimee is now guarding the key more carefully." Looking at her, he said, "If you want, you could give it to Zahir for safe-keeping."

Passing it behind Uncle Louis' back, Aimee gratefully handed the key over to Zahir.

"Really?" he questioned uncertainly.

"Please?" she begged.

A dark look passed across his face as he reluctantly took the key from her hand. Aimee didn't understand why he was so unhappy. She was very disappointed by his reactions to the special mission. "Have I made a mistake?" she asked herself again. "Was I only thinking about my own feelings and not what is best for everyone?"

Then Zahir asked the Professor a question. "Is it possible for Aimee and me to invite others to join us in this cave?"

"Who do you want to invite?" the Professor asked curiously.

"Definitely Kenzie," Zahir stated. "He should be here with us tonight. He might wonder where we are. He will be upset tomorrow to hear that he missed out on this, and I don't want to tell him any lies."

Uncle Louis and the Professor exchanged glances; they hadn't expected such a request. Both missed Aimee's elated look of surprise, but the one who made the suggestion did not.

"I will trust you and Aimee to make those decisions," the Professor decided hesitantly. "As I've warned you, this phone can be used for good or for evil. It was important for all of you to grow up and enjoy living life without this device. However, now you are adults and the Internet is a valuable tool for problem-solving and educational purposes. It's also a vital way to stay connected with me. If you and Aimee can find a way to share the phone and keep everyone safe, then by all means you can do so. Just keep in mind that I don't want anyone to become addicted to the harmful material that is easily accessed or use the phone to discover how to endanger others."

Uncle Louis, Zahir and Aimee all looked at each other.

"We can share it?" Aimee echoed happily.

"Yes," he smiled. "As long as you think carefully about how best to keep everyone safe. I realise that trying to keep all these secrets has been cumbersome. I don't want you to feel you have to lie or be dishonest. We must think of a better way moving forward."

Once again, Zahir had an idea, "I think it's time for all of us to meet *you,* Professor," he begged. "We could easily divide on so many matters. None of us have a position of respect like Uncle Louis does."

Aimee and Uncle Louis nodded.

"I have contemplated this possibility," the Professor acknowledged. "I agree it may help. We should discuss it further. For now, I hope I will hear from you once a day, if possible," he said. "Evenings or mornings are usually the best for me."

"We will try," Aimee promised, with a more cheerful expression. She was greatly relieved that Kenzie would be asked to join them in the cave.

Turning to Uncle Louis, the Professor said, "I'll leave it to you, Louis, to show them how to use the phone in profitable ways. I love you all. Good night, everyone," he smiled.

They all returned his good night greeting and waved.

The Investigation

Chapter 37

I need to know if the Bible is true," Uncle Louis told the two Tinys on either side of him. "If you aren't too tired, let's investigate tonight. Let's sort this out."

"I'm fine," Zahir replied. "I'm not tired."

"Same with me," Aimee agreed.

Earnestly, Zahir requested, "Please, could I run and get Kenzie? I know he would want to be in on this."

Since the Professor had changed the rule, Uncle Louis readily granted Zahir permission.

While they waited for him to return, Uncle Louis showed Aimee the Bible App that he had installed on the phone. He demonstrated how to look up passages, search for words or topics of interest, and find detailed meanings of words.

"I'd love to have this up in the Crisis Room!" Aimee exclaimed. "It would make it much easier to answer our questions."

"It would," he agreed hesitantly. "But a Smartphone in the mansion would create many other problems."

Finally, Zahir came back without Kenzie. "I couldn't find him," he mumbled, slumping into his chair. "I didn't want to wake anyone up. We'll have to tell him about it tomorrow."

"You will have plenty of opportunities to share this with him in the future," Uncle Louis acknowledged. Eager to show them some of the discoveries he had made before the fire, he smiled, "Let me take you on an amazing tour. We've heard a lot about the land of Israel while we've been reading the Bible. Let's go there!"

"What?" Zahir remarked in surprise. "Really?"

In an instant, Uncle Louis had clicked on 'Google Earth' and typed in 'Israel.' The leaders-in-training were astonished as they saw the revolving planet, glowing bright blue and green against the deep black atmosphere. Quickly, they zoomed closer and closer to the earth until they reached a brown coastline along the edge of an ocean.

"Wow!" Zahir exclaimed, fully impressed. "The earth is *enormous!*"

For half an hour, Uncle Louis took them to various places they had read about, showing cities on hills, ruins in plains, old mosaic tiles by the seashore and archaeological digs.

"So, the Bible talks about *real* places on earth," Zahir expressed eagerly. "And we can see them! They really exist!"

"And these locations are described accurately in God's Book," Uncle Louis nodded. "If the Bible were a fictional account, that may or may not be the case."

"How will you investigate if the Bible is *really* true?" Aimee pondered.

"Well, this is one way," Uncle Louis assured her. "We can research the details that it records and see if they are correct... like the geographical features. But here's another way – the way I've been hoping to explore for a while." Typing into the Google search box bar, Uncle Louis wrote 'Is the Bible true.'

So many hits came up on the screen. Some were articles in full support of the Bible, and some were aggressively against.

"There is so much to read!" Zahir marvelled as Uncle Louis scrolled down the list.

"There is," Uncle Louis nodded, "and I'd like to get through as much as I can *tonight.* I hope you can both do this with me. I feel we should decide together if there is enough evidence to prove the Bible is a precious message that can educate us and make Paradise a better place, or if it is part of the destructive influence that we need to avoid."

Some muffled noises suddenly caught their attention. Aimee thought she heard someone say something about a light. Zahir thought he heard Odin.

"Who is there?" Uncle Louis called out loudly.

A great deal of scuffling was heard, but no one answered. The noises faded away.

Uncle Louis sent a message to the Professor telling him that they had heard noises outside the cave around midnight.

Aimee and Zahir were keen to delve into the investigation. The first article Uncle Louis wanted to read claimed there were more than a thousand contradictions in the Bible. "This is one of the Professor's foremost arguments against the Bible," he relayed. "I have to read this through."

Remembering that this issue had come up in one of their earliest discussions about the Bible, Aimee and Zahir were curious.

As they skimmed through an article, which listed the top hundred 'contradictions' in the Bible, they found the differences to be mostly small spelling mistakes, numbers that weren't the same in both accounts and details that had been recorded in one place and not another. Apparently, not all scribes had hand-copied the manuscripts with one hundred percent accuracy. However, the majority of differences – called 'variants' – between the accounts were mostly tiny, insignificant errors that did not affect any important Bible teaching.

Looking at articles in support of the Bible's accuracy, Aimee read from an article entitled, "Isn't the Bible Full of Contradictions?"[128]

---

[128] Thacker, J. https://www.bethinking.org

"It is important to stress that the degree to which these manuscripts agree far outweighs the degree to which they disagree, and none of the discrepancies concern major theological issues. Nevertheless, both the Old and New Testaments have a range of variant readings scattered throughout. One reason for this is that scribes made errors as they copied the manuscripts across the centuries. The contradiction regarding Jehoiachin's age is probably this type of error."

Later another article caught their eye under, "How Accurate is the Bible?"[129] which said,

"Because of the great reverence the Jewish scribes held toward the Scriptures, they exercised extreme care in making new copies of the Hebrew Bible. The entire scribal process was specified in meticulous detail to minimize the possibility of even the slightest error. The number of letters, words, and lines were counted, and the middle letters of the Pentateuch and the Old Testament were determined. If a single mistake was discovered, the entire manuscript would be destroyed.

As a result of this extreme care, the quality of the manuscripts of the Hebrew Bible surpasses all other ancient manuscripts. The 1947 discovery of the Dead Sea Scrolls provided a significant check on this, because these Hebrew scrolls predate the earliest Masoretic Old Testament manuscripts by about 1,000 years. But in spite of this time span, the number of variant readings between the Dead Sea Scrolls and the Masoretic Text is quite small, and most of these are variations in spelling and style."

One article went on to describe several insertions found in later New Testament manuscripts but not in the earliest records. Again, most of these weren't longer than one verse, but two were significant sections. It was possible, they read, that the account of the 'woman

---

[129] Boa, K. https://kenboa.org

caught in adultery' in John chapter seven had been inserted at a later point in time,[130] as well as verses nine to twenty in the last chapter of Mark's Gospel.[131] However, these later insertions did not impact any essential Gospel teaching and weren't vital to establish any doctrinal truth.[132]

Among the four Gospel accounts there were also some small variations, for instance, Mark recorded one angel was at Jesus' tomb, while Luke recorded two. But Mark didn't say there was only one, he simply *referred* to only one. Other so-called 'contradictions' were also of little significance, and, as one article stated, when verifying authentic eye-witness accounts, it is realistic for there to be small discrepancies depending on what details the eyewitness chose to record, but none of the variations directly contradicted one another in any essential matter.[133]

As they scanned various articles, they discovered that each Gospel writer shared a unique perspective on Jesus, which meant that different details of his life were important to include in one book but not in others. For example, Matthew set out to prove Jesus was the Messiah and referred to scores of Old Testament prophecies that he had fulfilled. Mark wrote about his experiences as a suffering servant. Luke was writing to a Gentile audience and was concerned with chronology, listing many specific, historical details. John's Gospel was reported to be the most theological, using very spiritual language to describe the Son of God. All four had different themes and audiences to address. One article stated that if everything matched up perfectly, it could indicate collaboration with the intention to deceive,

---

[130] Knust, J. https://www.bibleodyssey.org
[131] Hixson, E. https://www. thegospelcoalition.org
[132] Childers, A. "Another Gospel?" (2020), pg.132 – 133.
[133] Ibid. Footnotes in more detail in Bibliography.

rather than an honest recounting of the event from unique perspectives.[134]

Uncle Louis summed up the supportive articles, saying, "'We may not have the original manuscripts, but it seems to me, that for so many thousands of copies to be essentially the same message in all languages and parts of the world, this is powerful evidence that the Bible was copied accurately. We can read it with the assurance that we have God's essential message.'"

"That answers one question in my journal," Aimee smiled.

Her reluctant teammate, who was becoming more intrigued as the night wore on, found a quote that he wanted to read. It had been taken from a book called, "Another Gospel?" He read, "'...one of the traits of authentic eyewitness testimony that historians look for in ancient writings is called the 'criterion of embarrassment.' It basically means that one of the ways we can judge whether someone was telling the truth is if they didn't leave out embarrassing details about themselves or their story. In this way, the Gospels are incredibly embarrassing.'"[135]

"That's interesting," Uncle Louis agreed, repeating, "historians look for a 'criterion of embarrassment.'" Reading more of the quote out loud, he pondered the concepts. "If someone wants to promote themselves on Social Media," he read, "they will generally only record their best experiences. They will show everything in the most attractive way possible, hide or delete mistakes, foolish reactions, ugly expressions, failures, and so on. However, the Gospel accounts, and really the *whole* Bible, portray human life with all the good, bad and the ugly. Jesus' disciples sometimes argued about who would be the greatest. Sometimes their attempts to heal didn't have any effect because they lacked faith. They often didn't understand the simple things Jesus was trying to teach them – like 'leaven,' 'the source of

---

[134] Warner Wallace, J. "Cold-Case Christianity"
[135] Childers, A. "Another Gospel?" (2020), pg.132 – 133.

evil,' or even that their Master had to die, when he had explained it clearly on numerous occasions! They ran away in fear when Jesus needed them most. Sometimes Jesus had to rebuke them for trying to persuade him to disobey God's will for his life. If those disciples had written the Gospels on their own, in an attempt to start a new religion, maybe hoping it would bring them fame, money, power or help overthrow the governing bodies, would they write themselves into the stories with all their foolish actions revealed? Or," the older Tiny read thoughtfully, "did God want the authors to purposely record the moments of weakness, to encourage everyone that mistakes can be forgiven?"[136]

"I like that," Zahir agreed enthusiastically. "It is encouraging to read about the disciples' mistakes and lack of courage. It does give *us* hope."

Nodding, Uncle Louis added, "I'm thankful God has shown us the good and the bad. It helps us to remember that our Father in Heaven doesn't expect us to be perfect, just humble enough to admit our mistakes and try better the next time."

With a sigh of relief, Uncle Louis settled back happily. These questions had been bothering him since the first day he had heard that there were 'thousands of contradictions.' "Well, I don't see anything that directly contradicts the essential message," he remarked confidently. "Nothing is substantially inconsistent from one book to the next, there are just many insignificant differences among the thousands of manuscripts, due to spelling mistakes, missed details, and a few insertions made at a later date. I think that is quite acceptable for a book that is so old!"

Aimee recalled another point she had read, "Or there are some things that look like disagreements, but when we examine them

---

[136] See also: Childers A., "Another Gospel?" (2020), pg.142 – 143.

carefully, we find the variations enhance our understanding of the account."

Zahir was eagerly scrolling through more articles and found one claiming that highly advanced medical instructions to ward off contagious disease were recorded in the *earliest* books of the Bible, thousands of years before 'modern science' had discovered them.

Under the heading, "The Public Health Value of the Law of Moses,"[137] the article claimed that the medical requirements in Leviticus, Numbers and Deuteronomy were in keeping with the latest understandings of medical science known to be most important in stopping the spread of infection among groups of people and avoiding the entry of contaminants into the human body. The Law of Moses directed the use of running water for cleansing hands, bodies, clothes and bedding; isolation to prevent disease from spreading; advised against using any standing water into which a dead organism had fallen – thus appreciating the spread of bacteria. There were warnings concerning the danger and growth of mold, and many regulations against eating "unclean" animals prone to parasites and contamination. All these excellent health rules had been written down nearly four thousand years ago in the Bible, long before humans had discovered organisms that were invisible to the human eye, such as germs, spores and viruses. Even though modern science had only fully adopted and understood these safe measures in the last few centuries, they had been recommended in the Bible for millennia.

"So, if these laws had been followed," Zahir marvelled, as he read further, "it would have saved many people from dying of cholera, dysentery, fever and other highly contagious diseases... whatever they are."

Curiously, they investigated some of the diseases mentioned in the article and hoped that Paradise was never infected with any of them!

---

[137] Palmer, S. "The Public Health Value of the Law of Moses." (2001)

Aimee was impressed that the Bible's health instructions still held true *thousands* of years later, even with all the advancements in scientific knowledge.

Uncle Louis found another article that listed all the foolish notions people had believed, over the years, were 'helpful ways' to cure various illnesses. Lobotomy, bloodletting, electric coils, and radioactive water were some of the medical suggestions now referred to as 'quackery.' Drilling holes in people's skulls to let out evil demons, sounded terrible to Aimee. "It's hard to believe people actually thought that would help with mental illness!" she exclaimed.

"This is all really significant," Zahir marvelled. "If unsafe health practices were promoted in the Bible, that would demonstrate that it was written by people who didn't know what they were talking about and were just passing along the popular ideas of the day. For the Bible's health practices to still be effective four thousand years later, it's good evidence that whoever wrote it had a perfect understanding from the start!"

"It is a very good proof," Uncle Louis agreed. "The Law of Moses was even far ahead of *nineteenth* century science. The importance of hand washing was not understood even three hundred years ago."[138]

"Really?" Zahir remarked. "And that's just basic good sense!"

"You learned the hard way," Uncle Louis smiled.

The dark-haired Tiny agreed. "Yes, I sure did!"

Aimee smiled. Her hands had never been so clean as they had in the last three weeks.

Hour by hour, they sifted through articles, both for and against. Some reviews the older Tiny had already seen before the fire, so he readily summarised them. Others they all read together.

They examined an article that tried to disprove that God had created the world in six days. Uncle Louis wasn't impressed by the

---

[138] https://theconversation.com

suggested alternative, that everything had started with simple life and gradually evolved from one organism into another. "That sounds like the Professor's book," he said. "How can they prove that this is the way life began? No human being was there at the beginning to witness evolution."

Another article clarified the matter, saying, "If God didn't create the Universe, then who or what did? Likely any evolutionary answer to that question will involve a force that is uncreated, self-existent and capable of creating.[139] Atheists believe that the material world always existed. Creationists believe that God always existed. The atheists' view on the origin of life is no more probable or scientific than the Creationist. To believe that the material world always existed is an unproveable assumption based on faith."

Looking at a review of a movie called *"Dismantled,"*[140] Uncle Louis read, "'Avoid speculation on anything that can't be experimentally verified.' Evolution is a *historical* theory about the beginning of life. It is not a *scientific* theory because it cannot be verified through experiment."

"There's so much to discover," Zahir blurted out somewhat anxiously. "We could spend weeks down here!"

"We could," Uncle Louis agreed. "But we don't want to be consumed by all that is available. We just need enough information to answer the questions we have at the moment. This can be overwhelming."

They skimmed through articles on the consistency of the Bible message, which relayed that many different authors had received God's words and carefully recorded them over a period of about two thousand years. The message, the theme, the symbols, the hope, and

---

[139] Ferrar, H.M., "Mama Bear Apologetics." (2019) Pg.105–108.
[140] *"Dismantled: A Scientific Deconstruction of the Theory of Evolution."* Creation.com (2020)

the lessons were reported to be consistent from beginning to end. Such consistency would be very difficult, if not impossible for so many human beings to get right over such a long period of time.

"So, the Bible is a collection of many different books written by many different people," Aimee considered.

"Yes," replied Uncle Louis. Reflecting on the articles, he said, "I agree that a consistent message across so many centuries is solid proof that God is really the author and the people who were involved only recorded what God told them to write. How else could they have remained in agreement with one another?"

And then they found an article on the way in which Bible prophecy proved Divine inspiration. As the hours flew by, the excited Tinys examined Old Testament prophecies concerning Tyre, Egypt and Babylon, each time taking a fascinating tour with Google Earth to see where each place was and how it looked in the 21st century. Babylon was stark. In Jeremiah 51, God had said it would never be rebuilt. They looked at the ruins of the great city, broken down and sticking up out of mounds of sand. Apparently, it had once been one of the most beautiful places on earth. Googling 'Babylon,' they visited the Pergamum Museum in Berlin and were awestruck by the fascinating blue brick walls with lion decorations. They read about a man called Saddam Hussein, who wanted to rebuild the city and started the process but lost his life before getting far along in his renovations. Babylon was *still* a city of ruins, just as the Bible had predicted.

It was Uncle Louis who found information on Bible prophecies concerning Israel, as he had heard Evan mention while he lay in the Emergency bed. Outside the cave, dawn was breaking as they read about Ezekiel's prophecies of Israel's demise and regathering.[141] They also read that because the Jewish people had refused to follow God's laws, they had been scattered throughout the world and their capital

---

[141] Ezekiel 6; 36–37

city, Jerusalem, had been downtrodden by other nations,[142] until the regathering in the 1900's.

"This is all *recent* history!" Zahir repeated, fascinated.

"Yes," the older Tiny nodded. "The Jewish people have become a nation again in *their own land* after two thousand years of suffering, just like God said."

Aimee was reading on in the article. "And look," she said, "one of these prophecies speaks of God's Son – Jesus Christ – returning to be the king![143]

"Returning to this planet Earth?" Zahir asked with astonishment. "Will he come back from heaven?"

"Will we get to meet him?" Aimee wondered, looking over at Zahir with eager anticipation.

"It's all a part of these prophecies in Ezekiel and Zechariah!" Uncle Louis exclaimed. "If so much of it has already come true, then surely the rest will as well!" He pondered thoughtfully, "I believe the whole Bible either stands or falls together. All the way through, this book claims to be *a direct revelation from God,* where God spoke, and people recorded His message." Typing a few words that he remembered into the search bar of the Bible app, he found Second Timothy three, verse sixteen, and read the passage out loud, " *'All Scripture is breathed out by God and profitable for teaching, for reproof, for correction, and for training in righteousness, that the man of God may be complete, equipped for every good work.'*"[144]

Looking at his helpers, he said, "Either the Bible is what it claims to be, or it is an extremely well-designed fraud."

---

[142] Luke 21:20-24; Romans 11
[143] Zechariah 12, 14; Joel 3; Acts 1:10-12; Revelation 1:7
[144] See also 2 Peter 1:19-21; Deuteronomy 6; Joshua 24:26-27; Jeremiah 20:7-13; John 12:48-50; 2 Peter 3:15-17; 1 Peter 1:10-12; Hebrews 4:12-13; 1 Thessalonians 2:13

"I think we have found very good evidence to believe this book is true," Zahir proclaimed. "I don't agree with the Professor's objections."

"I believe it is true as well," Uncle Louis nodded. "So, that means that I have to act on it while I still can."

"What do you mean?" Aimee asked. "What do you need to do?"

Uncle Louis searched for the word 'baptized', and quickly found Acts twenty-two. They read, " *'And now why do you wait? Rise and be baptized and wash away your sins, calling on his name.'*"[145]

"I want to be baptized," he said. "God has granted me an extension of life, but I don't know how much longer I have." Looking at them both earnestly, Uncle Louis asked, "Aimee and Zahir, I need you to help me get to the lake. I need you to put me under the water, but keep me from drowning," he smiled. "I need to confess my sins and commit my life to God and His Son. Do you think you could help me, *please?*"

"Now?" Zahir asked.

"Yes. This is the best time," Uncle Louis smiled. "You've already helped me down the hill. We just have to walk to the lake."

---

[145] Galatians 3:27-29; Romans 6:3-11; Mark 16:16; Acts 2:38; 8:12

Into the Lake

Chapter 38

*I*t was a long journey in the sunrise to get to the lake. Leaning on their shoulders, Uncle Louis hobbled along slowly with frequent rests. Beautiful golden-edged clouds stretched across the sky. Pale pinks and blues melded into one another behind the criss-crossed expanse. Colourful lorikeets swooped over the sparkling, rippled water, riding breezy currents of air. Loons called out, beating their wings against the surface as they rose up out of the lake.

Once the water lapped gently against their feet, Uncle Louis breathed deeply with a peaceful smile. "We've made it," he said. Looking up to the sky, he rejoiced, "Father, I'm so thankful you've brought me to this!"

Following his direction, Aimee and Zahir waded out with Uncle Louis, deeper and deeper until the water reached past his waist.

Then Uncle Louis stopped. Resting his hands on their shoulders, he prayed, "My Father in Heaven," he said. "I am so thankful that you have blessed us here in Paradise with Your life-changing message and Your incredible hope of salvation. I am so thankful that You have extended my life to learn about You and that I'm no longer alone in this quest! You have answered my prayers in astonishing ways. I confess that there is so much that I still don't know. I pray You would help Zahir, Aimee and Kenzie to understand Your ways and bring everyone in Paradise to You. And I beg that You would open the

Professor's eyes, that he may also find Your salvation. Heavenly Father, today I confess all my sinful thoughts and failures to you. I pray for forgiveness for times of impatience with those in my care, and for things I viewed online that I completely regret. I know that you see every thought and examine our motivations. I recognize my need for forgiveness through the willing sacrifice of Your Son. I believe in Your Son, the Lord Jesus Christ. I love Your Son, our Lord Jesus Christ! I love the example he left for us to follow. I earnestly look forward to the day when Your Son will return and raise the dead to immortality. I want to be there, Father! I long to see Your Kingdom established on this earth. Please accept me as one of your children today. Please remember me when You call the dead to rise. In the Name of the Lord Jesus Christ, Your loving and obedient Son, I pray. Amen."

Opening his eyes, Uncle Louis smiled at the wide-eyed Tinys. "Now you can put me under," he said. "Completely under."

Zahir and Aimee put their arms around him securely. They tipped Uncle Louis backwards until the water came over his head. Then they brought him back up, sputtering and coughing a little.

"Are you okay?" Aimee questioned anxiously.

With a radiant smile, Uncle Louis looked at them both. "I've never been better. Now, I can go in peace." Looking up to the sky, he spread his arms out and said, "Thank You, Lord! Thank You for Your graciousness to me!"

As they helped him wade back to shore, Aimee saw that tears were streaming down Zahir's face once again. Uncle Louis' prayer had been deeply moving. She was impressed with her elderly brother's example that this was the way to forgiveness – confessing your sins and committing your life to Christ in baptism. She was very intrigued to learn more.

One phrase troubled her, and she asked uncertainly, "Uncle Louis, what do you mean by 'go in peace'? We still need you. We can't do this on our own."

Stumbling out of the water, Uncle Louis shook his head. "You're not alone... you have each other. Treasure your friendship and each other's insights. You have Kenzie and Ponce, Evan and Seth... and most importantly, you now *know* that you have a Heavenly Father – the Creator of the world... and His Son, our Lord Jesus Christ!"

Breathing heavily, Uncle Louis pointed to the sand, and they all sat down together. "You're not alone – *not anymore,*" he panted. "You have more on your side... than I ever did... and yet, I had all that I needed..."

Suddenly, he groaned in agony and brought his hand over to grip his left arm. "I'm sorry," he said weakly. "I need to lie down..."

Aimee and Zahir helped him to lie back in the warm sand. Uncle Louis' face became ashen. The sun had risen above the hazy horizon, and the beach boys were rising too.

Damien and Georgia were walking along the beach with their arms around each other. Curious, they drew closer to see what was going on. Uncle Louis was breathing fine, and his heart was still pumping, but his eyes were closed.

"We need to get the stretcher to get him back home," Zahir fretted anxiously. "He's exhausted."

"Is he dying?" Georgia inquired with a worried expression. Her long blond hair shone brilliantly in the early morning sun.

Aimee shook her head. "No, just sleeping," she replied, anxiously observing the older Tiny's grey face and keeping her hand on his heart. "But he's not doing well."

Looking up at Damien, Zahir begged. "Could one of you please run up Rainbow Hill and bring us the stretcher? Uncle Louis needs help getting back up to the mansion."

"Well, what were you dunking him under the water for, Scar Man?" Damien replied dismissively. "That was risky! Look, I've got three people coming for morning swims in a few minutes. What's wrong with your legs?"

Zahir didn't respond, but suddenly Lema dashed over. "I'll get the stretcher," he offered. "You stay here and help Uncle Louis."

Looking up gratefully, Aimee watched their tall, dark friend tear off towards the hill. She wondered if he had seen the baptism.

"Come on, Gorgeo, let's get in!" Damien called out, picking his blond girlfriend up in his arms and racing into the water.

Feeling the spray, Aimee and Zahir sat in the warm sand beside their uncle and dear friend. Holding Uncle Louis' hand, monitoring his pulse and hoping he wouldn't stop breathing, they waited anxiously for Lema's return. Resentment burned in Aimee's heart as she considered Damien's refusal to help and his derogatory name for Zahir. "Don't let his names bother you," she whispered. "I love your scars."

The dark-haired young man on the other side of Uncle Louis didn't look up but he shook his head dismally.

Amidst the laughter as the two swimmers frolicked in the lake, Uncle Louis spoke softly. "Let me go now," he begged. "Don't try to revive me. I have... found... the *greatest treasure.*"

In a few minutes, Lema came running back, carrying the stretcher. Kenzie and Ponce were close behind. Together they all managed to get Uncle Louis back up the hill and safely into his bed. Half-asleep and worn out, Uncle Louis was thankful for soft pillows and a comfortable place to rest. He fell asleep immediately.

Zahir flopped into his own bed nearby. "Good night," he said wearily. "I'm *so* tired!"

Ponce left to get breakfast, but Kenzie was puzzled.

"Why did you take Uncle Louis down to the lake?" he questioned Aimee. "I came up this morning to an empty room. I didn't know where anyone was."

"Uncle Louis wanted to be baptized," Aimee replied joyfully.

"Baptized," Kenzie echoed. "So, he's sure the Bible is true?"

"We spent the whole night researching."

"Here?"

"No... in the cave," Aimee explained. "The cave where I go to talk to the Professor."

Kenzie frowned. "I wish I'd been included."

Zahir looked up wearily. "I tried to find you," he implored. "I looked all over. I knew you would want to be in on it."

"Did you look up on Mining Hill?"

"No," Zahir replied. "Why were you up there?"

"That's the farmer's lookout," Kenzie smiled. "I was talking to Vinitha. It's probably just as well that you didn't find me."

"Is she really upset?" Zahir questioned.

"Yes, she is. We talked for hours."

Aimee saw a blissful glow spread across Kenzie's face. She was pleased to see his happiness.

For a moment, no one was sure what to say, then Zahir promised, "We'll take you to the cave, Kenzie. We'll show you everything we learned." He yawned. "For now, I'm so tired..."

The yawn was contagious; Aimee couldn't help herself. Covering her mouth, she took a few steps towards Lily's room. "We have so much to tell you," she added, "but right now I need to get some sleep too."

"No wonder you're both exhausted!" their curly-haired friend smiled. "Have a good sleep!"

A Mystery Resolved

Chapter 39

*E*van arrived early that morning, having been awoken by a cheerful bird outside his window. He and Jacques had planned to meet at nine and discuss a possible breach in the cave security. Planning to get a head start on their investigation by scrolling through the Internet history, he strode into the Paradise Room just as the sun was rising. Rays of sunlight were streaming through the greenhouse glass and sparkling across the water. He stopped for a moment to admire the beautiful scene. Movement in the lake caught his eye and to his great surprise, he saw Aimee and Zahir on either side of Uncle Louis as they all waded in.

"What is happening here?" he wondered curiously. He drew closer.

Over the speakers came the most heartfelt prayer. It sent a shiver down his spine. Uncle Louis was asking to be part of God's family and submitting to baptism! Evan was enthralled.

Pulling out his phone, the tall assistant took pictures as he watched the proceedings, pleased to see that the older Tiny had discovered the Gospel message and the hope that God offers to the whole world. "He certainly has been reading the Bible," he said to himself. "I'm so thankful we were able to send it in!"

Quickly, he sent the pictures off to Seth, knowing that his friend would be ecstatic!

It was alarming for the young researcher when Uncle Louis collapsed on the beach. Evan was distressed by Damien's unwillingness to help and his unkind name for Zahir. He was thankful that Lema once again was ready and willing to help. Riveted to the dome, he watched the Tinys move the older man to a stretcher and get him back up the hill.

Seth texted back, "This is the best news ever! I'm so glad you were there to see it!"

"Thanks to an early morning bird!" Evan typed in. "Otherwise, I would have missed it."

Once Uncle Louis was back in the Caring Centre, and Damien was running his lively surfing lessons with Georgia and Diya, the tall blond scientist saw Vinitha ascend Mining Hill alone. The dusky girl with the long black hair was crying.

"Poor Vinitha, her heart is broken," he murmured, wishing he could talk with her. He knew exactly how she felt. "Right now, she can't imagine it will ever heal, but it will. If I were her dad, I'd be really happy for that sweet girl to find a loving, committed friend. I hope her heartbreak leads to someone who will appreciate her value."

With an hour to go before he was due to meet with the Professor, Evan took a moment to count all the fallen trees. They had lost about a third of all that they had planted. On the steep side of Rainbow Hill, over a hundred lay dying. It was a sad, brown blemish on the rolling green landscape. He was glad to see the farmers were using some of the dead timber to build walls around their chickens. It would be a while before the tiny trees the Professor had germinated would be big enough to be sent in and planted by the Tinys. The newly programmed wind stress would help them to develop much stronger roots.

Sitting down at the computer, Evan searched the files of recorded Internet history. What he found disturbed him greatly.

Jacques arrived whistling a happy tune.

It was the first time Evan had ever heard him whistle and he looked up in surprise.

"Guess who was in the cave with Louis last night?" the grey-haired researcher boasted to his assistant. "Aimee and Zahir have finally worked it all out... I think," he smiled happily.

"You sound a little unsure..."

"Yes... well, they didn't seem as happy as I thought they might... But they were together!"

"So, Aimee has chosen Zahir," Evan reiterated.

"Yes, I knew she would eventually... it just took time."

Turning around in the office chair, Evan nodded happily. He didn't tell Jacques about the baptism or what he'd just discovered on the computer files. He decided to allow his mentor a moment to savour his long-awaited good news. But with a wry grin, he added, "Yes, time... and a little *suffering,*"

"Suffering?"

"The last few weeks have changed the dynamics in Paradise in ways that nothing else seemed to effect."

The Professor nodded slowly but he didn't respond. "Zahir will be an excellent leader," he declared, very pleased with the situation. "He has already made wise suggestions to the way we've handled the phone."

"Such as?"

"Well, he and Aimee would like to share the phone with others. He doesn't want to lie about it. I explained my concerns and left it up to them to figure it out."

"That's a huge task!"

"The Tinys are now adults," Jacques admitted, "and as I hoped, they've learned to enjoy life without artificial entertainment. Louis won't be doing school with them anymore unless he improves dramatically. We need a better way, a more open way for all of them to continue their education. And it seems that the phone has already

317

been discovered by those who would use it for harm. The secret is already out, so we will need to work with them all."

Evan agreed. He asked about the key, and the Professor told him that Aimee had entrusted it to Zahir. They both surmised that Lily may have been taking the key at night, while her roommate was asleep.

"We should have put a code on the door, instead of a lock," Jacques regretted.

"Well, we can put a code on the phone."

"Yes, we can!" Jacques agreed. "First, let's see what happens tonight. Right now, I'd like to make a journal entry, and then investigate a little," he said.

"Well... first, you need to look at this," Evan said sadly, pointing to the computer.

Striding over, the Professor looked at what Evan showed him on the screen. He was shocked to discover how many terrible sites had been visited even with the website blocker in place. He was alarmed by the many hours of YouTube videos that had been watched.

Shaking his head, he murmured, *"Ça alors!* So, this has all been taking place between the hours of midnight and four in the morning. No wonder they can't wake up till lunch. Why didn't I think to check this out before?"

Looking up at Evan with despair, he answered his own question. "I suppose I thought I had put enough safeguards in place. I didn't think this was possible." Scrolling through the records, the Professor was horrified to realize the early morning access had been taking place even before the fire! It had been happening for nearly two months! Initially, the sites were mostly educational or simply entertaining, with only the occasional red flag. After the fire, there had been a two-day hiatus. But in the following weeks, the quality of hits had quickly degenerated!

"*Oh là là!* What are we going to do about this?" he despaired.

318

"It's quite serious," Evan agreed.

"Let's do our journaling, while we think about it," Jacques suggested, looking very pale.

Taking their black books from off the shelf, the Professor and Evan headed to the north side of Paradise. In his book, Jacques jotted, "April 30th," at the top of his page. It had been a full three weeks since the fire.

"We've had a serious breach of security," he began, listing out everything they knew or assumed so far. *"I have made a huge mistake thinking I could keep the phone a secret! I should have realised they would all discover it one day. I needed to prepare them to choose good over evil! I just didn't think it would come to this – so soon, or that children raised in such a wholesome world would want to look at such perversion."*

Once he had detailed the types of sites that had been visited and lamented over the loss of their innocence, Jacques looked in at the charred trees, wondering if Odin and Franz were awake. He observed all the changes that had taken place and then wrote, *"The forest has been cleaned up and is now being revamped as an adventure park. They call it 'The Fun Forest.' I see rope swings, a target practice, tree-top treks, and a ball-launcher which is incredibly well-designed. I was quite surprised by the creativity displayed in this forest, but sadly, I now know that these marvellous ideas came from unsupervised use of the Internet."*

Quite behind in his journaling, the Professor continued to write, *"Odin initially took full responsibility for the damage he did and had a remarkable change of attitude. He helped tremendously in the first two days and was receiving a lot of positive feedback from the others. Once he found the ruby, he felt it paid off his debt to the community, and he slipped backwards again. He is rarely seen outside of the forest, aside from meals. There have been confrontations between him and Damien, and I am concerned it may end up in serious blows.*

319

Odin is now seen more often with Franz than Ponce, but of course, his old friend was restricted to the Caring Centre to heal.

Apparently, Ponce and Lily plan to get married. Surprisingly, weddings have become a popular idea among the Tinys – another result of their investigations online... and a more positive one."

Evan stood nearby, examining the same area and noted in his book, *"Today, on April 30th, Uncle Louis was baptised in the lake! His prayer of confession and commitment was wonderful. Aimee and Zahir helped him and witnessed the event. I'm sure it will have a huge impact on them. The Bible could have a powerful influence on everyone in Paradise.*

"On a tragic note, I confirmed today that some of the Tinys have found a way to access the cave and use the phone for evil. I am disappointed how quickly they chose perverse material and am fearful for the impact this will have! We are bound to have some behavioural problems now that there is a knowledge and desire for these activities. I assume Lily borrowed the key from Aimee when she was asleep. The Professor has also given Aimee and Zahir permission to share the phone with everyone, so all of this will begin an interesting new phase in our experiment.

"In the North Forest – actually the 'Fun Forest' now – they are creating an upscale target practice and Franz has figured out how to make bows and arrows... very well-made bows and arrows! I'm sure I'll find the exact pattern online. We now know why this group often misses breakfast and arrives yawning at lunch time – they've spent half the night awake."

As they both stood nearby on the other side of the glass, the trap door in the ground opened up, and Odin stumbled out.

Waking up grouchy, Odin began using choice words.

Evan and the Professor looked at each other sadly. There was no doubt where he had learned the foul language.

Glancing back at the piles of dirt and nearby shovels, it suddenly occurred to Evan that Odin was a tunneller. He had built an underground den. "Is there any chance they might have *dug* their way into the cave?" he whispered anxiously.

"That would be a substantial feat!"

Immediately, the two scientists walked over to Rainbow Hill and examined it carefully. With all the trees lying in messy piles, it was almost impossible to see if there might be a hole in the ground. However, they noticed a faint trail in the grass that led from the North Forest behind Cascading Mountain, right to the back of the hill in question.

"I'm going to stay up tonight," the Professor stated firmly. "I'm going to see what's happening when we aren't watching."

Conflicted in his mind, Evan asked tentatively, "Do you mind if I head home? My mom is expecting me to be at a barbeque this afternoon... and we're having *steak!*"

"Enjoy your barbeque!" the Professor laughed. "I'll call you if I need your help."

"Thanks," Evan said, as he turned to leave. On his way out of the Biosphere, he thought to himself, "The Internet can be such a great resource for good. It has been the source of our communication, Louis' education and so many of the most important things that the Tinys have learned. Our first little man may never have found God's Book without it. But what is available online can also lead someone into the very depths of evil. It all depends on the choices that are made. Instead of locked doors and secrets, we should have been developing strong consciences!"

In the Night

Chapter 40

*H*aving picked up dinner at the Reptile Café, the Professor sat down at his desk to enjoy the bowl of shrimp chowder and one very large Americano, which he hoped would help him stay awake for most of the night. He made himself comfortable at his desk. The soup was delicious. Online there were plenty of scientific debates to watch and articles on Intelligent Design to read. Deep into his own investigation, his mind was opening up to new possibilities that he hadn't yet discussed with anyone. He intended to make good use of his time. Turning up all the speakers that were linked into the microphones in Paradise, the Professor settled into his work. He wanted to make sure he didn't miss any suspicious noises, especially from near the cave.

With his eyes on the screen, he began reading the transcript of a recent debate, "We can only know to be true what science has demonstrated," the Atheist began. "Anything that science cannot methodically examine cannot be known to exist."

"But you can't explain the existence of DNA by purely natural causes," the Creation Scientist reasoned. "How did simple atoms write their own elaborate software? How did the four-dimensional genome form itself in such perfect fashion? You know that it's impossible for information to come from nothing, yet you believe that the vast variety of self-reproducing, complex lifeforms simply *evolved?* Which is *more* impossible – an intelligent, supernatural

Creator designing everything you see, or a primordial soup struck by a source of unguided, meaningless energy, forming the very building blocks of life? Your ideas on the origin of life are no more scientific or probable than mine. You are still left with an 'unproveable assumption based on faith.'"[146]

Uncomfortably, Jacques shifted in his chair. As he read the debate, his ears were tuned in to Paradise and the speakers were picking up even the most distant voices. He could hear all the laughter from Rosa's Hill, Odin's foul language in the Fun Forest and even the four Tinys in the Caring Centre as they read from Genesis chapter six. Looking in briefly, he was surprised to see Lema and Sanaa on the swinging bench, just below Aimee's open window. "Are they listening in?" he wondered. "Or just enjoying their own private conversation?"

Tonight, Zahir was reading, *"The Lord saw that the wickedness of man was great in the earth, and that every intention of the thoughts of his heart was only evil continually. And the Lord regretted that he had made man on the earth, and it grieved him to his heart. So, the Lord said, 'I will blot out man whom I have created from the face of the land, man and animals and creeping things and birds of the heavens, for I am sorry that I have made them.' But Noah found favor in the eyes of the Lord."*

"The great catastrophe," the Professor thought to himself, as he saved the interesting debate to his files. "Six chapters into the first book of the Bible and God destroys His whole creation! I just don't get it!"

Inside the Crisis Room, he faintly heard Aimee ask, "How many years after creation did God bring this flood?"

Uncle Louis had looked into this when he first began to read the Bible. "Around a thousand, five hundred years had passed before the

---

[146] Hillary, H.P. "Mama Bear Apologetics" (2019), pages 105-108.

flood," he replied. "That's a lot of years, and people were living much, much longer than they do today."

"That's two hundred and fifty times our lifespan," Zahir chuckled, now wide-awake, having slept most of the day.

Kenzie and Aimee marvelled.

"And this flood surrounded the whole earth?" the curly-haired nurse questioned.

They looked at the record more carefully, noting that God intended to destroy everything that breathed, *everything* under the heaven and on the *whole* earth.

"Forty days and nights of rain!" Zahir noted. "That's a lot! Our little world was nearly submerged in a few hours."

"What does it say about the mountains?" Uncle Louis prodded.

Reading from chapter seven, Zahir replied, *"all the high mountains under the whole heaven were covered. The waters prevailed above the mountains, covering them fifteen cubits deep."*

"If water covered all the mountains under the whole heaven, that indicates to me that the whole earth was covered. Water always seeks a level."

In agreement, Zahir read the next few verses, *"'Everything on the dry land in whose nostrils was the breath of life died. He blotted out every living thing that was on the face of the ground, man and animals and creeping things and birds of the heavens. They were blotted out from the earth. Only Noah was left, and those who were with him in the ark...'"*

"Sounds like *every* land animal that wasn't on the ark died," Kenzie observed.

"Why would God destroy His whole creation?" Aimee asked.

"It says that He was sorry that He made people," Zahir suggested.

Uncle Louis spoke up, "And it says that God was greatly distressed that His earth was filled with violence, and that humans had 'corrupted their way,' and their imaginations were filled with evil."

"I wonder how this happened," Kenzie mused. "How did they get to this very bad state?"

On the other side of the glass, the Professor stopped his research for a moment to listen to the discussion. "How *did* humans become so bad back then?" he wondered. "This was long before the invention of the Internet. How did they develop these terrible imaginations? What influenced them?"

Zahir was looking closely at the Bible. "There's another one of those references written in the margin," he said. "I'll look it up."

"Certainly," Uncle Louis encouraged.

Finding Mark chapter seven, Zahir read the passage, *"'What comes out of a person is what defiles him. For from within, out of the heart of man, come evil thoughts, sexual immorality, theft, murder, adultery, coveting, wickedness, deceit, sensuality, envy, slander, pride, foolishness. All these evil things come from within, and they defile a person.'"*

Surprised, Kenzie clarified, "All this evil is from our own hearts?"

Uncle Louis nodded and explained, "Ever since Adam and Eve ate from the Tree of the Knowledge of Good and Evil, human beings fell from the 'very good' state in which God had made them. Since that day, there has been a sinful side in every one of us that can easily be inflamed by what we think about and do, or we can *choose* to restrain it... with God's help and the influence of goodness into our lives."

Aimee was thinking it through. "So, at the time of the flood, all the people were choosing to follow their evil imaginations," she pondered. "All except Noah. That must have been a scary world! I don't think I'd want to live in a place *full* of violence and corruption."

On the other side of the glass, the Professor reflected, "When I first set Paradise in motion, I thought all the Tinys would choose good, since they would never see evil. Yet," he pondered thoughtfully, "most of those 'evils from the heart' have shown up in Paradise. Thankfully, we haven't had a murder... *yet*... but there have been threats. Odin and Franz have made weapons... And now, some are choosing perverse behaviour. What would I do if Paradise became full of evil? What would I do if the Tinys were afraid to live in their own world? What if there were only a few who cared about doing good, and they were under attack?"

As he considered the scenario, the Professor could feel his blood pressure rising. It had been easy enough in the past to condemn God for wiping out countless people and animals and making so many rules. But now with his anxious thoughts about what some of his Tinys were choosing to bring in, he recognized that a world full of violence and wicked imaginations, such as he had heard described in Genesis, would be a terrifying place to live. As humans dismissed their high calling and chose to give in to their own selfish desires, more and more rules would need to be added... and enforced!

Aimee didn't make her regular call that night. He could hear the occupants of the Crisis Room read a chapter from his book. For the first time ever, he squirmed uneasily with his own strong language.

His daughter read, "Religion is damaging to the human psyche as it encourages us to accept foolish notions as truth. The concept of 'faith' is applauded by Christians as something we should 'strive' to develop, yet it leads many to accept antiquated, unproveable superstitions as hard facts. Christianity developed when humanity was still ignorant of the great scientific discoveries that have revolutionised the modern world. We now know and understand the mechanisms behind natural forces and are no longer mystified by powerful storms, floods and earthquakes once attributed to a Higher Being. We now understand mental illnesses and are no longer so foolish as to think that supernatural forces are behind schizophrenia and epilepsy. Scientists today would not be dazzled by the miracles recorded in the Bible. They know everything can be explained by natural causes. While 'magic' shows are a source of entertainment even for those who understand it is all about a cunning sleight of hand, a magician deceives only those who are so ignorant as to believe he is some great one. In reality, he has no more power than you or me. Yet, from what I have observed in religious circles, the less evidence available to believe in a Higher Being, the more 'faith' is put forth as a virtue!"

Jacques frowned. "I don't feel the same bitterness that I once did," he thought. "I worded things rather harshly back then."

"But faith is based on evidence," Aimee argued. "That's why we did so much research."

"And we found evidence," Zahir added. "Powerful evidence!"

"Then hold onto it," Uncle Louis encouraged. "And let's pray that the Professor goes in search for evidence as well."

On the other side of the glass, the Professor nodded his head slowly. "Well, he is searching," he smiled. "So, we'll see if this old, radical skeptic can reasonably sort through what he finds."

As he continued to make his way through various online articles, discarding some and riveted to others, he heard the Tinys react in shock to some of the statements they were reading in his book. Often, he agreed with their sentiments, not his own. "I might need to write a new book," he smiled sadly. "I don't agree with myself anymore."

Eventually, the Tinys began to tell Kenzie about all they had discovered down in the cave the night before. Occasionally, Jacques looked up the 'evidence' they were discussing and read the articles through himself. Little by little, his perspective was changing. There was a powerful case on the Creation side that he wished he'd examined more thoroughly years ago.

When the talking ceased around eleven-thirty, he heard Aimee say goodnight to the others as she headed to bed. Approximately half an hour of peaceful quiet settled in across Paradise, as the Professor continued to research. A few loons called out, a cow mooed, snores echoed from the farmland, there were a few groans from the mansion, and then the Professor heard a soft thump.

327

Walking over to peer into the dome, he could see movement by the Caring Centre. In the glow from the twinkle lights, a petite figure was running off into the forest. Lily was awake!

Watching her run down the hill and across the meadow, Jacques was fairly sure where she was heading. In a couple minutes, she had reached the North Forest, knocking quietly on both Ponce's cabin and Odin's den. A few minutes later, Odin, Franz, Ponce and Lily were scurrying around the back of Cascading Mountain.

Glancing at his phone, the Professor saw that it was just after midnight.

"I get to see *my* show first," Odin was whispering loudly. "I love those shoot-em-ups. We have to figure out how to make guns for the Fun Forest."

"Guns and *cars,*" Franz added. "Only there wouldn't be enough room to drive a fast car anywhere!"

"And to think we thought go-karting was fun!" Odin added.

"Yeah! Paradise is way too small!"

Odin chuckled, "We have to get out of here! We are definitely missing out on the good life." Throwing in a few choice words, he added, "We live in a kid's world. The real fun is outside of this cage."

"Can I watch my show tonight?" Lily pleaded.

"Another kissy episode?" Odin complained.

"Come on," Ponce argued. "She says she missed out the last time. I'd say Lily's show should be first."

"But we *all* had to miss out last night," Odin growled. "It's no fair when some hog it for the whole night!"

"Please," Lily begged.

"Oh, all right," Odin growled. "But only if you give us time to look at pictures!"

"We'll be leaving before you do that," Ponce said in dismay. "You guys really should stop looking at those!"

"What? You've spent too much time up in that mansion," Franz protested. "If you don't like what we're doing, go back to them!"

"I'm really glad that I spent time up there," Ponce argued. "It was good for me. There's a book I'd like to show you..."

"Reading? I'm not doing any more school," Odin dismissed. "Make up your mind, Ponce. Either you're with us, or you're with them."

"But it's changed my life," Ponce pleaded. "You see, the Professor isn't the one who made us. There is a God who made the Professor's world and everything in it. He wrote a book to tell us about Him and how He wants us to live. There's a right way and there's a wrong way and He's going to judge us for what we do..."

"Shut up!" Odin exclaimed. "If you're going to keep talking like this, you're not on our side *anymore!* Do you hear me? Go back to your friends on the hill!"

"But real friends do whatever they can to help... even if it hurts!"

Odin stopped and crossed his arms. "I don't want to hear this stuff! Leave!"

Ponce shrugged. "I'm coming with you," he said.

Franz spoke up. "Then stop talking!"

On the other side of the glass, the Professor shook his head in dismay. "Ponce is trying hard," he thought. "I hope he doesn't get pulled back to his old ways."

Watching his lanky, troubled son, follow the stocky youth in front the Professor whispered, "Franz, what are you up to?" As the four Tinys disappeared quietly into the hill, Jacques murmured, "Why do you and Odin keep making poor choices? I am so disappointed. I am so sad!"

Unable to hear the conversations inside the cave, the Professor was too distraught to continue any profitable work. Mechanically, he began cleaning files on his hard drive, all the while keeping an eye on the control monitor to see what was being accessed on the phone in the cave. The first hour was fairly harmless. "Lily is getting her way," he observed. He was intrigued that the Greenville University page held their attention next and then a DIY site was investigated with details on how to make a flying fox.

A rustling noise alerted him that some were leaving the cave. The rainmaker was passing overhead, programmed to come on when everyone was asleep.

"Perfect timing!" Lily exclaimed to Ponce, out in the open again. "I'll stand in the rain and get all cleaned off. I don't want Aimee to get even more suspicious. It's so dirty in that tunnel!"

As the two Tinys laughed and washed off in the rain, the Professor was dismayed to see the names of various Internet sites now coming up rapidly on his screen. There were things he'd never thought to put on his blocker. In anguish, he realised, "Franz and Odin are choosing corruption. How I wish I'd encouraged Louis to give them some guidance. How can their lives be simple and innocent after this? They may never erase these images from their minds. How is this going to affect the way they treat others in Paradise? I fear for my girls, especially. Is my world still safe, or is everyone in danger? What can I do to combat this?" With a sinking feeling inside, he realized he didn't have any easy answers. He didn't know how to counter the powerful alure of human depravity. He didn't know how to save his wayward young men.

Running to the bathroom, the Professor was physically sick. When he returned, weak and shaken, he determined that he needed to set up an automatic shutdown of the Internet from midnight to six in the morning. "I will encourage Aimee and Zahir to put a password on the phone," he thought, "so that no one can access it without them. They may want to share it with everyone, but unsupervised access of evil will ruin Paradise." Sighing deeply, he wondered how the two young men would react if he turned off the Wifi. With the click of a button, he tested it out.

A few minutes later two Tinys emerged on the far side of Rainbow Hill and they were blazing with anger.

"But that's never happened before," Franz was arguing.

With many interjections of foul language, Odin complained, "Something's gone wrong. It better not happen again, or I'll smash my way out of this place! We have oxygen tanks! We can leave anytime we like."

Astonished, the Professor thought, "What? Did they steal Louis' oxygen tanks?"

"I'm coming with you," Franz boasted. "Paradise is so boring and there's not nearly enough girls!!"

"Not when one guy takes *three!*"

"Three?" the Professor wondered. Then he realised that Damien had stolen Vinitha's heart and was now flirting with Georgia and Diya. He had to admit it was a little unfair. It was then that the Professor heard the young men come up with a plan that left him anxious and afraid.

"The Professor put us in a cage," Odin scoffed, "so we can do the same to someone else!"

"Exactly! And our new den is perfect. No one knows about it but us!" Franz agreed.

Heading home to the forest, the schemers discussed how best to capture their prey. Jacques swallowed hard.

"Paradise is no longer a safe place!" he fretted, pacing outside the dome. "What will I do? I can't allow these two to bring any more suffering on the others. The girls will be terribly distraught if one of their friends goes missing."

He remembered the constraint triangle that Seth had showed him months ago. "You can have two of the three," he recalled, "'A Loving Community, Free Will, or Everyone Lives.'"

"Well, I will certainly never put anyone to death," he told himself proudly and then he remembered the threats. "Damien might! There

331

could be a terrible struggle! And what will I do with a murderer? Oh dear! What can I do?" he asked himself desperately. An idea popped into his head. "I could consign these two young men to the nursery and do some intensive counselling with them one-on-one! That's it!... But how do I get them in there?"

Still feeling greatly distressed by what he had uncovered, he stroked his goatee. "What if I hadn't overheard this plan and a third disaster had occurred tonight?" He sighed deeply. "If only I could reverse this miniaturization and take everyone out!" Pulling out his phone, his hand trembled. *"Oh là là!* I need to call Evan!" he said.

Two Choices

Chapter 41

*E*van was sound asleep, but he woke up when his phone began to ring. He saw Jacques' name on the screen and was instantly wide awake. The Professor would only call at two in the morning if there was some type of emergency!

Accepting the call, Evan sat up in bed. "What's wrong?" he asked anxiously.

Jacques spilled out the distressing story, while he watched Odin and Franz take down a swing and wind up the rope. Briefly and urgently, he relayed the scheme he'd overheard the boys plotting. "What do we do, Evan?" he pleaded. "The Internet has *corrupted* their minds."

"The Internet isn't the *source* of the problem," Evan argued, based on his new understanding. "Their own hearts are bent to evil.[147] Odin and Franz have inflamed their lusts with what they've chosen to view, but they may have come up with a plan like this without ever finding the phone."

"But what do we do now? Should we confine them to the nursery?"

"How would we get them to go in there? They hate the nursery."

"I know!" Jacques despaired, imagining the scene. "We'd need to ask several of the young men to capture them and force them in. There's no way they would willingly enter the doors."

---

[147] Mark 7:15-23; James 1:13-15,19-21; Romans 6:12-23

"They have weapons," Evan recalled. "They could end up taking other innocent lives..."

"But to leave them in Paradise means that every night and *every day* from now on, we will have to have someone on guard to ensure that they don't carry out their plan. And if we don't think of a way to stop this, it may be carried out *tonight.* How can we warn anyone this late at night? How can we stop it from happening?"

"We *have* to stop it, immediately!" Evan agreed. "We can't let anyone be taken captive like this. If Odin and Franz have given themselves over to selfish, harmful actions like this, I'd say they've chosen their destiny."

"What do you mean?"

"We will give them what they want," Evan suggested.

"Quoi?" the Professor frowned, watching Franz coil the rope around his arm. "Evan..."

"They've always wanted to break out of Paradise," Evan reminded him. "I think it's time to let them go free..."

"But they will die. Although," he pondered thoughtfully, "they stole Louis' spare oxygen tanks, so they will have an extra hour..."

"We could allow them to experience the big world in the train supply room, and then confront them," Evan suggested. "If they see the tunnel door is open, I'm sure they will go in! We can give them the choice of confinement in the nursery or perhaps we could oxygenate the supply room and they could become our loaders and stockers."

The Professor considered the idea, his mind racing. Keeping a wary eye on the young men as they snuck out of the forest, he thought it through. "I think confinement in the nursery is safer," he reasoned. "Louis grew up in isolation and turned out well. And maybe Odin just needs a little more empathy and persuasion. If they see that I am real, they may be convinced to change."

"True, but I'd *love* to put them to work," Evan stated. "I think it would benefit them to lose their freedom and be required to labour all day long until they appreciate how fantastic their life used to be. Based on their ongoing harmful actions with no real remorse, they have lost their privilege to live in Paradise. We don't want to force the other Tinys to confront them or be harmed by their actions. And... we don't want anyone to take justice into their *own hands...*"

Thinking of all the significant controls in the supply room that could possibly be reached with enough time and ingenuity, the Professor didn't like the train loading scenario. He explained his concerns to Evan, fretting, "They are too smart. We just can't risk them finding their way back into Paradise *unreformed.* I think private counselling in the Nursery is the best option. But..." he considered, "I like your idea of allowing them to explore, just so they realise we have been protecting them, not depriving them. We could let them experience the effects of low oxygen."

"I like that!" Evan agreed. "They need to feel it to believe it."

"Then, get here as fast as you can," the Professor called out, dashing toward the elevator passageway. He ran through the tunnel that led to the supply room. He could see the troublemakers had gathered supplies and were now heading toward the meadow. Pressing the button to open the train entrance, the Professor desperately hoped the foolish young men would see their chance to escape and choose this option over the other.

As the gates creaked open, the Professor ran to the window in the viewing tunnel. He gazed anxiously through the dark pane.

Odin was first to hear the noise and he turned around curiously. "Well, well, would you look at that!" he exclaimed. "The entrance just opened up, and the train isn't coming through! This is our lucky night! Let's make our escape!"

The breeze picked up, programmed as it was, to intensify after the rain.

Franz wasn't so easily diverted. "But we have a better plan," he argued, pushing back his thin straggly hair that was now blowing across his face. "Maybe the gate opens every night at this time. We can escape tomorrow night. Or maybe Evan is watching us..."

"Are you kidding?" Odin mocked. "He's sound asleep in bed like everyone else. I'd say something has malfunctioned with that door." Becoming agitated, Odin was anxious to seize the opportunity. "Look, I've been waiting for this to happen all my life," he considered eagerly. "There's no way it happens every night. This is a chance occurrence. We've got to take it, Franz. We have oxygen tanks in the den! Come on, we're so prepared!"

"What are you worried about oxygen for? You said that was just a big lie to keep us in the cage?"

"It is! I'm sure of it. But... well... just in case it isn't."

The two looked at each other long and hard, as they deliberated what to do. A tree fell over in the Fun Forest with a loud thump. Both Tinys turned to look.

"Oh, that's the one we hoped to attach the new bridge to!" Franz fretted. "What's wrong with all these dumb trees?"

"Everything is getting wrecked around here!" Odin complained. "If there is a Professor, he sure doesn't know what's going on!" For a moment, the two Tinys looked back and forth between the farmland and the tunnel.

On the other side of the window, the Professor hoped with all his heart that they would choose the tunnel!

"I'm going!" Odin declared, turning around. "It will be so much better in the big world! There will be *plenty* of girls, cars and *freedom!* I'm getting those tanks!"

Franz stood still for a moment, wavering between the options. As Odin ran off, he threw the rope down angrily and followed his friend.

The Professor breathed a huge sigh of relief. On his phone he found his control apps and video access to the supply room security system.

Once the toggle switch was ready and visible on his screen, he waited breathlessly.

With the oxygen tanks under his arms and the masks trailing behind him, Odin ran to the tunnel. Reluctantly, Franz followed.

As soon as he saw them step inside the supply room, the Professor hit the switch. In a moment, the foolish Tinys found themselves well and truly on the other side of Paradise. The gate closed behind them.

Evan burst through the office door, joining the Professor in the viewing tunnel. Quietly, they watched the Tinys on Jacques' screen.

"It just closed!" Franz' anxious voice called out.

Odin was looking around curiously in the dim lighting. "This looks like the store," he observed. "It's full of supplies. We'll have to remember this room...just in case..."

"It's so dark in here," Franz complained. "I hate that red light! It's eerie!"

"So many lies! Everyone lies," Odin fretted. "Ponce said it was so bright that he couldn't see!"

"Maybe it's bright in the daytime?"

"The only way to figure things out is to see it for yourself," Odin muttered. "No one can be trusted."

Walking back and forth on the train tracks that ran along a shelf, Odin assured his partner, "We'll find a way out. This isn't the big world... Maybe it's behind that door. It's such a gigantic door! First, we have to get down to the ground!"

Franz ran back inside the train tunnel. The scientists heard loud thumping on the tunnel entrance gate. Looking over at the Professor, Evan whispered, "I think he's trying to get back in."

"Maybe ten minutes will be long enough," the Professor replied compassionately. He looked at his phone. It was two-thirty in the morning. "At two-forty we'll confront them."

Ten minutes seemed like two hours, as the Tinys began to panic. Hollering profanities back and forth at each other, Franz was angry that Odin had spoiled their plans for the night to lead them into a dark, confined storage room. Odin fell from one shelf to another with a dull thud. He cried out in pain.

Worried for his safety, the Professor opened the door one minute early and turned on the light.

The two runaways screamed in terror when the scientists appeared like massive, dark giants filling the enormous doorway. Once the young men recognized Evan, they calmed down.

Looking directly at the Professor, Odin demanded, "Who are you?"

Folding his arms across his chest, Jacques replied with a smile, "I'm the one you've been waiting to meet. I'm the Professor – the Mastermind of Paradise. Why are you here, Odin?"

"We've broken out of your cage!" the stocky Tiny stated angrily.

"You have indeed," the Professor agreed, "and you won't be going back for a long while."

"What do you mean?" Franz challenged anxiously. "You're going to leave us here?"

"I prepared a safe and beautiful place for you in Paradise," the Professor responded calmly. "I gave you everything you needed to enjoy life, but you despised it. You have damaged my world in the past and hurt my family. I heard your evil plans tonight. I'm not going to allow you to harm any more of my children."

"But *your* world knows about us!" Odin taunted. "I've seen us on YouTube! You're in enormous trouble for putting us in that cage! The Governing Board will be on our side!"

"You chose to escape," the Professor reminded him, although he did wonder what the Governing Board might say. "No one forced you out."

Kneeling down to their level, Evan smiled, "So, we have two choices for you. You can go into the Nursery where it's safe, or..."

Odin was defiant. "No way! I wouldn't go back in there if my life depended on it! And besides, we've been totally fine without masks! That 'oxygen' thing is just a big lie, isn't it?"

Looking at his friend for confirmation, the hefty Tiny scoffed, "Do you feel any different?"

"Not at all!" Franz retorted.

Crossing his arms, Odin turned back to the Professor, "You've been telling us lies to keep us in that cage," he shouted. "You didn't make enough girls or give us a big enough world. I don't like being in your experiment! We want to see the *real* world! I want to drive cars and travel to a city!"

Evan nodded calmly. "You have about half an hour more until you'll feel the effects of the lack of oxygen," he said. "We *are* telling you the truth. But if you don't want to live safely in the Nursery, your other choice is to explore the Rainforest next door. With the oxygen bottles, you may last another hour or two."

Concerned for their safety, the Professor piped up, "But, we'll warn you that in the Rainforest you may be eaten or stepped on if you stray from the path. Wild animals and birds roam in the cages next door."

"And they are *our* size, not yours," Evan reminded them.

"I killed the spider!" Odin protested bravely. "I'm not afraid."

Franz shouted frantically, "This is a mistake! I want to go back to Paradise! Please may I go back?"

The Professor shook his head. "No, you may not. Not while you're making harmful plans for others like what I overheard tonight."

Swearing at Odin, Franz shouted, "This was the dumbest idea you've ever had! We should never have left! I'm going to kill you!"

"It wasn't *just* my idea," Odin retorted. "You suggested..."

"So, what will it be?" the Professor interrupted. "An hour or two of exploration in the big Rainforest world, or life in the Nursery?"

"Not the Nursery," Odin grumbled to Franz. "The oxygen thing is definitely a lie... don't let them mislead you. We're feeling fine. Let's go explore."

With some more deliberation and hateful remarks about the boring Nursery, both Tinys finally agreed. They wanted to see the big world.

Evan picked up the Tinys. In a compassionate gesture, the Professor grabbed two building boards from the shelves and handed them to the tiny brave warriors. Remembering that they had killed the spider with the sticks, he thought it would give them some protection.

Accepting the gift with an ungrateful shrug, Franz scoffed, "I should have brought my bow and arrow. What good is a dumb stick!"

Odin and Franz stood tall on Evan's hand as he strode through the hall to the office door. Once he stepped into the beautiful glass Biosphere, they gazed around in amazement. All the displays were softly lit, and moonlight shone through the magnificent, glass greenhouse enclosure above. For a few moments the Tinys were speechless.

"I'm going to give you a tour," Evan said, glancing quickly at the Professor.

Motioning with his hand, Jacques let him know they had approximately twenty minutes left till the lack of oxygen would begin to affect the young men.

Walking through the mirrored hall, Evan took them to see the monkeys, which started a howling racket that woke up all the other animals. Franz was initially terrified by the loud noise and clung fearfully to Evan's sleeve, but Odin's jeers soon had the lanky young man standing stoically tall.

One monkey jumped from tree to tree and both the Tinys gasped.

"Wow! That is awesome!" Odin exclaimed. "I'd love to do that. What did you call those creatures?"

"Howler monkeys," Evan replied. "There are a few Spider monkeys too. They are most active in the mornings."

The large cats in the next exhibit were only barely visible in their dark caves. Disturbed by the visitors and the noisy monkeys, the jaguar's eyes glared at them from his safe haven. He growled angrily.

"He's not so friendly," Odin remarked.

Franz was in awe. "I didn't know cats grew *so big!*"

"They aren't housecats, like the ones you have in Paradise," Evan explained. "These cats could actually harm someone my size if they were free."

"Are there any *friendly* animals in here?" Franz asked, his voice wavering.

"Not for a Tiny," Evan replied. "You'd be a tasty morsel for most of the wildlife we have in here. But *we* interact with them on a regular basis."

"Let's show them the lizards," Jacques suggested, feeling they were running short of time.

"Now this is more like it!" Odin shouted, as they approached the cascading water near the Reptile Café. Soft coloured lights lit up the plummeting water in a brilliant, ever-changing display. "What a gigantic waterfall!" the stocky Tiny exclaimed. "And look at the colours! See, Franz – it's just like we thought. It's *so much* better than Paradise!"

"It is!" he agreed.

Odin was fascinated by the lizards, having never seen anything like them before. Illuminated by the continuous colour exhibit, the iguanas' scales shimmered in the dancing light.

"What is that long, rope-like creature?" Franz asked suddenly.

The large rope-like creature was in a glass enclosure of its own. Soundlessly, it slithered forward, coiling effortlessly around the branch over their heads. A little light reflected off its beady eyes and its forked tongue sensed the air.

"That is a snake," Evan told him. "I'd stay far away from him if I were you."

341

"They are all in cages, right?" Franz asked warily.

"Yes," Evan assured him. "If you stay on the pathway, you won't be eaten. But don't enter *any* cages. And if you're still here in the morning, I'd advise you to stay off the pathways, or you could be stepped on by other people like us."

"Cages! More cages!" Odin complained. "If anyone sees us, they'll help us escape," he boasted. "We'll tell them how bad it is in Paradise and they'll force you to let *everyone* out. Then *all* the Tinys can go exploring."

"Good thinking!" Franz agreed. "This time they'll all thank us!"

"You might want to investigate this tunnel on your own," Evan suggested, as he lowered the Tinys to the ground near the insect and spider display. Since the creatures inside were so small, the glass enclosures held no miniscule gaps that Tinys could slip into. With a smile he said, "After all, Odin is the spider hero. Enjoy your tour, guys."

"I'd get those oxygen masks on, if I were you," the Professor warned. "You may not be feeling the effects just yet, but you will very soon."

"If we need them, we'll put them on!" Odin said defiantly, waving his building board from side to side like a club. "You're just trying to make us afraid with all these *useless* warnings! But I'm not afraid of anything!"

Leaving the courageous Tinys on the walkway, the Professor and Evan sat down at one of the café tables, waiting for the inevitable.

Unwilling to lug around the heavy oxygen tanks, the boys entered the tunnel without them. Dim white lights lit up the various floor-to-ceiling displays. A large tarantula had attached itself inside the glass wall in close view.

"That spider is taller than us," Franz remarked in awe.

"And he's in a cage too!" Odin retorted loudly. "Is everything in a cage around here? This is not freedom! Where are the cars and all the people? That's what I want to see!"

For ten minutes, the scientists could hear the young men alternatively marvelling and complaining as they strode by the various exhibits. There were tidy rows of unique butterfly chrysalis, a Goliath bird-eating spider, jumping spiders and bullet ants.

They heard Franz protest, "I don't see cars, or girls. It's just one dumb spider after another. This is so boring! Why did we escape?"

Another angry argument broke out. The Professor looked at his phone. The Tinys had been without enriched oxygen for thirty-five minutes. Glancing at Evan, he showed him the time.

Suddenly, they heard Odin call out, "Are *your* hands shaking?"

"And my arms," Franz replied warily. "I don't feel so well..."

"We better go back and get those tanks," Odin murmured. "Oh no! Now my knees are starting to shake. Hurry, Franz, hurry!"

Standing up, the two researchers knew the young men were beginning to feel the effects. They had seen this happen with animals several times in their years of experimentation. They knew that if intervention didn't occur quickly, major seizures would soon take place, followed by unconsciousness and death.

The Tinys didn't make it back for the tanks. Overcome by the lack of oxygen and too far away to get relief, they succumbed to seizures on the floor. Scooping up their trembling bodies into his hands, the Professor hurried over to the mirrored hallway, and took the drop floor exit. With Evan on his heels, they raced through, fumbling codes and opening doors until they reached the backside of the nursery. Sliding the young men in through an unlocked exit, Jacques laid their limp bodies on the floor, and sealed the Nursery shut.

Striding forward to the controls, he and Evan made sure that everything was in functional order, checking the oxygen levels, filling up the Wonderdrink machines and turning on the security cameras.

"It's never been used as a jail before," Evan pondered. "I hope we don't have any weak spots they can break out of."

"*Oh là là!* If we have a weak spot, they will find it," Jacques murmured. "Unfortunately, it will be to their own peril, without any fast cars or girls."

"What's your plan with them?" Evan queried, as they watched the young men slowly recover and begin to realise where they were.

Odin groaned. "Not the Nursery! This is worse than death!"

"I believe we should to try and counsel them," Jacques replied. "Let's give them a few days in isolation and then maybe they'll be receptive to some heart-to-heart talks."

As the scientists turned off the hallway lights and followed the underground exit, they discussed the various online programs they could use to help the young men break free from the destructive mental habits they had developed. They knew there were many available. The Professor was also determined to find productive ways to harness their brilliant, energetic minds.

"Maybe if Franz knows he is my son, he'll be motivated to try harder..."

"Possibly... but then how does that make Odin feel?" Evan deliberated. "I think they need to know who their *Heavenly* Father is. He is a Father they both share. Nothing has motivated me to change more than coming to know there is a Creator God who loves me and yet calls me to account for my actions."

Jacques looked over uneasily, yet deep down he knew Evan was right. Opening the door to such knowledge was already having an impact on his own life.

Stepping outside into the very early, mild May morning, the researchers breathed a huge sigh of relief. This time they had stopped the schemers before any harm had occurred to anyone else. Yet, there were changes to be made. Jacques realised he needed to increase restrictions on the source of good and evil that streamed freely through the device in the cave, and more importantly, educate *all* the Tinys to choose wisely. And they were both fully aware that, even if new measures were put in place, the Tinys had entered a phase of maturity, where those who chose to do good could do much good in many ways, but those who loved evil could ruin the beautiful, serene world for everyone. With or without the Internet, one Tiny choosing to live in a selfish, perverse way could be just as frightening and dangerous as any of the poisonous creatures in the Rainforest biome.

Evan was convinced more than ever that a force of good was necessary to counter the cravings of fallen human nature. Entering his car, he took a moment to pray. He was so thankful that their intervention had been successful, and that God's Word – *the true source of goodness* – was now being actively read and shared in the Paradise dome.

In the Cave

Chapter 42

*I*nside the beautiful dome world on that rather grey morning, no one noticed the missing Tinys for the first few hours. It was quite normal for Odin and Franz to skip breakfast.

At lunch, Ponce and Lily mentioned that they thought it was strange their friends were still sleeping in. When they went to check the den, it was empty. Damien found rope coils lying on the edge of the forest. Lily was very upset that her new swing had been cut down. By mid-afternoon, those from the Fun Forest had searched all the forests and the cabins, and Lily had even secretly visited the cave.

Aimee, Zahir and Uncle Louis were outside the mansion on the deck, telling Kenzie a few more things they had discovered online about the Bible when a breathless Lily and Ponce ran up to them.

"We're really worried about Odin and Franz," the freckled, petite girl panted anxiously. "We can't find them anywhere!"

Ponce added, "We've searched all their hiding spots, and they are nowhere in the forest."

"Are any boats missing?" Uncle Louis asked, sitting comfortably beside Zahir on the bench swing.

Lily turned to Ponce, "That's it! Maybe they've taken a boat out. Maybe they are fishing."

"I doubt it," Ponce frowned.

"Hey, why not?" Zahir interjected with a wry grin. "What could be more fun than fishing?"

Ponce laughed.

"Let's go check," Lily called out, running out of the room with Ponce close behind.

The conversation on the veranda switched back to the evidence they had discovered, and the action Uncle Louis had taken based on the hope he felt was real, true and intensely satisfying. Sitting on the deck beside Aimee, Kenzie wanted to know more.

For the rest of the afternoon, the deep conversation was occasionally punctuated by Lily and Ponce's unsuccessful quest to find their missing friends. After dinner, Uncle Louis suggested to the new leaders that they should report the absence to the Professor. "I can't come with you tonight," he remarked sadly. "It's too much effort. But my search is complete. I am content that I've found truth."

A few rainbows danced on Uncle Louis' blanket as the sun suddenly shone through the clouds and the breeze intensified. Looking up, he saw a remarkable rainbow high in the sky above the criss-crossed black lines. "Look at that!" he pointed out.

Aimee jumped up to view it away from the veranda roof. "It's enormous!" she exclaimed.

"It must be raining in the Professor's world," the older man remarked quietly. "We haven't read about the rainbow yet. It's in the next chapter..."

"Of which book?" Zahir inquired curiously.

"God's Book," Uncle Louis smiled. "In Genesis. The rainbow was a special sign of God's promise to never flood the earth again,"[148] he relayed. He reminded them of the hot day when the rainmaker had helped to cool things off, producing a beautiful arch of colour above the hill, which is why it had been named 'Rainbow Hill.' Uncle Louis

---

[148] Genesis 9:8-17

explained, "God intended us to see the rainbow and remember that He made a covenant between Himself and all the people on the Earth – a covenant He expects us both to keep. This was the first promise He made after the flood destroyed the world that was full of violent and wicked imaginations. God has promised not to flood the Earth in this way again, but that doesn't mean we are free to do what we like. He has bound the whole earth in this covenant with Him, and He remembers His part of the agreement every time He sees the bow. If we turn away from Him and His laws, we are breaking our part of the covenant."[149]

"That makes it extra special!" Aimee declared, watching the huge arch in the sky begin to fade away. "All these little rainbows can remind us of God, too!"

Zahir jumped up from the bench. "I'll go read the chapter," he suggested eagerly. "You'll hear me from the window."

The others sat outside and listened while Zahir read about Noah leaving the ark and God's promises to His newly cleansed world.

The sky was a dark, smoky grey when the young man came back down to the veranda. There were still shouts and laughter coming from Rosa's Hill. Zahir looked over at Kenzie. "You'll come with us tonight?" he begged.

"For sure!" Kenzie said.

The young men assisted Uncle Louis up to the Crisis Room and helped him get ready for bed. Aimee gave him his medicine. Zahir covered him with a blanket.

"Thank you for today," Uncle Louis smiled, reaching out to clasp Zahir's scarred arm, since he was still close by. "I'm so thankful for all of you. I know you will do well. Stand strong on the foundation we've discovered. Don't forget how much I love you, and that your

---

[149] Isaiah 24:4-6, 19-23; 2 Peter 3:3-13

Heavenly Father loves you even more. I want to see you in the world to come."

Aimee came over and pressed her face close to his. "Goodnight, Uncle Louis," she said kindly. "I love you, too."

Kenzie and Zahir shook his hands affectionately.

With the key in his pocket, Zahir led the way through the dark forest, over fallen trees and down into the valley. Having been overcast all day, darkness had settled in early. Opening the door, he turned on the lights. Immediately, he noticed the messy state of the phone. "Someone is definitely coming in here when they shouldn't," he said. "I wonder if the Professor discovered anything last night."

"But how are they getting in?" Aimee puzzled. "There is only one key and it's been with you."

Kenzie looked around curiously, while Aimee wiped the phone clean and turned it on. Since the device hadn't been shut down properly the night before, a disturbing image came up on the screen. Zahir immediately swiped it away. "Is this what they were looking at?" he exclaimed in disgust. "Is this poison?"

It wasn't the introduction they had hoped to give Kenzie. However, they had already explained so much about their communications with the Professor that their guest was well aware of what it could do. Aimee and Kenzie sat down on the chairs.

Zahir hesitated. Picking up the empty chair next to Aimee, he brought it around to the other side of Kenzie.

"What are you doing?" Kenzie frowned, with a slight chuckle of amusement.

"I don't want you looking at my bad side," he laughed.

"But it doesn't matter to me," Aimee protested.

"Or me," Kenzie stated.

"It does to me," Zahir mumbled.

Giving her dark-haired friend a quizzical look of dismay, Aimee reached out to make a videocall to the Professor.

"This is nice and early," the Professor remarked when he came on the screen. "I hoped I would hear from you today. And good evening, Kenzie!" he smiled, a little unsure of how to understand the seating arrangements. "I'm glad you're joining us."

Kenzie was in complete awe. "Thank you," he sputtered. "I'm really thankful to be invited."

Aimee told him of Odin and Franz' disappearance. Zahir explained the state of the phone.

"I know all about it," the Professor acknowledged sadly. "Look around the room and see if you can find a hidden entrance."

In alarm, the three Tinys perused the room. Kenzie thought to look under the table that was covered with a cloth. "There's a tunnel here!" he called out.

"As I thought," the Professor replied. "At least four Tinys have been entering the cave with or without the key for the last *two months.*"

The news was astonishing to Aimee, but so many things made sense now. The messy phone. Lily's nightly excursions. The dirt in her roommate's hair.

"First things first," the Professor smiled. "The phone is no longer a secret, so I'd like to suggest that we put security measures into the system. Then you'll never need to worry about someone else finding the key or creeping through the tunnel. And if you want to share information on the phone with others, you can choose to do so in accountable ways."

All three liked the idea, so the Professor gave them various options to lock the screen and asked which one they thought would be best."

Zahir spoke up. "Let's do the face recognition," he suggested. "Anything else might be guessed in time, or seen if we invite others and have to type it in."

"Yours or Aimee's?"

"Aimee's of course," Zahir replied, before she could say otherwise.

Working together, they set up the new system and ensured the phone would only turn on when Aimee stood in front of it.

Returning to their seats, the Professor slowly broke the distressing news about what had happened the night before. He explained the things that he had overheard and gave them a basic idea of the types of sites that had been visited.

When he told them about the threat to the girls, Aimee trembled. Had Zahir not been sitting so far away, she would certainly have reached out for his hand. Instead, she clasped Kenzie's arm tightly.

Looking over at her with concern, Kenzie's freckled face was very drawn and white.

Zahir looked over as well, and then he sharply turned away.

"I know this is disturbing information," Jacques apologized, seeing the dismay on all their faces, "but as leaders, these will be some of the things you will face and need to decide how to manage in the future."

They all agreed that the decision to allow the Tinys to escape had been the right one, and Aimee was secretly very thankful that Odin and Franz weren't coming back any time soon.

Anxiously, Zahir asked the Professor, "What would we have done if you hadn't overheard their plan? What if Odin and Franz had actually carried it out? They wouldn't have listened to us. Would we have had to fight them? What happens if someone else tries to harm another person?" Bewildered, he asked, "How do we handle this?"

The Professor went over the most important precepts of servant leadership - Listening, Empathy, Healing, Awareness, Persuasion, Foresight and Building Community. He reminded Zahir to think of the way Uncle Louis had handled conflicts, but Aimee sensed that her dark-haired friend was not confident those methods would work.

"I do have good news for you - especially Zahir," the Professor relayed, hoping to bring a little joy back to the young man's troubled gaze. He explained about 'fathers and mothers' and how a family structure works in the big world. With apologetic overtures to Kenzie, he explained in a rather confusing manner, that some of the Tinys were based on unknown combinations, but that Zahir and Aimee were not. He told them about Aimee being his daughter and her relation to Uncle Louis. Wide-eyed, the young men listened to everything he said and tried to absorb the new, highly significant information.

"Zahir," he continued kindly, "you have parents in my world who are very dear friends of mine. I've worked closely with them over many years. They know that you are their son, and they have asked to meet you."

Awestruck, Zahir didn't know what to say. Aimee and Kenzie looked over with excitement.

"I'll send you through their phone number," the Professor told him. "When you feel up to it, you can give them a call in the same way that you call me."

Saying good-bye, the Professor sent through the number.

"You have parents!" Aimee cheered, standing up and clapping her hands together. "This is so exciting, Zahir!"

Looking over, Zahir said, "And so do you! Why didn't you tell me that the Professor was *your father?*"

"I wasn't allowed to tell," she explained. "He doesn't want anyone to feel less important. He wants *all* of us to be his children. You and Kenzie are just as much a part of his family as anyone else."

Kenzie nodded slowly but he didn't look convinced.

Zahir was contemplative, trying to process the new, impactful information.

"Should we call them?" Aimee asked eagerly. She knew how wonderful it had been to discover her own family relations, and she longed to meet Zahir's parents. She thought it might boost his floundering confidence to speak to the people most closely related to him. She anticipated they would love him a great deal.

"I suppose," he replied. "It's rather intimidating..."

"Intimidating," Kenzie agreed, "but also very exciting! You are *so* lucky!"

Aimee clicked on the tab to set up a new contact. She wrote in 'Zahir's parents,' and looked over at him with a smile. Raising his dark eyebrows cautiously, he smiled back.

With her finger hovering over the number, Aimee asked, "Do you want me to make the call?"

Taking a deep breath, Zahir nodded slowly. Eagerly, Aimee pressed the button.

In no time at all, the call was answered. A beautiful dark-haired woman with lovely blue eyes appeared on the screen. "Zahir," she gasped in surprise. "You called us! Oh my! Let me just find your father. This is wonderful... *so wonderful!*"

They saw her call out to Farouk, telling him that his son was on the phone. In a moment, two eager faces appeared on the screen and three Tinys looked back.

"Hello," Zahir said nervously. "The Professor has just told me that you are my mother and father," he began uncomfortably.

Watching the parents and son exchange awkward introductions, Aimee noticed that Rachel's stunning blue eyes were very similar to Zahir's. Farouk had the same skin-colouring and perhaps the same gentle spirit. This was the first family she had ever seen – a husband and wife standing together... with a son in Paradise who shared characteristics of both of them. It was all so special, and she was fascinated.

Having introduced themselves, Zahir's parents asked about his time in the Caring Centre and how he was healing. Aimee was thankful when they assured their son that his scarring was perfectly normal for the injuries he had sustained.

"In fact," Farouk replied, "I'm surprised how well you've healed, Zahir." Looking at Kenzie and Aimee briefly, he flashed a grateful smile. "We saw you when you were first injured," he told his son. "Whoever looked after you has superior nursing abilities..."

Suddenly a young face appeared on the screen in front of his parents. He had the same colouring as Zahir, but his big eyes were very dark like his father's. His smile quickly faded into concern as he noticed one of the Tinys' scars and his cloudy eye. He turned and whispered something in his mother's ear and pointed to the screen.

Kenzie put his arm around his friend.

"This is your brother, Jordan," Rachel introduced warmly. "He's five years old."

Aimee was ecstatic! Zahir had a little brother!

Turning to the curious five-year-old, his mother gently explained, "Your brother, Zahir, was badly burned, trying to save another Tiny. Zahir saved Ponce who was trapped under a burning beam."

"Wow! You're *very* brave!" Jordan smiled with full admiration. "That must have hurt... a lot!"

The dark-haired Tiny smiled. "It did," he agreed, "but thankfully, I had two very kind nurses who fixed me up."

"Did they only look after you?"

With a quick smile in his friends' direction, Zahir turned back to those on the screen. "No, they are kind to everyone. They looked after Ponce and Uncle Louis too. They really do have superior nursing abilities!"

Farouk and Rachel glanced at each other in a loving way.

Jordan looked bewildered.

"I'm really glad to meet you, Jordan," Zahir smiled.

"Me too," Aimee piped up.

"And me as well," Kenzie added.

With a quizzical expression on his face, the boy asked, "Can you all come to my house?"

Chuckling, Zahir shook his head. "We would really love to, but we can't right now."

356

"As soon as the Paradise exhibit opens, we will go to see Zahir in his world," Rachel assured her younger son. "And we'll see Aimee and Kenzie and all the others," she added.

"Where is Paradise?" Jordan asked.

"It's where we go to look after all the animals."

"But where? I've never seen these people before..."

Jordan was full of questions, but his parents sent him back to bed.

"He will absolutely *love* watching you in Paradise," Rachel laughed.

"So, *you've* seen us?" Zahir clarified.

"Yes," his mother nodded. She explained, "Your world is right next to where I work in the Rainforest Biosphere. You can Google the Greenville Biosphere online and see what it's like. I am an animal doctor, so I take care of the birds and the animals." Looking over at the young lady beside Kenzie, she said, "Aimee, I hear you love animals too. I've watched you care for them. We have so much in common! We'll have to have a chat one day. Often in the mornings before work or after I am done, I look in to see how everyone is doing. I love watching the go-karting, and the surfing shows and just everyday life. Your world is beautiful!"

The Tinys nodded. It was very strange to imagine other people looking in at them. However, Aimee understood their curiosity. She was eager to Google the Rainforest Biome and see what their world looked like!

"We saw you stand up to Odin when he wanted to find a way out of Paradise," Farouk spoke up, looking fondly at his son. "We were very impressed by your courage... and yours too, Kenzie," he added. "And, Zahir, we know how you took charge in the fire and rushed in to help Ponce. We are very proud of you."

Aimee and Kenzie smiled warmly at their brave friend, but he seemed to be uncertain of how to respond.

Rachel spoke up saying that she would like to give her son a new name – a middle name - which was a strange concept to all three Tinys. He was now to be Zahir Haniel, as a token to her father, and his father before him. "It's a Jewish name," she smiled. "Zahir is Arabic, like your father. Haniel is Jewish like me."

"Jewish?" Aimee interjected. "We've been reading all about Jewish people in the Bible. Is Zahir *a Jew!*"

Zahir's eyes widened in surprise. With a wild expression, he glanced quickly over at Aimee and then back to his parents on the screen.

"Technically, yes," Farouk agreed.

"Did you say that you've been reading... *the Bible?*" Rachel asked with a slightly concerned tone.

Zahir nodded. "It's an amazing book!" he stated confidently. "Uncle Louis started reading it to us while we were all confined to the Crisis Room. We've learned so much."

Rachel shared a worried glance with her husband. "Does the Professor know about this?" she questioned.

"Oh yes," Aimee piped up. "He sent in his own book as well, and we're comparing the two."

"I see," Rachel frowned. "I am surprised. Personally, I wouldn't recommend the Bi..."

Farouk placed his hand on hers, and Rachel stopped and looked up at him uncertainly. He shook his head.

Clearing her throat lightly, Rachel didn't finish her sentence. Instead, she smiled in her son's direction saying, "Well, we have something special we'd like to offer you, Zahir - you and your friends with their *superior* nursing abilities."

Aimee had noted the silent communication on the screen. With amazement she pondered, "Her husband didn't say a word and yet she understood his message perfectly! Is this part of 'being one'?"

358

Rachel was relaying her idea. "I don't know if the Professor has told you, or not," she said, "but your father and I are *both* doctors. Doctors are like nurses, but they know even more. I look after animals, and your father cares for people in hospitals... I suppose you would call them 'Caring Centres.' We look after the sick and wounded and bring them back to health. We sent in all the medications and creams for your recovery."

With surprise, Zahir thanked them gratefully.

Thinking of all the pages they had stuck to the walls in the Caring Centre, Aimee's face glowed, "Were all the instructions from you?" she asked.

"Yes. That was my writing," Rachel nodded, pleased that Aimee had asked.

"The notes were really helpful, and thanks for all the medications," Kenzie added.

"You're very welcome," Farouk replied.

"A doctor is truly needed in Paradise," Rachel encouraged. "You may face other emergencies or illnesses. Having someone with expertise inside the dome could be very useful and save lives. If you are interested, Farouk and I can set you up with a course. You could learn to be a doctor," she smiled at her son, "like your father and like me."

Stunned, Zahir hesitated. Aimee saw the dark look pass over his face. "But... that's what Kenzie and Aimee do," he said slowly. "They would both be... *fantastic doctors.*" Turning to his friends, he pleaded, "I'm sure Kenzie would love to take a course. And you too, Aimee?"

Aimee sensed his uneasiness and wished she was sitting close beside the one she loved best. Kenzie reached over and clapped his friend's shoulder. "And you, Zahir!" he assured him.

"We'd like to do this with you all," Rachel replied earnestly, speaking to her son, "if you are interested, that is. It would be a great opportunity for us to develop a relationship."

359

Farouk put his arm around his wife's shoulders. Changing the subject, he asked kindly, "What do you like to do, Zahir? What are your interests?"

"Well, before the fire happened, I caught fish every morning," Zahir smiled. "That was my time to have chats with the guys, and fried fish is the best breakfast! Since the fire I've been learning about the Gospel message and God's Son – Jesus Christ. This has had a *powerful* effect on my life, especially," he added soberly, "with all that I've gone through. I want to search it out more and be certain it's true. If it is, I want to share this hope with everyone."

Rachel turned and looked at Farouk uneasily.

"He has his own life," Zahir's father said quietly to her. "He doesn't live in our world."

With a loving smile, Rachel suggested, "Maybe you can do both. It would be really nice if we all had something that we could enjoy together..."

"Perhaps we can talk again soon," Farouk suggested. With proud eyes, he said, "Zahir, we are very impressed by the valour you have demonstrated inside Paradise. We want to be a part of your life, somehow. Give some thought to your mother's suggestion. There's so much we could share with you that will benefit your entire community."

Including the others, his father added, "Aimee and Kenzie, we're very thankful that you followed the directions with such diligence. We can't thank you enough for nursing Zahir and Ponce through such serious injuries. We know it wasn't easy. Had you not been so dedicated to their care, they may not have healed as well as they did. We are very, very grateful and impressed with your abilities."

The conversation ended in a loving way. When the screen went dark, Aimee noticed the brooding look on Zahir's face. Having been in close proximity with her favourite patient every day for the last three weeks, she was beginning to understand some of his expressions. She longed to hold his hand. She sensed his need.

Kenzie suggested Googling the Rainforest Biome. For a while they had fun exploring the world around their world, admiring the animals and plants and massive greenhouse structures so close by. Finally, they understood why the sky was criss-crossed with black lines and realised that high above it was a beautiful, unblemished expanse.

They had plenty to share with Kenzie, showing him some of the highlights from the night they had spent with Uncle Louis. But when they finally turned off the phone and locked the cave door behind them, Aimee could see that her dark-haired friend was troubled. "What's wrong, Zahir?" she asked kindly.

"That was a lot to consider, tonight," he mumbled quietly. "I need some time to think things over."

"Your parents seem really nice," Aimee encouraged, as they climbed the hill back toward the Caring Centre, "and I *love* your little brother!"

"He is really cute," Zahir agreed flatly. Reaching over, he passed Aimee the key out of his pocket. "This isn't so important anymore. You should keep it, since only you can turn on the phone."

Aimee took it back reluctantly.

"How do you like your mom and dad?" Kenzie asked as they trudged up the rock stairs, keeping a wary eye on the swaying trees. "Or was that all a bit much?"

"It was a bit much," he sighed. "They do seem really nice," he replied earnestly. "I'm just not sure we have anything in common..."

Stopping still, Aimee asked, "Why?"

"Well, they are doctors," he explained wistfully, standing behind her on one of the large flat stones, "they aren't fishermen. And it doesn't seem like they have a very good impression of the Bible. I'm not sure that the things that matter most to me are meaningful to them." With a deep sigh, he relayed, "Uncle Louis is the only parent I need. I want to be like *him*. He appreciates me for who I am, and I appreciate him."

"We do too," Aimee pleaded, speaking for herself and Kenzie. Tentatively, she reached out for Zahir's hand, but he stepped off the stairway and trudged past her up the hill.

"I need some time to think," he begged, as they reached the clearing and felt the full force of the wind. "I'm sorry, Aimee. *Please don't be hurt.* I'm just not sure I'm the right one for any of this." With a heavy sigh, he said, "Good night." Then he turned around and headed quickly towards the mansion.

Aimee fought back tears.

Kenzie hesitated uncertainly. "I think we should give him some time and space," he mused. "It would be rather overwhelming to meet your actual parents, when you didn't know you had any. I know I'd need time to deal with it... if I was so lucky!"

Nodding dismally, Aimee agreed. "You're such a good friend to him, Kenzie. I really appreciate how much you care for Zahir."

"He's my *best* friend," Kenzie stated. "I'm really glad you care for him too." Looking down at the meadow, he said, "I think I'll go visit the farmers, but I'll be back later tonight." He shrugged and said, "Maybe then he'll want to talk."

Following his gaze, Aimee could see silhouettes on Mining Hill.

Hesitating, Kenzie asked, "Are *you* okay?"

With a sad smile, Aimee sighed, "We all need time to think."

"We do," he agreed. Giving her a quick hug, Kenzie said goodnight and took off down the nearly finished stone stairway.

Aimee sat down on the hill and looked out over the windy orchard. Trees were swaying in the breeze. Sunflowers looked like they might topple over. Small waves rolled across the lake. Once again, she felt hurt and confused. She knew it was normal for burn victims to feel a whole range of emotions, but she didn't understand why Zahir's doubts and questions were causing him to push *her* away. "Does he just need time and space," she wondered, "or am I doing... or saying something wrong? If he loves me, why doesn't he want to be with me? It seems like he'd rather pass me off to Kenzie... but wouldn't that make him jealous if he cares? But Kenzie encourages me to tell Zahir how I feel... and... well, I *still* haven't," she reflected. "I'm just not certain he feels the same way anymore... if he ever did. Surely, *my* feelings have been obvious! Or ... maybe they *aren't*," she sighed. "Is that the problem? Does he actually need to hear a few simple words to believe?"

Watching her nurse mate run across the meadow and up the slope of Mining Hill, she considered, "Maybe Zahir wants nothing to do with leading Paradise. Maybe he just wants a quiet life without so much responsibility. But my father has chosen me for this role and Uncle Louis wants me to try my hardest. I don't want to let them down. I have to think of what is best for everyone... not just me. Maybe Zahir isn't the best choice... Maybe I've got it all wrong. Oh, I really need to talk to Uncle Louis about this!"

Weary and unsure about love, Aimee headed home to bed. As she lay quietly in the darkness, she thought about the lovely relationship she'd witnessed on the screen. "How beautiful to just understand each other without a word," she marvelled. "Did Zahir's parents always have that understanding? Or did it happen over time? Do they ever disagree, or doubt each other? Were they each other's *first* choice? What is it like to be *married* to someone?"

Hope

Squawking lorikeets woke Aimee up as the first light of dawn brightened Lily's room. Rising with the morning sun, Aimee pulled on her favorite blue dress with the glittering spirals that Diya had made. She noticed a long white dress hanging inside Lily's closet door. "Lily has her dress!" Aimee smiled. "Now she and Ponce can get married. I wonder if Nancy has hers?"

A loud knock sounded on the door, followed by another.

"Aimee, are you up?" Kenzie called out desperately.

Immediately, Aimee sensed the urgency in his voice. She ran to turn the handle.

"It's Uncle Louis," her friend cried out, when she opened the door. His big, grey eyes were filled with anguish. "Come! Please come!"

Zahir was kneeling at Uncle Louis' side, sobbing. Uncle Louis lay in the bed, completely still.

Running over, Aimee laid her hand on the older man's chest. He was cold. In a panic she tried his vital signs. He wasn't breathing. He had no pulse. "Should I try CPR?" she cried out, attempting to tilt back his head. Uncle Louis was very stiff. She recoiled in fear.

Kenzie laid his hand on her shoulder. "He's dead, Aimee," he said soberly. "It's too late. He must have died in the night."

Wanting to do something, anything to help, Aimee looked for Uncle Louis' oxygen tanks, but they were missing!

"Tell the Professor," Zahir begged, between sobs. "Ask him what we should do."

"Do you want someone to come with you?" Kenzie inquired.

Seeing the distress of her dark-haired friend, Aimee shook her head. She felt it would be better for Kenzie to stay with Zahir. "Thank you, but I'll be okay," she assured him. Running down to the cave, she burst in through the door. The face recognition worked well, and she tried a video call. Thankfully, the Professor answered right away.

"Uncle Louis died!" she blurted out. "He's cold, he's stiff. Kenzie told me not to do CPR." Breaking down in sobs, she cried, "What do we do?"

Months ago, such an outcome would have been the Professor's worst nightmare. The unsubstantiated, controversial science of cryonics was only 'effective' if performed *shortly* after death. Months ago, he would have thrown all of Paradise into a frenzy, trying to get Louis out as soon as possible, hoping beyond hope that even if he was cold and stiff, an EEG might show a little brain activity. But all his research and study were leading him to realize the miracle of life was far beyond human ingenuity. Nevertheless, he longed to bring Louis to his side. To hold him one last time and bury him, himself. Louis was his beloved son!

Tears were running down his own face as he gave instructions to Aimee. "Please bring him to me," he pleaded. "I'll send in the train. Please carry Uncle Louis down and put him on it. Aimee, my darling, I'm so sorry! I wish I could give you a hug – you and all the Tinys. I know this will leave such a deep hole in everyone's hearts."

Sobbing, Aimee nodded, yet even through her sadness, little rays of hope were breaking through. Uncle Louis had told her not to try and revive him. He had said he was at peace. He believed something far better was coming, and death was only a part of the transformation. Deep emotions welled up inside her heart. Looking up at her father with a tear-stained face she blurted out, "I don't understand why *you* are so against God! God gave Uncle Louis hope!"

Knowing that they were both emotionally distraught, the Professor didn't feel it was a good time to engage in a discussion of this nature. "Aimee," he said kindly. "I wrote what I believed at the time. It's... it's quite possible that I've been wrong... and if I'm wrong, I will have huge apologies to make. For now, please just send Louis to me. I will talk this over with you, when *both* of us aren't so upset."

With a grateful, sad smile, Aimee nodded, realising the Professor was grieving just like she was. "Okay. I'm sorry... *Dad,*" she apologized earnestly. "I'll go tell the others."

The train whistle sounded as Aimee reached the Caring Centre on Rainbow Hill. Together, Kenzie, Zahir and Aimee lovingly laid Uncle Louis on the stretcher and brought him down to the tracks. Everyone had gathered for breakfast and was there to witness the tragic departure. There were many tears.

A brown envelope lay in the train car with the names of the three leaders. Picking it up, Zahir handed it to Kenzie for safe keeping.

Watching the train head back through the tunnel with Uncle Louis on board was devastating to all the Tinys. Some expressed hope that maybe he'd be back again the next day – after all, that was what had happened the last time. Others wondered how life would go on without him. Many were weeping and hugging each other. The Orchard girls stood in a tight circle. The farmers had their arms around each other. Sanaa and Lema were hugging Ponce and Lily, and Kenzie stood alone, silently reading the letter.

The sound of the train alarms blaring only added to the chaos that everyone was feeling. Leaning against the post of the store veranda, Aimee burst into tears when the entrance gate closed, and the loud noises were silenced. Her most important and reliable source of comfort, advice and affection was no longer in Paradise. He could no longer answer all the questions she had. Looking over at her friends, she saw Zahir walking away! His head was down, his shoulders slumped; he wasn't sharing his grief with anyone. Disheartened, she didn't understand why he was leaving. Her dark-haired friend looked back for one quick moment, and then he continued on his way. Feeling abandoned, Aimee wasn't sure she could bear the sorrow she felt. With her face in her hands, she sobbed deeply, but then someone placed a hand on her shoulder.

"Zahir told me to give you a hug," Kenzie murmured compassionately. "I'm so sorry, Aimee."

Aimee appreciated the hug. It was a friendly, caring hug, even if it wasn't a Zahir hug. Feeling the loss of Uncle Louis who had always been there for her, and crushed by Zahir's repeated desertion, Aimee was grateful that someone cared. She cried and cried, and Kenzie didn't leave. He even passed her a spare cloth that he kept in his pocket so she could wipe her nose and face.

Aimee knew that Uncle Louis would not come back to Paradise. The last few weeks he had struggled to hold onto life; he had reached the end, and she was now fully aware that there was nothing more the Professor could do. As she cried over her beloved brother, his words kept echoing inside, round and round in her mind in a strangely comforting way - "Now I can go in peace... I have found the greatest treasure."

At last, when the tears had run out and she was able to pull herself together, she thanked Kenzie gratefully. But then, in a pitiful voice she asked, "Why didn't Zahir want to hug me? Why does he want to be alone? I don't understand him *at all!*"

Kenzie shook his curly brown head and smiled sadly. His own face was wet from crying. He tried to explain, "Something is really bothering him, and I kind of understand his point of view... but I don't agree with his conclusions." He smiled. "The two of you need to sort this out. *You* need to have a long talk with Zahir."

Standing up straight and wiping her face one more time, she considered his advice. She was confident that Kenzie knew his friend well. She remembered a time when Uncle Louis had told her, "we don't always know what is bothering people, but if we're a good friend we ask them and find out." For months it had been difficult to talk to Zahir privately, but it wasn't any longer. It was time to overcome the fear of rejection. Before she could make any big decisions, she needed to understand what lay behind her friend's confusing actions. "I'll talk to him," she said with determination. "As soon as he comes back, I will talk to him *today.*"

Kenzie nodded. "I hope you do," he said.

Lily came running over, with a tragic expression. "We still haven't found Odin and Franz," she cried. "Did you tell the Professor? I sure hope Damien didn't drown them!" she wailed. *"Everyone is dying!"*

Aimee put a hand on her roommate's shoulder. "They aren't dead," she assured her.

"Then, where are they?" she mourned.

Kenzie looked around and saw that many of the others were looking over. Some had heard Lily's complaints and were heading his way. He waited until most of the group was within hearing distance and then he called out. "We have news about Odin and Franz."

Everyone came close.

"As you all know," Kenzie explained, "there is a cave in Paradise where Uncle Louis and the Professor used to meet." He launched into a full explanation of what a phone was, and all the ways in which it could connect with the outside world. He told them that Odin and Franz had dug a tunnel to access this device and used it to gain harmful information and ideas. "This was the Professor's fear from the very beginning," he stated, "that instead of seeking the helpful things from this device, we would indulge ourselves in the bad."

Many questions were asked about the phone and the cave, and Kenzie and Aimee did their best to answer. Damien protested that it was extremely unfair that some knew about it and others did not. Aimee assured them all that this was going to change in the future, but with some limitations.

"What are the limits?" Lema wanted to know.

"Aimee has to be with you," Kenzie explained. "The phone will only turn on if it sees her face."

"What?" Lily retorted. "That's not true. I can turn it on myself."

"Not anymore," Kenzie replied.

Hands on her hips, Georgia challenged, "And why *Aimee?*"

Kenzie pulled out a letter from the brown envelope he had found on the train. "This is from the Professor," he told everyone.

Vinitha came close to view the letter. Aimee looked up, waiting to hear what it was about.

"I'll read it to you all," Kenzie said. There was complete silence as he unfolded the piece of paper and cleared his throat.

> *"To all my beloved family,"* it began. *"I know today is a very sad day for all of you. Losing Uncle Louis will leave a big hole in your lives and hearts. His guidance, support and love has been wonderful and in many ways is irreplaceable. I'm grieving today, just as you are! Uncle Louis was very special to me!*
>
> *In order to maintain communication between myself and Paradise, I have given this responsibility to Aimee, Zahir and Kenzie. From this day forward I am choosing them to contact me when supplies are needed, problems arise, or decisions need to be made. However, tomorrow morning, after breakfast, I'd like to meet all of you in the cave and talk to you over the phone. We have many things to discuss.*
>
> *With love from your father,*
>
> *The Professor."*

For a few moments the invitation caused a major stir of excitement. It was good news at a very sad time. Kenzie and Aimee answered many questions, and then Damien remembered the first question that had still not been answered.

"So where are Odin and Franz?" he challenged. "You said you had news about them."

Without giving too much detail, Kenzie explained that the Professor had heard the two Tinys plot another catastrophe, worse than the first two, based on things they'd seen on the Internet. He told them that the two schemers had been banished to the Nursery.

Of course, everyone wanted to know *how* they had been 'banished,' and Kenzie told them that they had chosen to walk out through the open train entrance.

Once all the questions had been asked and everyone felt somewhat satisfied with the answers, they began to head back to their homes.

"I'm going to clean up the Caring Centre," Aimee said to her curly-haired friend. "I can't bear to walk past Uncle Louis' bed tonight and know that he's gone."

Shrugging his shoulders, Kenzie replied. "I'll help you. It's a big job. I think Zahir plans to go home tonight and Ponce has already gone back to his cabin. You can finally have your room back."

Vinitha came over to the curly-haired nurse with a shy, hopeful expression. "I promised Vahid I'd help him dye the wool today. He's waiting for me. But will you be at the hill tonight?" she asked.

With a smile, Kenzie nodded. "I'll be there," he promised. "See you then."

Nodding warmly, Vinitha headed off to the farmland.

Observing the friendly interactions, Aimee was pleased. "This is nice," she thought. She wanted Kenzie to have someone special in his life.

Together, the two nurses walked back up to the Caring Centre to clean up. There were some tearful moments when they first walked into the room and saw all three beds lying empty. In between many tears and fond reflections, they sorted through the supplies. Bandages and gauze were no longer needed, and most of the medication had been consumed.

For a while they worked steadily, carting used bottles to the store deck to put on the train. Diya joined in to wash and sort the blankets. Charley was summoned to help Kenzie pile the mattresses downstairs in the house. Beds were moved around and organized so that everyone could have their own room again.

"Where should we put the Bible?" Kenzie asked Aimee, as they stood in the newly uncluttered room looking at the window seat. "I think it should be somewhere accessible to everyone."

Deciding they should take it down to the living room area, Aimee walked over to where it lay. She stooped down to look at the pages. The Bible was open to First Corinthians fifteen. Glancing down, the copper-haired nurse saw the word 'resurrection.'

"Look at this," she said.

Kenzie joined her.

Scanning the words quickly, she cried out in astonishment, "This whole chapter is about *resurrection!*" Tears began running down her face.

"Let's take it downstairs," Kenzie encouraged. "We can read it out loud and maybe others will hear and join us."

Picking up the heavy book between them, they took it downstairs and placed it carefully on the large table that was never used for eating and surrounded by several chairs. With a large wall of windows, the kitchen was always brightly lit in the daytime.

"Maybe we could bring the solar lights in here," Kenzie suggested. "Then we can have an investigation every evening after go-karting, for anyone who wants to come."

At that moment, Sanaa and Lema walked in. Seeing the Bible open on the living room table, Sanaa's eyes lit up. Curiously, she asked, "Is this the book that we're not supposed to know anything about?" Then she giggled.

Aimee and Kenzie nodded.

With his arms across his chest, Lema laughed. "Is it down here because we're *finally* allowed to be part of the investigation?" he challenged.

"Yes. It's time to share it with everyone," Aimee relayed, explaining the reason for keeping it a secret.

"Oh, we know all too well," Sanaa replied, with a happy sway. "We've been listening in right from the start. And we want to hear more!"

Kenzie was pleased. He told them about the Bible being left open to First Corinthians fifteen and that he and Aimee wanted to read the chapter through. Sitting down on the white furry rug, the four Tinys read it together, commenting from time to time with the occasional flood of tears. Lema finished the encouraging words, reading, *"For the trumpet will sound, and the dead will be raised imperishable, and we shall be changed. For this perishable body must put on the imperishable, and this mortal body must put on immortality. When the perishable puts on the imperishable, and the mortal puts on immortality, then shall come to pass the saying that is written: 'Death is swallowed up in victory.'"*

Feeling great encouragement, Aimee piped up, "This is the reason Uncle Louis died so peacefully. God is going to overcome death - *the great enemy!* Mortal bodies will be made immortal!"

Sanaa exclaimed, "I love this hope! God can give Uncle Louis and all of us life again! We need to share this with everyone!"

The others agreed happily.

Lema noticed a reference written in the margin. When he asked what it meant, Kenzie said, "Let's look it up."

Showing the others the book title tabs, Kenzie helped Lema find Revelation chapter twenty-one, verse three.

Resting against her dark friends' arm, Sanaa read, *"Behold, the dwelling place of God is with man. He will dwell with them, and they will be his people, and God himself will be with them as their God. He will wipe away every tear from their eyes, and death shall be no more, neither shall there be mourning, nor crying, nor pain anymore, for the former things have passed away... The one who conquers will have this heritage, and I will be his God and he will be my son."*

"Oooh, this is wonderful!" Sanaa rejoiced, getting up and dancing around. "We can all be part of God's family! *No more tears! No more death!"*

Nodding his head, Kenzie pondered thoughtfully. "I suppose when we're made immortal, all the things that cause tears and pain will be gone. This is the future that God has promised *forever!"*

There was another handwritten reference, so Lema turned up First Thessalonians four, verses thirteen to seventeen. They read it through with interest and Aimee summarised, "We aren't to 'grieve as others do who have no hope.' Uncle Louis is just asleep, waiting for Jesus to return and raise the dead. We will see him again!"

"And the living and the dead will be gathered together to be with Christ at his return," Kenzie smiled, wiping his eyes. "What a day that will be!"

"Aimee," Sanaa spoke up suddenly, clapping her hands together. "I know what we need to do. We need to get everyone together tomorrow and have a special remembrance for Uncle Louis. We can read this chapter to everyone and tell them that this was Uncle Louis' hope!"

The others nodded eagerly.

"Great idea, Sanaa," Kenzie agreed. "I'm sure Uncle Louis would have made the same suggestion if he were here."

"And we can sing songs about him," Lema nodded.

"Yes, songs! We should all do songs!" Aimee smiled. "And share stories of our favourite times with him."

373

Sanaa's eyes sparkled. "And the things he said that we need to remember," she added.

"I really, really like this idea," Kenzie enthused. "Maybe Vinitha... and even Georgia could make a beautiful sign in his memory."

"And we should have food," Sanaa reflected. "Like all of Uncle Louis' favourites... fried fish, fruit salad, maybe even *honeybuns!*"

Aimee smiled sadly as tears welled up again in her eyes. "But just *one* for everybody," she teased.

The others chuckled.

"Let's go and see who wants to be involved," Sanaa said, standing up. "We'll go talk to Nancy... and Charley about the food."

"I'll find Vinitha," Kenzie said quietly.

They all walked to the door.

Outside on the deck, Aimee hesitated. "I'm going to try and find Zahir," she said resolutely. "If any of you see him," she begged, looking around at her friends, "please tell him that I want to talk to him."

Sanaa and Lema nodded and rushed off to organize the meal.

Kenzie hung back with encouragement. "Be brave, Aimee," he said. "Just keep talking till Zahir has a smile on his face."

Looking up appreciatively, she promised, "I will."

As her steady, helpful friend with the kind grey eyes turned to leave, she called out suddenly, "Kenzie, just one more thing."

Raising one eyebrow in a quizzical fashion, he stopped.

"Thank you," she said sincerely. "You've been a true friend to Zahir and to me." With a laugh, she added, "I hope we don't have any more emergencies, but if we do, I will gladly work with you again."

Reaching out to playfully shake her hand, Kenzie agreed. "Me too, Nurse Aimee. It's been my pleasure."

374

Finding Peace

Chapter 44

As the nurses parted ways and Aimee left the Caring Centre that was now restored to a home, she wondered where Zahir might be. There were a few possibilities, such as his house, or down by the water, or possibly somewhere in the large forest on Rainbow Hill. She was fairly certain that he wanted to be alone, or at least that he *thought* he did. She understood that sometimes being alone was the best way to sort through troubled emotions. But she also remembered the saddest moment of her life, when she thought she wanted isolation and was surprised to discover a kind friend could turn darkness to light. She hoped it might be her turn to rescue him.

As the laughter echoed from Rosa's Hill, Aimee went first to Zahir's house in the forest, but no one answered the door. She tried calling his name, standing on the hill, but no one replied.

Making her way down the winding path to the beach, a small object caught her eye. Someone was out in a boat on the lake, a *red* boat, a boat that she had once named 'The Red Bird.' "Of course," she smiled. "He's gone fishing."

Walking down to the pier, she knew eventually the boat would come in to dock. Until then, she decided to wait. Sitting down on the pier, Aimee dangled her bare legs in the cool, flowing water. A gentle breeze blew steadily across the lake. After all the sadness of the day, it was refreshing to have some peaceful, quiet moments. She thanked

God for nineteen wonderful months with Uncle Louis, and that He had helped them to find a hope for life far beyond six years in Paradise. *Forever* was just the perfect amount! She thanked God that the burn victims had healed so well and that she hadn't made any disastrous mistakes. Then she prayed for the courage to say the right things to Zahir and sort out all their misunderstandings.

A calming, tranquil hour went by as she watched the red boat head further and further away. Loons bobbed up and down on the water and occasionally disappeared below the surface. For a wonderful moment, five lorikeets landed on the beach boys' boat and looked up at her curiously. She stretched out her hand, but none of them were brave enough to come so close. With a few squawks, they rose back into the air. At one point, she was sure she saw a bat swoop over the water; bats were rarely seen!

As the sun dropped low in the sky and the dinner bell rang out, Aimee didn't move. She took the time to reflect on her precious memories with Uncle Louis, trying to decide what she would share with the others. She was sitting close to the place where he had comforted her after she had nearly drowned. Watching the distant Red Bird move slowly along the perimeter of the dome, she remembered various things her beloved brother had told her, little sayings that she would always keep in her heart. He had led them to Jesus – his new 'role model,' and the one who would never leave them alone. For a few minutes she wondered what Jesus would tell her if he was there by her side. She imagined he might have the same kind expression that often shone from Uncle Louis. In a peaceful reverie, she hoped he might say, "Aimee, I love your compassion for others, and your desire to do what is right and save lives. It is through these qualities that you can best share my message to the world." Then with a prick of conscience, she wondered if he might add soberly, "And I know that you struggle to love Georgia, and that's something you need to work on, but I'm pleased that you want to try. I'm willing to help you if you take my advice from God's Book. It's all there to help you live well and treat others right."

As she reflected dreamily upon such comforting and guiding thoughts, gradually, the sun began to set, and bright colours intensified in the clouds above. The group of lorikeets flew overhead again, squawking noisily. Even a few bluebirds could be seen circling the pier. A fish jumped out of the sparkling pink and gold water. The loons glided by, eyeing her warily and then diving deep and out of sight. In a few minutes, she heard them call out far away.

The Red Bird was slowly drawing closer, gliding in on the current. She thought back on her friendship with Zahir. "We both struggle with doubt," her dark-haired friend had once said. She remembered her fears of driving after the accident and thought about the way he had patiently helped her to overcome her anxiety. His full confidence in her ability, his gentle determination to wait for her to try, and his loving smile had put all her fears to rest. Somehow, she had to try to do the same for him. She hoped that Zahir wanted a caring friend in his life.

Suddenly, on the breeze, she heard faint singing. The voice she loved best in Paradise was singing a new song. Enthralled, she strained forward to listen carefully. Her heart thrilled with the hopeful melody.

"I have found life," he was singing, *"I have found hope, I have found God, and Jesus Christ, my Lord.*

I'm never alone, not anymore."

Aimee swallowed hard. Uncle Louis had said, 'You're not alone, not anymore.' Zahir was already composing the perfect song for their remembrance ceremony! She was eager to hear what followed. Her friend was still quite a distance away.

"I have been loved," Zahir sang. *"I have been cared for, and someday soon, I'll see Uncle Louis again.*

But I'm never alone, not anymore.

377

I have found a real Father, the Creator of all, He always sees me, And knows when I fall.

I'm never alone, not anymore.

I will see Jesus; he's coming back soon. He gave his life for the world, enduring the pain.

So, when tears run down, and my heart wants to break, I'll sing my song joyfully, with my eyes looking ahead, for the day still to come, the best day of all..."

Having picked up the tune, Aimee joined in on the chorus, "I'm never alone, Not anymore."

Zahir stopped singing abruptly as though he had just realised exactly who was sitting on the pier. As the Red Bird floated closer without any oars, Aimee tried to determine the expression on his face, but it was getting dark. It was hard to see. Gazing happily across the water at the young man in the boat, Aimee yearned to be his helper.

While the one she loved best was still being tossed around by unreliable emotions, he had embraced an unmoveable rock. Zahir's trust was in God and so was hers! They were both discovering the way to find true peace. She hoped they could find it together.

The Best Son

Chapter 45

*D*eep remorse lined Farouk's dark-skinned face. Quietly, he confirmed, "I'd say he's been dead for at least eight hours. I'm sorry, Jacques. I'm *very* sorry for your loss. I'm amazed that Louis lived as long as he did. His heart was quite weak when we sent him back in."

Stooped in a chair, with his head in his hands, the Professor nodded with a dismal expression.

Evan wiped his face and blew his nose.

"I must get back to the hospital," Doctor Khalid said, his dark brown eyes filled with sadness. "I am sorry, Jacques. I wish there was something more that I could do."

"I'm very thankful that you asked to come, Farouk," the Professor mumbled gratefully. He stood up and shook the doctor's hand. "I really appreciate your involvement with this project. It means so much to both of us!"

Evan nodded and also shook hands with the doctor. "Thank you so much for rushing over here," he replied appreciatively. "I know it was difficult for you to get away."

"And I'd like to thank you for the opportunity to speak to Zahir the other day," Doctor Khalid smiled. "He's a very special young man. I am *fully* invested in this project. Call me whenever you need me."

Once the doctor had left the laboratory, Evan sat down beside the Professor. He put his hand on the older man's shoulder.

Looking up through his tears, the Professor acknowledged Evan.

For a while, they sat together in silence. Occasionally, Evan glanced over at the tiny lifeless body on the emergency bed. Louis was still hooked up to wires and machines, but there were no signs of life. Occasionally, Evan patted the Professor's shoulder and passed him tissues. He didn't know what to say.

Finally, the Professor spoke, "I knew this day was coming," he murmured. "I just hoped it wouldn't come yet."

"It's not something you can ever be prepared for," Evan agreed, wishing he could think of something more comforting to say.

Minutes passed by, while the scientists mourned the loss of the lifeless Tiny in the emergency bed.

"He was a good man," Evan murmured finally. "No," he clarified, "Louis was the best! He *gave his life* for the Tinys. He always did whatever you wanted him to do. He rarely argued or complained and when he did, he had a good reason to do so. He asked for very few favours - he was just completely dedicated to raising your family. He was a true 'servant leader.'"

For a long moment, the Professor didn't respond. Then in a quiet voice, he said, "He was the son I always longed to have. He just didn't live *nearly* long enough!"

Standing up, the Professor walked over to the small bed. Slowly and carefully, he picked up the body and cradled Louis in his hand. "You were the best son," he wept. "We had five and a half wonderful years together."

Weeping, the Professor held his aged son close. Eventually, he reminisced with Evan about the fire and how Louis had overextended himself to help Zahir lift the heavy catapult from Ponce's back. "You gave yourself to save Paradise," Jacques sobbed, "and all I could give you was sixty-six months of life. You deserved so much more!"

As Evan sat listening to the outpourings of grief, the many discussions he'd had with Seth came into his mind. Over and over, he considered the things he had learned and deliberated whether or not there was a gentle way to share it. He didn't want to add to the Professor's misery, but the finality of death accentuated the injustice of keeping the offer of salvation from any of the Tinys. "Yes, Louis did deserve more," he thought silently to himself. "I am so thankful that he made the decision to investigate his options and find hope. For most of his life, his worldview was decided for him by those who thought they knew what was best – but we were wrong."

Finally, Evan could stay silent no longer. He walked over to the Professor and put his arm around the older man's shoulders. "I want you to hear me out," he said gently. "I want you to think about what I say, for the sake of all the Tinys who are still left in Paradise."

The Professor looked up at him sadly. "Go ahead," he said. "Say what you need to say."

"You didn't ask your son to save Paradise," Evan began. "You didn't even want him to risk his life in the fire. You asked him to lead, and he led the best way that he could. But he also chose to do everything in his power to save lives when it was necessary and to stop unexpected catastrophes. He did *more* than you asked, with a very willing heart. You were proud that he put others first and had such courage. You raised a wonderful son and for that you can be very happy. Louis fully enjoyed his life as the uncle to twenty children."

Nodding sadly, the Professor agreed.

Evan swallowed hard. "But think about this," he added, with his arm still around Jacques' shoulders. "God *did ask His Son* to save the world. And He let His Son know *ahead of time* that such a sacrifice would be a very painful, terrible experience. He didn't hide anything from him. He made him fully aware of the cost."

The Professor nodded. "But how can a *loving* Father ask such a thing?" he murmured.

"I think this is what you're missing," Evan told him earnestly, "God's Son *willingly* chose to go through with that sacrifice, even though he knew full well what it entailed. He loved the world so much that he *wanted* to do his part to die a sinless man! God didn't *force* Jesus to go through with the crucifixion – Jesus said he could have called on *thousands* of angels to stop his arrest, if he wanted to.[150] And God didn't force anyone to mistreat His Son. The hatred and torture that Jesus received was a result of his decision to speak up and expose lies that proud men didn't want exposed. His divine healing power provoked envy in some, rather than gratitude.[151] God foresaw that this would be the reaction from many because those who love evil *hate* good.[152] It's been that way right from the beginning."

The Professor was nodding slowly.

"And when it was all over," Evan said softly, "God brought His Son *back* from the dead."

Hanging his head sadly, the Professor saw the point, but Evan intended to finish with a positive message. In a gentle voice, he continued, "God resurrected His Son and He gave Jesus His Divine nature *for eternity*.[153] Jesus will never feel pain, or suffering, or death, ever again. God took Jesus to be with Him in heaven for the last two thousand years, and He's promised to send him back to rule the whole world for a millennium.[154] God rewarded His Son in an incredible way! How can we ever say that our Creator is unfair?"

Jacques Lemans couldn't speak. Carefully, he laid Louis back down on the incubator bed and then he broke down weeping.

Evan stepped forward and gave the Professor an awkward hug. It seemed like the right thing to do.

---

[150] Matthew 26:53
[151] Mark 15:10; John 11:45-53
[152] 1 John 3:11-15; John 15:18-25; Amos 5:10; Isaiah 29:20-21;
[153] 1 Cor. 15:20-23, 42-58; Philippians 3:20-21; Romans 8:29
[154] Acts 1:11; 1 Thessalonians 4:13-18; 2 Thessalonians 1:5-10; Revelation 1:5-7; Zechariah 14:1-5; Revelation 5:10; 20:1-6; Daniel 7:18; 1 Corinthians 15:22-26; Revelation 21

When Jacques could speak, he admitted, *"C'est vrai.* I can never reward any of the Tinys in such a remarkable way, regardless of what they deserve. Six years is a pittance!"

"It's true. We aren't God and I'm *so* thankful we're not! And you know, Jacques," Evan added kindly, "we aren't the only ones who feel pain in this relationship with our Father in heaven."

"What do you mean?"

"This is what I've learned from Seth," Evan explained, moving away and pacing the floor. "Sometimes we only see *our* sufferings. We expect God to be hard and resilient and not to have any emotions. Yet, He has told us that He is *grieved* when He looks down from heaven and sees a world that doubts His words, despises His promises and rebels against the commands that were only made for our benefit."[155]

Looking over at the Professor, Evan sighed. "After these last nineteen months, we both know how that feels! Imagine when God looks at His marvellous creation today and sees so many of us dismiss His incredible handiwork as random chance happenings with no purpose, love or intelligent thought... or, they tinker and re-engineer His designs like we did.[156] God called Jesus His 'beloved Son,' and says it was because He *loved the world so much* that He allowed His Son to fall into the hands of abusive sinners who didn't deserve to be saved – with the purpose of saving *them!"*[157]

Jacques nodded solemnly, feeling very unworthy of such love!

Standing in front of the older man, Evan put his hand on his shoulder. "You know how difficult it was for you to watch Louis walk into that fire. You would likely have preferred to give yourself, rather than see your beloved Son hurt by those he tried to save. Do we stop

---

[155] Genesis 6:5-6; Isaiah 63:7-14; Psalm 78; 1 John 4:9-10
[156] Romans 1:18-32
[157] John 3:14-18

and think how deep God's love is? Do we appreciate the hurt He feels when we don't return His love?"

"I'm not sure I understand," the Professor said sincerely.

Meeting the Professor's curious gaze, Evan realised he had said a lot already, but lately his talks with Seth had helped him reach some important conclusions that he yearned to share with the man who was his mentor, his friend... and someone he loved like a *dad*.

"This enormous experiment has given me a new appreciation for how God views our world," Evan told him earnestly. "I no longer want to be like Franz or Odin, grumbling, complaining and unthankful. I recognize the magnificent effort God put into designing the perfect world for us. I now appreciate the joy our Creator must feel when even *one* of His children demonstrates they trust Him or takes the time to turn and thank Him for all that He has done. And after these last nineteen months, I fully empathize with God's disappointment when He looks down from heaven to see His children consuming all His good gifts, without any acknowledgement to the giver of those gifts."

Pacing the floor, Evan proclaimed, "If I'm going to commit to Him, Jacques – I'll be all in. Why should any of us expect our Creator to be satisfied with half-hearted relationships, meaningless words, or actions that stem from pretence?[158] I wouldn't want that in a close relationship. Would you? God gave us freewill so that His love for us can be returned in a satisfying way – in a real, willing relationship, the kind of loving relationship that we all long for."

For a moment the two stood looking at each other and pondering all the things that had been said. Reaching out to steady himself against the wall, the Professor was deeply moved by Evan's passionate appeal. "Franz?" he repeated silently and fearfully to himself. "*Ça alors!* Does God look down from heaven and see me as I

---

[158] Deuteronomy 6:5-6; Matthew 22:36-38

see those two young men?" He pondered the matter inwardly, "I haven't acknowledged God as my Creator. I've turned people against Him. I've blamed Him for my suffering even as I've benefitted from living in His amazing world. I don't thank Him for anything..."

"Am I like Franz... and Odin?" Jacques blurted out. "Is Franz *like me?*" Swallowing hard, he trembled from head to foot. The Professor had always identified himself with Louis, but now he had to reconsider. "Why would God even want *me?*" he asked his friend.

Evan paused. Gently he prodded, "How would you feel if Odin or Franz earnestly begged for your forgiveness? Would you want *them?* Would you accept them back?"[159]

It wasn't hard to answer that question. "I'd be overjoyed!" Jacques nodded sincerely. As the remains of the dark veil of bitterness fell from his eyes, the Professor took a few steps forward and embraced his assistant. "Evan," he said, "You are so much more than just my assistant. You have been like ... a son... a *wonderful* son! I've been wrong! I've been so wrong... all these years. God *is* gracious! He is more gracious than I am! Help me, Evan! Please help me to change."

"We have been through a lot together," Evan acknowledged compassionately, patting his mentor on the back. "I'm with you, Jacques, all the way. Together we'll make a change. We have so much to share with the world."

For a moment the scientists embraced warmly, thankful to be back in harmony once again, with the same purpose and direction for all of the Tinys in their care.

"And just so you know," Evan smiled, as they drew back. "Louis committed his life to his Heavenly Father just before he died. That three weeks he had with a Bible gave him time to sort things out and find the hope."

"He did!" Jacques exclaimed. "When? How?"

---

[159] 2 Peter 3:9; 1 Timothy 2:4; Ezekiel 18:23, 32

Before Evan left that evening, he told the Professor the whole story. He was thankful he had been there to witness the special event and take five precious pictures that he now could share.

Carrycarts of Pain

Chapter 46

*D*arkness had fallen when The Red Bird glided close to dock. There were no oars in Zahir's hands, and he didn't meet Aimee's eyes. Reaching out to the pier, he tried to bring his boat up against the wood in a gentle fashion.

"Please may I sing that new song with you?" Aimee begged wistfully. "I love it! Uncle Louis would have loved it."

"Of course," he nodded uncertainly, as the boat bumped up against the wooden structure. Tying it up to the pier, he then spoke with quiet confidence, "I'd really like to investigate the Bible more thoroughly just like Uncle Louis did. Just like he said, I feel like this is the greatest treasure we could find..."

Aimee stood up. "And so do I. Kenzie, Sanaa and Lema do as well."

"That's great to hear," he said.

"Maybe we could all talk to Evan and his friend Seth about this," Aimee suggested. "They know a lot about the Bible. I've talked to them before."

Looking interested, Zahir nodded. "We should," he agreed. "That might be helpful." Beginning to walk away, the dark-haired man stopped when Aimee didn't follow. "Are you staying... *here?*" he questioned.

Aimee swallowed hard. "I've been waiting... to talk to *you,*" she confessed.

With a quizzical expression, he asked, "Is everything okay?"

There was a lot Aimee could have told him about their plans for remembering Uncle Louis the next day, but she knew it was finally the right time and place for a difficult conversation. Forcing herself to begin, she said, "Zahir, something *isn't* okay... something between us. Please, please tell me what's bothering you."

The scarred man didn't look up, but he spoke firmly. "There's nothing *bothering* me," he said, avoiding her gaze. "The Professor – your father – told us that we needed to think about what is best for Paradise... not necessarily for... ourselves. I thought about a lot of things last night," he relayed, shifting uncomfortably on the pier. "I hoped to talk it over with Uncle Louis," his voice wavered, "but I was too late." He wiped his eyes. "I know God loves us all but, we each have different roles. I really don't think I'm the right one to help you... or the Professor."

"Zahir..."

Pointing to his face, he explained rather bitterly, "How can I help you lead Paradise when I look like this? And what if I go completely blind? What if I become a burden to *everyone?*" A tear ran down his cheek, and he shrugged helplessly. "Great! I'm crying again! This is *so* embarrassing," he murmured. "Look, I'm still not myself. I don't even understand who I am anymore. You're better off to lead with... well... Kenzie, than with me. Damien wasn't right for you – he wouldn't treat you well. But Kenzie will be amazing. He will help you communicate with the Professor and make all the important decisions. You can both learn from my parents and be great doctors together."

Aimee tried to protest, but Zahir stepped back with his hands up. "Don't worry about me," he said almost harshly, as his words tumbled out. "I'll be fine. I have God and Jesus Christ in my life now. I'm not alone. I have all that I need. I'll keep fishing and investigating the Bible, and... well, I'll help out wherever I can."

The unexpected reply caught her off guard. Old doubts came sweeping back in one enormous wave. "Zahir will 'be fine' without me?" she pondered. "Really? Do I matter so little to him? Is God all that he needs? Why is he always pushing me away? Is Kenzie wrong about this?" Aimee longed for a comforting hug from Uncle Louis!

Inside, she tried to stay balanced. "But *God* says it's not good for a man to be alone," she recalled. "That's why he made Eve. Trust what Kenzie said – tell him how you feel. Don't take it personally. Don't *fizzle out* before you've given this your very best try. He doesn't have a smile on his face, so you can't leave yet."

"Why?" she faltered sadly. "I don't understand..."

In a kinder tone, Zahir explained, "You deserve more, Aimee. Kenzie's a good-looking guy who cares about you. You both work so well together. He'll be a fabulous doctor. What more can you want?"

"Zahir," she pleaded. "I want to be with you. I love *you!*"

Flinching uneasily, the scarred man swallowed hard and folded his arms across his chest. "Aimee, you don't *have* to look after me anymore! I don't want you to feel sorry for me... or think I need a friend. That's... too... *painful.*"

A smile broke out on her face as Aimee felt certain what lay behind all his objections. "Is that what you think this is about?" she asked incredulously. "I *don't* feel sorry for you, Zahir! I *love* you."

"But that doesn't make sense."

"What do you mean?"

Darkly, he relayed, "All my life I've been trying to get your attention and you've *always* been looking the other way. Why would you suddenly be interested now that I'm an ugly... *wreck.*"

Astonished, she asked, "When have you tried to get my attention and not received it?"

As though he was surprised that she didn't know, he frowned, "Over and over when we were kids you were *always* more interested in... the *surfers.* But there was one night, about a month ago, when I...

I thought maybe you *did* care," he relayed bitterly. "But when I finally found the courage to tell you that... I *loved* you; you didn't even reply. You said nothing! You looked *scared*. If you love me, Aimee, why didn't you say so *then?*"

"But that was the night you turned my darkness into light," she exclaimed, astounded, suddenly realising that silence might sometimes be as painful as hurtful words. Was this the *'brutal'* experience he had talked to Uncle Louis about? Had she caused *more* pain than Georgia? Stunned, she tried to apologize, "I can't believe you went home feeling that I didn't care! I am *so, so sorry!*"

Tears began to flow on the anxious face across from hers, and Zahir hastily wiped them away.

Aimee tried to explain, "Zahir, there was a rule, remember – that dumb girls' rule? Georgia claimed you, so I was breaking the rules that night. I wasn't supposed to hug you, or say I loved you, or spend time alone with you. That's why I looked scared. Even when Uncle Louis got rid of the rule, I still didn't feel it was right to interfere. He told me that Jesus said we should treat others the way we want to be treated. And you were telling Georgia that you loved her every day, so I doubted you *meant* what you said to me." Her voice faltered. "This has all been breaking my heart too, you know."

Zahir wiped his eyes again as a bright smile shimmered through. "Really?" he questioned, trying to process this new information. "That's... all there was to it? You were just afraid of breaking a silly rule?"

"Yes, really," she smiled. "That sad song had *a lot* to do with *you!*"

Astonished, the scarred man relented. With a happy chuckle, he reached out and pulled her close. It was a true Zahir hug - warm and comforting! While the stars shone through the night sky and fireflies flittered around in the breeze, Aimee savoured the best hug in her world – the one she had been waiting for. She was deeply thankful

390

that she had finally discovered what was troubling her very best friend.

After a little while, Zahir said, "It might have saved some confusion if you had told me how you felt earlier, but I appreciate your integrity. No, actually... I admire your integrity! You did the right thing, Aimee. I've been just trying to live by the 'no hurting' rule. I didn't think about all those other restrictions." A lop-sided smile crept across his face, and he added, "You didn't write those on your board..."

Recalling her attempt to qualify the rules, Aimee laughed, "No, it was a *secret* rule," she relayed, "until... it wasn't anymore."

"You are definitely someone I can trust," he sighed. "But then I guess I haven't been fair to you," he apologized. "I'm sorry, Aimee."

"What do you mean?"

Zahir explained his side of the story. He had been devastated when he had been told that she only cared for him as a friend. He had realized that she loved Damien much more than him. Georgia had showered him with attention and helped mend his broken heart. "But lately," he confessed, "I found *myself* speaking meaningless words to someone who was not my first choice, but I thought I cared enough about to make it work." He sighed. "Aimee, if I had realised that I was hurting you, I would have ended that relationship right away... even though it would have... hurt Georgia..." In anguish, Zahir added, "It's really hard to get this all sorted and not hurt anyone!"

"It is," she agreed, "and misunderstandings are *so* painful when you love someone this much."

Zahir begged, "Aimee, why do you love *me?*"

Thankful to finally have the freedom to speak without any others looking on or previous claims to consider, the copper-haired girl looked up earnestly. It was time to ride the wave. "I can't fully explain why *your* smiling face makes me so happy..."

"My face? *My ugly face?* But you cried when you saw the pink..."

"Zahir," Aimee implored, "I cried for *your feelings* – because I knew it would matter *to you.* There's no other face I'd rather see."

He was shaking his head, but she smiled, happy to remind her friend who he truly was. "That's not all there is to it," she began, "I love your honesty, Zahir, your incredible music, and all your emotions. Even your *tears, "* she laughed kindly as they began pouring down. Smiling, Zahir shrugged helplessly. This time he didn't bother to brush them away. She reached up and did it for him.

"You want to be like Uncle Louis... *and now Jesus, "* she continued, "and so do I. You risked your life to save Ponce. I only *wish* I were brave enough to do what you did! You care about right and wrong, and so do I. You knew how to change my sad song into hope, and I *love your* songs! I want to sing them all with you. You care about other people's feelings... even people that don't deserve you. And... well," she shrugged happily, "you give the *very best* hugs in Paradise – the *only* hugs I need!"

Enveloping her in another one of those wonderful hugs, Zahir lamented, "I wish we had talked earlier... *much* earlier. We could have saved each other so much heartbreak."

Snuggled in her best friend's arms, Aimee cheerfully disagreed, "Without the pain, it wouldn't be so good now."

"What are you saying?"

With her head on his shoulder, she explained. "Zahir, I'm so sorry for the hurt I caused you, but all this has helped me to realise just how special you are! I appreciate you *more* because of the pain."

Zahir quietly pondered her words.

"Okay, but let's be done with hurting each other, or anyone else," he begged. "From here on it's you and *only* you for me." Earnestly, he pleaded, "If I give you my heart, Aimee, I won't be able to share you with Damien... *or Kenzie...* or anyone else - not in this way. On top of everything else, jealousy has been driving me crazy."

A big smile spread across Aimee's face. It was a relief to hear that the one she loved was jealous of her affections. It was a satisfying confirmation that he truly had deep feelings for her. With a happy laugh, she teased, "Well, then it's a good thing I didn't let you pass me over to someone else!"

"I know!" he agreed, chuckling sadly as he pulled her closer. "I'm sorry for how I've been acting, Aimee. I would have understood if you had chosen Kenzie... and I really thought that's what you wanted. I need to be sure that you'll be happy with me, for my sake and for yours."

"You are the one I love, Zahir," she promised earnestly.

"You'll *marry* me?" he challenged.

"Zahir, I *need* you by my side. I want to marry *you!*" she exclaimed.

Among the twinkling fireflies and the distant call of the loons, two very happy Tinys enjoyed their budding new relationship. "This time I wasn't a whoosh," Aimee sighed inwardly, feeling very happy and content, "and finally, we understand each other."

Looking over at their boat nearby, Zahir asked, "Do you want to go for a ride on the water?"

"Sure!" she replied joyfully. "How long has it been since we rode together?"

"Way too long!"

Out on the gently rolling water, it took Aimee a few tries to remember how to steer the boat in a straight fashion against the current, but once they were back in sync, Zahir encouraged her to head for the moon's shimmering pathway. "Let's see if we can stay in the light," he said eagerly.

It was fun, pushing against the breeze on the rippled water and attempting to stay in the glow. Loons bobbed up nearby and sang out to each other. Laughing, the two reconciled Tinys tried to make the call themselves. They congratulated each other when one bird replied.

When they reached the far edge of the lake where the breeze blew strongly, Zahir pulled in his oar. "Let's drift for bit," he said. "I tried this out today. It's fun. The waves will take us back in."

Sitting together with the oars in the boat, the waves gently rocked them side to side. The soft steady breeze blew Aimee's hair around. Happy to be the one sitting close beside her best friend, she smoothed the bumpy scar tissue on the arm she had cared for day after day. "How did you *not* feel all the love that I poured into healing these wounds?" she teased.

The moon was full and bright above the hazy horizon. Zahir took her hand and chuckled. "I did feel love," he expressed kindly, "but I wasn't sure it was specific to *me.* You are kind to everyone and... well, do you know how hard it is to have the one you want to impress see you helpless, smelly... *rotting...* emotional? It was wonderful to have your care, but sometimes it was... well, *humiliating.* Does that make any sense?" His voice trailed off, "I just didn't feel worthy." With a sigh he added, "I thought I was doomed to another rejection."

"Is that how you felt?" she mused, having never considered what it might be like to be the helpless patient. "But couldn't you see I was guarding my job jealously?" she laughed. "I finally had the chance to care for you and I wasn't sharing it with anyone... not even *Kenzie!*"

"You weren't just following orders and trying... to make up... for the accident?"

"That was only a small part," she clarified, smiling. "It was an easy answer at the time. I know that forgiveness in Christ is what will set me free."

"Yes, it will," Zahir agreed with a happy sigh. "Forgiveness is a beautiful concept! I need it too."

Resting her head on his shoulder, Aimee loved their new closeness and understanding. Leaning against the back of the boat, they looked up at the vast expanse of stars as their red-waxed aluminum vessel gently rocked on the flowing water. Out in the middle of the lake, only the black criss-crossed lines obstructed their view of the heavens. Slowly, they drifted toward the shoreline.

Suddenly, Zahir said, "You know, maybe I've been seeing this all the wrong way."

"What do you mean?"

"I'm probably overthinking... apparently, that's my biggest... well, never mind." The dark-haired man shook his head dismissively. "Aimee," he said with his loving, somewhat lop-sided smile, "I was just thinking that the last time we were close like this, we were both grieving over our losses... our pets and maybe a few other things?"

She nodded fervently.

"Now we've just lost Uncle Louis," he said soberly. "Pain is definitely a consequence of losing something or someone you love. But maybe," he speculated in a happier tone, "maybe pain is the trading commodity for love. The deeper you love, the more pain you are required to trade, and you never know when you'll need to bring carrycarts full."

"Carrycarts of pain," Aimee considered merrily. "I hope we've traded enough to last a long while."

Wrapping his arms around her, Zahir sighed happily. "This is so nice, *believing* that you love me and being here with you. I love you, Aimee, more than you know! Regardless of how much it might cost, I'm willing to pay *full* price!"

Two Prayers

Chapter 47

Sitting at his desk, writing his reflections in his journal, the Professor was fully aware that a very important conversation was taking place on the pier, one that made him happy beyond words. He didn't go over to look, wanting to give the two Tinys some privacy. However, the intense exchange that was drifting quietly over the speakers explained why they had continued to misunderstand one another for so long. Rachel's son and his daughter were finally working things out and he couldn't be happier. He was astounded that Zahir had felt unworthy of Aimee's love and her father's good favour. "If only he knew!" he sighed, shaking his head.

Scribbling all his thoughts on the blank page, he contemplated various things he had learned, now that he saw his experiment in a completely new light. "Even in ideal circumstances," he wrote, as a few teardrops fell on his page, "without any oppression or natural catastrophes, it is possible for people to feel unworthy, unloved and alone, even when it's not true.[160] Human doubts and fears can keep us from acknowledging love that is real and genuine, regardless of all the strong evidence we see. In an attempt to avoid pain we may inadvertently cause and receive far more."

Pausing thoughtfully in the privacy of the Paradise Room, Jacques stared out his window for a few moments, before continuing, "We

---

[160] Ferrer, H. M. "Mama Bear Apologetics" (2019), page 171.

also have a tendency not to trust that our superiors truly want what is best for us, whether that might be our board of directors, teachers, parents or even... *our Father in Heaven.*" With his pen poised in the air, he reflected, "Maybe doubts, fear and a lack of trust in their Father's love caused Adam and Eve to listen to that snake."

"Some," he wrote, "rail against the concept that any Higher Being should tell us what to do or judge our actions adversely. However, in our desire to live as we please, we may unwittingly place ourselves in bondage to something or someone else... even if it's just our own selfish desires."[161] In brackets he wrote, '(me, Odin, Franz).'

"There are others," he continued, "who seem content to live their daily lives without any strong pull in any direction. They have much less anxiety and fewer 'ups and downs,' but they may also lack the motivation to dig for treasure."

Considering Zahir's new song, which had come across the water and the speakers quite clearly, Jacques was thankful the fire had not affected the young man's voice. "And then there are those," he wrote, "who find great comfort believing there is a Higher Being who guides our way, gives us hope and gave us His greatest treasure – *His perfect Son* – in order to save those who are doomed to death." In brackets he wrote, "(Seth, Louis, Zahir, Aimee, Kenzie, Evan, Sanaa, Lema, maybe even Ponce, Lily and Vinitha - and now me!)."

He heard Aimee explain to Zahir that without the painful mistakes and experiences, she would never have realised how much he meant to her. "Suffering brought those two together," he acknowledged. "All my feeble attempts to give them fun projects that they could do together only tore them further apart. I would never have chosen a fire, dreadful burns, and weeks of healing, but that's what helped in the end. If we can avoid turning bitter, maybe suffering can help us to

---

[161] Romans 6:15-23

398

appreciate and value the gifts we are given, and to recognize true treasure when we find it."[162]

Laughter rang out from his beloved daughter and soon to be son-in-law as they headed out in the boat. The building board oars slapped quietly against the water. Hearing them laugh together brought such joy to his heart. He sat back in his chair.

Overhearing Zahir express that carrycarts of pain might correspond with the depth of love, Jacques Lemans nodded his head. "They do indeed," he acknowledged thoughtfully. "Would I have refused twelve happy years with Wendy, had I known it would cost *fifty* carrycarts of pain?" He shook his head. *"Ça alors!* I never wanted things to end, but if I'd seen a price tag, I would have agreed to pay. So, why then, did I turn against God? I should have been thanking Him for the time He gave me. My beautiful wife was a priceless gift in this 'fallen' world."

His thoughts on suffering took him deeper, as he considered Evan's comments and an article he had recently read. "Jesus *chose* to suffer for us," he recorded, "Jesus went through deeply distressing and painful times[163] – he willingly paid with 'hundreds of carrycarts of pain,' but now he is in heaven enjoying life with his Father. He will never experience pain, death or suffering again. And Christians say he is coming back for 'his bride' – the bride for whom he was pierced."

Pausing with his pen in the air, Jacques was relieved to hear a happy young man commit to leadership in Paradise now that he was sure that Aimee loved him. "I couldn't work closely with you and be the second-best guy," Zahir explained. "It would break my heart."

As the two discussed their plans for the future, they both agreed with Uncle Louis' suggestion that the best way forward was to share

---

[162] Psalm 119:67,71; Romans 5:3-5; 1 Peter 1:6-9; James 1:2-4; Heb. 10:32-39; Hebrews 12:11-15
[163] Hebrews 5:7-8

God's Book with the others. "If the Gospel message governs everyone's hearts and guides their actions," he heard Zahir tell his daughter, "we won't have groups trying to kill each other. We can set the Bible up in our house and invite everyone to come and read it with you, me and Kenzie."

"*Our* house," Aimee repeated happily. "That has a nice ring to it!"

"It does!" he laughed.

She considered who else might be interested in reading the Bible with them. "I'm sure Ponce will bring Lily," she said, "and Kenzie has good connections with all the farmers. No doubt, Vinitha, Sanaa and Lema will be eager to come!"

With a pleased expression, Jacques listened as the young couple discussed their ideas. He chuckled when he heard their eager desire to show Google Earth to the others, so that they all could see the vastness of God's creation and realise the superiority of His power. Wistfully, he jotted a few more notes in his journal.

He was pleasantly surprised to hear Zahir say, "I'm really thankful Kenzie will be helping us. He's sure and steady and will keep us both grounded. And my parents can teach you to be the best doctors."

"All *three* of us can learn from your parents," Aimee encouraged kindly. "They said they don't mind extras joining in, but they really want to share their time and learning with *you*. They love you, Zahir."

"But I've only learned how to be a good *patient,*" he jested. "I can drink when you tell me to, and hold back some hollers... if not the *tears...*"

Aimee laughed. "Actually, I think you will be the best doctor," she determined, "because you've been the patient. You will have real empathy." Then she added, "And besides, as we keep learning about the Bible, we'll have something to share with your parents. It can be a learning experience for all of us."

For moment, Zahir was quiet and then he said, "Aimee, let's pray. I want to thank our Father in Heaven for all His good blessings. We both believe we'll see Uncle Louis again and meet Jesus Christ and live forever! And you finally love me the way I always hoped you would. It's awfully nice! *You*... this new *hope*... my one *good* eye - these are *my* treasures! I am *so* happy, Aimee! Let's thank Him."

An email flitted across Jacques' screen. "Full Tribunal Hearing Scheduled for June 1st."

"Treasures!" Jacques repeated to himself. "I couldn't agree more. They can take away all my money, destroy my reputation and dreams of success, but I still have my tiny family and my close friends. What more can anyone ask than to be loved by loyal friends, to have a hope of life beyond the grave, live in an incredibly functional body... and to know... to truly know that the Creator of the Universe *is gracious* and kind and wants us to be His children forever!" These are priceless gifts that no one... except our own foolish pride... or doubtful minds... can take away."[164]

As the two Tinys began a grateful prayer, Jacques leaned forward on his desk, with his head in his hands and listened. When they were done, he continued on with his own words. "I'm so sorry, Lord," he pleaded, as tears ran down his cheeks. "I have done foolishly. I have been just as stubborn and willingly ignorant as the young men that I removed from Paradise. I allowed my anger and bitterness to blind me to all Your brilliant designs, to all Your faithful provisions and evidence of love. I held tightly to my pain and refused to let it go. I don't know how many students I turned against you, but I confess that I purposely tried to turn away as many as I could. I thought I could do better than You, but I have done so much worse. I have been terribly biased. I have let the Tinys down when they needed me the most. And," the Professor sobbed, "I tried to persuade my son, my faithful, beloved son, not to investigate. I tried to deny him the opportunity to know You and find salvation. I thank You from the

---

[164] Romans 8 – especially vs. 18-39; Hebrews 4

bottom of my heart, that *Your grace* was greater than my resistance. You found a way to give Your precious hope to Louis in the last few months that he had left to live. I am so, so thankful!"

Tears poured down Jacques' face as he thought of all the accusatory statements he had written and encouraged so many to read. "For all this," he sobbed, "I am not worthy of Your mercy. I don't deserve forgiveness. It's hard to believe You could still love me, or *want* to save me... but I recognize that I am a sinner, and Your Son chose to die to save *sinners.* I am wrong and *You* are right. You *are* *gracious!* You are the giver of light and immortality. I should never have tinkered with Your creation and miniaturised Your children, but You have provided the way to restore them to You. I pray that You would help me to lead all of Your precious children to life. Dear Father, please forgive me for these sins and help me to turn things around, both in the Tinys' world and here at the Biosphere. May I lead more to You in the future than I've driven away. I ask this in the name of Your Son who willingly chose to endure the terrible pain and give his life for all of us. Amen."

It took a while for Jacques to regain his composure. While he wiped his face with a tissue, he heard Aimee beg to practice Zahir's new song with him, so they could sing it the next day in remembrance of Uncle Louis. As their voices rang out harmoniously across the water, Jacques Lemans recorded it on his phone. "Wait till the world hears this one!" he smiled. Then he emailed Tom Freeman, "I'm ready to do an interview," he typed. "Call me anytime you like. I have made some conclusions that I'd really like to share."

The End

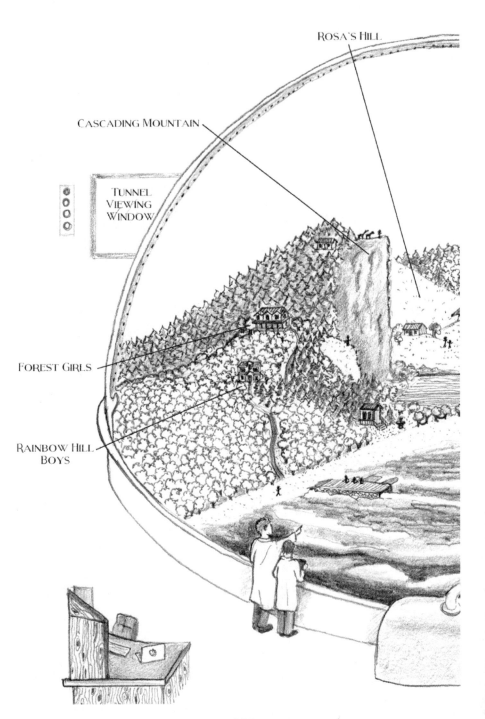

ROSA'S HILL

CASCADING MOUNTAIN

TUNNEL
VIEWING
WINDOW

FOREST GIRLS

RAINBOW HILL
BOYS

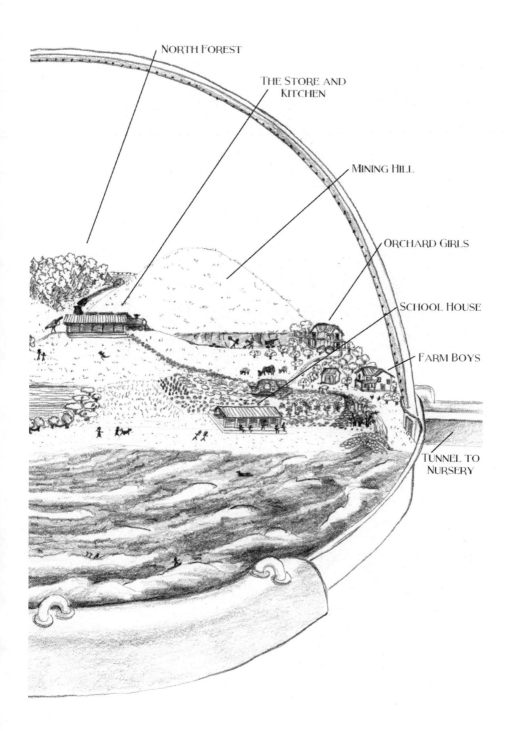

NORTH FOREST

THE STORE AND
KITCHEN

MINING HILL

ORCHARD GIRLS

SCHOOL HOUSE

FARM BOYS

TUNNEL TO
NURSERY

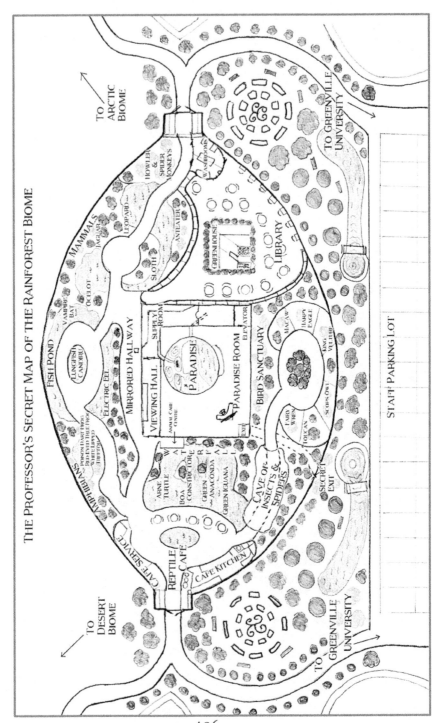

THE PROFESSOR'S SECRET MAP OF THE RAINFOREST BIOME

TO ARCTIC BIOME

TO GREENVILLE UNIVERSITY

STAFF PARKING LOT

TO GREENVILLE UNIVERSITY

TO DESERT BIOME

MAMMALS
HOWLER & SPIDER MONKEYS
LEOPARD
JAGUAR
SLOTH
ANTEATER
OCELOT
VAMPIRE BAT

FISH POND
LUNGFISH
CANDIRU
ELECTRIC EEL

AMPHIBIANS
POISON DART FROG
RED-EYED TREE FROG
WHITE-LIPPED TREE FROG

MIRRORED HALLWAY

VIEWING HALL
SUPPLY ROOM
PARADISE
PARADISE ROOM
ANIMAL CARE CENTRE
EXIT

GREENHOUSE
LIBRARY
ELEVATOR

BIRD SANCTUARY
MACAW
HARPY EAGLE
KING VULTURE
SCOPS OWL
FAIRY WREN
TOUCAN

SECRET EXIT

ARNE TURTLE
BOA CONSTRICTOR
GREEN ANACONDA
GREEN IGUANA
W
T
R
E
P
T
I
L
E
S

CAVE OF INSECTS & SPIDERS

REPTILE CAFE
CAFE KITCHEN
CAFE SERVICE

Bibliography

Many helpful ideas for this series have come from the Bible and our Christadelphian fellow believers. The following books and websites also provide some useful scientific insights and logical arguments to counter Postmodernism and New Atheism, and we have gratefully incorporated some of these concepts and answers. However, we don't endorse every book, movie or article in the following list as doctrinally sound.

Since this is a fictional novel, ideas and information from various sources maybe referred to, but are not always directly quoted, in the following chapters:

Chapter 9 – THE BASIS OF MORALITY

L. W. King. "The Code of Hammurabi" The Avalon Project. https://avalon.law.yale.edu/ancient/hamframe.asp

Paul Copan. *"Is God a Moral Monster? Making Sense of the Old Testament God"* (Baker Books, 2011)

Chapter 11 – SKEPTICISM

Matti Leisola & Jonathan Witt. *"Heretic – One Scientist's Journey From Darwin to Design."* (Discovery Institute, 2018)

Scott Hann and Benjamin Wiker. *"Answering the New Atheism – Dismantling Dawkin's Case Against God."* (Emmaus Road Publishing, 2008)

Hillary Morgan Ferrer. *"Mama Bear Apologetics."* (Harvest House Publishers, 2019)

Lawrence Mykytiuk. *"Did Jesus Exist? Searching for Evidence Beyond the Bible"* (Biblical Archaelogy Review. 2015) www.biblicalarchaelogy.org

Christopher Klein. *"The Bible Says Jesus Was Real. What Other Proof Exists?"* (History Stories, 2020) www.history.com

Alisa Childers. *"Another Gospel? A Lifelong Christian seeks Truth in Response to Progressive Christianity."* (Tyndale House, 2020)

Scott Hann and Benjamin Wiker, *"Answering the New Atheism – Dismantling Dawkin's Case Against God."* (Emmaus Road Publishing, 2008)

Hillary Morgan Ferrer. *"Mama Bear Apologetics."* (Harvest House Publishers, 2019)

Dr. Robert Carter. Creation Ministries. www.creation.com. https://creation.com/four-dimensional-genome. https://www.youtube.com/watch?v=fXFKJhUGNS8

John Launchbury. *"Change us Not God – Bible Mediations on the Death of Jesus."* (WCF Publishing, 2009 – wcfoundation.org)

Lawrence Mykytiuk. *"Did Jesus Exist? Searching for Evidence Beyond the Bible"* *(Biblical Archaelogy Review. 2015)* www.biblicalarchaelogy.org

Christopher Klein. *"The Bible Says Jesus Was Real. What Other Proof Exists?"* (History Stories, 2020) www.history.com

Alisa Childers. *"Another Gospel? A Lifelong Christian seeks Truth in Response to Progressive Christianity."* (Tyndale House, 2020)

Josh Byers. *"Did Jesus Rise From the Dead?"* [Infographic] www.joshbyers.com

David Burges. *"Wonders of Creation. The works of the Divine Designer"* The Testimony, 2017; http://testimonymagazine.com

Chapter 12 – SUFFERING

Tony Benson, *"Stormy Wind Fulfilling His Word".* Christadelphian Scripture Study Service. 1983

John Pople, *"To Speak Well of God – An Exposition of the Book of Job,"* 2009, page 26. madenglishscientist@yahoo.com

Scott Hahn & Benjamin Wiker. *"Answering the New Atheism"* 'Dawkin's god, Chance.' Emmaus Road, 2008, 2019. Pg. 65, 68

Greg Palmer and Phil Shaw. "Hard Questions? Real Answers!" The Christadelphian Magazine. 2022

Chapter 27 - THE PROFESSOR'S PERSPECTIVE

Charles Darwin, *"The Descent of Man,"* Pt. I, chap. V, p. 168.

Scott Hann and Benjamin Wiker, *"Answering the New Atheism – Dismantling Dawkin's Case Against God."* (Emmaus Road Publishing, 2008)

Chapter 28 - THE PLAN OF SALVATION

Mark Vincent. *"Life's Biggest Questions."* A Brief History of Sin. The Christadelphian. 2019

Chapter 30 - JUSTICE

Alisa Childers. *"Another Gospel? A Lifelong Christian seeks Truth in Response to Progressive Christianity."* (Tyndale House, 2020)

Miroslav Volf, *"Free of Charge: Giving and Forgiving in a Culture Stripped of Grace"* (Grand Rapids: Zondervan, 2006), 138-139.

Chapter 37 – THE INVESTIGATION

Greg Palmer and Phil Shaw. "Hard Questions? Real Answers!" The Christadelphian Magazine. 2022

Alisa Childers. *"Another Gospel? A Lifelong Christian seeks Truth in Response to Progressive Christianity."* (Tyndale House, 2020)

Justin Thacker. "Isn't the Bible Full of Contradictions?" https://www.bethinking.org/is-the-bible-reliable/isnt-the-bible-full-of-contradictions

Ken Boa. "How Accurate is the Bible?" https://kenboa.org/apologetics/how-accurate-is-the-bible/

Jennifer Knust. https://www.bibleodyssey.org/en/passages/main-articles/woman-caught-in-adultery

Elijah Hixson. https://www.thegospelcoalition.org/article/was-mark-16-9-20-originally-mark-gospel/

Alisa Childers. "Another Gospel? A Lifelong Christian Seeks Truth in Response to Progressive Christianity." 'For the Bible tells me so?' Tyndale Momentum, 2020, pg.132 – 133.

J. Warner Wallace. "Cold-Case Christianity: A Homicide Detective Investigates the Claims of the Gospels"

Bible Contradictions Explained: 4 Reasons the Gospels "Disagree" (September 19, 2017) https://zondervanacademic.com/blog/bible-contradictions-explained

Stephen Palmer. "The Public Health Value of the Law of Moses" http://testimonymagazine.com/back/may2001/palmer.pdf

https://theconversation.com/ignaz-semmelweis-the-doctor-who-discovered-the-disease-fighting-power-of-hand-washing-in-1847-135528

"DISMANTLED – A Scientific Deconstruction of the Theory of Evolution." 2020 DVD by Creation Ministries International.
https://creation.com/dismantled-movie

Matti Leisola & Jonathan Witt, *"Heretic – One Scientist's Journey From Darwin to Design."* (Discovery Institute, 2018)

Christadelphians, *"Babylon"* https://bibletruth.net.au/babylon/

Richard Morgan, *"Prophecy Proves the Bible True"*
http://www.christadelphia.org/pamphlet/p_prophecy.php

Stephen Palmer. "Read Online/The Middle East and Bible Prophecy" The Christadelphian Daily Journal.
https://thechristadelphianjournal.com/read-booklets-online/the-middle-east-and-bible-prophecy/

Robert K. Greenleaf. *Servant Leadership.* (Paulist Press, 1977)

Chapter 47 – TWO PRAYERS

H. M. Ferrer "Mama Bear Apologetics"– Chapter 10, 'Follow Your Heart; It Never Lies', page 171. Harvest House Publishers. 2019

Acknowledgments

All profits from "THE ENORMOUS TINY EXPERIMENT" series will be donated towards Agape in Action. Agape in Action is a Christadelphian charitable organization helping underprivileged children, widows and families in Africa and India. Support to Agape in Action is provided through child sponsorship, project sponsorship and general donations.

Although the needs are enormous, Agape in Action aims to affect change one child at a time, one family at a time, one community at a time. The name Agape in Action reflects our intention of putting love ('agape') into action by responding compassionately to those who are in need. Providing wells for water, basic nutritional and hygiene programs, schools and scholarships, homes for orphans, help for widows, and in-depth Sunday School and Bible tuition, Agape in Action seeks to assist children and families living in extreme poverty.

http://www.agapeinaction.org/

With grateful thanks to our Heavenly Father for answering my prayers and strengthening my effort in many ways. A huge thankyou to Carrie Reynolds as my foremost editor, who persevered through illness, work and family demands to give so many great suggestions and encouragement. My husband always cheerfully takes on a lot of the editing and technical support; I could not have finished this project without him. Thanks also to those who encouraged me to finish this project and made important editing contributions, in particular: Frank and Dorothy Abel, Faith Imhof, Bailey Moore, Katie Stedman, Olivia Badger, the Gore family, and Mary-Jane and Eden Styles.

A special thankyou to Linda Beckerson who advised me on the medical issues involved in this story.

A special thanks to those who cheerfully modelled numerous times for the pictures - my husband, Abel Sales, Tom Mansfield, Josh Jackson, Ben and Beth Aback, Kyla and Kailyn Abel. ☺

Printed in Great Britain
by Amazon

22577128R00235